KT-130-701

Nora Roberts published her first novel using the pseudonym **J.D. Robb** in 1995, introducing to readers the tough as nails but emotionally damaged homicide cop **Eve Dallas** and billionaire Irish rogue **Roarke**.

With the **In Death** series, Robb has become one of the biggest thriller writers on earth, with each new novel reaching number one on bestseller charts the world over.

For more information, visit www.jd-robb.co.uk

Become a fan on Facebook at
Nora Roberts and J. D. Robb

J.D. ROBB

LEVERAGE IN DEATH

piatkus

PIATKUS

First published in the United States in 2018 by Berkeley,
a division of Penguin Random House LLC
First published in Great Britain in 2018 by Piatkus
This paperback edition published in 2019 by Piatkus

1 3 5 7 9 10 8 6 4 2

A CIP catalogue record for this book
is available from the British Library.

ISBN 978-0-349-41788-2

Printed and bound by CPI Group (UK) Ltd, Croydon, CR0 4YY

Papers used by Piatkus are from well-managed forests
and other responsible sources.

Piatkus
An imprint of
Little, Brown Book Group
Carmelite House
50 Victoria Embankment
London EC4Y 0DZ

An Hachette UK Company
www.hachette.co.uk

www.littlebrown.co.uk

I cannot think of any need in childhood
as strong as the need for a father's protection.

SIGMUND FREUD

Nothing is sacred to a gambler.

JACQUES SAURIN

1

Thou shalt not kill.

Paul Rogan didn't consider himself a religious man, but that commandment played over and over in his head as he stepped into the lobby. As his wing tips clicked on the polished marble floor, those four words beat inside him.

As he'd done every weekday morning for eleven years – minus holidays, sick days, and vacations – he swiped his company ID at check-in.

Stu, manning security, gave him a nod. 'Monday again, huh, Mr Rogan.'

'Monday,' Rogan muttered and turned, as he did every Monday morning, to the elevator banks.

Behind his back, Stu smirked a little. It looked like Mr Rogan had himself a big-ass Monday morning hangover.

Rogan stepped into an elevator along with a handful of other execs, some admins, a couple of assistants. He wore a dark, pin-striped suit over an athletic frame, a crisp white shirt, and a blue-and-red-chevron-pattern tie in a single Windsor knot.

Despite his cashmere topcoat, the cold seeped into his bones as he listened to the voice in his head.

Cecily. Melody.

The voice spoke the names, again and again even as four words pounded out a rhythm.

Thou shalt not kill. Thou shalt not kill.

And yet.

He stepped out on the thirty-second floor – executive level, Quantum Air. The logo, the silver whoosh of it, streaked over the wall behind the curve of the reception counter. Already the 'links and comps beeped and hummed. The waiting area, empty at this hour, sat quiet and plush. Another wall, all tinted glass, opened the room to New York, its sky and skyline.

Blue today that sky, so blue, he thought as he stared a moment. How could it be so blue, so clear?

He turned from it and, without his usual words for the trio at reception, walked to the double glass doors.

They opened, splitting the logo's whoosh in two. He understood what it meant to be split in two.

Cecily. Melody.

Thou shalt not kill.

He passed assistants, admin stations, offices. Though it was still just shy of nine, men and women in sharp suits sat at desks, opened briefcases, sipped their fancy coffees while studying reports.

His own admin jumped up. So young, so bright, so earnest, Rogan thought. He'd been the same, just the same, once upon a time.

'Good morning, Mr Rogan. I updated your tablet for the nine o'clock conference. It's on your desk. If you're ready to go over some of the updates—'

'Not necessary. No calls, Rudy.'

Rudy opened his mouth to speak, but Rogan closed the door to his office. Though he frowned when he heard the *click* of the lock, Rudy decided his boss just needed a few before the big meeting.

Inside his office, Rogan begged, bargained, pleaded. The voice inside his head never changed in tone. Utterly calm, utterly cold. When another voice came through, desperate and terrified, he wept.

He trembled as he removed his topcoat. Once again he stared through a glass wall at the blue sky, as he stood in an office he'd worked diligently to earn.

It all ended today, as February dribbled into March 2061. Eleven years since he'd come aboard Quantum as a junior exec.

The voice gave him only two choices, so he had no choice at all.

Surrendering, he followed the instructions inside his head and opened his briefcase.

At eight-fifty-six, he stepped out of his office. Rudy popped up again.

'Mr Rogan, I wanted to tell you I added a few more notes, some personal data on Ms Karson. Just chat points.'

'All right, Rudy.' He paused a moment, looking into that

young, earnest face. 'You do good work. You've been an asset to me, and to Quantum Air.'

'Thanks.' Rudy brightened. 'It's a big day.'

'Yes, a big day.'

Feeling the weight of it, Rogan walked to the conference room. 'Please stop,' he murmured as his heart beat like a brutal fist inside his chest.

Inside the conference room, the blue sky, the sweep of downtown Manhattan, the glint of the river gleamed through the tinted glass. On the wall, the screen held steady and silent with the silver logo.

On the long, polished table, silver trays held glossy pastries, perfectly ripened fruit, pitchers of water – sparkling or still. China cups waited for assistants to fill them with tea or coffee.

Reps from EconoLift – one male, one female – sat studying tablets with cups and glasses at their elbows. Two of Rogan's associates did the same. Lawyers and accountants from each company filled more seats.

'There needs to be another way.'

At Rogan's murmur, Sandy Plank – senior VP, accounting – gave him a quizzical glance.

But Rogan only heard the voice in his head.

At nine sharp, the doors opened again. Derrick Pearson, Quantum's president and CEO, stood for a moment surveying the room. His black and silver mane flowing, he entered along with Willimina Karson.

In heeled boots, Karson – Econo's president – stood six

foot one inch. They made an imposing pair, Pearson in his severe black suit and silver tie, Karson in her straight-line red dress and short jacket.

Everyone around the table stood.

'Good morning, everyone,' Pearson said in his lion's roar of a voice. 'Let's bring in Chicago, New LA, Atlanta, London, Rome, and Paris.'

As he rattled off cities, the screen flashed into sections, those sections flashed with other conference rooms or offices, more people in suits.

The voice in Rogan's head spoke incessantly, sharper and sharper. Then added screams.

Rogan took two staggering steps forward, interrupting Derrick's opening greeting.

'Paul.' More surprised than annoyed, Pearson touched a hand to Karson's arm. 'Willimina, you've met Paul. Paul Rogan, our VP of marketing.'

'Derrick ... I don't have a choice. I'm sorry.'

Something in his voice, something in his eyes, had Karson stepping back even as Pearson stepped forward.

'Are you all right, Paul?' he asked, gripping Rogan's arm.

'I'm sorry. I'm so sorry.'

Rudy, dashing toward the conference room with the tablet Rogan had left on his desk, got within three strides of the doors before they blew.

Lieutenant Eve Dallas stood amid the carnage. The air stank of blood, charred flesh, piss, and vomit. Water from the sprinkler system soaked into the carpet so it squished underfoot. With her boots and hands already sealed, she studied the room.

The blast had blown off the doors, shattered most of the mega screen, blown chunks off the table, sent chairs and people flying – and some burning.

The thick carpet now bore a wide, blackened hole, and the walls as well as the floor carried spatter – blood, brains, other bodily fluids.

Lieutenant Lisbeth Salazar, heading up the Explosives and Bombs Unit, stood with her.

'Eleven dead, nine injured. The dead include the bomber. We're picking up the pieces there . . . '

Both women watched the sweepers in their protective white suits, the boomer hounds in their thick gray, comb the room.

'But we've got some wits from the other side of the room, more shaken than stirred, who state Paul Rogan, VP of marketing, revealed a suicide vest seconds before he detonated it. I can tell you from the extent of the damage, it was either designed for short-range effect, or it piffed and that's all he got. I'm estimating a range of twelve to fifteen feet.'

'You're saying it could've been worse.'

'Oh, a whole hell of a bunch worse.' Salazar – an imposing woman with skin the color of well-steeped tea, eyes of flaming green – gestured. 'He was facing away from the table, angled toward the door – toward Derrick Pearson, CEO. He blew Pearson with him, and the people at the front section of the table. It looks like some of the DBs took chunks of the table and the shrapnel as COD rather than the actual explosion.

'We've swept,' Salazar added. 'And we're sweeping again – the entire building. But I'm saying this was the only device, this was the only bomber.'

Eve noted the spears of wood and metal impaled in the walls, the webbing cracks on the wall of glass. But the bulk of the damage, the radius of the blast? Yeah, around twelve feet.

'How'd he get it in the building?'

'Briefcase – lead-lined. He breezed right through the standards, and he's worked here nearly a dozen years. Security had no reason to wand or ray him. I did a run, the guy's got no record. Married going on fourteen years. An eight-year-old daughter.'

'Where are they, the wife and kid?'

'I sent some uniforms to pick them up. You and the ME make the call, Dallas, but this looks like homicide to me. It's not terrorism, domestic or otherwise, on the face of it. Maybe the guy flipped out, who knows? Some big deal supposed to go down today – here. Maybe he didn't want it to go down. We'll pick up the pieces, and we'll tell you what kind of boomer.'

Eve stood tall and lean in the long leather coat. Her hair, short, choppy, and brown, haloed a face of angles, with a shallow dent in the chin. Her eyes, brown, sharp, and all cop, swept the room again.

'You handle your end, I'll handle mine. Let's see where we end up.'

'Works for me.' Salazar pulled out her signaling communicator. 'Salazar.'

'Lieutenant, neither Cecily Greenspan nor Melody Rogan showed up at the school this morning where the kid attends and the mother is assistant principal. The mother texted in that the kid wasn't feeling well. They don't answer their 'links.'

Salazar's brows lifted, and Eve gave her the nod.

'Officer, I'm passing you to the primary in charge. Lieutenant Dallas.'

Eve took the comm. 'Get to the residence. If there's no response, you have probable cause to enter.'

'"Probable cause"?' Salazar said as Eve passed the comm back.

'Eleven dead, nine wounded, and a missing wife and daughter. That's more than probable for me. I'll let you get back to what you do. I'll start doing what I do.'

Eve walked to the doorway. 'Peabody!'

Her partner hustled down the ruined corridor in pink cowboy boots. 'This is ours. Treat it as a homicide until it looks otherwise. Bomber, deceased, was Paul Rogan – do a run. Officers are en route to his residence to locate his wife and daughter – neither of which is where they should be this morning.'

'Devoted family man.' As she looked into the conference room, Peabody blew out a breath. 'According to one of the wits who survived that. A Sandy Plank, another VP, minor injuries, treated on-site. Hardworking, loyal, smart, and crazy in love with his wife and daughter is how she describes Rogan.'

'The loyal don't generally blow up their boss and co-workers,' Eve pointed out.

'Yeah. She's a mess – Plank, I mean. She states he didn't look well, and she heard him mumbling to himself. She thought he said: There needs to be or has to be another way. And when his boss and Willimina Karson – head of EconoLift – came into the meeting, Rogan walked over to them. Plank said she was watching Rogan because she thought he must have been feeling ill. She heard him say he didn't have a choice. He said he was sorry. He was, according to her, crying. Then he opened his suit jacket. Boom.'

'Run him, and let's find out what this meeting was about. Details. Any idea where his office is?'

'Down and left, second right. Salazar put a man on the door.'

'I'll take it.' She started down, stopped. 'Pearson, deceased, was top dog. Let's find out who's top dog now.'

Eve made her way to Rogan's office, badged the officer on the door. Inside she closed the door, stood, scanned.

Big window due to VP status, she mused, and a refreshment station with AutoChef. Curious, she checked the AC for previous orders.

Nothing since Friday at 16:22. A tube of ginger ale.

The desk was angled, giving Rogan the window and the

door view. A good desk chair, two sturdy visitors' chairs, club style in a smooth coffee-brown leather. A sofa – navy-blue gel – with a long table. Walls, light brown, decorated with aeronautic art.

An evolution of air travel, she realized – from those early deals that made Eve wonder how anyone had had the balls to jump into them, up to sleek shuttles. With them, a child's drawing in bright primary colors of a plane flying in a sky with white clouds and a yellow circle of sun.

The artist had signed it in careful block letters. MELODY.

The daughter. Devoted family man, Eve thought, who framed his kid's drawing and hung it on his office wall.

On the desk, in addition to a top-grade data and communication center, a brightly painted cup held a bouquet of paper flowers, all clearly handmade. Eve lifted the cup, looked at the bottom.

HAPPY BIRTHDAY, DADDY
LOVE,
MELODY
JANUARY 18, 2061

The desk held a triple frame, an attractive mixed-race female, late thirties, and a seriously beautiful girl – Melody, no doubt – with mad toffee-colored curls, laughing eyes of pale green, and a joyful smile that showed the gap where she'd lost a couple of baby teeth. They flanked one of the family, the child cuddled between Rogan and his wife.

The visual said happy, loving, attractive family.

If there'd been problems on the home front, it didn't show here.

She sat behind his desk.

'Computer, open ops.'

It fluttered on to a holding screen. **Password required** . . .

Ignoring that for now, she opened desk drawers. Standard office supplies, some file discs, some hard copy files. And a memo book.

She switched it on and, as it wasn't password protected, paged to the current date.

- ECONO! Meeting/signing★ 9:00. Final presentation and reveal. Don't sweat it!
- Confirm cupcakes and champagne for department thank-you by 11:30. Send department memo for meeting (surprise party). Set for 4:15. Prepared remarks – brief.
- Personal bonuses for Rudy and Kimmi for job amazingly well done.
- Home by 6:00 – stop for flowers for your amazing girls! Act surprised at the celebration dinner those amazing girls have been whispering about for a week.
- One hour post-dinner to resume Dragon Spear tourney with Mel – too long postponed. Tuck Mel into bed, and make love to your beautiful wife – way too long postponed.
- Get some damn sleep!

Eve sat back, swiveled to look out the window. Why would a man so obviously looking forward to a day – business and personal – blow it all up, himself included?

She paged ahead, noted several appointments – again, business and personal – in that same easy stream-of-thought style. She paged back, found several weeks of an intense work schedule, much of which revolved around Econo strategy sessions, planning sessions, marketing campaigns – aside apologies to his amazing girls for missing dinner or dance practice.

Nothing to indicate depression, anger – frustration here and there, yes, but not anger. Nothing to indicate he'd bought or acquired explosives or had the knowledge to create a suicide vest.

'Doesn't fit,' she muttered, looking at the triple-frame photos. 'You don't fit.'

As she pulled out her comm, Peabody gave the door two knuckle raps, then poked in.

'Pearson – son and daughter – will probably cohead the company. Son was in London handling that area, and daughter in Rome when things went boom. Both are on their way back. As for Paul Rogan—'

'Clean as they come?' Eve finished.

'You got that. Financially secure – no signs of trouble there. Nothing to show any knowledge or interest in explosives, in political fringe associations. Company man, in charge of marketing for the last three and a half years. Worked his way up with over eleven years in the company.

The same goes for the wife. I ran her. Actually, she had an assault charge brought when she was in her twenties – dropped. And the guy who brought the charge was subsequently charged with spousal and child abuse.'

'Okay, it doesn't add up.' Eve reached for her comm again, and it signaled in her hand. 'Dallas.'

'Lieutenant, Officers Gregg and Vols. We're at the Rogan/Greenspan residence. Greenspan's been worked over, and was bound, locked in a basement storage room. The minor child's unharmed except for some bruises and minor lacerations. We called the MTs for the woman. Both she and the kid claim home invasion.'

'That adds up. Secure the scene. If the MTs need to take Greenspan to a med center, one of you goes with her, one sits on the residence. I'm on my way.

'Peabody,' she said as she clicked off. 'Inform Salazar of the situation, and contact EDD. I want all Rogan's e's – office and home – taken in. I want an e-man at the residence to go over security. I'll seal this office and get a team in here. Move. Meet me at the car.'

She bagged the memo book, sealed and labeled it as she contacted her bullpen.

'Yo, LT,' Detective Baxter said.

'Are you and Trueheart clear?'

'Clear enough. What do you need?'

'I need you at Quantum Air, coordinating with Lieutenant Salazar.'

'On the boomer.'

She sealed the office as she barked out orders.

'Bring a couple of uniforms. Peabody started getting statements. You finish. Everybody, down to the cleaning service. Two honchos are coming in – family of CEO. I'm going to want to talk to them as soon as possible.'

'How many dead?' Baxter asked.

'Eleven, so far. Nine injured.'

'It could've been worse. I'll contact Salazar, let her know we're coming in. Are you on scene?'

'I won't be. I've got a second crime scene. I'll brief you when I know more. Dallas, out.'

It could've been worse. Baxter said it, she'd thought it. The thing was, when things could be worse, they usually got there.

Eve beat Peabody to the car, and peeled out of the slot the minute Peabody hopped in. She wove through the underground lot at a speed that had her partner gripping the chicken stick.

'You said it added up.' Peabody's eyes, dark brown and widening at every swerve, closed to spare her brain the visual of a crash. 'I'm putting some of the numbers in columns. Somebody broke into Rogan's house, threatened his wife and kid, and forced him to kill himself? I don't get the two-plus-two.'

'Somebody says take this boom vest to work Monday morning, strap it on, and wear it to the meeting at nine. Blow it up. Do that, or we kill your amazing girls.'

'His amazing girls?'

'That's what he called his wife and kid. In his memo book. I don't know why this guy, why this meeting, why this company, or why this method, but that part adds up.'

'Wit statements say he was alone in his office, at least for a few minutes before the meeting. He doesn't call for help?'

'Could've had him wired. I would have. Let him hear the wife getting slapped around, or the kid crying for her daddy.'

'That's unbelievably cruel.'

'Nothing cruel's unbelievable.' She arrowed out of the underground, zipped into traffic. 'Why the marketing guy? They needed somebody who'd not only kill for his wife and kid, but die for them. But how did they know he would? We need to know more about this Quantum-Econo deal. Was the deal the thing? Was there something about it that made someone willing to kill – to use what appears to be an innocent man and his family as the weapon?'

'I use Econo a lot,' Peabody said. 'Or did before I had a mag partner with a magalish husband who lets me use Roarke's private shuttles.'

She'd used Econo herself, Eve thought, before Roarke. They were as bare as bare bones got, and therefore affordable if you had to use air travel. She wondered if Roarke had ever used them, before becoming one of the richest men in the known universe – and one who had his own transpo lines as well.

She'd tap that source, she thought, that expert

15

consultant, civilian. If anybody knew the ins and outs of the QuantumAir-EconoLift deal outside of the particulars in the deal, it would be Roarke.

She swung in behind the mobile medical unit. Since it was already double-parked, horns and curses were already blasting anyway.

As she stepped out, the Rapid Cab driver behind her laid on his horn, stuck his head out the window. 'Gimme a fucking break, girlie!'

Eve held up her badge, smiled with all the warmth of the early March wind. 'Lieutenant Girlie. What would you like me to break?'

He steered around her, shooting her his middle finger on the way.

'You know Charles and Louise live just down the block,' Peabody commented.

'Yeah.' The doctor and the former licensed companion had an elegant brownstone within easy walking distance. 'Nice neighborhood.'

Upper-class, Eve thought. Reasonably quiet and safe. Brownstones and townhomes tucked back from the sidewalk, often with little front gardens or paved rear courtyards.

This one had a front garden – dormant now, but neat – with a walkway leading to a short set of stairs, a pair of bold blue double doors. One of the doors hung crookedly.

The house rose up three stories – decorative (and she'd wager effective) bars on the lower windows. All the privacy screens were engaged but for one on the second floor. Someone had broken that window. She noted the shards of glass and some sort of good-size ball, cracked, in shades of red and orange and brown.

'I think maybe that's Jupiter.' Peabody frowned at the ball, tipping her head back to look up at the window.

Eve avoided the shards, studied the security as they approached the doors. 'It's one of Roarke's systems, so it's good. Palm plate, voice ID, solid locks and alarm, double cameras.'

The door opened. 'Lieutenant. Officer Vols.'

'Status.'

'Sir. Officer Gregg and I arrived, rang and knocked. Automated security engaged. The comp said no one was currently in residence. Before we attempted a bypass, Gregg stepped down to check windows, go around to the back. And the ball back there? Planet Jupiter?'

'I knew it,' Peabody said with quick triumph before Eve shut her down with a cold stare.

'Well, it nearly beaned Gregg. And the kid who managed to throw it through the window started screaming for help. Gregg called up to her, told her we were the police. She said she couldn't get out of her room.

'We couldn't get through security, LT, had to use the battering ram.'

'Did the alarm go off?'

'No, sir, it didn't. Disengaged. We found the kid upstairs – holding on to herself pretty well. She said they'd hurt her

17

mom, and had taken her away. They'd taken her dad away. Then we heard the pipes. The mother managed to bang on the pipes in the basement room. We found her down there, beat up, tied up. The kid fell apart a little then.'

A ripple of emotion ran over his stony cop's face. 'She thought they'd killed her mom. Two men, they both state, broke into the house sometime in the early hours of Saturday after all three were in bed. From what the wife said, it sounds like they may have drugged the husband while he slept, taken him out that way, then they dragged the wife out of bed, smacked her around a little, tied her up, hauled the kid in. Tied her and the father up.'

'Did you get a description?'

'Masks. Both say white, featureless masks. Hoods, gloves. They both say male going by voice and build, but they can't give us race, facial features, hair or eye color. I'll tell you, we didn't push too hard, Lieutenant. The mother needed medical attention, and the kid . . . She holds it together, like I said, but she's pretty shaken up. We haven't given Greenspan notification on Rogan. She and the kid asked about him, but we didn't want to step in it on that.'

'Okay. You and Gregg stand by. I've got an e-man coming to evaluate the security breach and pick up all electronics. Where do you have them?'

'There's a family area in the back of the house, off the kitchen. Gregg's sitting on them.'

The two MTs walked out from the rear of the house, equipment in hand. 'She won't go to the hospital,' one of them announced. 'The adult female. The minor's mostly just shaken up, but the adult female could use the hospital.'

'What's her status?'

'Two cracked ribs, bruised kidney, sprained wrist, deep lacerations on both wrists and ankles from fighting against the zip ties, broken nose, severe facial and torso bruising, and lacerations from repeated blows. She was dehydrated, suffered a mild concussion.'

'We'll see what we can do about getting her to agree to the hospital.'

The other MT shook his head. 'Won't budge. Wouldn't take a tranq, either. We've got her splinted, wanded, stabilized, but she needs to go in.'

'Got it,' Eve said as the MTs walked out.

'She's afraid to be a foot away from the kid,' Vols told Eve. 'Like the kid's afraid to be a foot away from the mom. You can't blame them.'

'Yeah. I got that, too. Good work, Officer.'

With Peabody, Eve started back to tell a woman that her husband was dead, and a child that her father wouldn't be coming home again.

2

The kid sat, hollow-eyed, glued to her mother's side on a wide sofa covered with big, bold red flowers. She wore baggy cotton pants, thick pink socks, a purple sweatshirt. The bruises on her wrists added more purple.

Her mother kept a protective arm wrapped around her.

Bruises rioted over Cecily's face. Eve noted the swelling and blackened rays at the edges of the ice patch on her left eye.

NuSkin bandages wrapped around both of her wrists. Violet-and-yellow bruises spread around her unpatched right eye.

When she shifted, the flicker over her face told Eve there was still considerable pain.

'Ms Greenspan, I'm Lieutenant Dallas. This is Detective Peabody. We have some questions. We can speak to you at the health center of your choice, as the medics who treated you strongly recommend further examination and treatment.'

'The MTs treated us here. We want to be home.' She

looked down at her daughter, who cuddled a little closer, nodded. 'No one will tell us about Paul, about my husband, Melody's father. We'll answer all your questions, but you have to answer one first. Where is Paul?'

Eve sat. Eye-to-eye was better, though there was never a better. 'I regret to inform you, your husband's dead. We're very sorry for your loss.'

The girl stared at Eve for a long, trembling moment, then pressed her face to her mother's side. She made a sound like a small animal in terrible pain.

Cecily turned to gather her daughter in, and the pain, all the levels of it, drained her face of color until the bruises stood out like banners.

'Are you sure? Are you sure? Are you—'

'Yes. I'm sorry, but we're sure.'

'Is there someone we can call for you?' Peabody asked. 'Can I get you something? Water, some tea?'

'How? How?'

'Detective Peabody can take Melody into another room,' Eve began, and Melody pushed away from her mother, aimed a ferocious look at Eve.

'I'm not leaving my mom. They made me leave her, and they kept hurting her and Daddy. I'm not going to leave. They made him do something awful. They made him because they kept hurting Mom and said how they'd do things to me. One of them had a knife and told Daddy he'd cut me, and he pulled my hair really hard to make me yell. I tried not to, I *tried*, but it hurt.'

'It's okay, Melly. It's okay, my baby.'

'They killed Daddy, and he didn't do anything. They hurt Mom, and she didn't do anything.'

'Neither did you,' Eve said. 'Did they do anything else to hurt you?'

'They put the plastic tie things on my wrists and my feet, really tight. They hurt. When the one took Daddy away, the other came in and . . . he made the ties looser so they didn't hurt so much. But he said if I didn't yell for Daddy to help me in the 'link, he'd kill Mom.'

'Oh, Melly, oh, baby.'

'I had to do it. I had to. And I could hear Daddy crying. He was crying, but he said it would be okay. It's not okay. They killed Daddy.'

'Tell us what happened,' Eve said to Cecily, 'from the beginning.'

'I heard Melly scream. We were all in bed. I don't know what time exactly, late Friday night, early Saturday morning. I know it was after midnight because Paul and I didn't go to bed until about midnight. I heard her scream, and I started to get up and run to her room. Something hit me. Someone.'

She touched a hand to her face.

'I fell, and he pulled my arms behind me, used the zip ties. I called for Paul, but he dragged me back to the bed, hit me again, and bound me to the headboard. I could see that Paul was still sleeping. At first I thought he was somehow sleeping through it, but I realized they'd used something – a pressure syringe. He was unconscious, helpless. The other one came in with Melly, bound her to the chair.

'I kept asking what they wanted, begged them not to hurt my baby, told them to take whatever they wanted. They didn't say anything, didn't speak. They dragged Paul to the other chair. They tied him, then used another syringe. It brought him around. He tried to fight, but . . . '

'They hurt Mom again. They kept hurting Mom.'

'I'm all right now, Melly, I'm okay now. They hurt me, threatened to hurt Melly to torture Paul. They laughed when he cursed them, threatened them, begged them. They just laughed. Then one sat on the side of the bed, beside me – touched me.'

Cecily's eyes met Eve's, said all.

'He said it would get worse, a lot worse. And did Paul want to save his wife and child? Did he want to protect them? Would he do anything to save them? Of course Paul said yes. He said he'd do anything.'

'They took me away, even though Mom and Daddy begged,' Melody said. 'One of them carried me into my room and used another of the zip things to tie me to my bed so I couldn't get up. I was scared, and I kept calling for Mom and Daddy, but the one who locked me in, before he did, he said everything was going to be okay. He told me not to be scared, but to stop calling for my mom and dad. So I stopped calling for them. He wanted me to, so I stopped.'

'You're smart and you're brave,' Peabody told her.

'They still killed Daddy.'

'Daddy saved us,' Cecily murmured as she pressed her lips to her daughter's hair. 'The one sitting on the bed told Paul he had to do one thing to save his wife and child. One thing, and they'd leave us alone. If he didn't do what they said, they'd keep hurting me, they'd ... violate me, and then they'd start on Melody. If he still wouldn't do it, they'd kill all of us, him last so he could watch them kill his wife and child. They kept saying that – or the one did – wife and child.'

'What did they say he had to do?'

'Kill. Take lives to save lives. His wife and child, didn't they mean more to him than anyone else? Paul said he would but he was lying, and they knew it. The one said he needed more time, more persuasion to make the deal. Then he advised me to convince my husband to save me and my child. They left us alone. I don't know how long.'

'They left you and your husband alone in the bedroom?'

'Yes. Paul tried to get free. I tried. He kept asking if I was all right, telling me he'd find a way. We told each other we loved each other. He swore he'd never let anything happen to Melly.'

Cecily shuddered, took a moment to try to regulate her breathing that had gone ragged. 'I think they had a recorder in the room because the one, when he came back in, mocked some of what we'd said to each other.

'It went on and on and on. One would come in, hit me or touch me. Then do something to make Melody call out. Ask Paul if he'd do anything to save his wife and child. Hours.

Hours and hours. Then they dragged me out. I fought, and one of them hit me and knocked me out, I think. They took me to the basement, locked me up, but they put up a camera. I think they wanted Paul to see me, locked in, cold and hurt, afraid. I was so afraid. I never saw them again. I never saw Paul again.'

Tears streamed down her face, a river of grief, as she rocked her daughter, stroked Melody's hair.

'I was alone down there until the police came. Now I know Paul did what they asked. He did what they asked to save us. They tortured a good man, a good husband and father, until he did what they asked.'

Turning, Cecily tipped Melody's face up to hers. 'Don't ever forget that. Whatever Daddy did, whatever people say about him, he loved you more than anything in the world. He did what he had to do to protect us, to save us.'

'They made him wear a bomb.'

Cecily jerked back. 'What? How do you—'

'Ms Greenspan,' Eve interrupted. Focusing on Melody, she asked, 'You saw the explosives?'

'No, but I heard them talking. One came in, and I pretended to be asleep. It was dark in the room – they kept it dark a lot, but it was dark outside, too – and I pretended to be asleep. And the other one came, like, to the door. They talked about the bombs, and the one – the one that hurt Mom – he said how my daddy would wear it, how he was almost there, how he'd do what they said.'

'Do you remember anything else they said?'

'They were talking really quiet, but I guess, like, they were really excited, too. I don't know how to say it.'

'I get it. Anything else?'

'They were going to Fat City.'

'Fat City?'

'They'd be in Fat City at nine. And the one who came in my room most of the time came over and sort of nudged me. I just sort of rolled over and kept pretending I was asleep. He said he was glad I was getting some sleep. And the other said ...'

She looked at her mother, tipped her head to her mother's arm. 'He said the bad word that starts with "f." The bad "f" word and "the kid." And they went out. Then I did fall asleep, I think, because it got light out. The one that mostly came in let me get up and pee. It's embarrassing. Then he put the tie things on my wrists again, and I had to get back on the bed. But he got tagged on his 'link, and he got excited and said the bad word again, a lot, but excited, not mad, and he walked out, still talking – he locked the door.'

Melody took a long breath. 'He didn't come back. Everything got really quiet. I almost fell back to sleep, or maybe I did, but then I saw he hadn't tied up my feet again, or tied me to the bed like before. He was excited. He forgot, maybe. So I tried to get out, but I couldn't get the door open. I couldn't get the windows open. I yelled, but nobody could hear me. I saw Mr Benson across the street going out of his house, and I yelled and tried to bang on the windows but he didn't look up. And I saw the police, and they came to the door, but nobody was going to answer. I saw my solar system, and I knocked Jupiter off, and I picked it up. I dropped it at first because it was hard to hold it, but then I threw it as hard as I could at the window. It broke the window, and I yelled and yelled for help. And the police came in.'

'Smart,' Eve told her. 'Seriously smart.'

'But my daddy—'

'Your mom was trapped in the basement. Hurt, cold, scared. She couldn't get help. You could, and you did. It would help now if you took Detective Peabody up to your room, and showed her how you did it. It would help.'

'I don't want to leave Mom.'

'I'm going to stay with your mom.'

'My daddy didn't want to wear the bomb.'

'I know. I think he'd want you to help us now, as much as you can.'

'Go on, Melly.' Cecily kissed the top of her head. 'Be brave for Daddy.'

'Don't take Mom away.'

'Never going to happen,' Eve promised.

She waited as Peabody led Melody out. If anyone could get more out of the kid, Peabody could.

'Ms—'

'Could I have a minute? I think I want to get some tea after all.'

'Sure.'

Eve watched her walk into the kitchen area with the careful, stiff-bodied movement of the injured.

'I've been knocked around a few times,' Eve began. 'I hate hospitals, but sometimes you need them.'

'I can't and won't leave Melly. We can't stay here, I know that. We won't be able to live in this house.'

She began to weep. 'I know it's just a house, but it's home. Our home, and they killed that, too. My husband, my baby's father, the home we made together.'

She fought the tears back, swiped at her face. 'I need to talk to my mother. She and my stepfather live in New Rochelle. We can stay with them until we decide what to do. Once I know Melly's with my parents, I can see a doctor there.'

'We'll arrange to get you to your mother's.'

Cecily nodded as she programmed tea. 'I have to keep going. I have to think of Melly first and last. Paul . . . I don't know, I don't know what I'm going to do without him, but I can't think about that yet. I can't think.'

'Can you describe the men?'

'They wore black, all black, with hoods like skullcaps. Tight over their heads, high on the neck. Thin black gloves. And the masks were white, they almost glowed in the dark. No features, slits for eyes.'

'Height, weight, build?'

'Not tall or short. Paul's six feet exactly. Maybe about his height. Fit. Not bulky, but fit. One slimmer than the other. The one who hit me had more muscle. I . . . '

'Keep going.'

'It's just an impression, but I think the one who hit me liked it. He liked hitting me, and watching Paul react. The other one didn't – as much. He slapped me, but he never punched me, and it seemed like it was more because the other one was watching.'

The cup and saucer rattled in her hand when Detective Callendar walked in.

'This is Detective Callendar, with our E Division,' Eve said. 'We're going to need to go through your electronics. Did your husband have a home office?'

'Yes. Second floor, directly across from the master bedroom. I can show you.'

'We'll find it. We'd like your permission to examine any and all electronics and security systems, communication devices. We may need to take them in for further analysis.'

'Yes, anything.'

Eve moved to Callendar. 'Check the security first, then the home office.'

'On it.'

'Ms Greenspan, was there anything about their voices? Accents, syntax, colloquialisms?'

'They kept their voices low, often in whispers.'

'Okay.' Change directions, Eve thought. 'How did your husband get along at work? Was he happy in his job?'

'He loved his work. He loved the company. He worked hard, but he enjoyed it. He ran the marketing department, and thought of his team like family.'

She walked back to the couch, sat with that same stiff-bodied care. 'Lieutenant, please, please tell me what happened. Please tell me what they made him do.'

'Are you aware of the meeting this morning?'

'The merger with Econo. It's the biggest campaign Paul's worked on in years. It's taken months for the deal to get approved and pushed forward. He and his team have been working on the marketing for the expansion. I don't understand.'

'This morning your husband went into the meeting wearing a suicide vest.'

'Oh God, oh God. How many? How many?'

'Eleven dead, nine injured at this time.'

She set the tea down, covered her face with her hands. Sobbed. 'They made him a killer. They made my Paul a killer. Why? Why would they do this? Why would they force him to do this?'

'Did he have any enemies?'

'No, no, no.'

'How did he feel about this merger?'

'He – he wasn't sold on it initially. Quantum's luxury travel, high-end, all the amenities, and Econo's cut-rate. But Derrick – Derrick Pearson – wanted the expansion, liked the idea of adding levels, and more hubs. Econo has hubs everywhere. Paul got on board, looked at his end of it as a challenge. He's a company man, Lieutenant. His loyalty is always to Derrick and to Quantum.'

Her eyes widened. 'Derrick. Is Derrick all right?'

'I'm sorry.'

'Oh my God, Derrick was practically a father to Paul.'

She reached out for Eve, gripped Eve's arm with a hand

that shook. 'I swear to you, I swear on my life, Paul loved Derrick. Loved, respected, admired him. There isn't a violent bone in Paul's body. Oh God, God, God, Rozilyn, Derrick's wife. They've been married for nearly forty years. What will she do? What will she do?'

'Have you noticed anyone in the neighborhood who doesn't belong? Did Paul mention anyone who made him uncomfortable?'

'No. Just no. He's been working long hours these past few weeks especially. On this campaign. He's been tired and distracted, but excited. It was coming together, and today was the day. Friday, when he finally came to bed, he snuggled in with me, promised as soon as this deal went through, the three of us were going to take a long weekend anywhere I wanted to go. He fell asleep with a smile on his face. And then, then they were here.

'They were here,' she repeated. 'And nothing will ever be the same again.'

'Your security. Who has your codes?'

'Paul, Melody, and I, of course. Iris. Iris Kelly, our parents' helper. She's been with us for nine years. We hired her while I was pregnant. She's like family.'

'I'll need her contact information.'

'Yes, but Iris would never have given away our codes, would never have had a part in this. Oh God, I have to tell her what happened. Tell her about Paul.'

'She doesn't work on Mondays?' Eve asked. 'On weekends?'

'Not unless we need her. With Melly in school full-time, and since Iris got married last year, she generally comes in on Tuesday, Wednesday, Thursday. Lieutenant, I trust her with my child, and that's trusting her with my life.'

'No one else has the codes?'

'No, just – Oh, I'm sorry. My mother, my stepfather. They have them. Paul's parents live in Sedona, so . . . Oh God, oh God, Paul's parents. I have to—'

'We'll do the notification. How often do you change the security codes?'

'I guess maybe once a year or so. We never had any trouble here. We never had anything bad happen until . . . Paul. When can I see Paul?'

What there is to see, Eve thought, you just don't need to see. 'I'll give you the information on contacting the medical examiner. Ms Greenspan, I'm going to have one of the officers go upstairs with you. You can contact your mother. You should pack what you and your daughter need. We'll have you taken to New Rochelle. I need a contact number for you.'

'What will you do?'

'I'll do my job.'

'My husband isn't a murderer, Lieutenant.'

'Ms Greenspan, I'm sitting here and telling you, your husband was a victim. I'll do my job, and do everything possible to find the men who hurt you, terrorized your daughter, and killed your husband.'

*

32

Eve tracked Callendar down in the home office.

'Nothing hinky on his devices with a standard pass,' Callendar told her. 'A lot of work shit – a lot especially over the last six, eight weeks. Personal shit, reminders, basic correspondence. He mostly played word games to unwind, it looks like. We'll take a deeper look in the lab.'

'House security?'

'That's the hink in the hinky.' Callendar pulled a little wrapped square of gum out of one of the multitude of pockets in her cherry-red baggies. 'Want?'

'Pass.'

'So, it's a good system,' she began as she unwrapped and popped the gum in her mouth. 'Seriously mega good. They didn't stint. You don't compromise a security cover like this one like butter, right? And they didn't. They've been working on getting through for a couple months.'

'"Months"?'

'We'll check it at the house, but what I get on-site with portables? A good thirty flicks and pushes at it, starting back end of December. Every flick and push between two and three in the A.M. Flicks get longer and deeper, pushes harder. What they did, see, is go a layer, then take that data back, work it, come back again, go down a layer, and like that.'

She blew an impressive pink bubble, snapped it back.

'I'm getting the vics didn't change any codes over that period, and these guys just steadily hacked through. Couldn't manage a slide, couldn't just jam-o-rama. They had to chip and hack by layers. Took time and patience, some reasonable skill, and damn good equipment.'

'So they targeted these people, this location, back before the first of the year,' Eve concluded. 'They didn't have the codes, didn't have the skills to compromise the system straight off. They didn't have the skills to compromise in a few attempts.'

'Exactamundo.'

'And the residents didn't notice the flicks and pushes?'

Callendar shoved at the hair she wore short, spiky, and deeply purple. 'They would have if they'd paid real attention. Most don't, Dallas. You set and forget.'

'Take everything in. We'll want to go deep on all the devices, including the wife's, the kid's. Who's on the Quantum location?'

'Feeney and McNab. It's a big one. The cap shuffled to cover it.'

Eve nodded. Having Feeney, captain of EDD, on the case meant the e-geeks would analyze every byte.

'Everything, Callendar, down to the memo cubes. We'll be in the field.'

'You got it. Dallas, you get a good sense of a person when you pry open their personal e's. This dude loved his work. Seriously got into it. But his family? Number one, all the way.'

Eve stepped out, called in the sweepers. She wanted every inch of the house covered. To give Cecily and Melody time to pack and be transported, she went down to the basement.

Another family area, sprawling and casual with a big screen and a gaming area, a mini-kitchen setup, a big dollhouse that made her think of Bella, some puzzles, some toys, a half bath.

The maintenance area was behind a thick door – broken by the first on scene. Pipes, an old iron sink, the guts of the house where Cecily had been imprisoned. Some blood on the pipes where she'd struggled. No windows to let in even a sliver of light. Thick brick walls to absorb sound.

Eve imagined being trapped there in the dark – cold, terrified, not knowing what happened or was happening to her husband and daughter.

She searched the room, found fresh scrapes in the dust where she concluded the captors had secured a camera. One angled to show Paul Rogan his bruised, battered, helpless wife.

She turned when Peabody came to the doorway.

'The uniforms are taking the wife and kid to the wife's parents. They're wrecked, Dallas. Greenspan's holding on by a thread for the kid, but it's a really thin thread.'

Like Eve, she scanned the room. 'Jesus,' she murmured. 'I don't know how she grips that thread.'

'They targeted these people specifically,' Eve said. 'That means they had to know enough to believe, to be all but certain, Paul Rogan would press the button to save his family. They stalked them, spent – according to Callendar – about two months working to compromise security and get in clean.'

She shook her head as she walked out, circled the family area. 'If the target had been Derrick Pearson, they'd have spent their time on him. All of this to blow up a meeting, and at least some of the people in it. To kill the merger?'

With another shake of her head, she started up the stairs. 'There have to be better ways to kill a deal. Easier ways. Did you get any more out of the kid?'

'She thinks maybe they had a cam in her room, too. And she said the one who stayed with her more made her cry into the 'link a couple of times. He made her say: "Please, Daddy, help me."'

'Yeah, into a 'link. That's for recording. They had the poor bastard wear an earbud, had his kid crying in his head. Probably recorded the wife, too. And I'm betting they put a recorder on him so they could watch. He makes a move to contact the police, he wavers, his amazing girls scream in his head.'

'From the way Melody talks, I lean toward the one who spent more time with her father, instead of the one with her, being in charge.'

Eve continued up to the bedroom level. 'Why leave them alive? Once Rogan did what they wanted, why not finish the wife and kid? No wits then. Nobody left to give us an accounting.'

She walked into the master. Blood-spotted, rumpled sheets, clipped zip-tie restraints littered the floor. More blood on a chair where she imagined Rogan struggled.

'How well did they know the house before Saturday

night?' she wondered. 'Had one or both of them been in here before, as a guest, as a repairman? Deliveries, some maintenance deal? Not necessarily,' she continued as she moved around the room. 'They gave themselves two full days with the family. Time to pick their spots, to find the master and the kid's room. They didn't tear things up,' she added. 'Didn't take valuables – didn't compromise or take electronics. Cecily had a wedding set thing on. Not a real flashy diamond, but it looked like an easy few thousand, and they didn't take it.'

She stepped into the walk-in closet – a large his and hers – found, as she'd expected, a small wall safe.

'Safe's locked, and I'm betting whatever was in it still is.' She tapped her fingers on the lock pad.

'Wow, you're getting really good at that.'

Eve spared Peabody a glance. 'Not that good.' Not Roarke good, she thought. 'I got the combo from Cecily. And here we have some cash, some decent if not flashy jewelry, and a couple of high-end, dressy wrist units, passports, and so on.'

She shut the safe again. 'They didn't care about a few thousand here and there, however easy the pickings. Or what they could get fencing the art and e's. Focused, one purpose. Patient.'

She wandered into the master bath, out again.

'Patient, focused, purposeful.' As she spoke, she went out, found her way to Melody's room. Girlie, but not obsessively, Eve thought. Neat – except for the broken glass, the scattered solar system – but not regimented.

'Did he forget to strap her back to the bed, to bind her ankles, or did he want her to be able to get up? Kept her hands tied,' Eve mused.

'Just a kid. He wasn't worried about her, that's how I see it. Once they had what they wanted, this one just wasn't worried about the kid. Not in charge.'

Nodding, Eve turned to Peabody again. 'I agree. The one in charge of her wasn't and isn't the leader. This one left a loose thread. He loosened her ties – maybe a soft spot for kids. Only a kid, but not an idiot, and strong and smart enough to figure out how to get attention. Maybe it didn't matter to them we found them so fast. We'd have found them in short order anyway. But it might've taken another hour. Didn't matter.'

She walked over to the broken window. 'Really didn't. Long gone by then. Off to Fat City.'

'Which is not an overweight urban area,' Peabody put in.

'How does blowing up a marketing exec, a meeting, a merger, and/or the head of Quantum lead to Fat City?'

'Sounds like a Roarke question.'

'Yeah, it does. Here come the sweepers,' Eve said as she saw two vans pull up. 'Let's get them started.'

3

As the domestic lived in a building within easy walking distance of the Rogan/Greenspan home, Eve decided to have a talk with Iris Kelly before moving on to the injured. Eve mastered them inside, stepped across the small lobby.

One of the two elevators let out a pair of women speaking rapid Spanish, both carting handbags the size of baby elephants. The younger pushed a thumb-sucking baby in a stroller with little animals dangling – including a baby elephant. The kid's eyes looked glassy with pleasure as it snacked on its own thumb.

'What do they get out of that?' Eve wondered as they stepped into the vacated elevator. 'How good could your own thumb taste?'

'It's not the taste, it's the sucking action. Oral satisfaction and comfort.'

'So, basically, they're giving themselves a blow job?'

For a couple of seconds, Peabody's mouth worked silently. 'I . . . I can't possibly answer that without feeling really dirty and weirded.'

With a shrug, Eve rode up to the fourth floor. Decent building, Eve thought, decent security. Solid working class with residents who took enough pride of place not to litter up the lobby, elevators, hallways.

She pressed the buzzer on Kelly's door, waited.

The intercom hummed as it engaged. 'Yes?'

'Lieutenant Dallas, Detective Peabody.' Eve held up her badge. 'NYPSD. We'd like to speak to you, ma'am.'

Locks clicked, the door opened, and Eve saw Iris had already gotten the news. Sky-blue eyes, swollen and red-rimmed, dominated a face the color of Irish cream. Sunshine hair was sleeked back in a long tail. She wore straight-legged black pants, a shirt shades quieter than her eyes, and a simple black cardigan.

'On the screen. I heard the report on the screen. Paul . . . I can't reach Cecily. I can't reach her. Please.'

'Can we come in, Ms Kelly?' Eve asked.

'I'm sorry. Yes. I slept late,' she continued as she stepped back. 'It's a day off. I slept late. I turned the screen on for company while I did some chores before I went out to run errands. I can't reach Cecily. Melly. Oh God, please.'

'Ms Greenspan and Melody are on their way to Ms Greenspan's mother in New Rochelle.'

'Oh. Oh.' Iris sank into a chair in the living area, covered her face, burst into tears. 'Thank God. I thought . . . I was afraid . . . It's all craziness. They're saying Paul killed himself and all those other people at his office. He never would, never, but they keep saying it and saying it. And I couldn't reach Cecily.'

'Why don't I get you some water?' Peabody suggested.

'Thank you. Thank you. I don't understand why they're saying Paul did something like this. He'd never hurt anyone. Please, he's a good man.'

'We believe Mr Rogan was coerced.'

'"Coerced,"' Iris repeated slowly.

'Ms Kelly, has anyone approached you, asking questions about the family, their home, Mr Rogan's work?'

'No. No. I mean to say, I talk about the family the way you do, with my husband or friends, my own family. Except they're family, too. They made me family.'

As she swiped at tears, she rocked herself for comfort. 'I was there when they brought Melly home for the first time, just a little pink bundle. I'll share things, like how well Melly's doing in school or her dance recital, or something funny Paul said – he likes to joke – or something Cecily and I did. Just casual talk.'

'Someone outside your friends and family,' Eve pushed as Peabody brought Iris a glass of water. 'Someone making a delivery to the house when Melody was in school and her parents were at work. Or a repairman. Anyone.'

'No, I promise you. I might talk to the people who run the market when I do the marketing. They might ask how I am doing, and how the family is doing. I might brag about Melly now and then. She's next to my own. I might say how well she did in school – she, she wants to be an astronomer. I might speak to one of the mothers or nannies if I went to the school to get her. Sometimes

41

Cecily has to stay for meetings, and I pick Melly up and take her home.'

'Did anyone make you uncomfortable? Anyone you spoke to, anyone you saw around the neighborhood?'

'I can't think of anyone. I know some of the neighbors, and the people who work for them. You chat sometimes. I met my Johnny when he was working on the house next door. He redid the kitchen for the Spacers, and we chatted.'

'How long ago was that?'

'Nearly four years.'

'You have the security code to the residence.'

'Yes.' Her streaming eyes went wild. 'Yes, I—'

'Have you given it to anyone?'

'Oh no, no one. Not even Johnny. You can't break trust.'

'Do you have it written down?'

'No.'

'How do you remember it?'

'It's easy. It's all the initials of our first names, in order of age. PCIM – the numbers of the alphabet for them. So it's sixteen – one-six, that is – three, nine, thirteen. I don't understand. Did something happen at the house?'

That part of the report hadn't hit the media, Eve thought – or it hit after Iris turned off the screen. 'Two men broke in – got through security. At this time we don't believe they knew the code.'

Her breath started to hitch. 'You said Cecily and Melly were all right. You said—'

'They will be. Ms Greenspan was hurt, but her injuries

aren't critical. You can contact her through her mother when we're done here.'

'Melly?' Rocking faster, Iris fisted both hands over her heart. 'Did they hurt Melly?'

'Nothing serious. Do you answer the 'link when you're working?'

'Yes. Please, I just need to talk to them.'

'Melly threw Jupiter out her window to get the cops' attention.' Peabody added a smile to her soothing voice. 'She's smart, brave, and she's fine.'

'She is smart. She is.' More tear swiping. 'Okay. They're okay.'

'Have there been any contacts,' Eve continued, 'repeat contacts you don't know personally, surveys asking questions, anything like that in the last six months?'

'Nothing I can think of.'

'Think back to December. What was going on?'

'Oh, the holiday prep. Melly was so excited as we counted down to Christmas, even though she doesn't believe in Santa anymore. I helped with the decorating, as I always do. We make a party of it. There's extra marketing and shopping. I'd pick up things for both Paul and Cecily. Paul especially this year, as he was already working hard on a campaign. And of course, Melly and I would go out to shop – our secret shopping and wrapping. For her parents, and a few of her girlfriends, her grandparents.'

'Nothing unusual.'

'I can't think of . . . Well, unusual for me, but I don't see—'

'Anything.'

'I had my 'link and wallet lifted, right out of my purse. And I know better. Born and raised in New York, so I know how to be careful, and still.'

'How, when?'

'We'd been shopping, Melly and I, hours of it, and had lunch out. A busy Saturday. I don't work Saturdays as a rule, not for a couple years now, except sometimes over busy times and in the summer break. We were loaded down, and I was a little tired. I got careless. We were on the subway platform, crowded, noisy, and Melly was so excited. I had her hand, firm grip. And there was some jostling as the train came in. That had to be when it happened, as I'd just used my 'link to scan us through the turnstiles. And when we were on the train, and I went to get it out – just to let Johnny know I'd pick up a curry on the way home – my 'link and my wallet weren't in my purse.'

'Did you report it?'

'I did, only because Paul and Cecily insisted. Who would find them? I couldn't say who took them, only when I thought. I had to cancel the debit card I carry, and the other apps on my 'link and so on. I hadn't had but a little cash. Well under a hundred dollars, but I had photos in my wallet that meant something to me.'

'But not the codes for the security system?'

'No. Detective – I've already forgotten your name.'

'Lieutenant Dallas.'

'I'm sorry, Lieutenant, I'll swear to you on all I love,

you'll never meet a man more decent and caring than Paul Rogan. If he did what they say he did, it's as you said. He was coerced. More than even that. I don't know what the word would be, but more than even that. Please, can I try to reach Cecily and Melly now?'

Eve rose. 'Go ahead. If you think of anything else, however insignificant it might seem, contact me or Detective Peabody. Cop Central.'

'You have my word on it. I'll do anything I can to help find who did this to my family.'

'December,' Peabody said as they rode down to the lobby

'Before Christmas, so before the flicks and pushes. They gave it a shot, figured maybe Kelly had the code in her wallet, on her 'link. She didn't, so they had to start working through the system. Let's find out when this merger started rolling, who knew as far back as December. And let's get the incident report on the stolen wallet and 'link.'

Eve stepped out into the brisk air. 'We'll run Kelly's husband just to cover the bases.'

'She has pictures the kid drew on her kitchen board – and a Valentine's Day card from the kid, along with one from the husband.'

'It's not going to be the husband. We run him anyway, cover those bases. He wouldn't have to lift the 'link and wallet to try to get the code. He'd just check for the code when she wasn't looking. But maybe somebody he's done a job for, or there's someone he works with, hangs out with, who wanted a shortcut to Fat City. Pump him for info, start hacking the layers just like they hacked the security.

'We'll head to the hospital,' Eve decided. 'But let's see who might've been released. If there's any on the way, we'll take them as we come to them.'

By the time they got to the hospital, they had statements from three people who'd been treated and released. All ran along similar lines. Paul Rogan – family and company man, creative team leader – had appeared 'off' or 'ill' or 'not himself', had approached Derrick Pearson and Willimina Karson as they'd entered the conference room.

And boom.

Eve hoped to start at the top with Karson, but the severity of the Econo exec's injuries had her in ICU, in a coma, and off-limits. Switching tacks, Eve badged them into Rogan's admin's room.

Against the white sheets of his hospital bed, Rudy's face shined raw and red under its coating of burn gel. A stabilizer cast covered his right arm from wrist to shoulder. Sutures closed a gash running from the crown of his head to his left ear. Skin exposed by the thin hospital gown showed nicks, punctures, bruises, and burns.

'Mr Roe, I'm Lieutenant Dallas, and this is Detective Peabody.' She slipped her badge away again as she approached the bed.

The room, the patient, reeked of the sweet, green smell of the gel. Rudy's blackened eyes welled.

'I don't know what happened. I don't know.'

Ease him in, Eve thought. 'What time did Mr Rogan come into the office this morning?'

'Eight-forty-five. I was worried because I expected him by eight-thirty, latest. It was the big day, and we were going to go over the bullet points of the presentation before the meeting. I'd made some more notes – just chat points – over the weekend.'

'Did you send them to him?'

'No, but I texted him yesterday to tell him, and to remind him of a couple of things.'

'Did he answer?'

'He just texted back to relax. Um, "Chill, Rudy. We're locked on."'

'"Locked on"?'

'Yeah, I didn't get it for a minute, then I figured he meant we had the presentation locked down. Sort of.'

'It wasn't one of his usual expressions?'

'I don't think so. I mean, I never heard him use it.'

Military, Eve thought. First mistake.

'How did he seem when he came in this morning?'

'Distracted. Tired. I figured he worked all weekend even though he told me not to worry.' A tear leaked out, slid down the slick gel. 'I wanted to give him my notes, but he went right into his office, told me no calls. And – and he locked the door. I heard him lock the door. He never locked the door before. I should've known something was wrong, really wrong.'

Peabody reached down, took Rudy's uninjured hand. 'You couldn't know.'

'He wasn't acting right, he wasn't, but he came out just before nine and he stopped, and he looked right at me. He told me I did good work, and how I was an asset to him, to the company. It felt good, you know? He always made sure to tell us when we did a good job. He went to the conference room, and I finished up some other work before I went into his office to put a file on his desk. I saw his tablet. He hadn't taken his tablet to the meeting, and he'd need it. I grabbed it, and I ran because he'd need it. I got to the doors, or maybe I opened the door. I can't remember. Something exploded and everything was hot and loud, and it felt like I was flying. Then I don't remember until I heard screaming, and somebody was dragging me. I think. It's all mixed up after.'

'It's all right. Did Mr Rogan get any contacts at work – appointments, correspondence, tags – that seemed unusual, that concerned you?'

'No, ma'am, I swear. Paul wouldn't do what they're saying. He'd never do this.'

Because he was hurt, and grieving, she let the *ma'am* go. 'Did anyone in the company have an issue with him?'

'No, ma'am. I mean there are disagreements sometimes, debates, and things got tense a few times during the campaign and the negotiations. But nothing harsh. I loved working for him. Is he really dead?'

'I'm sorry.'

'Maybe it wasn't him,' Rudy mumbled, looking away,

looking at the wall. 'Maybe it was somebody who looked like him. Like a clone. I'm really tired.'

'If you think of anything else, contact me.' Eve signaled for Peabody to leave a card on the table beside the bed.

'Do you have anyone who can come hang with you?' Peabody asked him.

'My mom's flying in, and my brother.' The misery in his eyes lessened when a woman came to the door. 'Kimmi.'

Though she'd obviously been crying, she carried a cheerful clutch of flowers.

'NYPSD,' Eve told her.

'Oh. I can come back.'

'No need. We're wrapping up. Relative?'

'No, I work with Rudy.'

'Peabody, why don't you take the flowers, stay with Rudy. Can we talk outside for a few minutes?' Though she had asked Kimmi, Eve simply took her arm, led her out.

The petite brunette with the sad doe eyes twisted her fingers together. 'I wasn't even there,' she said before Eve could speak. 'I mean, I was at my desk when . . . I heard the explosion, only it didn't sound like I thought an explosion sounds. I guess because I wasn't close to the conference room. But then I heard shouting and screaming, and people started running, and alarms were going off.'

'Did you see Mr Rogan this morning?'

'For a second, when he walked by my desk. He didn't say anything. He always says something, but he didn't.'

'How much did you interact with him at work?'

'Paul interacted with everybody. It was his leadership style.'

'Personally?'

'I've only been with Quantum a little over a year, but I went to the party he has at his house for the holidays. None of this makes sense.'

'What's your position at Quantum?'

'I'm Lia Berkell's assistant.' She squeezed her eyes shut. 'Was. She— she died in the explosion. They told me she died. She was the digital marketing manager. She was in the meeting. Um, she and Rudy and I worked tight with Paul on this campaign. But it wasn't just work.'

She brushed a tear away. 'We were really a team. You had to be there for each other. Like, when my apartment got broken into, Lia let me stay at her house until my roommate got back in town, so I wouldn't be alone.'

'When did that happen?'

'Last December. My roommate was on a business trip, and I went on a date. I got home and somebody'd broken in.'

'What was taken?'

'My comp, spare 'link, my tablet, my wall screen, the wrist unit my parents got me when I got my MBA, my emergency cash. The police said it was probably somebody looking for a quick score, but they messed up my place, and scared me. It doesn't matter now.'

'Did you have work on the comp?'

'Sure, but it was passcoded and fail-safed. And I always backed up on disc, and I take the disc with me if I go out. Just habit. So I had everything backed up.'

'You had data on the Econo deal on the comp? Office emails regarding it, that sort of thing?'

'Yes. It's why I had the fail-safe.'

Nothing, Eve thought, was fail-safe.

She filled Peabody in as they went up to ICU to try another check on Karson.

'December again.'

'December eighteen – just after Kelly had her wallet and 'link lifted. We'll want that incident report.'

'I'll get both. The best I can get – until I get more – is negotiations between Quantum and Econo started wrapping up the end of November, or close enough they had the deal pretty much nailed down. Rogan's domestic has her wallet and 'link lifted in December, and now one of Rogan's team gets her comp and e's taken in December. Coincidences are bollocks, right?'

'As rain,' Eve agreed. 'Though I don't know what the hell makes rain so right. It's going to be about the deal, not the people. Blow up the deal – and follow the money. Who benefits, who loses, that's the first line.'

They stepped into the ICU lobby. The guard dog nurse at the desk shot them a hard and suspicious look. A scattering of people sat in chairs. All looked weary. One had the shine of burn gel down his left cheek, a walking cast on his right ankle, and his right arm in a sling.

Eve walked to the guard dog, palmed her badge. 'What's Willimina Karson's condition?'

'I'm going to verify that ID.'

51

'Go ahead.'

The nurse scanned it. Her stony expression clicked down to stern. 'I had some media types try to get past me before. Ms Karson's critical. If you want more, if you want specifics, you'll have to speak to her doctor, and you'll have to wait. It's been a hell of a morning.'

'All around. I'd appreciate being informed about any change in her status.'

'I'll note it down.'

'How many up here from this morning's incident?'

'Two now, including Ms Karson. There were three, but she didn't make it.'

Twelve dead, Eve thought, turning her attention back to the man with the sling and cast.

Middle sixties, she thought, with a lean, distinguished look despite the sweatpants and the I ♥ NEW YORK sweatshirt. Both of which looked fresh off the rack and incongruous with the black dress shoes.

'Let's check him out,' she said to Peabody.

She crossed to him, showed her badge. 'Do you have someone in ICU?'

He eyed her carefully, though the left eye was shot with blood. 'I do. I'm legal counsel for EconoLift and Willimina Karson's adviser.'

'You were in the meeting. I'm primary on the investigation. My partner, Detective Peabody.'

'I know who you are. An easy case for New York's top murder cop, isn't it, as you already have the killer. Or what's left of the son of a bitch.' His good hand fisted on his knee, rapped twice. 'I wish to God he'd lived through it so I could think of him rotting in a cell for the rest of his life.'

'Peabody, see if there's a more comfortable, more private place we can talk to — Your name, sir?'

'Loren Able. I won't leave Willimina.'

'No, sir, but I need to speak with you, and I need to give you some facts.'

Peabody managed to secure a small break room — a single table, four chairs, a pair of vending machines, and an AutoChef that looked older than Noah. And somehow, being Peabody, she'd come up with a small pillow.

'Mr Able, the nurse told me you should have your foot elevated.' She set the pillow on the fourth chair, angled it.

He sighed. 'That's kind of you.' He lifted his leg with his hands, set his foot carefully on the pillow.

'Can I get you some water, some tea?'

'I would give you my firstborn, if I had one, for some decent black coffee.'

'Let me see what I can do.'

When Peabody went out, Able shut his eyes a moment. 'I read the Icove book. Haven't seen the vid, but I read the book. It appears Nadine Furst captured the detective very well. You're fortunate in your partner, Lieutenant.'

'I am.'

'Facts, you said. I'd like to hear the facts.'

'Not all of this will filter through the media,' Eve said. 'Not at all while the investigation's active.'

'I've been a lawyer for thirty-nine years, Lieutenant. I know how to keep my mouth shut.'

'I'm going to tell you about Paul Rogan.'

As she spoke, he closed his eyes again so she couldn't read them. But the burn on his face became an angrier red as she described the home invasion.

When she finished, he said nothing for a long moment. Then he opened his eyes. 'You're saying, essentially, he was told to make a choice. His life and those of us in that room this morning, or the lives of his wife and child?'

'All evidence points to that, yes.'

He drew in a deep breath. 'I came out of that room with some broken bones, some bruises. A woman I've known since birth is fighting for her life. A woman who's a daughter to me in all but blood. If I'd had even seconds of warning, I would have tried to shield her with my own body. I wouldn't have hesitated. I may, eventually, be able to accept that Paul Rogan made the only choice he could make, as I may have done the same. If Willi dies, I'll curse him with my last breath.'

'How well did you know him?'

'Not at all.' He looked over as Peabody came in with a to-go tray and three cups. 'You're resourceful, Detective, as that smells at least decent.'

'I don't know if it'll hit much above that.'

'Thank you. I didn't have any direct business with

Rogan,' Able continued as he took the first sip. 'I worked with Quantum's in-house counsel. He's in ICU along with Willi. I hope he makes it. I got to know Derrick Pearson well over the last few months. A very good man, shrewd and fair, from my standpoint. My priority was to help craft the best deal for Econo.'

'Did you?'

'I believe so, yes.'

'What happens to the deal now?'

'With Derrick gone, and Willi ... The ground's shaky. The paperwork, the legalities would have been cemented today, after the meeting, the marketing reveal, and so on. The deal was done in spirit last week.'

'But unsigned.'

'Yes. There may be some board members, on both sides, who balk now. But Derrick's children will push for the deal, because that's what he wanted. And it's a good one for Quantum.'

'And Econo? I'm sorry, if Ms Karson is unable to speak for Econo.'

'I would be majority stockholder. Her shares of Econo would be divided among me, her half brother, and her closest friend, one she's had since childhood.'

'Where are the brother and the friend?'

'Javier – her mother's son with husband three – lives in Barcelona, where he's studying medicine. Both he and Willimina's mother are arranging travel. They should be here by tomorrow, latest. Juliette is on her way here already.

She lives in Santa Fe with her husband and daughter. She's pregnant with her second child. I told her to wait, not to travel, but she's coming.'

'If you'd died in the blast? Who gets your shares?'

'Interesting. Willi, but if she predeceased me, they're to be divided between my brother and sister.'

'Could you give me the names and contact information for all the beneficiaries?' Peabody asked.

'I'm afraid you'll have to contact my office – and I'll clear that. I lost my 'link, memo book, and everything else in the blast. I had to beg an orderly to get me something to wear. Except for the shoes.' He frowned at his elevated foot. 'They made it through.'

Once Peabody had helped Able back to the waiting area, Eve decided she'd done enough in the field, enough interviews, enough impressions.

She needed to get back to Central, needed to set up her murder board, her book. And she needed to think.

'Let's grab a conference room, coordinate with Baxter and Trueheart. I need time to write this out, report to the commander.'

'Could we maybe get food – any food whatsoever – from the go place off the hospital lobby?'

'You want hospital food?'

'So hangs my desperation.'

'Fine.' Eve pulled out a handful of credits. 'Get desperation food, meet me at the car.'

It would give her time to start reviewing her notes.

A lot of players, she thought as she walked out-side. Deals and the wheels inside them. Shares of this, shares of that.

Somebody, she concluded, had wanted more than their fair share.

4

Peabody hopped in the car, handed Eve a go-cup.

'Soup. Vegetable Beef.'

Eve took a sniff, then a swallow before she started winding out of the underground lot. It smelled like pepper and tasted like spicy, liquefied cardboard, heated to cautiously approach lukewarm. 'Beef of what?'

'They didn't say, and I thought it wiser not to ask.' Peabody took a gulp, coughed a little. 'It's bad, it's bad. I should've gone for the mini berry pies.'

'They had mini berry pies and you went for liquid mystery meat?'

'And veg.' Peabody choked down another swallow. 'I told myself to be an adult, to think of loose pants. Is it gamey? There's a little bit of gamey aftertaste. Gak.'

'It could be rat. Liquefied, peppered rat.' Eve shoved her cup into Peabody's hand.

'It's a hospital! Hospitals don't serve rat.'

As she wound, Eve swung toward a recycler, stopped. Pointed. 'Dispose of the rat soup.'

'It's not rat. I didn't drink rat.' But Peabody fumbled the door open, juggling go-cups. She hotfooted it to the recycler, dumped the cups. She slid back into the car, downtrodden. 'Can I get a diet fizzy from the AC?'

'What flavor washes away the taint of rat soup?'

'It wasn't rat, but any.' She ordered up cherry, and a tube of Pepsi for Eve. 'The lawyer came off on the level,' she began. 'Still, if both he and Karson went down in the explosion, that's the big bulk of shares in Econo. And with Pearson gone, that's the majority of Quantum.'

'We'll take a look at all beneficiaries. It's a weird-ass way to inherit. Risky and overly complicated. What if Rogan loses his nerve, doesn't hit the button? What if the main shareholders survive the blast? And Karson may.'

'Why explosives?' Peabody picked up. 'Killing multiples rather than homing in on specifics – if inheritance is the motive?'

'Point,' Eve agreed. 'More probable someone with a grievance against one or both of the companies. More probable someone who benefits from – ha ha – blowing up the deal. You toss both companies into chaos, postpone or kill the merger, while the new leadership comes in to deal with the fallout.'

'I don't get what's gained if the merger goes south, especially if it's just postponed.'

'That's what we'll ask our expert consultant, civilian.'

'McNab and I are giving Roarke ten thousand to invest for us.'

'What?'

'I asked Roarke awhile back, and we're not there yet, but close. We're going to do five each, and give it to Roarke.'

The idea made Eve's stomach sink a little. 'That's a lot of scratch to gamble on detectives' salaries.'

'We might want to buy a place one day. An apartment or even a townhouse. If you wanted to invest, who would you trust with it?'

'Roarke,' she admitted, 'since I know pretty much squat about investing.'

'Exactly.'

'He bought a farm,' Eve muttered.

'He bought the farm? You're mixing up your idioms again.'

'A farm. An actual farm, somewhere in Nebraska, because I made some comment that turned into a challenge in his head. So he bought this shithole farm in Bumfuck, in *my* name.'

'You're going to live on a farm in Nebraska?'

'Jesus Christ, Peabody, did a glug of rat soup melt your brain? He's going to do something with it, who knows what? Make it something or other and sell it or something. It's a craphole of a house with weird craphole buildings on a bunch of scary, empty land in the middle of nowhere Nebraska.'

'And you own it.'

'Technically.' Which bugged and baffled her – which she knew stood as reason number one he'd done it in the first damn place. 'What I'm saying is whatever he paid for this bullshit is a game to him. Even if he loses the challenge, he'll be, you know, amused. If you give him your money, it won't be a game to him. He'll be careful with it.'

'I know it. The idea's a little scary, but exciting, too. And it wasn't rat soup. There's maybe, possibly, a scant ten percent chance it was squirrel.'

Eve pulled into Central's underground lot. 'What's the difference?'

'Squirrels are sort of cute and fuzzy. And they can have personality.'

After zipping into her slot, Eve shifted in her seat. 'Look in a squirrel's eyes next time you see one scampering along like a fuzzy rat. Right in the eyes. They're lunatics.'

As she swung out of the car, her communicator signaled. She saw Whitney's office on the readout. 'Dallas.'

'Please report to the commander's office as soon as possible.'

'I'm in the house. I'm on my way up.' She clicked off. And there went her thinking time. 'Get the conference room set up for the briefing with Baxter and Trueheart. Start runs on the beneficiaries,' she continued as she strode to the elevator. 'We need to check in with EDD, get the status, and check like crimes for anything that rings with the home invasion.'

In the elevator she ran through a host of other things she needed. She'd start on them herself once she'd met with Whitney.

The minute the elevator stopped so more cops could crowd in, she abandoned Peabody, headed for the glides.

She pulled out her 'link on the way, tagged Roarke.

It went straight through so that face – carved by the gods with eyes of impossible, soul-spinning blue – filled her screen. 'I guess you're not real busy buying a recently discovered solar system.'

'On my way back from a very long lunch meeting.' With those magical wisps of Ireland in his voice, he smiled with that perfectly sculpted mouth. 'Did you manage a midday meal, Lieutenant?'

'I had some rat soup.'

Eyebrows as dark as his mane of black silk lifted. 'How adventurous of you.'

'I'd rather have pizza. Anyway, I need an expert consultant, civilian – with a specialty in business. Big business. Mergers, specifically.'

'You're on the bombing at Quantum.' His smile faded. 'Twelve dead at last count. Is Willimina Karson still living?'

'She was when I left the hospital. In a coma, critical, but among the living. You know her?'

'Only a bit. I knew Derrick Pearson a bit more, but not well. Still, I'm sorry for it all. A disgruntled employee who snapped is the line coming through the reports. I take it that's not altogether accurate?'

'Not even close. Can you carve out time tonight? It might take awhile.'

'I can, and always will. But I might be able to do better. I need an hour or so yet, but after that I can come to you at Central. Or wherever you may be.'

'Likely here at this stage. I'd appreciate it. I can't get the meat when I don't understand the ... menu,' she decided.

'Then I'll come to you when I finish up. Meanwhile, see if you can get my cop something more appealing than rat soup.'

'Yeah, thanks. See you when you get here.'

She clicked off as she approached Whitney's outer office and admin.

'Go right in, Lieutenant,' the admin told her. 'He's expecting you.'

She stepped in.

Whitney stood at his wall of windows, his hands behind his back in parade rest as he studied his view of New York. He had broad shoulders, and they carried the weight of command well. His close-cropped hair had gray shot through the black.

'Before you report,' he began without turning, 'I'll tell you my wife and Derrick Pearson's have been friends more than twenty years.'

'I'm very sorry, Commander, for her loss, and yours.'

'Thank you. Anna and Rozilyn Pearson are and have been close. While I consider her and considered Derrick friends, Anna and Roz are more like sisters. This is a very difficult day.'

He turned then, his wide, dark face solemn. 'I want to add that when I informed Anna you'd taken charge of the investigation, she expressed relief, and told me she'd comfort Rozilyn by telling her we have the best seeking answers and justice for Derrick.'

Rather than going to sit at his desk, he stood where he was, the towers and spires of Manhattan rising into the pale blue March sky at his back. 'What answers do you have at this time?'

'You're aware, sir, of the home invasion on the Rogan/ Greenspan residence?'

'I have the report from the first on scene.'

'Two men — as both the wife and daughter identify the assailants as men — entered the residence in the early hours of Saturday morning. Detective Callendar is, at this time, analyzing, but reported on scene that the security on the home had been compromised gradually, layer by layer, over several attempts since December. Also in December, when the negotiations for the merger of Quantum and Econo began to solidify, Rogan's domestic, and the only non-family member to have the security code, had her wallet and 'link lifted from her handbag. She reported same.'

'Ah' was all he said.

'Further in December, an assistant in Rogan's department returned home to find her apartment broken into. Her comp — with work data on it — was among the things taken.'

Whitney nodded. 'It's my understanding Rogan was marketing. He wasn't finance or legal, or someone who would have been intimately connected with the terms of the merger or in its negotiations.'

'No, sir. But he and his team had worked on the market-ing campaign for the merger, and he was to present that at the meeting this morning. Commander, they tortured him and his wife, his eight-year-old daughter for more than two full days. They beat his wife in front of him, let him know they could and would rape and kill her – and his daughter. They had cameras in the basement room where they moved and held the wife, and another in the daughter's room where she was restrained to the bed.'

'I understand the duress, but Rogan walked into that conference room alone, and twelve people are dead.'

'I don't know if it's altogether true he was alone, sir. Some of the statements we've taken indicate he seemed to be speaking to someone, and they forced the daughter to call for her father into a 'link, to specifically cry out for him to help her.'

'Recorded it,' Whitney noted. 'Most likely to play that through an earbud.'

'Yes, sir. They may have put a recorder on him as well.'

'To threaten him if he hesitated or attempted to contact the police.'

'That's my belief, Commander. Sir, I'm not saying he had no choice, but that he believed he had no choice. He pulled the trigger, there's no question of that. But he pulled it, the evidence at this point shows, to save his wife and daughter.'

Whitney expelled a breath. 'I didn't know Rogan, but Derrick mentioned him more than once. I know Derrick thought highly of him. Fondly of him and his family.'

'He had plans for a celebration with his team after the meeting, Commander. He'd arranged for refreshments with a caterer, was putting bonuses through for two assistants. He noted down to stop on the way home Monday for flowers for both his wife and daughter as a thank-you for understanding how much time he'd put into the work. He didn't leave Quantum Friday evening with plans to bomb the meeting. There is no evidence we've found to show he had any connection to explosives, or the knowledge to build or acquire the vest.'

Whitney nodded. 'What do we know about the two men?'

'The sweepers were covering the house when I left it. Frankly, sir, I don't expect them to find much of anything we can use. These men were careful. They'd planned this for months. But I believe at least one of them is military or police, active or former. I lean military, and when Salazar and her team examine the bomb fragments, I believe they'll show some experience with explosives.'

She detailed the rest – the interviews, the angles, the upcoming briefing, and her working theory.

'I've asked Roarke to consult,' she added, 'for the business angle, the ins and outs of a merger on this scale. And the ups and downs of it. Straight terrorism, Commander, there'd be a statement by now. Some group would take credit. A vendetta against one or more of the individuals in the meeting? It's too broad and complicated for that.'

'So a strike at one or both of the companies,' he concluded, 'or the merger itself.'

'Unless something comes out that leads me otherwise, that's the direction I'm going. Pearson's wife, son, and daughter are beneficiaries. I'll need to interview them.'

'Understood and expected.'

'Could you tell me, Commander, if Pearson spoke to you about the merger?'

'I haven't seen him since the holidays, though I know Anna and Roz have gotten together a few times since. We rarely talked business, Lieutenant, his or mine. I do know his children. Anna knows them better than I do, but my impression is they're both bright and dedicated to Quantum. I can help clear the way for the interviews. Tomorrow morning, at their family home?'

'That would be fine, sir.'

'I'll set it up. Keep me informed, Lieutenant. I won't get in your way.'

'You'll have a report from Baxter and Trueheart directly after our briefing. I'll send you a report of my consult with Roarke as soon as possible.'

He nodded. 'Good hunting. Dismissed.'

And he turned back to study his city through the glass.

She opted to swing by EDD before heading to her office and, calculating, headed to the lab first. She passed a few e-geeks in their eye watering colors and patterns as they bopped their way to and from, but avoided Geek Central as she veered off to the lab.

There she spotted Feeney, his silver-threaded ginger hair sproinging out in every direction. He'd discarded what she assumed was a shit-brown jacket to go with his shit-brown pants and wore the sleeves of his wrinkled beige shirt rolled up.

At a station to his left, McNab stood with his long tail of blond hair streaming down a shirt the color you might get if you electrocuted an orange. His skinny hips ticktocked in carnival-striped baggies. On the other side, Callendar perched on a stool in her red baggies and pink polka-dot shirt. Her purple hair bounced as she shook her shoulders and rolled her head side to side.

Eve rubbed her eyes, then risked them and went through the glass door.

Despite the hips ticktocking, the shoulders shaking, and Feeney's cop-shoes tapping, no music played. Just in their heads, Eve thought. What the hell did they hear in there?

Feeney spotted her, held a finger in the air to hold her off as he used his other hand to swipe and dance over a screen.

He grunted, turned to her.

'Got anything?'

'Got all kinds.' He gave his droopy, basset-hound eyes a quick rub. 'Not much that's going to help right now. Callendar, hit it.'

'Okay, so it's like I said on scene. I've broken down the security – and it's mega good. But they sanded off the layers bit by bit. Spent like maybe twenty hours since December wearing it down – that's just on-site time. Who does that on a residence? Even a nice one?'

'Somebody who wants in bad enough.'

'Yeah, that. A lot of work, a lot of time. On the comms inside, they switched them so the residence got incoming, but nobody could do outgoing.'

'In case one of the captured got to a 'link. Smart. Keep the incoming,' Eve continued, 'so they could monitor, deal with anything over the time period that might bring somebody around if unanswered.'

'You got that. They did get a couple. One tag from the wife's mom on Saturday – and they texted back how she and the kid were going to the vids and shopping and blah-blah because the husband was locked into work all day. Husband got two tags – work-related. They answered one from his admin   probably because it sounded like he'd just keep tagging. Texted him to—'

'"Chill,"' Eve finished. 'They were locked on. The admin gave me that.'

'That's it. What they did with the second, and to the system – smart, too – is programmed an auto response on how he was switched off until Monday morning. And Sunday night, they texted the contact on the wife's 'link for the principal at the school saying the kid was sick, so she was keeping her home Monday and sticking with her.'

'So nobody from the school would wonder or tag or go by on Monday when they didn't show up. The domestic doesn't come in on weekends, on Mondays, so they're clear. But they had to know the schedule to make it work. They watched the house enough to know the routines. What about the house comps?'

'That's on McNab.'

'Yo,' he said, scooting his bony butt onto a stool and swiveling it around. 'The wife's e's have a lot of school stuff, administrative, like, and correspondence with other administrators, teachers, some parents. Some way bitchy parents, just FYI. She handled them smooth, it strikes me. Stuff for her kid. More correspondence – her family, some pals. Nothing hinky. She kept the household accounts – and nothing out of line there, either. His, work stuff. Most of the work over the last couple months is the flashy deal for the merger. Slogans, digital ads, screen ads, and one's like a mini-vid. Pretty frosty. Work correspondence, calendars – work and personal. He did a lot of notes to self in his memo book. Lots of photos on his and hers. Mostly family, vacations, holidays. She does some social media, but he didn't.

'The kid?' McNab shrugged. 'Schoolwork, a few games. Parental controls. Her tablet's full of books. Must be a big reader, and she leans toward science and science fiction. Social media blocked. Any texting had to go through the parental account. I'm still going down layers, but nothing's under any so far. SNNTS. Situation Normal, Nothing to See.'

'I want anything on the merger – the ads, the mail, notes, all of it – copied to my units. Home and office.'

'Can do.'

'Feeney?'

'I started with Rogan's office e's. Same as McNab on them. Merger data is priority. Nothing out of line, no correspondence that doesn't check out, no tags out or in office that doesn't jibe. Did you see his office memo book?'

'Yeah.'

'So you know he planned a party for his team, buying flowers for the wife, taking her and the kid on a long weekend. The guy didn't leave work on Friday planning to blow himself up on Monday.'

'No. I just said exactly that to Whitney.'

'If anybody tried hacking in to access data, it doesn't show. Moved to his admin's next. I gotta say, the kid needs a life, and he oughta make a move on this Kimmi he's got the hots for.'

'Really?'

'Comes over,' Feeney said with a shrug. 'But he spends most of his time at work or thinking about work. Few personal emails – a few friends, his mom – in which he usually mentions this Kimmi, but mostly work oriented. Not a single damn game. No photos. A lot of reminders to remind his boss, calendars – his and Rogan's – contacts – office, personal – Rogan's. Birthdays and anniversaries listed in the personal sections. No sign of hacking, no contacts that read off. And he had a reminder to buy this Kimmi flowers and Rogan a bottle of wine over the weekend for congrats on the campaign. The kid wasn't just not up to no good, he was up to too much good, you ask me. Needs a life outside work.'

'Kimmi visited him in the hospital, brought *him* flowers.'

'Maybe he'll make a move there. Anyhow, I started on the big guy's – Pearson's. So far, nothing off, but I've got a ways to go.'

'I'm working on getting you toys from Econo.'

Feeney puffed out his cheeks. 'I'm gonna need more boys. You're looking inside job?'

'I'm just looking. I've got a briefing downstairs. And Roarke's coming in – not for EDD,' she said quickly. 'I need somebody who knows what the fuck about big business mergers.'

'If he wants to play after the what the fuck, I'll take him. I'm gonna walk you out. Fizzies?' he asked his geeks.

'Solid,' they said in unison.

'So,' Feeney began as they walked out. 'You know that Oscar deal's coming up.'

'Oscar who?'

He scratched fingers through his wiry hair. 'Jesus, Dallas, even I know about the fricking Oscars. The vid award thing.'

'Right. I knew that.' Somewhere, in some corner of her brain.

'You're not going?'

'No.'

'The Icove vid's up for a shitload. Nadine's up for one. Why aren't you going?'

Inside her head, she sulked at the question. 'I don't want to. You have to get all fancied up and talk to other fancied-up people, and sit there with them, right? And you have to do it in New LA with the media all up in your grill asking idiot questions like: Who are you wearing?'

'Yeah. I'd want to stun myself first, but it's a BFD anyway. You know Peabody and McNab got invites to it.'

'No.' Eve stopped, more than surprised. 'Are you sure? Peabody'd be nagging me brainless about it.'

'I'm sure. I got it from Callendar because McNab's keeping it down low, too. And I figure they're not nagging us brainless because we just gave them five days off, and you gave them the place in Mexico to recharge. So they're not saying anything about it because they don't want to be greedy assholes.'

'Okay.'

He sent her that basset-hound look as he ordered up the fizzies at Vending. 'It's a BFD, kid. Likely a once-in-a-lifetime BFD. I'd be willing to spring McNab for it if you spring Peabody.'

'We just caught a case with twelve vics. Shit, shit, fuck! When is it?'

'Sunday.'

'The what? Like the next one coming?'

'Yeah, like the next one coming. But Sunday. They could take the weekend, be back Monday if this is still going hot. Tuesday, maybe, if we nail it – because it goes late, I guess. What I'm saying about that admin kid runs true. We gotta have a life. Don't say anything yet. Give it a day or two.'

'Fine,' she grumbled as he armed himself with fizzies. 'Now I've got to ask Roarke, if I decide to spring her, to provide transpo.'

'You oughta talk to Nadine about that. She's going, for sure. She's probably got something lined up they could hitch to.'

'Maybe. Shit. It's bad enough she did all this with Icove, now she's got me reading the manuscript deal she's done for the Red Horse case.'

'Yeah? How is it?'

Eve's shoulders sagged. 'It's fucking good. I *hate* that. I've gotta go.'

Oscars, my ass, she thought as she strode away. How was she supposed to think about the freaking Oscars when she had twelve in the morgue? Most of them in pieces.

She put it aside to worry about later, hopped on a glide. And put her brain in the job.

She strode into Homicide, blinked once at the bug-eyed multicolored fish on Jenkinson's virulent blue tie, and kept on going until she hit the comforting dull colors of her office.

Because the swallow of rat soup still sat uneasy, she locked her door before stepping over to her AutoChef. She programmed an alfalfa power smoothie, her latest hiding place for her candy stash.

'Son of a bitch!' She pulled out an actual alfalfa power smoothie. 'Son of candy-stealing bitch of a bastard!'

Not only had the nefarious Candy Thief snatched her chocolate, he/she had taken the time and trouble to replace it with the actual item on the freaking menu.

She had to respect that.

When she caught the son of a bitching bastard – and she would, oh, she would – she'd hang the thief out her window by the heels. Naked.

But she'd do so with respect.

For now, she unlocked her door, programmed black coffee, then set up her book and board.

To satisfy herself, she started a couple of runs while she updated her notes, requested a search-and-seizure warrant for electronics at Econo's New York base, and for Willimina Karson's personal e's.

She heard Peabody's familiar clomp as she finished up. 'We're ready when you are, Dallas.'

Eve gathered her files. 'The Rogan/Greenspan's domestic's husband had a ding back when he was sixteen,' she said as they walked. 'Underage drinking at an unsupervised party where the kids were stupid enough to get so loud the neighbors called the cops. Otherwise, he's clean. He's worked for the same company for twelve years. They live within their means. And a check on Loren Able verifies everything he told us.'

She walked into the conference room, scanned the board Peabody had set up, approved.

Baxter and Trueheart sat at the conference table. Trueheart, young and earnest, went over his notes with a tube of ginger ale at his elbow. Baxter, slick in his suit, kicked back with cop coffee in one hand while he studied the board.

'A lot of players, LT,' Baxter said.

'There'll be more to come. I'm getting warrants for Econo. EDD will go through the office data, and Karson's personal electronics, to start. Pearson's son and daughter and his wife will be available for interview tomorrow morning. Whitney just informed me his wife and Pearson's are close friends.'

Baxter winced. 'That's a not good on top of the already bad.'

'What have you got?'

Baxter looked at Trueheart. 'Head it up, partner.'

'Sir, we took statements from a total of thirty-three Quantum employees. The company has three floors of offices at that location, and most had been evacuated when we arrived. Those who'd stayed to help the injured or had come back after the all clear we were able to interview. We'll follow up with the others.'

'We focused initially on what we'll call Ground Zero,' Baxter continued. 'Most who weren't in the conference room did the skedaddle. Can't blame them. Some came back – loyalty or curiosity. I'm going to say nobody stood out on the first round. Trueheart's started a standard run on the full list of employees, so we'll take a closer look once we have the results.'

'If you knew a bomb was in the building, in the possession of or on the person of an individual under extreme duress, what would you do?'

'I believe I'd be late for work,' Baxter answered.

'Let's find out who wasn't in the building. Who took a sick day, got there late, had a vacation day scheduled. Or just didn't show up. Cross-check anyone from Econo who missed the meeting, or was, again, late to arrive.'

She pushed back from the table, walked to the board. 'We're looking for two unsubs, likely male. Potentially average height, and in fit condition. We have no other description at this time. However, due to a response text to Rogan's admin, I lean toward at least one of them having some military training. If so, it strikes as most probable some of that training would be in explosives. And/or one or both of the unsubs has a connection to someone who can create a reliable, effective suicide vest or has the ability to build one himself.'

'Salazar's good,' Baxter put in. 'She should be able to ID some of the components. Bomb builders usually have a style, a signature.'

'We'll hope for that.' She looked at Peabody. 'You're up.'

5

Shifting, Peabody swiped her notepad. 'I ran it through IRCCA for like crimes. Most uses of these vests are political. But we've got a few where they were used in robberies. Usually financials. The closest to this is the abduction of a bank employee, two years ago in Chicago. The abductors strapped him into a vest, forced him to enter the bank. The abductors fitted him with an earbud, and held the controls for the vest on remote. Police responded to a silent alarm, surrounded the bank, but the guy relayed the threat that if anyone left the building, they'd blow the vest.'

'What were the demands?' Eve asked.

'Two hundred and fifty million wired to a numbered account. After four hours of the standoff, the owner of the bank opted to wire the funds. The guy in the vest? His son-in-law, and the father of two of his grandchildren. Once the transfer went through, the robbers contacted the hostage negotiator directly, told him thanks. They cleared the bank, the bomb squad deactivated the vest.'

'They didn't go boom,' Baxter commented.

'No, and they didn't get away with it, either. The bank guy, however scared shitless, paid attention. They wore masks, but they sealed up instead of wearing gloves. He caught a tat on the left wrist of the guy who strapped him into the vest.'

'Oh, those identifying marks,' Baxter said with a grin.

'Yeah. Prison tat. And though the second one didn't say much, the guy recognized his voice. Worked in the bank – and had a brother who'd done time. They tracked down the third guy – the bomb maker – on a beach in Mexico. Bomb signature.

'Anyway, it's not similar except for the use of the vest and the abduction. Though they snatched the guy on his way to work, strapped him up, sent him in after slapping him around a little.'

'And they didn't get away with it,' Eve added, studying the board. 'Only morons don't learn from their mistakes or the mistakes of others. No identifying marks, no direct connection to the tool you intend to use. Make him responsible – and make sure it blows. Any more like it?'

'Well, a couple where the bad guys used a dupe like this. We had one in New York about twenty years back, but the bomb went off during negotiations. Faulty switch. Another in Vegas where some bystander tackled the dupe, and boom. Every one I found that wasn't political was motivated by straight cash, and I didn't find one that worked.'

'It's interesting.' Eve walked up and down in front of the board. 'Here you have two guys. Could've been more who stayed out of sight or never came into the house, but let's go with two. Two's smarter, less chance of mistakes or rivalry or leaks. They don't snag a bank employee – though those assholes played a smart card by grabbing somebody who mattered to the main money guy. They don't rush it through. Grab, strap, go. They take some time, create fear, layers and layers of it because they're going to put the control in the victim's hand.'

'What if he couldn't do it?' Trueheart asked. 'If, even with his family on the line, he couldn't pull the trigger?'

'They lose the time and effort, but they walk away. They had to have him wired so they'd know what he was doing.'

Stepping to the board, she tapped Melody's photo. 'The kid said they made her call for him, scream for him into a 'link. Record that, play that through an earpiece. And still, if he balks, they walk. Maybe they kill the family, maybe they don't, but they walk. Mission abort.'

She set it aside to play with later.

'Here's what Peabody and I have.'

She ran them through the interviews, the evidence, the theories.

'So they've been at it since at least December,' Baxter calculated. 'Had Rogan as the mark. Maybe had others, too, before they settled on him.'

'I'd say the probability they had others as potentials is high,' Eve agreed. 'He suited best.'

'If it came down to balk and walk, what would they lose? A few months' work,' Baxter considered, 'whatever they paid for the e-toys and bomb – or paid a bomb maker. Not that big an investment.'

'What were they investing in?' Trueheart wondered. 'I can see a kind of domestic terrorism.'

When he paused, Baxter circled a hand in the air. 'Continue, young master.'

'Well, Quantum's a major company, one that caters to rich people. So maybe a fringe group with a political stance against the wealth, especially since they're about to hook up with a company that caters to the average Joe. Setting off a bomb at Quantum's main base, with its CEO and other brass there, it terrorizes, doesn't it? Who isn't going to think twice about booking a flight on Quantum for a while? And the company's shaken up.'

'Don't forget Econo,' Peabody pointed out. 'Same thing applies. Its CEO is hanging on, but that's more luck of the draw, and she might not make it. So both companies are shaking.'

'Econo takes a slap, maybe, for hooking up with rich guys.'

'It's an angle,' Eve said. 'Why hasn't anybody taken credit for the bombing? You want credit if you're going to make the statement.'

'Yes, sir, you do. Or they would,' Trueheart corrected.

'It's still big bucks in the mix,' Peabody said. 'Big bucks to the beneficiaries. But it seems off to hit your own company.'

'Some people'll sell off. Knee-jerk,' Baxter said.

'The beneficiaries?' Eve asked.

'Shareholders. The stock'll probably take a hit, both

companies. It's probably already taken a dive. Quantum can probably weather it unless they can't get the ship righted in the next couple days. I don't know how solid Econo is. The word is they needed this merger more than Quantum.'

Interested, Eve slid her hands into her pockets. 'You got that from statements from Quantum people at the crime scene?'

'No. Financial news, market reports.' Baxter got up to get more coffee. 'I dabble.'

'Killing the merger, blowing up the heads of both companies and other brass, that doesn't benefit the shareholders, the people who'd inherit?'

'I don't see how.'

'If hurting them's the motive, what's the gain? Unless it's not about gain, but bullshit screw the rich guys. Or revenge. And fuck me if it feels like revenge.'

She paced the board. 'We're going to dig down, particularly on Quantum employees – current and former. They picked Rogan for a reason. You don't pick him unless you know him or know enough about him to make him a mark. Maybe there's a cross in the Econo staff, so we'll look for it. And we need to find out if anyone outside the two companies knew the exact time, date, location of this meeting. Was that publicized, Baxter?'

'All I read about it was they'd cleared the legal hurdles and it was likely to snap together sometime this week.'

'So not in the media, but a lot of employees, and people talk. These two knew how much time they had, knew it was going down Monday morning, gambled – with damn good odds – Rogan would do what they told him to do. At the same time, if he didn't, they built the plan to walk away.'

'Lieutenant?' Trueheart didn't raise his hand, but sort of lifted it from the table like he'd been about to. 'Would the threat – the home invasion, the attack, strapping Rogan up and having him enter the building – even if he didn't pull the trigger, wouldn't it shake the companies anyway? Maybe nobody dies, but it's bad media.'

'That's a good point, Detective. If hitting the companies was the motive, if what Dabbling Baxter says holds, they'd have accomplished it. Not as hard, but yeah, bad media reports. Start by finding out who didn't show up for work – right down the line. Peabody, get on that. Baxter, you and Trueheart get back in the field, wrap up more interviews.'

She turned back to the board. 'Wait. Companies like that have food vendors and deliveries come in, right? Even if they have their own vending and break rooms. And they get package deliveries – messengers. Some of the execs probably use a car service. People sit in the back, babble on 'links. I'll take that end.

'Move out. Peabody, get a lock on this room. We might need it again.'

When her detectives left, Eve pulled out her 'link and pushed her way through the winding process of speaking to Rudy Roe.

He sounded both sleepy and hesitant. 'Uh, Lieutenant Dallas?'

'That's right. I have a question. Did Paul Rogan, or your

department, call in particular vendors? For in-office lunches or breaks?'

'Paul liked QT – Quick 'n Tasty. They've got a place on the lobby level. Elsa would bring him their muffin of the day at ten.'

'Elsa?'

'I don't know her last name. Or can't remember. She handles most of QT's deliveries for Quantum.'

'Did she deliver to him directly, in his office?'

'Most of the time she'd just drop off the order with me. He came out or called her in sometimes, just to ask how she was doing, but mostly she'd drop it off with me.'

'Okay. What car service did he use?'

'All Trans. I always requested Herbert as his driver.'

'Did he use All Trans this morning?'

'I . . . I don't know. I can check.'

'I'll do that. Can you tell me who generally made deliveries, which messenger or delivery company?'

'Quantum uses Global Express. For incoming, it depends on what that company uses.'

'Thanks, this is helpful.'

'Sissle. Sorry, I just remembered Elsa's name. Elsa Sissle.'

'Even more helpful. Get some rest, Rudy.'

Pacing, Eve contacted QT, was told Elsa was out on a delivery. As she started to contact Global, Roarke came in.

'Peabody said you'd likely be here.' As he walked to her, he scanned the board. 'A hard day's work, Lieutenant.' And skimmed a hand down her back.

'I'd rather have a hard day's work than a permanent day off, like the twelve on the board.'

'The twelve includes Paul Rogan, I see.'

'Dead's dead.'

'And dead makes him yours as well.'

'Being a victim made him mine.'

'How is he a victim?'

'Let's take it into my office, where there's real coffee.'

'Did you follow up your rodent soup with any actual food?' he asked as they started out.

'I was going to, but the goddamn Candy Thief found my stash.'

'Only in your world does candy qualify as actual food.'

'You eat it. It tastes good.'

They passed through the bullpen and into her office, where Roarke went to her AutoChef, programmed two coffees and a cup of chicken soup.

'When did chicken soup get in there?'

'When someone who loves his cop decided she might eat actual food if it was handy. You might check your own AC menu occasionally.'

'I programmed the candy as an alfalfa smoothie, but it didn't work.'

'No one who knows you would fall for an alfalfa smoothie.'

He had her there, so she dropped into her desk chair, ate the soup while she gave him the high and low points of the investigation.

'So he killed himself and eleven others to save his family. How did they know he would?'

Good question, Eve thought, but she expected no less from Roarke. 'I want to talk to Mira, but I believe they'd taken the time to target him specifically. There had to be other contenders, almost had to be. Then they took the time to torment him and his family, to keep giving him the choice, to keep asking the question: What would he do to save his wife and child? They broke him.'

'I'd like to go over the security system, particularly as it's one of mine. And the same with Callendar's analysis. From what you've told me, neither of them had the skills, or the access to someone with the skills, to circumvent the security without considerable time and effort, but they got through nonetheless.'

'Over two months of eroding it,' Eve pointed out. 'So they focused on Rogan back in December, or before. I have the beneficiaries, but from what I can tell, the merger would be a good thing, financially, from their standpoint.'

'It should be, yes.'

'Why didn't you go after a merger with Econo?'

He took a seat, carefully, in Eve's ass-biting visitors' chair. 'I already have an arm that competes with Econo. Buying them outright might have been interesting, but it would also have, almost certainly, tangled us up in regulations against monopolies.'

'Were they for sale?'

'Not currently.' With a shrug, he sipped at his coffee.

'Down the road a bit, that might have changed. They've had some cash flow issues the last year or so, possibly due to their COO retiring and a few other factors. The merger would have shored those up, I'd think.'

'So the merger is/was more beneficial for Econo than Quantum?'

'Initially, but Quantum would expand into areas where Econo's very solid and they're not.' Again, carefully, Roarke settled back. 'Quantum's exclusivity is part of its appeal to those who want and can afford to have five-star transportation. It's also their weakness, as the average person may want but can't afford.'

'Who benefits from it all going south?'

'Well now, I will — in the short term at least. And other competitors.'

'Why "short term"?'

'Because despite today's tragedy, the merger will almost certainly go through. It's a deal nearly a year in the making.'

'How do you know?'

He gave her a mild look. 'It's my business to know. There have been murmurs about it since last winter, and paperwork dealing with the regulations of such things were filed several months ago, as bureaucracy takes its time, and everyone else's.'

'Did you know it was going down this morning? The merger?'

'I did, yes.'

'How — and don't say it's your business to know.'

'It is, and there's been chatter on it. Pearson's son runs the London offices — and a bit of chatter came from there. His daughter left for Rome last week, another of Quantum's HQs. All the BOD who aren't based in New York traveled to New York last week. And the word has been the deal would be formalized today. Some window dressing first with a reveal of the marketing campaign this morning.'

'So, okay, your average Joe wouldn't know, or at least couldn't know the ins and outs, but somebody in the same business or someone within the two companies would.'

'Certainly. They've leaked enough to the media in the last few weeks that today's formality was expected. But they held back details so they could do the splash. If Karson lives, and I hope she does — or if she dies — the deal should still go through. Unless her and Pearson's heirs are idiots, all the reasons to merge remain in place. The negotiations are done, the deal is done but for the formal signing.'

'So why the hell blow it up? It doesn't make sense to do all of this just to kill Rogan, or Pearson, when a shiv in the throat in a dark alley's quicker and easier.'

'I agree. And if your conclusion is this wasn't about killing any individual, I agree.'

'What's the point then?' she demanded. 'What's the goal if blowing up the meeting doesn't stop the merger anyway?'

'To disrupt,' he told her. 'And in a big way, a media-frenzy way, a business way. What do people think of, instantly, when a suicide vest and bombs are employed?'

'Terrorism.'

'And what happens when terrorism is involved?'

'Panic.'

'Exactly. Not only do people panic, the markets panic. And in this case, Quantum Air and EconoLift are at the front and center of the attack. Due to that, the stocks of both companies took a deep dive this morning in trading.'

'So they're worth less than they were yesterday.'

'Considerably less than they were before nine this morning, as panic drives people to sell, and once the stocks inch down, that rolls on with a kind of groupthink, and more sell. And those who play on the margins will find their shares sold out if they fall too far over the next couple of days.'

She'd followed him, more or less, but now held up a hand. 'I don't know what that means.'

'It means those who use loans for part of the buy, hoping to maximize profit while risking more loss. Simply, they buy ten dollars' worth of stock, but borrow five, only having five of their own to invest. If the stock goes up to fifteen, they see a hundred percent profit. If it tanks, you'll likely have a margin call, lose your investment, what you borrowed, and the interest and fees attached to the loan.'

'It seems like a stupid way to do business.'

'Playing in the margins is a gamble,' he acknowledged. 'But can lead to profit. And you can use margins to create leverage.'

'Like an advantage?'

'It can be. In this case, leverage is taking on debt.'

Now she wanted to pull at her hair. 'Who wants to take on debt? People want to get out of debt.'

'You take on debt to make profit.' He all but saw her eyes glaze, had to smile. 'It's why loan companies exist – taking on debt to make profit. Investors, serious ones, look at a company's leverage, do an analysis. At this time, after the bombing, investors – those who either aren't serious or simply panic – sell off rather than hold and wait.'

'People dump the stocks so the price goes down. More people see the price going down, and they dump. That doesn't benefit the heirs, or anybody holding the stocks.' She frowned at the board. 'So what's the point?'

'What people sell, others buy. In a matter of hours stocks that were worth – to keep it simple again – a hundred a share are now selling for fifty. Buy them at fifty, wait until the dust settles and the merger goes through, sell them at a hundred, or likely more.'

'If it doesn't go through, you've lost fifty bucks – more if you worked the margin. Right?'

'True enough, but it will go through. I'd wager quite a few representatives from both companies will issue statements either by end of business today or first thing in the morning stating just that. Someone taking advantage of this window – someone expecting this window to, let's say, blow open? They'll make a pretty pile in a short time.'

She shoved up. 'All of this?' She swung a hand at the board. 'To play the fucking stock market?'

'All of this, if this was the goal, to make a considerable amount of money in a short amount of time.'

'How much? Ballpark it.'

'I can't say how much these people had to invest, but it's a deep dive indeed. The sort where, say, a hundred thousand as a stake might turn into a million or more, and in the margin, considerably more.'

'So we need to pursue the angle of investors. Look for people who plunked down investments when the stock took that dive.'

'And good luck with it, as both companies are global, and so are their investors. Add such information isn't readily available, or can be done under various covers and through shells. It's a bloody clever scheme, if it follows those lines.'

'It's a goddamn con, is what it is.' And at least she understood a con. 'Nothing but a goddamn con that took twelve lives, put eight more in the hospital, and scarred a kid and her mother.

'Why didn't they kill them, the kid and her mother?' she added. 'Why leave witnesses? It doesn't matter that they can't describe you, they're loose ends. If you were going to kill them if Rogan balked, why leave them alive once it's done?'

She turned back to Roarke. 'Unless they weren't going to kill them. That's one. Or they're too arrogant and cock-fucking-sure of themselves to think we'd get anything from the ones they let live. Hell, maybe both. I need to talk to Mira.'

She walked to her skinny window, stared out. 'What you laid out here, this theory? It makes the most sense of anything I've played around with in my head. It's cold and it's ugly, and it makes sense. How long do you figure before the stock goes back up?'

'It depends.'

She turned quickly, shook her head. 'Fuck "depends". You're the expert. If you were playing the game, when would you figure to cash in?'

'It should start to climb once the companies announce the merger's going through. It's late in the day for it to recover altogether before the closing bell. But if the companies issue statements, if Pearson's wife, son, daughter make them personally – which the board of directors will certainly push for – Quantum will start recovery. The same with Econo. And if they announce the merger as done, the stocks will rise as quickly and dramatically as they fell. The stock market runs, in large part, on emotions, feelings.'

'So a big profit within about twenty-four hours.'

'Yes. Unless all this is bollocks and someone inside one of the companies created all this for some sort of vendetta, and has a way – I can't think of one at the moment – to stop the merger altogether.'

'I was leaning that way. We'll keep it in the mix. I need to process this, and I'm probably going to have more questions on market bullshit. Do you want to talk to Callendar?'

'I'd like to, yes.'

'She's in the EDD lab, or was. Feeney and McNab are on this, too – and whatever other geeks he's pulled in. A lot of e's to sift through.'

'I can lend a hand there until you're ready for home.'

'Feeney's eyes lit up when I said you were coming in. He'll be glad to have you. So am I.'

He stood, walked to her, cupped her face in his hands. 'The dead weigh on you. Twelve with one blow, it's a great deal of weight.'

'It'll make locking the cage on these two more satisfying. With you? I've got leverage.'

He smiled, touched his lips to hers. 'I'll go play with my friends then, until we take this home.'

He'd do that, she thought when he left her. Spend his time working with cops, stick with her when she brought the dead home with her. Leverage, hell, she decided. He was her personal miracle.

She went to her desk, intending to contact Mira's office, shifted gears when her comp signaled incoming.

She read Lieutenant Salazar's preliminary report.

'I knew it,' Eve said aloud. 'Military.'

She contacted Mira, spent two precious minutes haggling with Mira's dragon of an admin before winning a short consult. In the bullpen she stopped at Peabody's desk.

'Salazar's team's starting to identify components of the explosive. Her analysis, so far, indicates some of them, at least, are military grade.'

'That's what you thought.'

'It's good to have some confirmation. I'm heading down for a consult with Mira.'

'I've got a list of Quantum and Econo employees who

were out sick or on scheduled leave. None of them were on the meeting agenda. I'm just starting runs.'

'Do that, and add Elsa Sissle – she delivered a muffin every day to Rogan. Works at Quick 'n Tasty, in the building. Rogan used All Trans, and a driver named Herbert. Global Express was his messenger service. If you don't get to those, I'll take them when I'm done with Mira. Roarke tossed in a theory. Baxter!' She signaled a come-ahead.

Both he and Trueheart got up from their desks. Baxter edged a hip onto the corner of Peabody's.

'Econo's and Quantum's stocks took a deep dive after the explosion.'

'You had to figure it,' Baxter said. 'I checked a few minutes ago. Still falling. A lot of people losing their shirts today, and the companies are going to be hurting. Somebody had it in for one or both.'

'Roarke has a different take. Do this to cause the dive, maybe work the ... margin or whatever, but buy when it tanks.'

'That's a hell of a risk, boss. It could take months for those companies to recover.'

'Roarke's convinced the merger's going through, and the stocks will start going up by end of business today or by tomorrow. Look for statements from the company brass. Look for announcements of the merger going through, and for the numbers to climb up. That's his take.'

'Wait, so he thinks all of this is so these assholes can buy low, sell high?' On a half laugh, Baxter ran a hand over his well-styled hair. 'That's fucking brilliant. Cold as it gets, but brilliant.'

'We need to look at this angle. Those absent for work? We want to dig into their financials. Same with employees close to Rogan or Pearson or Karson. He also said talk of the merger's been going on for about a year.'

'They kept it pretty down low then. But that gives the unsubs a lot of time to come up with the system, and how to play it.'

'At least one of them's military. He's going to have experience with explosives. Factor it in. I'm with Mira.'

6

Eve found the admin's desk unoccupied, Mira's door open, and inwardly cheered her luck. Mira stood at her AutoChef, her mink-colored hair swept back in sassy curls. She wore one of her slim, stylish suits, this one the color of ripe peaches, paired with needle-thin heels that hit somewhere between green and blue. Mira turned, soft blue eyes in a pretty face, smiled.

'You're prompt. Tea?'

'No, thanks. I appreciate you fitting me in.'

'I had a busy morning, but the afternoon's easier. Have a seat.'

The department's top profiler and shrink sat in one of the two blue scoop chairs, crossed her excellent legs, and balanced a delicate cup and saucer. 'My morning was jammed,' she continued as Eve sat. 'I did hear bits and pieces about the bombing at Quantum, but only that an employee, an executive, entered a meeting with EconoLift execs wearing a suicide vest. Twelve dead, more injured.'

'I'm going to send you full reports, but if I can highlight it for you, it'll save time.'

'Of course.'

'In the early hours of Saturday morning, two men circumvented the security on Paul Rogan's home,' Eve began.

She wound through it quickly while Mira nodded and sipped her tea. She listened, without interruption, until Eve finished.

'So Rogan was terrorized, tortured, and coerced by two unidentified men who held his family hostage. You've found no connection between Rogan and the men, no motive for Rogan to have been a willing part of the bombing. And from what you've learned, the men likely targeted him months before – when news of the potential merger leaked.'

'Exactly.'

'Everything you've learned of Rogan, from the contents of his desk, his home, his memo books, from statements from his family, his coworkers, his staff, describes not only a loyal, hardworking employee, a fair-and-balanced team leader, but more key, a devoted family man, a man who loved his wife and daughter. That makes him an excellent target, but it's hardly a guarantee he'd set off the bomb, taking his own life and the lives of others.'

'They weighed the odds, and gambled.'

'Yes. Well, what did they have to lose? If he refused, they lost nothing but time and effort. They simply walk away.' She paused, sipped. 'One did most of the talking, most of the violence on the wife, while the other kept watch on the girl, but didn't really harm her. Terrorized her emotionally, but not physically.'

'She said he loosened her wrist restraints a little, but the other yanked her hair to make her yell or cry.'

'So the parents, separated from her, would hear and not know what was happening to their daughter. They could've done much worse, even to the wife – no sexual assault, but the threat of rape, again to show Rogan what could happen if he didn't do what they asked.'

'His wife said the one who dealt with them kept asking Rogan what he would do to save his wife and child. What would he do to protect his wife and child. Not their names, but always "your wife and child."'

'A constant reminder they were his responsibility. It was his choice. It's psychological torture, as was separating him from his wife, locking her in a basement room, showing him how helpless and hurt she was. They knew what they were doing, or certainly the one – the more dominant – knew. He may very well have interrogated and/or coerced prisoners before. Your hunch that he's military seems sound.'

'I've brought Roarke in – expert on business, mergers, and all that. He has a theory. The stock of both companies took a dive – his word – after the bombing. Ah, he says the stock market's emotional.'

'Really? I never thought of that.'

'So it – the market – panics, the stock takes the dive. The unsubs buy a shitload, then wait for the merger to go through, or the announcement that it will, whatever.'

'The stocks climb again, and they make a great deal of money.'

'Roarke says a big profit. I get it, but it's a complicated, risky, and violent way to play the damn stock market.'

Mira set her tea aside, sat back. 'The fun's in the gamble, isn't it? Especially when you've nothing to lose, and have the money to risk. They'll have money to risk, so they'll have accumulated the stake one way or the other. They understand how the market works, know business. They, or one of them, knew enough about business and the merger to plot out the bombing. They have patience – it took months. And it took two days inside the Rogan home.

'The violence against the wife was nothing more than a tool. No real need to physically harm the child, especially as they kept her separated. The separation was enough, particularly with the recordings. So the dominant one may be no stranger to violence, but he uses it as a means.

'Sociopaths,' she continued, 'mature with military background, a knowledge of explosives and psychological tactics. They can and did profile Paul Rogan. They're intelligent, or surely the dominant one is intelligent when it comes to tactics, and trusts his partner. They've known each other, have a bond. They might even be related, but there's trust. They understand family,' she murmured. 'They understand that bond, and a father's love. One or both may have children or a child. And they're gamblers, ones willing to risk for a big payoff.'

'And arrogant?' Eve leaned forward. 'They didn't kill the wife and kid. I get the no need, but they left loose ends. They just didn't see it that way because they're so fucking clever. But the kid heard them talking, and leaving her alive I have more. The wife formed impressions, and same goes. Is it arrogance, overconfidence, or did they see it as keeping their hands clean?'

'The last is interesting, isn't it? Rogan's responsibility again? It's possible, and interesting.'

'It's one thing to send some guy out with a bomb, another to kill a woman and kid, both bound.'

'It becomes personal, and all the rest is, certainly to them, impersonal. It's just gambling.'

'Okay. Thanks.' Eve rose. 'They could bank a million, maybe a couple million. Maybe it's all they were after, but gamblers gamble. It worked, as far as they're concerned.'

With a nod, Mira recrossed her legs. 'Yes, they're likely to try it again, try to find a way to manipulate the market to their advantage. Whatever it entails. The fun's in the risk.'

'And when the stocks go up, they'll have a bigger stake.'

'One more thing.' As she considered, Mira tapped a finger on her knee. 'From what we have at this point, I'd say if they're related, one would be the older – older brother, cousin. Father and son is more a stretch, as they strike me more as contemporaries. If they worked together, one is more experienced, perhaps a kind of mentor. The dominant one is the older, more experienced, more tactical. And very likely more ruthless.'

'One yanks the kid's hair, the other one loosens the zip ties so they don't hurt.'

'Yes. I don't believe the dominant would have left the

child able to get up and cleverly break the window to alert the police. The police would have entered regardless, but it would have taken more time. This cut that down, and was, most likely, simple carelessness.'

'That's how I see it. Brothers,' Eve mused. 'Not necessarily by blood, but closely tied. That's an angle. Thanks again.'

On her way back to Homicide, she played with the gambling angle. Was it just stocks, the market, or did it extend? Cards, the tables, horses, sports?

Two men, closely tied, who liked to play risk and reward, calculate the odds, had enough of a stake to make it worthwhile. Patient, intelligent, and without conscience.

She tagged Peabody. 'Conference room. I've got a couple fresh angles.' After another moment's thought, she tagged Roarke as well. 'I'm going to brief the team on a couple new angles. I can fill you in later if you're into something in the geek lab.'

'I am, but I like angles. I'll come down, and get back to this.'

'Good enough.'

She moved directly into the conference room, began updating the board with Mira's profile.

'Dallas.' Peabody hustled in. 'Karson's conscious. She made a statement through her rep – and the Pearson family made one to coordinate. After the personal stuff on both sides – regrets, sympathy, grief – the upshot is the merger's on. They expect to finalize the deal tomorrow, with the Quantum reps signing with Karson in her hospital room.'

'That's fast. Contact the hospital, get us cleared to interview Karson.'

'Will do. Baxter and Trueheart are just finishing something up. They'll be here in a couple minutes.'

'That's all I need.' Eve continued to work. 'Roarke's heading down. He should be able to tell us what these statements do to the stocks. You need to go back to my office, get us all some decent coffee.'

'I can be all over that one.'

She started for the door when Baxter and Trueheart started in.

'I'm getting real coffee.'

'I'll give you a hand,' Trueheart said, going with her as Baxter wandered to the board.

'Brothers,' he noted. 'By blood, in-arms, by choice. That makes solid sense. Sociopaths – big duh on that one – but gamblers? That adds interest, and adds more solid sense.'

'When two experts – Roarke and Mira – use similar terms, I go with it.'

'Both companies' stocks took major hits. I checked about a half hour ago. Being an ethical son of a bitch, I refrained from calling my broker and saying buy me some of that, baby. But, kiss my ass, it was tempting.'

Curious, Eve glanced back. 'How much would you have tossed in?'

'If I didn't know about all this? Mmm, maybe five each. Knowing, double that.'

'Seriously. You're a fucking NYPSD detective, and you've got twenty large to gamble?'

'I have my ways.' He turned as Roarke came in. 'How much would you have laid on Quantum and Econo an hour ago?'

'Well now, if my cop wouldn't have given me the hard eye? Two hundred on each, as I know some of the players well enough to be reasonably certain on a fine return. And . . .'

He pulled out his 'link, tapped. 'I'd have already gained considerable, as both companies' stocks are on the move. Up.'

'Easy come.' Baxter sighed. 'Easy go.'

'Already going up?' Eve asked.

'With the statements some twenty minutes ago,' Roarke told her, 'they're inching up. They'll be higher than they were before the dive, I'm thinking, by end of business. Emotion,' he reminded her. 'Some will see this as courageous and strong. Others will just see the opportunity. Some who scooped up the bargain will sell, and others will buy what they see as a strong, solid stock.'

'It's a gamble,' Eve noted as Peabody and Trueheart came in with a pot of coffee and a tray of mugs, some creamer, some sugar.

'Run that part by them,' Eve told Roarke.

As he did, he took out his PPC and skimmed. 'Still moving up,' he added. 'If they're in for the kill, they'll likely wait until near close of the market, then sell off. I'd do just that in their place.'

'Can we track the sell-offs?' Eve asked him.

'If they're idiots, yes. From what I see on your board, they're not.'

'How would you do it, not being an idiot?'

'I'd be using numbered accounts in any of a number of locations that offer anonymity, on-planet or off. Myself, I'd lean to off, but it takes longer for the transactions. So for them? I'd lean on-planet, offshore, safe havens, and if they're particularly bright, they'd layer it in shells.'

'Could you dig them out?'

He shifted his gaze up to hers. Clearly, to him, she wondered if he could use his unregistered equipment to run deep, ethically shadowy searches. 'Eventually,' he said, and smiled.

'Peabody, start working on warrants.'

So not the unregistered, he thought, as yet. Pity.

'Meanwhile,' Eve continued, 'we're looking for two males, with at least one of them having some military background that would include working with explosives. They might be related, or have worked together. They trust each other. One is likely older and more dominant. Gamblers, sociopaths, and patient ones who take time to research and work out the details. They'll have some business knowledge, and understand the stock market.'

'It won't be their first investment,' Baxter put in. 'I'd bank against them plotting out a scheme like this first try.'

'Agreed. Possibly they've worked in the market. Financial advisers, stockbrokers. Dabblers, such as yourself.'

'As a dabbler, I'm with Roarke on the on-planet, offshore account. Maybe more than one?'

Roarke nodded. 'Almost certainly. It costs a bit more to buy and sell in increments, but adds another layer of that anonymity. No particularly large transactions through a single account.'

'Um.' Trueheart lifted a hand. 'How much could they make?'

'Well now, if they bought at or near the low . . . ' Roarke checked the numbers again. 'And again, in their place I'd have had one eye on the market, and the other on the media, watching movement on the first, and for statements or announcements on the other, and they hold on until near the peak? Considering the two companies to work with, the steep dive, the steady recovery? I wouldn't quibble they'll make ten times their investment, and that's a tidy profit.'

'Trueheart,' Eve said, 'start looking at employees, both companies. Former employees, too, and give a hard look at anyone terminated for cause. Dabbling Baxter, take a look at financial types, emphasis on those who lean toward high risk. Check for that military — add paramilitary background. Then see if there's any cross. And let's consider it's high on the probability scale that one or both of these fuckheads met or crossed paths with Rogan. Nothing overt, nothing that Rogan would have thought about. Maybe they used the same gym — at least during the stalking stage. Played golf at the same course, whatever. Any name pops more than once, we dig deeper. Questions?'

'Bound to have some once we start on it.' Baxter looked at Trueheart. 'We're going to be busy, my young apprentice, so let's get on it.'

'Peabody and I are in the field. Roarke?'

'I'll wander my way back to EDD for now. Let me know if you'll be back, and I'll ride home with you.'

'I'll be back. Peabody, with me. Grab your gear.'

She swung through Homicide, grabbed her own, swung out again as Peabody caught up. 'Are we clear to interview Karson?'

'The medicals agreed to fifteen minutes – and that's because Karson herself insisted. My impression is she's pissed as much as hurt, but that's my impression through her rep.'

'Wouldn't you be?' As she alternated elevators with glides to the garage, Eve thought it through. 'Family business. Successful one. She's about to make a deal that expands it, takes it up a level or two. Before she can clinch it, she's blown into a coma and wakes up in ICU. I'd be righteously pissed.'

'When you put it that way.'

Eve slipped behind the wheel. 'Let's see if it seems righteous or layered on. She knows business, and these businesses damn well. She's bound to know the market.'

'Do you think she could be a part of it – to sweeten the deal? Coma, ICU.'

'It's a gamble,' Eve said, pulling out into traffic. 'Long shot, but let's get an impression. And hell, let's check Pearson's medicals. It doesn't jibe, but let's check. He's terminal, sees a way to sweeten the deal for his beneficiaries. Finds a screwy way to self-terminate. Low, low, low probability, but let's not just ignore potential wackiness. After all, his wife and kids were out of harm's way.'

As she drove – stop, start, stop – she tapped her fingers on the steering wheel. 'Unlikely there's any third party in this. Neither the wife nor daughter heard their assailants talking to anyone but each other, not even on a comm. It's going to be the two of them. Brothers, by blood or choice. Or . . . lovers. That's a thought. They could be lovers, or spouses.'

Considering it, she turned into the hospital's underground garage, spent longer than she liked finding a slot.

'We're also going to see about the other patients who were in the meeting and ended up at this med center. Karson's priority.'

'They bumped her down a level. Out of ICU, condition serious but stable. The rep – Anson Whitt, and he might be a little sweet on her – said she has burns, a concussion, head lacerations, two broken ribs, a dislocated shoulder, and a serious wound in her side where a hunk of shrapnel from the conference table stabbed into her.'

They located the floor, badged at the nurses' station. The nurse on duty scowled.

'Ms Karson is in serious condition. She needs rest, quiet, care. It would be better if you came back tomorrow.'

'Maybe, but we're here now, and have clearance.'

'Yes, I see that. However, if the patient is sleeping, I won't wake her for you or anyone else.'

She rounded the station, a pint-size woman with chocolate skin and the air of authority in her hard eyes. Hard eyes that turned soft with compassion when she reached the snazzy private room Karson occupied.

'The police are here, sweetie. If you're not up to visitors, they'll come back.'

'Thanks, Jeannie. I've been waiting for them. It's fine.'

'Fifteen minutes,' the nurse said with another hard eye for Eve. 'You just have to buzz for me,' she told Karson, and then stepped out, eerily silent in her thick-soled shoes.

'Ms Karson.'

Eve approached the woman in the bed. Mixed-race female, with gel patches on burns, sutures running down her left temple to the middle of her ear. Eve saw the gray pallor under the wounds, the stabilized shoulder, while the monitors gave their quiet, steady *beep, beep, beep.*

'Lieutenant Dallas. And Detective Peabody.' She didn't smile. 'I'm told you were here earlier when I was ... unavailable.'

'We appreciate you seeing us now.'

'Five of my people are dead. People I knew, people who trusted me. I want justice for them, and I'll have it, even though justice is pale and weak for those who loved them.'

She closed her bold, bright blue eyes, sighed. 'I just sent my oldest friend – she came in from New Mexico – to my place to get me some personal items. But Anson, my admin, is around somewhere. He'll be back, he won't leave.

108

He could get you coffee or a cold drink when he shows up again.'

'We're fine. We're sorry for your loss.'

'So am I. It's incalculable, but I won't let them win. They won't win.'

'Win what?'

'The merger's going through.'

'You believe this happened to stop the merger?'

'Of course I do. What other possible reason is there?'

'Who would have motive to stop it?'

'I wish I knew, specifically. Maniacs, someone hell-bent on stopping this progress, this deal. Someone with a stake in other transportation companies.'

'Have you received any threats?'

'No. I discussed just that with Loren – you met him before. I convinced him to go home, finally. I had to work myself up into a state.' She smiled a little. 'I don't do states, but I managed this one, and got him to go home to rest. I haven't managed the same with Anson once they released him. He has a broken arm and burns, cuts and bruises. Maybe it's as well he stays, in case he needs more treatment.'

She started to reach for the cup of water on her tray, winced.

'Let me get that for you.' Peabody stepped up, handed Karson the cup with the angled straw.

'Thanks. God, it's irritating to be stuck here – and that's a terrible, selfish thing to say.' Those fascinating eyes welled up before Eve watched her will back the tears. 'I'm alive, and I'll recover. No threats, sorry.'

'Did you know Paul Rogan?'

'I came to know him during the course of the deal. His marketing concepts, angles, interest, were a plus for me. When this happened – only this morning? My God.'

She took a breath, sipped at the water. 'When I first came to, understood what happened, I was stunned, because I liked him, respected him. I was so angry. Then Loren told me about his wife and daughter, about what was done. I want to be angry, I want to be enraged at Paul Rogan. But I can't. I see his face now, how pale it was, his eyes full of tears, the way his hand shook. I can see that now, looking back. And, oh sweet Jesus, how Derrick walked right to him, laid his hands on Paul's shoulders in concern, asking him what was wrong. I stepped back – you see, I stepped away to give Derrick and Paul a moment. We hadn't merged yet, and this was Derrick's man, his company, so I stepped away. If I hadn't . . .'

'Did Rogan speak?'

'He said – I think: "I'm sorry. I don't have a choice." I think. I can't swear to it. And then it was like the world went white, blinding white, and I felt myself thrown back. A shocking, terrible pain.' Her hand crept to her side. 'Then nothing. Just nothing, until I woke up in ICU.'

'Have you had to let any of your employees go in the last year? Anyone who might have caught wind of the merger, any of the details.'

'The serious talks didn't begin in earnest until midsummer. We did begin sooner, of course, easily a year ago. Testing the waters, running the numbers, working out the legalities and regulations. But in earnest, with real purpose and direction, in July. We were able to keep it quiet and contained until the fall, but, of course, these things leak out. But to the point, there's always some turnover.'

'Do any stick out?'

'I don't micromanage my company.' That half smile again. 'I'm sure many would disagree there. But I believe in giving my department heads authority, or they wouldn't be department heads. Not all of my people were fully on board with the merger from the outset. They came around. If I knew or suspected anyone, absolutely anyone, capable of doing what was done, I'd tell you without hesitation. Is there anyone you suspect? Anyone?'

'We're actively following any and all leads.'

Karson hissed out an impatient breath. 'That's company boss talk. It takes one to know one.'

'It's still truth.'

A man, no more than thirty, handsome despite the burn gel, arm stabilizer, and the exhaustion in his wide hazel eyes, came to the doorway.

'Willi.'

'It's all right, Anson. It's the police.'

He walked to the side of the bed, took her hand. 'Why don't I talk to them outside?'

'When they're done with me.'

'Jeannie said to tell them their time's about up.'

'And she's fierce. Soften her up a little, would you? Get us another few minutes.'

'That's all right,' Eve told them. 'We have enough for now. If you think of any more, have any questions we can answer, you can contact either of us.'

'You need to keep me updated. There are memorials I won't be able to attend. I need to know what's happening.'

'We'll keep you informed.' Eve glanced at Anson. 'Why don't we step out?'

'Let me get you some fresh water,' Peabody offered.

'Thanks. I don't suppose you could talk Jeannie into some coffee? I'd settle for tea, even the herbal crap, but something that's not flat water?'

'Let me see what I can do.'

Eve stepped out with Anson. He angled himself out of view of Karson's bed, pressed his fingers to his eyes. 'Anything I can do to help. I thought she was dead. I couldn't do anything. My friend, one of my closest friends is dead. I watched it happen, and I couldn't do anything.'

'How long have you been Karson's admin?'

'Three and a half years. I was her admin's assistant, and when Marcia retired, I took the position.'

'You knew about the merger from the outset?'

'Yes.'

'How did you feel about it?'

'Willi – Ms Karson's got the smartest business brain I know. And she cares, genuinely cares about not just the company but the people who work for her. It's what makes Econo such a good fit with Quantum. Mr Pearson had the same qualities, at least from my point of view.'

'Anybody think differently?'

'There were a few doubters, some dissents, but as the deal took shape, that faded off. I don't understand any of this. I don't know anyone who would have done this. And anyone, absolutely anyone who works for, who knows Willi, would know she'd push through it. No way she'd let the deal fall apart.

'I don't like leaving her alone for too long.'

'Just another minute. As her admin, you'd see her correspondence, set up her appointments. Did anything strike you as threatening, even subtly?'

'I can't think of anything.'

'On a personal level? Someone who might want to harm her?'

'She has an ex, a jerk, but there's no way. Honestly, just no way. They're not friendly, but I'd know if he'd ever been violent. He's more of an opportunistic asshole.'

'Name.'

'Crap, crap. Okay. Jordan Banks. Trust-fund type, swanks around, pretends to work in the art world, but mostly swanks.'

'Don't like him much?'

'At all, but he wouldn't do this.'

'How about you – do you have a more personal relationship with Ms Karson?'

'Sure I— Oh, it's not like that. I mean to say, I love her – but not like that. I have a girl, a sort of fiancée. Well, I haven't asked her yet, but I'm going to. Going through this wakes you up. But I love Willi – just not romantically. That would be . . . just off. I work for her, and she's, well, older.'

Eve saw Peabody go back into Karson's room with a go-cup, wound things up.

'If you think of anything else—'

'I hope I do. My brain feels upside-down right now, so I hope I do. My best friend, Lieutenant, blown apart right in front of me. We went to the Knicks' game last night, and now he's . . . I can't get it out of my head.'

Eve let him go, joined up with Peabody.

'It sure seemed like righteously pissed to me,' Peabody commented.

'Yeah, it rings, for both of them. She has an ex. Jordan Banks. The admin doesn't like him – doesn't see him in this, but doesn't like him. Let's run him. And we'll see if the guard nurse can give us more names and locations in this place for the other injured.'

'She stopped scowling when I asked for coffee or tea for Karson. It was herbal tea, but she stopped scowling.'

'Then you take point,' Eve said.

7

They made the rounds at the hospital, but pulled no new information.

'We'll need statements from the rest of the wits, injured and not,' Eve said as they started back down to their vehicle. 'But it's unlikely any break's going to come from there.'

'I can't see anybody in that room being complicit, at least not knowingly.'

'We work on unknowingly. Connections, however negligible, to someone who fits the profile. A little careless chatter might have sparked something.'

'People brag,' Peabody agreed. 'Wow, we got a big deal in the works. Or they complain. I'm whipped with all this extra work.'

'Or a spouse or lover complains to a friend because of the overtime. Add in companies of this size, some are bound to be terminated – or opt to leave. We look there. And since there's no indicator Pearson had a sidepiece for sexing out info, we'll take a look at Karson's ex.'

As they got in the car, Peabody pulled up the data she'd already run on her PPC.

'Jordan Lionel Banks, age forty-six, Caucasian, one marriage at age thirty-three, one divorce at age thirty-four.'

'Hardly really counts,' Eve commented.

'Ten months from "I do" to "Get out". No offspring. Ex-wife, Letitia Alison Argyle, an heiress to the Argyle Communications empire, based primarily in Great Britain. Remarried, three years in. She's thirty-five, so some younger than Banks. Currently expecting her second child. Anyway.'

She scrolled down a bit. 'Banks is fourth-generation moolah. One of the Banks Information and Entertainment titans. BI&E does media, vids, home screen, digital, live theater. Just as an aside, FYI, *The Icove Agenda* is up against their blockbuster, *Five Secrets*, for best picture.'

Eve only grunted.

'Jordan Banks has residences here in New York – Upper West – and a beach place in the Hamptons. His ex-wife bought him out of their place in London when they split. He also owns a yacht, often spends part of his summer on the Med. Nice work if you can get it.'

'What work?'

'Exactly,' Peabody said. 'He owns an art gallery – called the Banks Gallery – again, Upper West. His official data says he's worth one-point-two billion. But.'

'What's the but?' Eve asked as she headed back to Central.

'The gossip pages tell a different story. Like, his ex-wife paid him handsomely to shake him loose. He rents out the beach house, and the art gallery's barely hanging on, as Banks ran it into the red. He, like, flits. Party to party, woman to woman — usually looking for a profit angle. Unlike his two siblings, his cousins, and the older generations, he doesn't actually put any real time into the family business, and gets away with that, drawing an income from same, as he's more trouble than he's worth.'

'Gossip-wise, they pay him to keep him out of their hair,' Eve concluded.

'That's my read,' Peabody confirmed. 'He's probably got less than half of what he puts on his official data, which is still a lot of the moolah. But his lifestyle and personal habits require more, I guess.'

'I'll pay him a visit before I go home. Take Roarke with me,' Eve decided. 'He's good for intimidating phony rich bastards.'

She pulled into the garage, checked the time. 'Okay, you can take your share home, wait it out for McNab, whichever works. I'm going to write this up, grab Roarke, and take a swing at Banks.'

'I'll write it up,' Peabody offered. 'You can probably grab Roarke quicker than I can McNab.'

'Fine. Anything fresh, tag me. I'm with Banks, then working from home.'

Eve sat where she was when Peabody left, sent Roarke a text.

In the garage if you're done.

Under a minute later: **I can be. Ten minutes.**

She sat, started to review her notes, then sighed. She had ten minutes to wait. She might as well get it over with. She contacted Nadine, who'd tried to contact her a half dozen times during the day.

'At last!' Nadine's camera-ready face filled Eve's dash screen. 'I need a one-on-one about this morning's bombing.'

'Not going to happen. I'm in the middle of it.'

'I can be fast,' the dogged on-air reporter pressed.

'Not fast enough. I'm heading back into the field. I can confirm the NYPSD investigation considers Paul Rogan a victim.'

'Will you confirm or deny terrorism?'

'Paul Rogan was not a terrorist or affiliated with any terrorist organization. I can confirm that he and his family were tortured and held against their will by two uniden-tified subjects for many hours, and the NYPSD is actively investigating.'

'How was he targeted? What were their demands? How—'

'I'm not going to give you any more at this time, Nadine. It's a touchy business. I've got something unrelated to ask you.'

Nadine's cat-green eyes sharpened. 'So, you get to ask me, but—'

'Yeah, I get to ask you if – and it's *if* – I can spring Peabody and McNab for this Hollywood thing, can you fix it for them to go?'

'Absolutely. It's already fixed. And you and Roarke—'

'Not going to do it, but if I can cut Peabody some time, and Feeney can cut McNab the same, I will and he will.'

'I've already got the transpo, and they're welcome. I have a suite with room for them, so they're welcome there. They have seats reserved in my section for the awards. They just need the duds.'

'Solid. When do I have to let you know?'

'I'm leaving Friday, I hope by early afternoon.'

'Then I'll get back to you on it.'

'I wish you'd come. Win or lose, it's a moment.'

'I'll watch on-screen. So ... The Red Horse book. It's good.'

Eyes narrowed, suspiciously. 'You finished it?'

'Nearly, and it's good. It's – hell, what do I know – it's maybe even better than the Icove book.'

Now Nadine's clever eyes closed a moment. 'I wanted it to be. It matters what you think.'

'It shouldn't, but since it does, good work and all that.'

'It matters,' Nadine repeated. 'And since we're on it, the director and the cast have signed on for the vid. Well, they're casting another Peabody, because, you know, dead actor but everybody else is on board. They're already asking for a third – to make it a kind of trilogy. I'm trying to decide which case to spring from.'

'Don't ask me. And don't say anything to Peabody about maybe going out to this Oscar deal. She'll nag the crap out of me with silence and puppy eyes.'

'Not a word.'

'Are you taking the rock star?'

'I'm taking the rock star. It's going to be a hell of a night if you change your mind.'

'I won't. Gotta go interview an asshole.'

'How about a name? Assholes make great copy.'

'If he connects, I'll let you know.'

Eve clicked off, opened the data Peabody had copied to her on Banks, reviewed it until Roarke opened the passenger door.

'Want me to drive while you work?' he asked.

'No, I've got enough. How's it going in EDD?'

'Plenty of data unearthed, nothing that seems to apply at this point. And where are we off to?'

'Karson's ex. What do you know about Jordan Banks?'

The DLE's passenger seat adjusted for Roarke's longer legs. 'Other than he's a wanker?'

'So that's a confirmation of Karson's admin's opinion and Peabody's famous gossip pages.'

'He's barely an acquaintance, but I can confirm, yes, a wanker, and a git on top of it. Wealthy family, most of whom seem to do something constructive with their lives and advantages,' he continued as she pulled out of the parking slot. 'I had a . . . closer acquaintance with one of his cousins.'

'Uh-uh.'

'A pleasant enough acquaintance with a woman of some intelligence and style, which contrasted sharply with her cousin. I'd judge Jordan has the brains of a bag of wet mice, but he's sly enough, and has a certain slick charm that he slithers into to convince the unsuspecting to invest or lend or offer him bounties.'

'Did he try that with you?'

'He did once. I happened to run into his cousin – my pleasant acquaintance – in Madrid. I was on business, and she was about to marry a Spaniard. She graciously invited me to the wedding, and I accepted. Jordan was there, naturally enough, and laid it on thick about some scheme or other. I told him to bugger off. It was quite a lovely wedding, as I recall.'

'So no business with him?'

He turned those amazing blue eyes on her. 'I rarely do business with wankers.'

'Is he afraid of you?'

'Why would he be?'

She just rolled her eyes as she negotiated traffic uptown. 'When you told him to bugger off, did he bugger off or keep slithering?'

Roarke smiled a little. 'I believe he buggered off right quick.'

'That's what I'm talking about. So you'll put on the coldly polite Roarke, which is scary enough, and if I need more, you can pull out the full scary Roarke. I don't know if he's got any connection to this, but since he was involved with Karson, he may know something about something.'

'Happy to oblige.' He shifted to look at her more fully. 'You've had a long one, Lieutenant.'

'Not so long. It's just . . . lots of DBs, a terrorized family, and all – it looks like – to profit off a stock-market gamble. It's such a stupid, self-serving scheme that it ends up being damn smart. Sure, they made mistakes. Leaving two wits alive, talking in front of the kid when they should've zipped it. But they selected just the right type in Paul Rogan. What would you do to save two people you love more than yourself, more than anything?'

Roarke laid a hand over hers. 'Absolutely anything.'

'You wouldn't have pushed the button.'

'Wouldn't I?'

She shook her head. 'You'd – we'd – have found a way out. It takes being smarter, meaner, more crafty. He may have been smarter – under other circumstances – but he didn't have the mean or the crafty, and that's how they got him to do it.'

'You wonder if they'll do it again.'

'Maybe it was a one-off. Maybe.'

'You don't think so.'

'No, but if so, they'll take their winnings and fucking celebrate. But even if, they'll want to do it again down the road. It worked. They won. And if it wasn't a one-off, they're planners. Detail men. They'll already have another target, another scheme.'

'I've thought the same, and so, I can tell you, does Feeney. Still, mergers of this magnitude don't happen every day – or every year.'

'So you'll help me figure out other ways they might manipulate the market.'

She pulled to the curb in front of a tower of silver and glass rising sleek as a sword into the evening sky.

'I'll deal with the doorman,' Eve said, jumping out to confront the man in classic black livery. Before she could speak, he smiled.

'How can I help you, Lieutenant? Sir,' he added as Roarke stepped out.

Eve shifted modes. 'Jordan Banks.'

'Of course. Mr Banks should be in. He arrived only twenty minutes ago.'

He moved briskly to the wide glass doors, which swept open to a deep lobby done in blacks and silvers, splashed with classy arrangements of red flowers. The air, fragrant with them, carried the hush of a church as they moved over the black tiles to the security desk.

'Lieutenant Dallas and Roarke for Jordan Banks,' the doorman told the man at the long counter.

'Of course. Sir,' he said, turning his gaze to Roarke, 'should I call up to announce you?'

'No,' Eve said, definitely.

'Fifty-first floor. Number 5100 for the main entrance.' He pushed a button that had one of the silver elevator doors sliding silently open. 'Enjoy your visit.'

'Thank you.' Roarke touched a hand to Eve's arm as they walked into the elevator.

'Your building.'

'It is, yes.'

'So you don't do business with wankers, but you rent to them?'

'I imagine I rent to scores of wankers, as even they need a roof over their heads.'

She looked up at the silver ceiling. 'Some roof.'

'It's rather nice, isn't it?' He leaned in, and though she sent a narrowed eye toward the security cam, kissed her. 'There's an equally nice restaurant just next door, as I recall, if you're hungry.'

'Home's better for that.'

'It tends to be.'

They rode up, smoothly, silently, to fifty-one.

A wide corridor, more splashes of red flowers, bursts of art against silver walls, and the double doors of 5100.

'Good security,' Eve commented, noting the door cam, the palm plate, locks. She pressed the buzzer, then stepped out of view so the camera would pick up only Roarke.

As she expected, the door opened without Banks or the security comp inquiring.

'Well, this is a surprise.' He glanced at Eve as she shifted. 'And hello.'

She supposed that was the slick charm – the slow smile, the deepening of puppy-brown eyes in a boyishly handsome face. A lot of tousled brown hair with streaks worked in from the sun, or a skilled colorist, framed the face. A sweater of pale gold and dark brown trousers casually covered a trim body.

About six feet, Eve calculated, and the right build according to Cecily Greenspan's description.

'Lieutenant Dallas, NYPSD.'

He barely looked at her badge, kept the puppy eyes on her face in a way she suspected most women would find flattering.

She wasn't most women.

'Of course, Roarke's wife. I've seen you on-screen. Read quite a bit about you. Please, come in. It's good to see you, Roarke.'

He extended a hand. Roarke shook it, coolly polite.

'The lieutenant's here on police business.'

'That sounds ominous.' But Jordan's smile never dimmed. 'Have a seat. I hope "business" doesn't mean we can't have a drink.'

'It does – but you can have all you want.'

The living area exploited the view with a wall of glass and a wide terrace beyond it. Twilight slid over the city, all soft light while buildings speared and lanced into the deepening sky. It fell glimmering on the river.

Jordan gestured to a conversation grouping of sofas and chairs, all in black and white, making Eve think of a chessboard. A long, narrow fireplace ran flickering along a wall. Over it ranged charcoal and pencil studies of nudes – male and female.

Quiet music gurgled in the background.

'I have an aperitif,' he said, picking up a glass of pale gold liquid. 'It's coffee, black for you, isn't it? My droid can see to that.'

'No, thanks.' Eve sat to put a stop to the pleasantries. 'You were in a relationship with Willimina Karson.'

'Yes. I – that is to say, we ended it several weeks ago. Amicably.'

He sat as well, comfortable, at ease.

'You're aware, are you not, Ms Karson was seriously injured this morning in a bombing at the headquarters of Quantum Air?'

His face fell into somber and sorrowful lines – as sketchy, to Eve's mind, as the charcoals. 'I heard this morning. It's beyond horrible. All those people! An employee of Quantum, an executive? I can't imagine the mind-set, just can't. Thank God Willi wasn't killed, and I'm told is expected to fully recover.'

'Who told you?'

'I . . . heard the bulletin. I confess I've been glued to the reports throughout the day, as I was sick with worry for Willi. The merger's going through, even after all this, and she's doing better already. Such a relief! Have you learned why this man, this maniac, did this?'

'You used some faulty glue if you missed the fact that Paul Rogan was as much a victim as the others who died or were injured this morning. You were aware Quantum and Econo have been in negotiations for several months?'

'Yes. Well aware, yes. Willi has an amazing head for business, and while my strengths run in the art world, she did share some of the ins and outs with me while we were romantically involved.'

He flashed that smile again, lifted his aperitif in an easy toast. 'Much as the Icove book and vid indicate you share some of your work with Roarke.'

'You knew the particulars?'

More sober lines replaced the smile as Jordan shifted,

126

leaned in just a little. 'It was, and will be, a major shift for Econo, and Willi. She's not in any way impulsive, and fac tors in advice, opinions as well as spreadsheets and figures.'

'She consulted you?' This from Roarke, baiting more than biting with a lifted eyebrow. 'On this major deal?'

Jordan lifted a hand, palm up. 'I do come from a business family, after all. A family that negotiates, deals, buys, sells – you certainly understand the scope. Naturally, Willi sought my advice and opinion, as, understandably, your wife seeks yours.'

'And did she follow your advice and opinion?' Eve asked.

'I believe she weighed them carefully. I certainly encouraged the merger. Econo, in my opinion, can use a kind of polish, and Quantum will provide it. Did you know Pearson?' Jordan turned his attention to Roarke again. 'A wonderful man. It's a tragedy. I've sent my condolences to his wife, his daughter, his son. Oddly, Liana, his daughter, reminds me of Willi. Fascinating women, businesswomen with considerable style.'

'And disposable income,' Roarke said with a cold, cold smile.

Jordan froze under it.

'Who else was interested in your advice and opinion on the merger?' Eve demanded.

'I'm not sure what you mean.'

'Who did you talk to about the merger, any details of it, as it was being negotiated and set up?'

He tried for insulted. 'Whatever Willi discussed with

me would have been confidential. I would never betray her trust in me.'

'Bollocks to that,' Roarke said mildly. 'You're a bloody sieve, as I learned myself at your cousin's wedding when you tried to rope me into investing in some deal you were working – and gave me plenty of *confidential* details in an attempt to sweeten the pot.'

'I don't recall—'

'I do, and could ... refresh you if the lieutenant would give us a moment alone.' Roarke leaned forward. 'Shall I refresh you?'

'I didn't invite you into my home to be threatened and insulted.'

'I didn't hear any threat.' Eve settled back. 'But we'll pass – for now – on the refreshing. You're going to want to think who you talked to, shared details with – trying to score a deal or impress someone.'

'I listened to and advised Willi out of affection.' He spoke stiffly now. 'I have more interesting things to talk about than some business merger. As I said, my interests are in the arts. Now, if that's all, I have an engagement this evening.'

'You're going to want to think,' Eve repeated. 'Because if Roarke says you're a sieve, you're just that. Twelve people are dead. The woman you were romantically involved with is in the hospital. I'm willing to bet when I check – and I will – you didn't contact the hospital to inquire on the status of a woman you parted ways with – amicably – only weeks ago.'

That brought on the faintest flush. Embarrassment, maybe, Eve thought. Anger more likely.

'You're going to want to think who you talked to about the merger, who may have pumped you for details. You're going to think carefully about someone with an interest in the stock market, someone who likes to gamble, someone who may have a military background.'

Banks set his glass aside. 'I know a great many people, and many of those have interests in the stock market, many enjoy gambling   '

'Do you?'

He broke off, picked up his drink again. 'I have financial advisers who worry about such matters. Art, as I said, is my field.'

'But the CEO of Econo consulted you regarding a major decision?'

'Pillow talk.' He brushed it away. 'And a woman's natural inclination to consult a man with some experience. Frankly, I had no real interest in Willi's business, and certainly didn't dine out on the details of it. In any case, we haven't been involved for weeks. Now, you'll have to excuse me.'

Eve rose. 'You're going to want to think,' she said again. 'Because if my investigation links you to the men who instigated the bombing, I'll find a way to tie you as an accessory. You wouldn't like it.'

His color rose deep this time, smearing away the charm. 'That's ridiculous. I've never harmed anyone in my life! I insist you leave or I'll be forced to call security.'

Now Roarke rose. 'It's my building, you arse, and my security. You'd be wise to heed the lieutenant's warning. Oh, and here's another: Liana won't give a wanker like you the time of day. Done?' he asked Eve.

'For now. Think,' she repeated before she walked to the door with Roarke. She glanced back to see Jordan's face, a mask of shaky rage.

Perfect.

'That was a good scary Roarke,' she commented on the way to the elevator.

'I'll add, you did a good scary cop as well.' He took her hand, kissed her fingers. 'Teamwork.'

'He'll think. He won't be able to stop thinking. Maybe it'll lead somewhere, because he damn well talked plenty about the merger. Puffing himself up with inside intel. It's all the fuck over him.'

She took a deep breath, rolled her shoulders. 'Let's go home, eat, keep up the teamwork. You can start the last part by finding out who the wanker's financial advisers are – and maybe how much he's invested in Quantum and/or Econo.'

'Delighted.'

She let Roarke drive so she could send a quick roundup of the interview to her team.

'I don't get why Karson, who comes off smart and steady, would hook up with a useless user like Banks. Sure, he looks good, but if that's a thing, just bang and move on.'

'The heart wants what it wants, sees what it needs to see.'

'The heart's just a pulsing muscle without the head.' She

angled to study him. 'You look good.' Major understatement, she thought. 'And that's a thing. I might've banged you if you'd been a useless user, but I'd have moved on.'

'I believe I was still on your murder board as a suspect when we first banged each other.'

'Technically,' she allowed. 'But I didn't figure you for it. If I'd been wrong, I'd have taken you down, slick. Maybe I'd have banged you one last time first, but I'd've taken you down.'

'Darling, that's so sweet – and oddly arousing.'

'The point is she strikes me as too smart and centered to fall for his bullshit.'

'He knows how to charm – and lays it on when he has a goal. He has intellect and can talk a good game.' Roarke shrugged. 'He's, at the core, a grifter with some skill. The smart and steady can fall for a well-oiled grift, especially those who play to the heart. One thinks: Oh, but it's different with me, or I can change him.'

She frowned as they drove through the gates, and home rose up into the deepening sky with all its wonders and welcomes.

'I was going to say polka dots don't change their spots, but sometimes they can. They do. You're married to a cop, and I'm living in an urban castle.'

He stopped the car, leaned over to kiss her. 'Polka dots are spots.'

'Until they get smeared and blend together. Then they're splotches.'

'That's both true and confusing,' he decided. 'So we've smeared our spots into splotches for each other.'

'Right, but Banks? His type's always going to be a polka dot.'

'I'm not completely sure how, but I'm forced to agree. And I suspect Willimina came to the same conclusion, and ended the relationship.'

'But not before she talked to him about the merger, about the negotiations. Not before he ... leveraged that to sound important, or even more. It just fits.'

They got out of the car, circled around to the door together.

'You do know it's leopards that don't change their spots, not polka dots?'

'A leopard's born, lives, and dies a leopard, so that's that.'

'That's rather the point of the adage.'

'Why need an adage on something that's just that? It's a waste of words. If people didn't have stupid sayings about the obvious, they wouldn't waste so many words and talk so damn much.'

She stepped inside the great foyer of her personal urban castle. There, the black-clad Summerset, back from his winter break, loomed with the fat cat at his feet.

Bony and cadaverous as ever, she thought, but he'd picked up some color in the tropics, and that threw her off. It just threw her off.

Worse, it made her wonder if the tropical color extended to other areas of that skeletal frame. And the wondering made her fear a brain bleed.

'Nearly on time,' he said in that snooty voice, 'and together.' His brows arched up. 'And with no visible injuries.'

'The day's young.' Eve pulled off her coat, tossed it over the newel post as the cat padded over to wind through her legs. 'You're not.'

She sailed upstairs as Roarke lingered to exchange some pleasantries. The cat trotted after her.

8

She went straight to her home office to begin setting up her board. By the time Roarke came in, tie and suit coat discarded, she'd made some progress.

He turned on the fire – a nice touch she often forgot.

'I've a bit of work to see to,' he told her. 'We'll say twenty minutes till dinner?'

'Thirty's better.'

'That'll do.'

With Roarke doing what Roarke did in his adjoining office, she finished the board, programmed coffee, created her book.

Then she put her boots on the desk, sat back with her coffee. Galahad leaped into her lap, and that was fine. She stroked him absently while she drank coffee. And gave herself thinking time.

No suspects. A gut-hunch that potentially tied a wanker – an excellent word – as a conduit of information or a suspect. An innocent man weaponized and his family shattered. Twelve people dead, two successful companies damaged.

She closed her eyes.

Gambling, stock market, profit.

'Explosives,' she muttered, opening her eyes when she sensed Roarke come into the room. 'You use explosives for impact, for creating not just loss of life, destruction of property, but panic.'

'And so?' He stood a moment, studying her board.

'There've got to be other ways to manipulate the market, less destructive and murderous ways. They weren't worried about the cops figuring out it wasn't Rogan – not willingly Rogan. But they wanted that initial impact, and the panic – and the results of both. Who died, how many? Just luck of the draw. One, a dozen, two dozen, that's not important, not really. Result-oriented, right? Risk takers, gamblers, but focused on results. Blast the window open, grab what you can while the time's ripe, then sell it at maximum profit.'

When she shifted, Galahad leaped down, sauntered over to her sleep chair, jumped up.

'It could be just a game, the gambling game,' she continued, and rose to join Roarke at the board. 'But I put that low on the list. They put too much into it – the time, the effort, the risk – and were too willing to kill an undetermined number of people – even after beating up a woman, terrifying a kid – not to reap a solid reward. But ... that's relative, isn't it? What might be a good profit for you, it's a different level than, say, one for Peabody.'

'Ten times an investment – likely more if they played the margins – is, regardless of the outlay, a very solid reward. If

Peabody, for instance, bought five thousand of Econo this morning, she'd sell off now, if she chose, at more than fifty.'

'I get that. And they may be more Peabody's level, or they might be yours. They're probably something between. Peabody told me she and McNab are going to give you ten K to invest.'

'When they've put it together, and are comfortable with it.' He glanced over. 'Does that concern you?'

'No. Maybe. No.' She paced away, paced back. 'No,' she said more definitely. 'It's their money, or will be, and you'll be careful. Probably more careful than with your own.'

She stopped, frowned again, paced again. 'That's a thing.'

'Is it?' He strolled over, opened the wall panel for a bottle of wine.

'They could save up the money, invest it themselves, but they don't know squat about the stock market or trading or investments. They could go to some brokerage house and get somebody to advise them, but why do that when there's you?'

Still frowning, she took the wine Roarke offered. 'So it's smart on their part. It's a smart way to invest, to — what do they say? — spend to make?'

'They do say that.'

'Trusting you with it, that's as close to a sure thing as it gets. And this?' She gestured to the board. 'That's what they put together. It's not so much a gamble if you stack the deck. Yeah, it can still go south, but you've skewed the odds in your favor. You've loaded the dice,' she murmured.

'And by the time the house is wise to it,' Roarke finished, 'you've taken your winnings and gone. We'll eat,' he added, 'then work on it. I think it's a night for red meat.'

She sat down to steak, tiny gold potatoes, tender spears of asparagus. After the first bite, she thought Roarke had been right again. It was a night for red meat.

'When you were still on my board,' she began, 'you roped me into having dinner with you here. Steak.'

'I remember, yes.'

'That was the second time I'd ever had real steak. The cow deal.'

He broke a roll in two, handed her half. 'You never said. When was the first?'

'When I made LT, Feeney took me out for a steak dinner. You get so used to the fake stuff, you think, What's the big deal?' She cut off a bite, studied it, ate it. 'Then you find out. First steak,' she asked him.

'I was eight, or about, and stole one when I was rummaging about in a big house in a fancy part of Dublin. People will hide valuables in their cold boxes, as if any thief worthy of the name won't look there.'

'Freezers,' she agreed, 'underwear drawers. Usually the top two. So, the steak.'

'Mick and Brian and I fried it up on a hot plate in our hideaway, and surely bollocksed that up altogether. And still, I've never had better, before or after.'

When she smiled, he topped off her glass. 'When Summerset took me in, we managed steak a time or two,

137

and I learned how it was meant to taste. And still, that hunk of burned meat in our little hole was ambrosia.'

'They won't be like us. Those two,' she said with a gesture back at the board. 'When you grow up hard, like we did, it can turn you mean, violent, vicious. It can warp you. Or it can make you remember the taste of something wonderful. Either way, that's not them.'

'Mean, violent, vicious? They don't qualify?'

'Sure, but it's thought-out, it's calculated, it's carefully orchestrated. Not striking out, not payback, not survival or some fucked-up version of it. They don't have to remember. They're going to have advantages, most likely come from decent backgrounds. I'm betting a solid education and/or training.'

Studying her, fascinated as always by her mind, its processes, he sliced a bite of steak. 'Why?'

'Okay, you gamble for a trio of basic reasons. For the hell of it, which includes the entertainment factor — and that means you can afford to lose, at least what you put in. Out of desperation or addiction, which usually means you lose even if you win because you'll end up feeding it back. Or because you want more, you just want more. I lean toward the want more. At least with what I've got now.'

She speared a tiny potato. 'I also bet you'd know about some high-stake games right here in the city.'

He cocked a brow, sipped his wine. 'I may.'

'It might be a thread to tug. You own some casinos,' she continued, 'but you don't really gamble. Cards, dice, like that.'

'The house always wins, so better to be the house than a guest in it. I've gambled here and there. It's a good way to while away some time, and make a bit of profit. But it was always as much for the entertainment as anything else for me, or for the insight into the other players, all of whom might serve as a mark down the line.'

'Every heist was a gamble,' she pointed out.

'True enough, but that was also a vocation.' He smiled again. 'A passion. Survival at first, then a way of life, then another kind of entertainment.'

'Richard Troy gambled,' she said, referring to her father. 'I can look back from this distance and realize, for him, it was as much a sickness as the drinking, as the abuse. Patrick Roarke gambled.'

Roarke nodded. 'He did, and it was much the same. Our bloody-minded fathers were much the same.'

'These two aren't like that, either. Not the types to lash out, to get shit-faced and pound on a kid. The more I think about it . . . This went so damn smooth for them. Sure, it took time, some investment, involved some risk, but it was clear profit in a matter of hours once it rolled. They're going to do it again. People just don't quit while they're ahead.'

'And so the house always wins,' Roarke agreed.

'Do you know of any other big mergers, major shifts in the works, something that could be used to manipulate the market?'

'There's always something cooking somewhere.'

'I think it has to be here in New York, almost has to be.

Otherwise, you have travel, more time to pull it off. You have to know a target to hit it. Would they try the same thing again? Would they risk that? Shit. I have to think.'

'Eat first.'

'Right.' She cut more steak, tried to clear her mind so it could brew on what lodged in the corners. And remembered other things, more personal things.

'Ah, anyway. I know that vid awards deal is Sunday.'

Angling his head, he lifted his wine. 'You surprise me.'

'Well, I didn't exactly know, then it came up, so I knew. And I know you like that sort of thing, but—'

'You have a case, and it's not the sort of thing you like whatsoever.'

'Still.'

Sometimes she wished he wouldn't be so reasonable. It brought guilt tugging. Then again, plenty of times he wasn't even close to reasonable, and that was a pisser.

So.

'I could probably work it to have you shuttle us out there in one of your fancy deals, but the thing is . . . '

He waited, half-amused, half-curious, while she struggled through it.

'It's just a major pain in my ass, Roarke, the whole freaking thing. Not just the getting into some stupid outfit and having stuff slathered all over my face, and having to talk to people in stupid outfits with stuff slathered all over their faces. I can handle that okay, sometimes. I do it with you, for your stuff.'

'You do, and it's appreciated.'

'Okay, good, but this? The damn book, the vid? I'll be doing my job, and some wit, even a suspect says, Oh hey, I read the Icove book. I loved the vid, whatever, and it's a weird pain in my ass. It wouldn't surprise me one damn bit to be reading some fuckhead his rights and have him say: Man, that Icove vid rocked it out.'

When he laughed, she scowled, ate more steak. 'I'm serious.'

'I know it.'

'And worse? Oh, it's worse. I'm about finished reading the Red Horse deal, because Nadine nagged the crap out of me about it. And it's good. It's goddamn stupid good, and I had to tell her because, friends. And even if I lied, said, Sorry, it blows, they'd publish it anyway, and make the next vid – they want a trilogy.'

She finished on a windy huff of breath, and he took a moment to choose his words.

'Darling Eve, I'm trying to be sympathetic, as your distress is very clear and obviously genuine.'

'Damn straight it is.'

'But you've gone and made a very talented woman a friend. A true and good one, and that's the breaks.'

'Goddamn breaks,' she muttered, and ate some more. 'I'm not going to the fancy awards. Just no.'

'One must take a stand, after all.'

'She'll probably win, just my luck.' Caught up, she brooded into her wine. 'So anyway, Feeney and I hashed it out, and we'll cut Peabody and McNab loose so they can go. They eat this stupid stuff with a spoon, and one of us should be there with Nadine, however it goes, even though she's taking the rocker.'

He said nothing, only stood, walked around the table, drew her to her feet. And cupping her face, kissed her soft and sweet.

'*A ghrá*, you are a marvel.'

'I don't—'

He kissed her again, then just gathered her in. 'I love you beyond comprehension.'

'Because I'm not going to some stupid dress-up party?'

'That actually factors. Shall I arrange a shuttle for them? A suite?'

She sighed, loved him beyond comprehension because he would do just that, without hesitation. 'They'll go with Nadine and the rocker. She's got it. I'm not saying anything yet because I won't get dick out of Peabody once she knows she's going.'

'Then we'd best contact Leonardo.'

Eve snuggled in. 'Why?'

'Our girl needs an Oscar dress – and shoes, a bag. You could lend her the jewelry.'

Now Eve yanked back. 'But—'

'He'll come up with something for McNab that suits. There's not much time, but I'll wager Leonardo can make it work, especially for Peabody and McNab.'

'Jesus, they already have clothes.'

'Not to worry.' Roarke simply patted it, and her, aside. 'I'll take care of this part of it. My contribution. Why don't you deal with the dishes, and I'll deal with this? Then we'll set our minds to murder.'

'Life was easier when all I had to do was think about murder.'

'Well now, you changed your spots to splotches, didn't you?' He kissed her again, then pulled out his 'link.

She muttered to herself as she gathered up the dishes.

'Leonardo,' she heard him say. 'And how are you and your girls?'

She dealt with the cleanup, a fair trade in her mind, as she didn't have to discuss fashion or accessories. By the time she got around to programming a pot of coffee, Roarke was tucking his 'link away.

'He's happy to help, so consider it done.'

'I'm not considering it at all. Jordan Banks.'

'Consider that all but done,' Roarke said, and strolled into his office.

The thing was, Eve admitted, she could. While he entertained himself digging into Jordan Banks's finances, Eve pulled her team's first reports from her incoming.

She scanned terminations first, highlighted any with connections to the military and/or finance.

She noted a couple of names – former employees of one company who'd shifted to the second. Those she earmarked for a deeper run.

*

While Eve worked and Roarke dug, Jordan Banks had an epiphany. The bitch of a cop had told him to think – and he'd done anything but. He didn't like being threatened or made to feel uneasy, so in his habitual way, he simply ignored the sensations and went to a party.

Cocktails, illegals, music, a little quickie with the wife of a friend in a butler's pantry. Some laughs, some gossip. He always filed gossip away for later use. Well utilized, gossip could be profitable.

More than a little high, he closed himself in one of the bathrooms to record some of the juice in his memo book. Family squabbles, who was cheating with whom, gambling debts – you just never knew when a little inside knowledge could pay off.

And it hit him.

Certainly he'd pumped Willi for information – subtly, of course. *Let me be your sounding board, cookie. You look so stressed, lover. Why don't you tell me all about it while I give you a back rub?*

He'd gotten enough bits and pieces to be useful – and more yet by accessing her files on her comp. Enough to tell his money man to keep an eye on Quantum. Enough to sound in-the-know should the conversation turn to business at a gathering.

Enough, he remembered now, to make a little loose change – always handy – for a little inside information.

But that was months ago, he thought. And only a bit of I'll scratch your back, you scratch mine. But when he thought it through, when he added in the visit from the bitch and the Irish bastard, it played out.

Who would have thought!

To his credit, Banks had a moment of distress. Mild and soon over. After all, he wasn't at all responsible for the regrettable violence. In fact, he was a victim.

Finding the softest route to victimhood was a particular skill he'd honed since childhood. It served him well.

He calculated it now, considered the speed, the turns.

He sat on the wide ledge of an apricot-colored jet tub big enough for four friends, fired up a joint of Erotica-laced Zoner he'd taken as a party favor, and contemplated. And, seeing the convergence of profit and victimhood, he took out his 'link.

'Hi, there,' he said with a flashing smile. 'We need to chat.'

When Roarke came in, Eve had two names at the top of her list.

She swiveled in her chair. 'I've got a couple to pull in for interview,' she began. 'Both male, both in their forties, and they've each worked for both Econo and Quantum. One has eight years in the navy, the other has a father still active-duty USMC. No specific links to explosives training, but. One's an IT specialist, and that's a good way to dig out data. The other's in accounting, and accounting knows finance. So.'

When she poured more coffee, Roarke twirled a finger for her to fill a second cup.

'Where do they work now?'

'Former navy and IT is still Quantum. He moved from Econo two years ago. The other started with Quantum, shifted to Econo – about five years in both companies. Now he's at a nonprofit called Resource of Animals Rights – or ROAR.'

'Well.' He sat on the edge of her desk. 'Criminal.'

'ROAR dude has some bumps, all related to protests. Major one at the Bronx Zoo, another for defacing a fur warehouse. That got him canned. Navy has a couple of minor scrapes – a drunk and disorderly and a pushy-shovy.'

She picked up her coffee. 'What have you got?'

'Jordan Banks is quite the scamp.'

'Scamp.'

'His art gallery is a colossal failure from which he draws a tidy salary for doing nothing much at all. He pays the staff a pathetic wage, offsetting that, from what I can see by allowing them to display their own art. If said art manages to sell, the gallery takes seventy percent. He also rents the space for private parties.

'A colossal failure,' Roarke repeated. 'On paper. But I'd deem it a reasonable success as a vehicle for laundering money. You'll want to pass on what I sent you from my little exploration to whoever handles that sort of thing at the NYPSD.'

'Whose money is he laundering?'

'I can't tell you unless you give me the go on crossing certain lines. But I can guess much of it comes from those high-stake games. He enjoys them occasionally. Nothing out of the ordinary, but he does have connections there.'

'I knew it.'

'Some might come from art. However poorly he manages his own gallery, he does have connections and contacts in the art world. Cash sales aren't unheard-of, and cash is easily washed. Still more may come from other areas, but washing cash he is. And even with that, he's a complete git.'

Eve shook her head. 'It bothers you more that he's a git than that he's a criminal.'

'Well, of course. He's a git, and money slides through his fingers. He has a couple of accounts reasonably well cloaked. A few million here, a few more there. He pays no rent for the gallery, as his family owns the building, but he lists rent on his expenses, and merely juggles it from one pocket to the other.'

'I want a biscuit,' he said, pushing up to go into the kitchen.

'I don't have any biscuits in there. What about investments?'

'He's with Buckley and Schultz,' Roarke said from the kitchen. 'It appears Buckley himself handled his portfolio until about eight years ago, when he passed it down the chain. Banks doesn't have enough personal wealth for Buckley to handle personally.'

He came back in with a plate holding two big cookies chunky with chips.

'Those aren't biscuits. Those are cookies.'

'I don't suppose you want one then.'

'Give me a damn biscuit.'

She took one, bit in. 'Warm. Good.'

'They are. Now Banks's portfolio is managed by Schultz's grandson, and competently enough, who appears above-board. Though my impression is he's passed it to another in the firm. But to confirm that, I'd cross the line you cling to.'

'Just keep going.'

'All right. Our boy bought a small chunk of Quantum stock in November, fifty thousand, in the margin. He put in an order to sell this morning, just after the bombing.'

'Panicked.'

'He did, but – perhaps just tiptoeing along that line – I stumbled over some correspondence. His broker advised him, strongly, to hold on to the stock, by rightfully telling him he had little more to lose, and ascertaining the stock would level at least.'

'Did he listen?'

'In his way. His response? *Fuck it, Tad. Whatever.* My take is he bores very easily. But his initial reaction leads me to believe he wasn't in on the scheme.'

'Maybe not. Maybe Tad was. Maybe he didn't know he was in on the scheme. Maybe being a scamp, a wanker, and a git, he was also a dupe. Whatever else, he's dirty. Money laundering's frowned upon.'

'A pity, as it comes out so crisp and clean.' He polished off the cookie. 'Willimina Karson paid his gallery thirty thousand and change – for art. Econo paid his gallery nearly a hundred thousand.'

'Interesting. And he'd get seventy percent of that. I'm

going to talk to her in the morning, push out what I can about what she told Banks on the deal. I'll go another round with him, and interview the two I culled out. Both of them would have had some access to Rogan, have means to study him.'

She pushed up, walked to the board. 'You'd have to have inside info. Sure, there's buzz about the merger, but they kept the lid on the details until they had it set. And this scheme took weeks, if not months, to refine. So they had to know more than the average onlooker, even money people. Speculation, sure, but enough to plot this out means solid data.'

She turned back. 'Am I wrong?'

'If you knew what to ask, how to ask, who to ask, you could find out more. Then there's the politics and bureaucrats. So you'd have information there, as the deal rolled through the red tape. You'd have some leaks.'

'So some assistant to some assistant with the right clearance could brag to his buddies over a brew about drone work on a big deal.'

'Possibly.'

'Yeah, I figured.' She pressed her fingers to her eyes. 'Okay. It's a heist.' She dropped her hands again. 'You know about heists, and you know about money, about business, about deals. You know how to cheat and steal.'

Thoughtfully, Roarke eased a hip onto her desk. 'I'm taking all of that as a compliment.'

'It's a heist,' she repeated, 'but at the base it's a con. You

149

know about those, too. It's not what you did, using innocent people, killing them, but you know how to set up heists, grifts, cons, thefts.'

'Still taking the compliment.'

'How would you do it? If you were a sociopath, didn't care about leaving a trail of bodies. How would you set this up? How long would it take? How much would you need?'

He blew out a breath. 'Well now, let's sit by the fire.'

'I want—'

'A brandy's what I want,' he decided, and strolled over to get one. 'And we might as well be comfortable while I'm planning out a job without worrying about the death toll.' He grabbed her hand as he walked, tugged her over to the sofa.

The cat slid off the sleep chair, bounded over and up to stretch out across both their laps.

'Cozy,' Roarke decided. 'The start could be from a variety of points – and there's where you'll have your issues. You might be inside one of the companies, or know someone who is. You might catch the word in the media, or on the street. You might be in finance, or again, the politics of it. But from there you have to know enough to have vision.'

'Crash the companies at the optimum time, buy, wait, sell.'

'In shorthand, yes. And if you're that sociopath, you'd think the optimum way at that optimum time to bring about that crash is blood and fear.'

'Explosion, loss of life, confusion. Nobody knows what the fuck for the first couple of hours.'

'Exactly. The world being what the world is, people rush toward terrorism at such moments, foreign or domestic. The market reacts. So if this is my plan, I'd want times, dates, names. I'd want the companies to rebound or it's not profitable, is it?'

He sipped brandy, calculated. 'I don't have to know, absolutely, the Monday meeting is the big marketing reveal and the finalizing of the merger.'

'I can't buy that. It's no coincidence.'

'Not at all,' he agreed. 'But I only have to know there's a major meeting. I already know about the merger, already know it's about to cross the finish line. But I need a time and place. I could make friends with an assistant or junior exec from either company,' he supposed. 'Meet them in a bar, a gym, strike up a conversation. Run into them a few times, have a drink, talk shop.'

'Loose chatter. Bragging or complaining.'

'Often both. All this person has to tell me is there's a big meeting on this particular date, and I can take it from there. Or I nudge for a little more, just conversation, just a couple of people blowing off steam after work.

'If I knew enough,' he continued, 'I'd know Pearson's heirs are safely away, as are Karson's. Only some of the BODs from each company were to be at that nine o'clock. This is a presentation, a formal introduction. The official signing will come after. So you'd need the names of who'd be at the presentation, as that's your optimum.

'Hit later, you take out too many of the bigwigs.'

'Both the biggest wigs were there,' Eve pointed out.

'From my standpoint? You're not worried about cutting off the heads of both companies, as they have more limbs to pick up the pieces. But too much damage, that dive will hold longer, and recovery might not come for weeks, if then.'

She nodded. 'The explosion was bad, but it was contained. One room, and the people in it. And those on the other side of the room – for the most part cuts and burns, broken bones but nothing really life-threatening.'

'The smallest impact for the biggest, if you follow. As I'm going to kill Rogan anyway, I might make contact with him. Friendly or businesslike. We jog in the park, frequent the same deli. Nothing that connects me to him particularly. Or, if not that close, the wife, the daughter, the assistant, a coworker.'

He sipped more brandy. 'If it's me, I'd cultivate more than one source. Casual – that after-work bar, a steam at the gym, a flirtation at a club. Bits and pieces add up if you know how to work it. When I have enough, I study Paul Rogan and his family.'

'Rogan's the key,' she agreed. 'If you're with Econo, why don't you pick somebody from Econo? Too close? Still, you have to *know* Rogan. You have to be sure of him, or gambling sure. Who's your partner?'

'Ah well, that's a tricky one, isn't it?' Roarke studied the brandy he swirled. 'I preferred to work alone, but you can't always pull a job on your own. You'd best be damn sure of any along with you. And this one's bloody, so all the more sure. If it's my job, my plan, I select someone who brings a skill to the table I need or want, and I know them. Personally and well. If I'm tapped for someone else's plan, the same applies.'

'Did you ever work with explosives?'

'Hmm.' He sipped some brandy. 'I preferred finesse, but when finesse isn't an option . . .'

'Did you build them yourself?'

He toed off his shoes, put his feet on the coffee table, and settled into the interrogation. 'It's wise to learn all aspects of a particular vocation, don't you think, Lieutenant? Blasting holes in things always seemed . . . crude, but there were times for crude, and needs must. For a big hole, now, I value my skin as much as any shiny object I might have coveted, so there's where a partner or an expert might come into play. Still, what you're dealing with here's a different thing. A bomb's a bomb in its results, but it comes in forms. And the building of a wearable one, that I've never done or had part in. It would take some study.'

'I've got Salazar for that. It's the broad strokes I'm after from you. And I've got a picture. The inside information's vital. You can't go forward without it. Inside information and the viable mark in Rogan, knowledge of the market, and the means to play it. Add to that the explosives – and most thieves, most market guys don't just have that at their fingertips – and you get a picture.'

She frowned over at the board. 'Okay.'

Roarke hefted the cat, dumped him on the other side of

the sofa, shifted, and nudged Eve back and under him, all as smooth as a dance.

She said, 'Hey. I'm working.'

'You're circling,' he corrected. 'And my consultant fee's due.'

'Put in the chit.'

He grinned. 'I intend to.'

It made her laugh even as his mouth came down to hers with a quick nip of teeth. So she gave in to the moment, the mood, wrapped arms and legs around him.

'How fast can you get it done?'

He slid a hand up her side, down again. 'Are you after fast or effective?'

'I know you, ace.' She arched up against him. 'You can handle both.'

'A challenge then?'

She arched again, heat to heat. 'You're up for it.'

He laughed as well even as he captured her mouth again.

Quick, quick, and oh yes, efficient, those hands skimming, those clever fingers tugging and pressing. A thief's steady hands, a pickpocket's nimble fingers, they stole her breath. And had her disarmed, naked to the waist before she caught it again.

'So far, so good,' she managed.

Then lost her breath again as his mouth ravished her breast. With her heart hammering under the assault, she fought her way under his shirt to flesh.

The fire smoldered, rolled out heat and light. The cat,

displaced and annoyed, plopped off the couch, stalked out of the room.

Roarke moved over her, savoring those long lines, subtle curves. He could make her tremble, always a thrill. And she could make him ache. Every gasp, every sigh he drew from her beat in his blood, tribal drums. Her hands, long and narrow like the rest of her, rushed over him, reached for him, unleashed him.

He drove into her, buried himself, filled her.

They held, breath ragged, eyes locked.

Her hands lifted to his face – one tender beat – then her fingers shot back into his hair, gripped, dragged his mouth back to hers for the hunger, mad and avid.

Then the movement, the hard and fast taking each of each, eclipsed all. The madness of need overtook with her arms chained around him, her hips flashing beat for beat.

When she cried out, flung herself off that whippy edge, he held on, held on, then fell with her.

9

Eve woke in the gray limbo before dawn, alone, naked, and to the alarm of her communicator beeping.

She fumbled for it.

'Block video. Dallas.'

Dispatch, Dallas, Lieutenant Eve. Report to officer, Jacqueline Kennedy Onassis Reservoir, Eighty-sixth Street. Possible homicide. Victim identified as Banks, Jordan.

'Crap.' She breathed it out. 'Acknowledged. Contact Peabody, Detective Delia. Dallas out.'

She rolled over. 'Lights on, twenty percent.' Headed for the shower.

'Who did you talk to, you asshole? Who did you talk to?' she muttered while the hot pulse of jets pounded her. She jumped out of the shower and into the drying tube. Closed her eyes while warm air swirled then grabbed a robe and strode into the bedroom just as Roarke came in the door with the cat at his heels.

'You're up early,' he commented.

'Banks is dead.'

'Ah, well. I'll get the coffee.'

Grateful, she dived into her closet. 'What the hell was he doing in Central Park?' She grabbed black pants, a shirt, a jacket. 'What was he doing at the JKO?'

'The reservoir?'

'All I know until I get there. Except this is damn well connected. No way in hell this bomb goes off yesterday, I talk to him, and he's dead by morning.'

She came out in the shirt – white – the pants – black – tossed a black jacket on the sofa in the sitting area, and grabbed the coffee Roarke held out to her.

'Thanks.'

'Should I go with you?' he asked as he wandered into her closet.

'No need.' She grabbed her pocket debris from the dresser as he walked out with a pale gray V-neck sweater and a pair of black knee boots with gray laces. 'Come on.'

'Not so much for fashion – though they work – but for practicality. The temperature dropped overnight, and it's sleeting, with some wind along with it.'

'Will winter never end?' She took the sweater, tugged it on, sat to pull on the boots.

Already dressed for the business day in one of his perfect suits, Roarke walked back to the AutoChef.

'I don't have time for breakfast,' she said, rising to strap on her weapon harness.

'For this you do.' He handed her a fat, toasted bread pocket.

'What is it?'

He smiled. 'Fast and effective.'

That got a smirk before she bit in. Eggs, creamy, bits of crispy bacon – and something sneaky like spinach.

'Tag me, will you, when you know something? After all, I talked with him as well.'

'Sure.' She downed the pocket, the rest of the coffee. After scooping a hand through her hair, she pulled on the jacket.

And Roarke pulled her to him, kissed her. 'Take care of my cop.'

'Got it.' She bent to give the cat a quick scratch before heading to the door. Stopped. 'Waffles or oatmeal?'

'Sorry?'

'When I'm not here, is it waffles or oatmeal?'

'I like oatmeal.'

She could only shake her head as she jogged downstairs, bundled in the damn winter gear, and headed out to meet death.

Sleet blew, wet and unpleasant, splattering her windshield. The sun had yet to make an appearance so the wet white streaks streamed in the nasty March wind as her headlights beamed. The streets gleamed black.

She passed a single maxibus, lumbering alone with its load of sleepy passengers fresh off the graveyard shift. She swung onto Eighty-sixth until she pulled up behind a black-and-white.

A uniform started toward her, nodding when she held up her badge.

'What do you have?'

'Well, we got a couple of college types in the back. They were out for a drunken stroll, saw the floater. The pair of them climbed over the fence, jumped in to pull him out. Beat droids called us in. We got them in the back keeping warm.'

'I'll take them first.'

Eve opened the door of the cruiser, took a look at the two men – maybe twenty – shivering under heat blankets.

She crouched down. 'Lieutenant Dallas. Let's hear it.'

'Man, Jesus, we were just taking a walk, right?'

'Right.'

He had smooth cocoa-colored skin, a little gray under it, and wide, wide brown eyes. She could smell the nerves, the water, and the cheap brew pumping off him.

'Your name?'

'Marshall. Marshall Whitier. We pulled like an all-nighter, and were walking it off, and messing around. Maybe jog around the JKO, right? And we saw the dude. So Richie says, "Holy shit," and I'm like, "What the fuck," and we climbed over and jumped in the water.'

'I tried CPR, even mouth-to-mouth,' the other man said.

'Name?'

'Oh, Richie. I mean Richard Lieberman.' He swallowed, hard.

He had skin so white his freckles popped out like ...

159

polka dots, Eve thought. And orange hair with tips of blue –
with a tiny pointed beard to match.

'I'm, uh, certified. I work summers as a lifeguard, so I
knew what to do. But, man, he was gone. You know, dead.
So we called the cops.'

'Did you see anyone while you were messing around, or
while you waited for the police?'

'Nobody. Well, there was a sidewalk sleeper, but he was
back on Fifth, before we came into the park. And well . . .'

'Well?'

'I guess we saw the beat droids back there, too, so we sort
of ducked in here.'

'Got any Sober-Up?'

Their eyes shifted to each other, then down.

'Look, I don't currently give a shit about your underage
drinking.'

'There was this party—'

'Don't care,' she told Marshall. 'I'm going to need your
contact information, then these officers are going to take
you back to – where?'

'We're at Berkeley. We, ah, sort of snuck out of the dorm
to go to the party, then—'

'Don't care,' she said to Richie. 'We're going to get you
back.' Impaired or not, she thought, they'd tried to save a
life. 'What are your chances of sneaking back in?'

That eye slide again. 'We're pretty good at it,'
Richie told her.

'Good. Do that. Dry off, get something hot – and

nonalcoholic – to drink. Here's what I care about: You tried to help someone, and when you couldn't, you called the cops.'

'You're not going to rat us out?'

'I'm not going to rat you out. If you don't have such good luck sneaking back in, have the person who busts you contact me. Lieutenant Dallas, Cop Central. Got it?'

'Yes, ma'am.'

'You lose points for the "ma'am."' She shut the door. 'Get them back,' she told the uniform. 'Make sure they get back inside.'

'Dumb-asses.' The uniform shook his head. 'But they got balls. Probably shriveled up right now, but they got 'em.'

In full agreement, she went back to her car for her field kit, started the hike to the jogging path and the reservoir.

The struggling sun turned the sky to a lighter, dirtier gray. In its pissy light, she spotted the beat droids – muscular issues, both male with square, serious faces. Unaffected by the wind and the wet, they stood flanking the body.

Eve held up her badge. 'Report.'

Their report added little to the witnesses' statements but for, in the way of droids, precise times. She had them stand by, then took a long look at Jordan Banks.

He lay faceup, and from the angle of his neck, the bruising harsh against the skin, she judged his neck had been broken before whoever broke it dumped his body in the water.

The droids had ID'd him with scanners, but she sealed up, took out her Identi-pad, made it official.

'Victim is identified as Banks, Jordan.' She rattled off the data for the record before taking out her gauge for time of death. 'TOD, oh three hundred twenty hours. Witnesses notified nine-one-one at five-twelve. He wasn't in the water long. He's not wearing a coat, a wrist unit, or shoes.'

She searched the pockets of his pants. 'No wallet, no 'link. It looks like a mugging, but it's not. Just not.'

Taking out her penlight, she examined the bruising on the neck. 'Not from a blow. Maybe a fall, but ...' She ran the light over the left side of the face, studied as she heard Peabody's clomping winter boots.

She rose, turned to her partner. 'Turn around.'

'What?'

'Just turn around.'

When she did, Eve stepped up behind her, cupped her right hand under Peabody's chin, pressed her left to the left side of Peabody face, gave her partner's head a quick – but gentle – twist.

'Hey!'

'Yeah, yeah.' Eve stepped back. 'Somebody knows how to kill, quick and quiet. No defensive wounds. He never saw it coming. Didn't expect it. Knew who was behind him, and wasn't worried. Could be they stunned him first, or had a weapon, but why kill covert, combat style, if you could just stun and toss him into the water to drown, or use the weapon?'

Peabody fussed the scarf back around her neck. 'This is Karson's ex, right? You interviewed him yesterday?'

'And he lied through his teeth. I could see it.'

'He was in this?'

'I don't know if he knew he was, but he was. And they didn't leave this loose end alive.'

Peabody stepped closer to the body. 'His neck's broken. Can you really break somebody's neck with just your hands?'

'If you're strong enough, and know how. Military, he's going to be military.'

She shoved her hands in the pockets of her long leather coat, stared over at the skyline, gray against gray. 'How the hell did they get him here? Three in the morning, he comes here, meets them. Or they come here together. No defensive wounds, no sign of struggle. He came willingly. Did he walk – he doesn't strike me as somebody who'd walk this far. Let's check for cabs, private car services for pickups at his address and for drop-offs in this area. Drop-offs between two and three-twenty this morning.'

She played her light over the grass, the path. 'We'll call it in, sweepers and the dead wagon. Crime scene might find something. Get that going. I'll finish with him.'

When she had, ordered the bag and tag, she left the beat droids guarding the crime scene and filled Peabody in on the witnesses' statements as they walked back to the car.

'The water has to be freezing.'

'I'd say they were too young and drunk to care.' Eve got into the car, said, 'Coffee.'

'Oh yeah.' Peabody programmed it. 'If Banks is tied in, it gives us a lead.'

'He's tied. So we're going to see Karson.'

'Now? It's pretty early.'

'Not for Banks.'

Eve dealt with the nurse – a different one but almost as disapproving – and bullied her way into Karson's room.

The patient was awake, with the morning reports murmuring on her wall screen. The nurse fussed over her, checking monitors, fluffing pillows.

'Lilian, I'd really love some coffee.'

'I'm going to order up your breakfast now.' She gave Karson a pat on the hand before sailing out.

'It's terrible coffee,' Karson said, 'and I know it's whining, but, God, I can't wait to get out of here. Do you have information?'

'Ms Karson, I regret to inform you that Jordan Banks is dead.'

'What? What?' She used her good arm to try to push up, winced, dropped back. 'Jordan? How? My God.'

'He was murdered in the early hours of this morning.'

'Murdered? How could – how? Where? Oh, my Jesus. I need a minute.'

She covered her hands with her face, rocked, rocked. 'Murdered. Dead. I can't ... I despised him. I came to despise him. He made a fool out of me, and I hated knowing I'd let him make a fool out of me. Now he's dead.'

She dropped her hands. Her eyes shone damp, but tears didn't fall. 'We were involved, for about eight months. Up until a few weeks ago.'

'I know.'

'Of course you know. It's your job to know. I can't think. I just can't think.'

'Would you like some water?' Peabody offered.

'I'd like a drink, a goddamn double of anything with a kick. I'd like for an hour to pass where people I know aren't dead.' She closed her eyes, seemed to breathe herself under control. 'How was he killed? Can you tell me?'

'The medical examiner will determine cause of death.' Eve weighed the odds. 'I believe his neck was broken.'

'He was in a fight? That's just impossible. He wouldn't know how.'

'No, not a fight. How much did you tell him about the details and timing of the merger?'

'I ... Too much.' As her breathing pitched again, she gripped the sheet in a fist. 'Are you saying Jordan had something to do with the bombing? I can't believe that – won't.'

'I don't know that. You gave him details?'

'I thought I was in love with him. I thought he was in love with me. His family ... they understand business. Jordan's more interested in the arts – and really that's not entirely true, either. He's more interested in women, and how to use them – wealthy women. But I thought he had an interest in my business – a caring interest – and I shared some of my thoughts, plans, hopes with him. He had advice, sometimes it was reasonably good advice. And he listened, he was supportive. And I was an idiot.'

'I don't think so,' Peabody put in. 'You cared for him, and

thought he felt the same. You thought of him as a partner, on a personal level.'

'I did. I thought . . . I really thought we had a future together. More fool me.'

'We need to be able to share with our partners,' Peabody continued. 'To talk to them, to have them listen. It's natural and human.'

'I hope I feel that way again someday – when I find someone worthy of trust. But now – I said I despised him, and I don't say that lightly. But I can't believe he'd have had any part in what happened. In terrorizing that family, in killing people. I might've died, too. We slept together for months, all but lived together.'

'Why did you break it off?' Eve asked her.

She sighed now. 'He'd started to ask for money. Just a loan. The first time, I didn't think much of it. Just a few thousand – cash. The second time, those few weeks ago, it bothered me. He'd never paid back the first, and obviously didn't intend to. I balked, he let it go. But then I found out he'd been cheating. Another woman – wealthy, of course, and married in this case. When I confronted him with it, he shrugged it off. Literally shrugged,' she added, her eyes glittery with temper.

'He'd needed the money I hadn't been willing to give him, so he'd tapped another source. Really, it was my fault – or so he said.'

'Ballsy,' Eve replied.

'I wish I'd kicked him in them. Still, I did kick him out,

then and there. It didn't seem to bother him a bit. In fact, he said he'd finished with me in any case.'

'*Despised* seems kind of a wussy word.'

Karson smiled a little at Eve. 'It does, doesn't it? Regardless, he's not a violent man. A user, an opportunist, a lazy, worthless son of a bitch, but not a man who'd kill.'

'He might have been a man who'd know others who would.'

'Oh, Christ, I don't know. What time is it? Early.' She answered her own question as she glanced at her wrist unit. 'Too early to tag up Juliette. My friend,' she added. 'Someone to lean on.'

'Tell me about his friends, his associates.'

'I don't know many of them well. I liked some of them. Fun, witty, interesting. Others? Well, fun for the short bursts, more biting than witty, and interested more in the next party or adventure. A lot of illegals – and after I made a point about that to Jordan, we didn't go to many parties. I have a business, a reputation. I wasn't going to get caught up and have my name and my company splashed over the media by being photographed at some party where Erotica and Buzz are offered like canapés.'

'Gambling?'

'Of course. Legal and, I'd assume, not. Most of these could afford to gamble.'

'Did any of them show an interest in your business, in the merger?'

'Lieutenant, these types – or the ones Jordan liked, particularly – don't worry overmuch about business or working.

They party, they travel. I might have had a few casual con-versations about Econo, but I honestly don't remember any particular questions or interest.'

'Did you know Jordan was laundering money through his art gallery?'

Karson let out a long breath. 'Was he? Of course he was. It makes perfect sense. How stupid could I possibly be? He wanted me to pay for the art I bought with cash – I wouldn't. I bought some for the company, through the com-pany – and there are rules. And I bought some for myself, but I wanted the paper trail.

'I told him too much,' she said dully. 'I trusted him too much, and he broke that trust in so many ways. He broke it by telling someone what I'd shared in confidence. For his ego or for money, both are the same to him, really. And because of that, people are dead. Because I wanted someone to lean on, and thought I'd found him.'

'You're not responsible.' Eve spoke briskly. 'If Banks was, he paid a price for it, a high one. But you're not responsible. And you're very likely not the only one who shared details with someone they trusted. The men responsible found ways to exploit that.'

They left her staring through a forest of flowers to the window and the gray sky beyond.

Pearson's Upper East Side redbrick mansion rose four stories. It stood dignified, its tall windows blank eyes as the sleet turned to rain.

'We're a little early,' Peabody noted as Eve stepped under the portico over the grand entrance double doors.

'They'll deal.' She noted the security, discreet but thorough, as she pressed the bell.

Good morning. The computer-generated voice carried a pleasant, neutral tone. **Due to a death in the family, the Pearson family is not currently receiving visitors.**

'Lieutenant Dallas,' Eve began as she held up her badge for scanning, 'Detective Peabody, NYPSD. We're expected.'

One moment please

The thin red line of the scanner swept over Eve's badge, turned green.

Your credentials are verified, Lieutenant. The family is being notified of your arrival. Please wait.

It took under a minute for a woman in black to open the door on the right. 'I'm sorry to keep you waiting. Please come in.'

She stepped back, a woman of about fifty with a smooth bob of dark hair. Dark eyes, red rimmed from weeping, held steady.

'May I take your coats?'

'We're good.'

'If you'll follow me.' She led the way, in sensible shoes, over floors of burnished gold, across a thick rug patterned in faded reds and blues. Centered on it stood a large round table, and centered on that a towering red vase of white flowers rose toward the lofty ceiling.

The woman turned to a deep arch off the wide foyer

and into a room large enough to hold three conversation areas. She chose one near the fireplace where flames simmered inside a frame of black-and-gray-threaded white marble.

'If you'd care to sit, the family will join you shortly.'

'How long have you worked for the Pearsons, Ms . . . ?'

'Mrs Stuben. Thirty-three years. If you'll excuse me, I need to check on the coffee and tea service.'

She started out, reaching the archway as a man stepped to it. Fully a foot taller, he put his hands on her shoulders, folded himself down to kiss the top of her head. He whispered something to her that had her lifting a hand to squeeze his before hurrying away.

He entered on wide strides. The black sweater and trousers added to the look of a walking stovepipe. His face, as gawky as the rest of him, carried the drawn, exhausted look of a man who hadn't slept.

'Lieutenant, Detective. I'm Drew Pearson. The rest of the family will be just a few minutes. Please sit.'

'We're sorry for your loss, Mr Pearson, and know this is a difficult time for you and your family.'

'We're shattered. People say that – like they're glass, I used to think. Now I know what it means.'

He sat, a kind of folding again, in a chair done in an elegant blue with a print of scattered roses.

'More than anything, we need to know who, and why. We have to get through today, tomorrow, and the rest, but how do we do that without knowing who or why? My father . . . It won't change that, but how do we get through unless we know?'

'The NYPSD will use all of its resources to find out. You were in London.'

'Yes. I'm based there. Or was.'

'But the negotiations, the presentation yesterday and the actual deal took place in New York.'

'Yes. I did a lot of shuttling back and forth the last several months, but we also worked by 'link and holo.'

'You were in favor of the merger.'

'I brought the idea to the table, and put out the initial feelers. And I've been asking myself for the last twenty-four horrible hours if bringing this to my father, helping to make the deal a reality, cost him his life.'

'No. The people who made the bomb and forced Paul Rogan to detonate it cost your father and eleven others their lives.'

'Are you absolutely sure Paul didn't – wasn't involved?'

'Yes. You knew him?'

'Very well. I couldn't believe . . . then didn't want to believe.' He pinched the bridge of his nose before gripping his hands tight together in his lap. 'Cecily and Melly – his wife and daughter – are they all right?'

'They will be.'

'We haven't – just haven't been able to reach out to them. My mother—'

He broke off, rose as three women in black came into the room, arms or hands linked so they presented a solid wall.

'Mom.' He walked to the women, took the woman in the center by the hand, then slid an arm around her and led her over. 'This is Lieutenant Dallas and Detective Peabody. My mother, Rozilyn Pearson.'

'Mrs Pearson, thank you for seeing us. We're very sorry for your loss.'

Her eyes, glazed from tranqs and red from weeping, slipped over Eve, brushed over Peabody before she sat. 'My husband's dead,' she said in a voice as dull as the day.

The other two women moved in, sat on either side of her. The one on the right took her hand. The daughter, Eve thought. They shared the same delicate bone structure, the same deep brown eyes. Though the daughter's were shadowed, they weren't glazed but hard with anger.

'My sister, Liana, my wife, Sybil.' Drew looked at his sister. 'Brad?'

'As soon as he can. My husband,' Liana told Eve and Peabody. 'He's upstairs with our son, and Drew and Sybil's children. Noah's only six, and Drew's children are so young. Noah and my father were especially close. He's upset.'

'We'll try not to take much of your time,' Eve began.

Stuben wheeled in a large tray holding the coffee and tea service.

Sybil rose quickly. 'Let me help you, Bessie. You'll have some tea, Rozilyn.' The educated British accent suited her roses-and-cream looks, the long fall of chestnut hair she'd pulled back in a tail. 'Lieutenant?'

'Coffee, black. Thanks.'

172

'And, Detective?'

'Coffee, regular.' At Sybil's blank look, she explained. 'Ah, cream – or milk – two sugars. Thanks.'

Obviously comfortable having a task, Sybil worked with Stuben to pour and serve. Eve gave them the time to settle.

'Mrs Pearson, do you know of anyone who wanted to harm your husband, his business, or this merger?'

'No. No. Derrick's a good man, a wonderful father and husband. He's a caring man to his employees. Everyone loves him. Isn't that right, Liana? Everyone loves your father.'

'Yes, of course.'

'He treated Paul like *family*!' Those glazed eyes cleared enough to show fury and terrible grief. 'Paul and Cecily were always welcome in our home. Melody played with our grandchildren! And he murdered my Derrick.'

'Mom, Mom.' Liana tried to get arms around her mother, but Rozilyn pushed her aside.

'Don't *tell* me Paul's a victim! Don't you tell me he was forced. That *murderer* made a choice. He made a choice and he killed your father. He killed my Derrick. My husband's dead.'

Her voice pitched high as the words spewed out until they rang on hysteria. Tears spurted and gushed.

'She can't do this,' Liana said, starting to rise.

'I'll take her upstairs.' Stuben walked around the sofa, leaned down, gathered Rozilyn up. 'Let's go on upstairs now, Miz Roz. You need to go up with me.'

'What will we do, Bessie? What will we do?'

'You need some rest,' Stuben soothed as she guided the sobbing woman out.

'She can't—' Liana broke off, looking away as she fought for composure. Sybil, silently weeping, sat beside her, gripping her hands.

'My parents—' Drew cleared his throat. 'My parents,' he began again, 'were married for thirty-nine years. They knew each other since childhood. She's just not able to do this now.'

'I understand. If you'd rather we came back to interview the rest of you—'

'No, please. God, let's get this done, Drew.' Liana pressed her free hand to her face. 'Let's just get this done. I spoke with Cecily.'

'You— When?' her brother demanded.

'Earlier this morning. I needed to. It was hard, for both of us. We got to be friends – or very friendly,' she told Eve. 'Her daughter's older than Noah, but they often played together – and with Drew's children when they were here – so we got to be friendly. It was hard, but she told me what happened to her, to Paul, to Melly. My mother can't understand, can't forgive, and I won't ask her to. But I can. I can. I have a child. You have children,' she said to Drew and Sybil. 'What wouldn't you do to protect them?'

She took a breath. 'I'm so angry, so angry. I can't push that anger on Paul and Cecily and that little girl. I wanted to, but I can't. What do I do with this anger? Who did this, to all of us?'

'We're working to find that out. Did your father have enemies?'

'Competitors – your own husband is one. Competitors and rivals, but enemies? Someone who wanted to kill him? To kill all those people? No. Just no.'

'You work in the New York offices, so closely with your father. Were there any serious disagreements regarding the merger?'

'Some, of course. It was a major step, a big change, but in the end a very good deal for everyone. Paul himself wasn't fully on board at the outset, but he got there.'

'Why weren't you in New York for the presentation?'

'Dad wanted a family rep in Rome. Drew's London, and Jean-Philippe – our cousin – is in Paris, but Dad wanted me in Rome. Willimina had key people in important hubs as well.'

'To give the presentation a global impact,' Drew went on. 'The big reveal,' he said with a ghost of a smile.

'Have any of you received any threats?'

'No.' Drew looked at his wife, his sister, got head shakes. 'This came without warning.'

'Who have you talked to about the merger? Outside of the business?'

'The media,' Drew said. 'At least in the last few weeks. Sybil handles most of that in Europe.'

'I'm media chief for Quantum Europe, based in London with Drew. I'd been on parental leave for more than a year, but I came back to take the lead on this.'

'You fed the media?'

'In small bites, strategic bites,' she added. 'Until we got the approval to push stories, we kept it locked down. An occasional leak – timed to stir some interest – but closed on real details.'

Eve shifted gears. 'How well do you know Jordan Banks?'

She saw the shock in Sybil's eyes before the woman cast them down. And her hand reached up nervously to smooth at her hair.

10

'I know that name,' Liana murmured. 'How do I Know that name? Drew?'

'It's not ringing for me, sorry.'

Sybil said nothing, just gave a quick shake of her head without making eye contact.

'He was involved romantically with Willimina Karson up until a few weeks ago,' Eve said.

'That's it. The Banks family, Drew? Communications, entertainment. The wastrel son.'

'Oh.' He frowned a little. 'I never met him, that I remember. I've met Morgan Banks. Is this his brother?'

'I think it is.' Liana seemed to settle, drank some of the coffee she'd ignored. 'I actually never met him, either, but I've heard things. I think I did know Willimina was seeing him at some point. I got to know her, of course, through the merger, but— Wait, wait, I *did* meet him. At a dinner party. It had to be months ago, maybe last fall. Why?'

'He's dead.'

Sybil froze; her color drained. Drew leaned forward.

'Is this connected? Was Jordan Banks somehow involved in the bombing?'

'We're looking into it.'

'But Willimina was in the room!' Obviously incensed, Liana set her cup and saucer down with a *snap*. 'She might have been killed. As it was, she was seriously injured. You can't tell me he engineered this to get back at her for ending their relationship.'

'We don't believe that was the motive, but he may have been involved, directly or indirectly.'

'He has a reputation as a womanizer, but this was evil. Just evil. Did he know Paul?'

'We haven't found any connection between them.' Eve kept her tone brisk, her gaze on Liana. Her focus on Sybil.

'I'm not able to share any more with you on that line of inquiry,' she continued. 'We don't want to keep you much longer, but it would be helpful if we could speak to each of you for a few minutes, separately.'

'Separately?' Drew repeated.

'It would be helpful, then we can leave you alone.'

'I'd like to check on Brad and the kids anyway.' As she spoke, Liana got to her feet. 'I could send Brad down, stay with Noah, if you want to talk to him.'

'That works. Mr Pearson, if you'd give us the room. We'll speak with your wife, then send her to get you. We'll work our way through this, and get out of your way.'

'All right.' He stood, skimmed a hand over his wife's hair, and went out with his sister.

Eve waited until she was certain they were out of earshot. 'Tell me,' she demanded.

Sybil blinked. 'Pardon?'

'You knew Banks. Denying it isn't going to work.' She kept her voice low and hard. 'Twelve people are dead. Thirteen including Banks. So you'll tell us. I'm going to read you your rights.'

'Oh God, my God.'

She unlinked the hands she'd gripped in her lap, wrapped her arms around herself as Eve recited the Revised Miranda. 'Did you have an affair with Jordan Banks?'

'No! No, no, it was nothing like that. I mean to say, it was only a ... flirtation. I never — we never — I couldn't, wouldn't betray Drew. It's just ... '

'Did you meet him in London?' Peabody asked, more gently than Eve.

'Yes. Over a year ago. The baby was only three months old. Jacey was just three months old — and Trey, our boy — had just turned two. We wanted to have our babies close together, you see.'

She linked her hands again. 'Drew and Liana are so close, so we wanted to have our babies near in age, so they'd have that kind of bond. And I just ... '

'Two kids under three.' Peabody offered a sympathetic look. 'Exhausting.'

'Yes. Of course, I had help. My mother, a nanny, but I—'

She broke off, pressed her fingers to her eyes. 'I have no excuse. Drew was just starting the ground floor of the merger, the meetings, the plans, the trips back and forth to sit down with his father, the board. And I felt overwhelmed and tired and neglected and – and undesirable. Selfish, I was selfish. Two beautiful children, a man I love who loves me and our babies, and I felt neglected because he had important work.'

'You were on leave. You'd been used to having important work outside the home,' Eve put in. 'To being part of it.'

'Maybe a little post-baby depression, I don't know. It's no excuse, but I bounced back so fast with Trey, and I just wasn't with Jacey.'

'How did you meet him?' Eve asked.

'There was an art showing I wanted to attend. An opening, and Drew had promised to take me. A night out, just the two of us. An adult night – no feedings, nappies, bedtime stories. I was all dressed, ridiculously excited, and he rang me up, and told me how sorry he was, but he'd gotten caught up in something and needed to deal with it.'

'You were upset.' All sympathy, Peabody nodded. 'Disappointed.'

'Crushed, beyond reason really. We'd already arranged for the nanny to stay the night. I'd bought a new frock. I just went. The hell with it. I wanted to go to this opening, I'd just go. So I did.'

'You met Banks,' Eve finished.

'Yes. He was there, and somehow we started talking about one of the paintings. He was so charming and attentive. I flirted, I did, partially because I was angry with Drew, but primarily because it felt so good to have someone pay attention.'

'You'd spent nearly two years of the last three pregnant.' Sticking with the theme, Peabody layered on more understanding. 'You wanted to feel like a person, a woman. Not just a mother.'

'Oh God, yes. It was wrong, but I had a drink with him after, and we talked, about art and literature and cinema. We just talked. He kissed my hand when he put me in a cab. Just my hand. But he said he'd only be in London for a few days, and wouldn't I have lunch with him. He hated to eat alone.

'So I did. The next day, I left my babies with the nanny and I went to have lunch with him, and flirt with him. And the next day I met him again. A drink, in the middle of the afternoon. It felt so wonderfully wicked. And this time he kissed me, and I let him. In the bar of his hotel. And he asked me to come up to his suite.'

She stopped, pressed both hands to her face. 'I almost did. I'm so ashamed of that. Part of me wanted to. But the rest of me was appalled. What was I doing? What was I doing with this man I didn't even know while my husband was working, while my babies were home with the nanny? I told him no. I apologized because it was my doing, it was my fault. I left, and I never saw him again. I swear to you.'

'What did you tell him about the merger?'

'The merger? We didn't really talk about—'

'You told him you were married,' Eve interrupted. 'You

181

wear a ring. Did he sympathize, say flattering things when you told him your husband was always working?'

'I . . . yes, I suppose so. Yes. He said – something like – he'd never be able to keep his mind on work with such a beautiful, vibrant woman at home. And he asked what was so important it kept him away.'

'And you told him.'

'I . . . ' She pressed a hand to her mouth. 'I did, just that it felt like the family business was more important than family to him right now, and he was so wrapped up in crafting this deal with Econo, he barely knew I was home.'

'You mentioned Econo specifically?'

'I did. Yes, I did.'

'Did he ask you more about it?'

'He might have. Yes, of course he did. I was complaining, and someone – a very attractive, charming man – listened to me, sympathized with me.'

'What did you tell him?'

'There wasn't much to tell, honestly. It was all just getting started. Things like Drew and his father, some others were meeting with Willimina Karson and some of her people. How Drew spent so much time traveling to New York, and in meetings. I resented it, all of it, and maybe because I wasn't part of it. Honestly, I was stupid and selfish, but there wasn't enough to tell. There weren't any real details. If he was involved in this, I don't understand, I don't understand at all.'

Eve did, but she let Sybil go. And though it was only for form, spoke with the others.

'Well, shit,' Peabody said when they got back in the car. 'Do you think she'll figure out she got the exploding ball rolling?'

'Maybe. But Banks took that fragment of a ball, rolled it over to Karson, and expanded it. Then, for ego or profit, he tosses the expanded ball around. Somebody else fields it, weaponizes it, and boom.'

'Do you think Banks set up Sybil?'

'No way he could know she'd come to that art opening, and come alone. He saw an opportunity – good-looking woman and wealthy, as the rock she's wearing on her finger would tell him. Also married, but alone. Strike up a conversation, get a feel. Okay, the lady's vulnerable, unhappy,' Eve said as she pulled into traffic. 'He just exploits that. Probably figuring he can get laid, maybe skin her for a few bucks. Then she drops the seed of the merger in his lap.'

'He does a little research,' Peabody continued, staring out into the rain as she thought it through. 'And look here, Willimina Karson – very attractive, unattached, and a good source for more information. Arrange to meet her, charm her, pursue her, attach, and milk her for whatever he can get. I think he probably figured to make some money on the insider trading part of it – or whatever it's called – and puffed himself up bragging about it. To the wrong people. Now he's dead, too.'

'It plays,' Eve agreed. 'Right down the line. Here's how I see it: The idiot contacted them, or one of them. He tells them he's figured it out, and wants a cut. Maybe he threatens to rat them out, maybe he's that stupid, but the wanting a cut's enough. Loose end.'

Eve made a fist, twisted it.

'Snap.'

'We're probably not looking for an inside man,' Eve concluded. 'Anyone on the inside wouldn't need the tidbits Banks could blather about. But he knew them, or at least one of them, well enough to brag, maybe offer the information for a small fee or favor. Well enough he walked into Central Park to meet up.'

'People like Banks? They do so much slithering and sliding they don't think anything's ever going to stick to them. He figured he had those two over a barrel.'

'Yeah. Let's go see what Morris can tell us about Banks falling off the barrel and breaking his neck.'

By the time Eve walked through the white tunnel of the morgue, the rain had eased to a piss-trickle of chilly wet, one that looked and felt as if it would continue to drip, drip, drip until somebody came along with a giant wrench and fixed the damn faucet.

The morgue smelled of chemical lemons and death, and through Morris's double doors, low-down blues played. He wore a protective cape over a suit of forest green with needle-thin gold stripes. He'd paired it with a shirt of dull gold and a deep green tie, and used both colors in cords wound through his long, dark braid.

With sealed hands he lifted the liver from Banks's splayed torso to weigh. Smiled over at Eve and Peabody.

'A morning made for blues and bed, but since we can't

have both . . . ' Still, he ordered the volume on the music to decrease.

'It's slowing down,' Eve told him. 'It's down to really freaking annoying.'

'Could be worse,' he said, cleaning the blood off his sealed hands. 'Could be snowing, and I've had enough of that this winter.'

'I'm forcing some narcissus – paperwhites – in the kitchen,' Peabody told him. 'They get me through the last of the winter.'

'I'll have to try that myself.'

'The dead guy probably doesn't care about rain or snow or whatever narcissus is,' Eve pointed out.

'A very pretty and fragrant flower,' Morris told her. 'A harbinger of spring. In any case . . . I'm told our dead guy was pulled out of the JKO by a couple of boys too insulated by various substances to worry about the filthy weather or the jump into the drink.'

'Young and stupid. Without the young or stupid, Banks would have spent another couple of hours in the water. Not a prime day for jogging in the park.'

'Your killer had to have some muscle to get Banks over the fence.'

'There were probably two of them.'

'Ah, that would help. Still, it took some upper-body strength and skill to break this neck manually.'

'Military training, most probable.'

'And logical. From behind,' Morris added. 'Dominant

right hand. The late Mr Banks didn't put up a fight. No defensive wounds, no other injuries. He'd consumed quite a bit of red wine along with some brie and herbed crackers – rosemary – two deviled dove eggs, about a quarter ounce of beluga, with the accoutrements: a few marinated olives, some goose liver pâté. He capped all that off with a few ounces of absinthe.'

'Party food,' Eve stated. 'Expensive cocktail party.'

'The goose liver and the absinthe? He'd have enjoyed that less than an hour prior to his TOD.'

'Left the party, went to the park. The killers may have been at the party,' she speculated as she studied the body. 'Or arranged for the meeting after. He knew them, told them I was poking around. So . . . ' She twisted her hands in the air. 'Snap. Tox?'

'Sent off. We should have the full results fairly quickly. He didn't just eat and drink at the party,' Morris added.

He picked up a clear sample case from his tray, held it up. Inside, Eve saw the single bright red hair.

'Pubic hair, combed out of his own,' Morris told her. 'I'll send it to Harvo at the lab.'

'It'll be female. There's nothing to indicate he was into same-sex play. DNA would be helpful.'

'If the owner's in the system, our queen of hair and fiber will track her down. I can tell you he's had a bit of work here and there,' Morris continued as he set the case back on the tray. 'Face and body, nothing major. As you can see, he believed in pubic grooming – of the permanent sort.'

Eve glanced at the narrow line of hair. 'Made it easy to spot the stray red hair.'

'It did. The evidence indicates he died well-fed, buzzed, and sexually satisfied. I don't suppose that's much comfort to him.'

'Or me, since I was looking forward to slapping him in a cage as an accessory. Thanks, Morris.'

'We're here to serve.'

As they walked out, he ordered the music up again, on a sob of tenor sax.

'Party and sex,' Eve said as they walked out. 'Hit those cab companies and private transpos, Peabody. We'll go by and talk to his money guy, see if we get any buzz there.'

She headed east, and by the time she approached the narrow streets and canyons of the Financial District, Peabody got a hit.

'Yeah.' She held up a hand to signal Eve. 'Can you patch me through to the driver? No problem. Rapid Cab,' she told Eve. 'Logged a pickup on West Ninety-sixth, two-twenty. Drop-off on West Eighty-seventh. Yeah, still here.'

Eve listened with half an ear as she negotiated in the shadow of the tall buildings. Some of the Gilded Age buildings with their fancy architecture had survived the Urbans. Others had been built up after the war, so sleek bullets married with high, festooned palaces beyond the bronze bollards, wet with rain, that shielded them from vehicular bombs.

She ruled out double-parking, not because it worried

her to piss off civilian drivers, but in order to avoid hiking blocks in the continuing piss-trickle. The street options were simply too narrow.

She found a lot, used her vertical option to squeeze into a stingy second-level slot.

'Confirmed,' Peabody told her. 'RC pulled up the ticket. Banks charged the ride, so we have that. The driver remembers him – solo fare. Says the fare was high and tight, talked to somebody on his 'link. Doesn't know or remember what he said beyond he'd be there in a few minutes. Fare called up a ride for pickup at 743 West Ninety-sixth, and came out about a minute or two after the driver tagged his arrival.'

Peabody got out as Eve did, started down the clanging iron steps to ground level.

'Banks paid via his 'link for the charge, got out, walked away.'

'Good. After we talk to the money people, we'll take a pass through Banks's apartment. He'll have an address book, so we'll find out who he knew at that address. We can talk to the partygoers, and hit his art gallery. We need to check in with Baxter and Trueheart.'

She'd hooked them for notification of Banks's next of kin.

'I want the family reaction, and we may need to interview them.'

They passed through the barricades, joined the throng of tourists who swarmed the Wall Street district with their cameras and craned necks.

She smelled street coffee from the glide-carts and the first of the steaming soy dogs as the morning eased toward noon. Purposefully, she avoided the diehards who marched or circled with their signs and their earnest, angry faces protesting the evils of capitalism. Others thronged around the Wall Street bull, gleefully posing in front of its snorting charge. To her mind, a bull – metal or flesh – was a cow with a dick. She gave it a wide berth.

And entered the vaulted, gilded lobby on Beaver Street.

Eve badged through security and headed up to the forty-third floor with Peabody.

No gilt, but plenty of plush in the lobby of Buckley and Schultz. And people looking very important as they watched screens full of stock reports or financial news.

One of the three receptionists looked soberly at Eve's badge. 'I'm sorry, but Mr Schultz is in off-site meetings all day today. He's not expected in his office here until tomorrow. Should I ask his administrative assistant to make an appointment for you?'

'I'll talk to the admin.'

'I'll see if he's available.'

Three minutes later, the admin came out.

Early thirties, Eve judged, with a kind of Trueheart cut of clean polished by a bankerly patina. Excellent suit, shined shoes, doe eyes in a youthful face.

'Lieutenant, Detective.' He glanced toward the plush, important, and prosperous. 'Please come with me. I'm Devin Garrison, Mr Schultz's admin.' He led the way by offices where people in suits sat or paced while they talked of money in a language as foreign to her as Greek. Or e-geek.

He turned into another office – a bit larger, good view, well-appointed. Upper-middle strata, to Eve's gauge.

Devin closed the door. 'I— Mr Schultz is out of the office all day. I just . . . I just heard a bulletin about Mr Banks. Mr Jordan Banks. I knew him. I can't believe . . .'

'How well did you know him?'

'Oh. Well, only really via 'link. When he wanted to speak to Mr Schultz. Or when I arranged a lunch or dinner meeting. I never actually met him in person. He didn't come to the offices. Mr Schultz went to him, if necessary.'

'When's the last time it was necessary?'

'Would you give me a minute to check?'

'Check.'

He went behind the desk, pulled up, Eve noted, a calendar. Mr Schultz was a busy man with few slots open most workdays.

'It looks like February eighteenth, for their regular monthly lunch meeting. They were scheduled for the next the middle of this month.'

'When did they last speak, that you're aware of?'

'Yesterday. Mr Banks contacted the office yesterday morning, first thing. Well, actually . . . Was Mr Banks really murdered?'

'He was really murdered.'

'I think you should speak with Agatha. Ah, you see, Mr Schultz was Mr Banks's financial adviser of record, but in actuality Agatha Lowell handled the account. The day-to-day.'

'Where is she?'

He led the way out again, and down to smaller offices. In one, a woman – a redhead, Eve saw with interest – sat at a desk working her comp with one hand, a 'link with the other. Her wall screen showed the same confusion of symbols as Roarke's tended to before breakfast.

She glanced over – blue eyes, annoyed and focused.

'I've got it. Yes, it's done. All good. I'll get back to you.'

She clicked off the 'link. 'What is it, Devin?' Her voice, thick with Brooklyn, all but snarled impatience. 'I'm more than swamped.'

'These are police. Mr Banks . . . He was murdered!'

'When?' Her eyebrows drew together, more in deeper annoyance than shock.

'Early this morning,' Eve told her. 'Thanks,' she said to Devin. 'We'll find you if we need to speak to you.'

'Okay. Aggie, should I contact Mr Schultz and tell him?'

'Text him.' She shifted her attention to Eve. 'Can we make this quick?' she said even as her 'link buzzed. 'I'm really busy.'

'And obviously broken up by the death of a client.'

'He was Mr Schultz's client. I barely knew him. I'm sorry when anybody dies, but people do. I've got work.'

'Devin said you handled the day-to-day business for Banks.'

She sighed, blew at her fringe of red bangs. 'Hold on.'

She picked up her 'link, tapped in a code. 'Cheryl, I need to forward my tags for the next few minutes. No, I need to.' She tapped something else, set the 'link down.

'Jordan Banks was a pain in the ass, okay? Senior Mr Schultz dumped him on Tad, his grandson, and basically Tad dumped him on me, but stayed his adviser of record because Banks figured females were for screwing or looking pretty.'

'Banks wasn't aware you handled his day-to-day.'

'Anything I dealt with for him I dealt with as Tad Schultz. I met with him a few times, but primarily stayed in the background.'

'Did you have a personal relationship with him?'

'Oh hell no.' At Eve's arched brows she sighed again, looked longingly at her 'link. 'He gave me the rush the first time we met, and I blocked it the way I've found is most effective. I told him I was gay even though when I actually have time for sex, I prefer men. It's just easier to block a client or an exec by claiming to play for the other team. Nobody gets insulted.'

'When's the last time you had contact?'

'Well, yesterday. He tried to get to Senior Mr Schultz or Tad, but he gets forwarded to me. He thinks – thought – I worked as a kind of admin, or messenger service. Whatever. I dealt with it – via text and email. He wanted to sell his recently acquired Quantum stock after the bombing, which was a stupid move. Emotional. Quantum is solid, and that stock was coming back up – which it did, and which I, in a text as Tad, told him. So I saved the client from losing many thousands of dollars, which I guess doesn't really matter to him now.'

'Did you have many who wanted to sell?'

'Some, and a few of the some refused to listen to me. They lost money. The ones who listened when I said buy now made money.'

'When did you last see Banks?'

'It has to be three months ago. Tad wanted to dump him on me, so he took me to one of the monthly lunches – which he still does to keep Banks mollified. He told Banks I was an up-and-comer and smart as they came – which is true, but he pushed it because he wanted to pass Banks to me. It was pretty clear Banks considered me just the cutest little thing, and that was enough for both Tad and me to decide the shift wouldn't work, at least not overtly. I agreed to the covert angle.'

'Why?'

'Because I'm an up-and-comer and smart as they come. I'm working my way up, and handling this account, doing Senior Mr Schultz and Tad a solid? It's a step on the ladder. Does that cover it?'

'Almost. Where were you this morning between one and three?'

'In bed – alone – sleeping.'

'Before that?'

'I was here until about seven-thirty. I met a client at eight for a dinner meeting that ran until after ten. I went home, where my roommate and I – platonic – bitched to each other about our day, then I went to bed.'

'Okay, thanks.'

Before Eve reached the door, Agatha was on her 'link. 'Cheryl, I'm back.'

'Redhead,' Peabody said as they walked out, 'but not that redhead.'

'Unlikely. We'll run her anyway, just cover that angle. Say she did bump uglies with Banks. He feeds her inside information, she uses it to advise clients and work her way up that ladder.'

As Eve drove uptown again through the drip, drip, drip, Peabody did the run.

'Jeez! She's seriously smart as they come. Yale grad, top of her class. I do mean top as in number one. She speaks four languages including Mandarin. Only child, no marriages or cohabs. Dallas, she's only twenty-five, and she speaks four languages. No criminal.'

Peabody looked wistfully into the rain. 'I wish I spoke four languages.'

'You speak two. Civilian and cop. That's enough for anybody. She half fits. She's focused, detail and goal oriented, and being in finance, a gambler. Not strong or tall enough to break Banks's neck. No military in the family?'

'No. Her mother was ambassador to Italy when she was a kid, so they lived there for three years – Italian's one of her languages. Father's a political consultant. They're based in East Washington, but have a place in New York. No military service there. Grandparents still living, both sides, but none there, either. Wait, wait, she has a cousin who served four years in the army – but he was a corpsman. And now he's a doctor – based in Atlanta.'

Eve let the angle go for now, and pulled up in front of Banks's building. A different doorman strolled over, but with the same deference as the night before.

'Can I help you, Lieutenant? Detective?'

'Access to Jordan Banks's apartment.'

'Of course. I heard the bulletin. It's shocking.'

'Has anyone inquired about Mr Banks this morning?'

'Not to me.'

He let them inside. A different security clerk – a black-suited, sharp-eyed woman – manned the desk.

'Rhoda, Lieutenant Dallas and Detective Peabody need access to the Banks unit.'

'I'll clear that immediately. We're all stunned by what happened.'

'Have you cleared anyone else into that unit?'

'No. I did check the log and I see that the night security recorded Mr Banks requesting a cab at eight fifty-three. One was ordered, and he departed the building at nine. He wasn't logged back in. I can contact the cab company and ask for his destination, if it's helpful.'

'I've got it.'

She moved to the elevator, got in with Peabody.

'Roarke's building?'

Eve scowled, just a little. 'Yeah.'

'It's nice.'

Eve only shrugged, shoved her hands in her pockets.

They got out, walked the same fragrant hallway to Banks's main door. Eve mastered in.

One glance had her weapon in her hand as she did a low sweep and Peabody did the same high.

'Shit,' she muttered. 'Shit, shit.' Knowing the weapons wouldn't be necessary.

Whoever had searched and trashed the luxury apartment was already long gone.

11

'Let's clear it,' Eve said, 'then go down, get copies of the security discs from nineteen hundred to oh-nine hundred. And I want to talk to whoever was on duty — door and desk — during that time frame.'

In a hurry, Eve thought as they cleared the two levels, a room at a time. Rushed work, sloppy work with drawers upended, art pulled from walls on the main level.

'Sloppy,' she said aloud as she holstered her weapon, 'but probably thorough. Get the discs. I'll contact the sweepers.'

'The security on the building's got to be the ult,' Peabody commented. 'It's Roarke's.'

'Yeah, but here we are. Grab the field kits while you're down there.'

Alone, Eve called in the sweepers, then backtracked to the kitchen and the security base directly off it. Banks had two domestic droids – both female. And the drives in both had been removed. So had the drives from the security base.

And she hadn't seen a single comp or electronic device on her sweep to clear.

She walked back out, studied the locks on the main-level door. Pulled out her 'link.

'Lieutenant.' Roarke's face filled her screen. 'Good timing. I'm just between meetings.'

'Yeah, well, I'm at Banks's place. Somebody beat me here. Down-and-dirty job's how it looks, but on a quick pass they scooped up his electronics and security logs.'

Those blue eyes went hard. 'Someone compromised the security?'

Eve glanced around the sleek, silvery kitchen where every drawer and cabinet door stood open, and two droids stood blank-eyed.

'Yeah, *compromised* is one word for it.'

'I'm on my way.'

'Figured,' she stated as he cut her off.

She left the kitchen, decided to start on the second level. Master, guest room, home office, linen storage. Frowning at the jumbled sheets and towels, Eve tagged Peabody on her comm.

'Find out if Banks used any outside cleaning service.'

She moved to the master. People, in her experience, often thought of their bedroom as a sanctuary, a kind of safe room. And often tucked things away in odd places.

In the master, Banks had gone for the gold. Gold posts speared up from the four corners of the bed, gold chairs stood in the sitting area, paintings framed in gold crowded the walls, gold drapes flowed at the windows.

The bedding – gold – lay in a heap on the floor while the

thick gel mattress sat crookedly in the bed frame. Sculptures and busts stood on tables or pedestals. If a table had a drawer, that drawer hung open.

She found an impressive collection of sex aids and toys still in a nightstand drawer. But no electronics. The master boasted two dressing rooms. One held Banks's equally impressive collection of clothing – suits with the pockets turned out, shoes jumbled. He'd used the second to store sports equipment. Golf clubs, skis – water and snow – tennis rackets, climbing gear, scuba gear. A shotgun, she noticed, and wondered if he'd had a collector's license for it.

Too late to fine him now anyway.

She heard the downstairs door, walked out, looked down at Peabody and the woman from the desk. The woman – Rhoda, Eve remembered – looked around the room with wide, distressed eyes.

'Up here,' Eve said, then went back to the master to start in the primary dressing room.

'This is just awful,' Eve heard Rhoda say. 'Just shocking and awful. I've worked here four years, and we've never had a break-in. Not a single break-in.'

Eve took a can of Seal-It from the field kit, sealed up, began to search, one article of clothing at a time. 'I need copies of your security feed.'

'I'm having it done right now. Lieutenant, I need to contact Roarke. It's imperative he—'

'He's on his way. Cleaning crew?'

'He uses our in-house service, twice weekly. Wednesdays and Saturdays.'

'How do they access?'

'I clear them. They don't have the codes, and have to be cleared by the desk and/or the resident.'

'Did anyone inquire about Mr Banks, were there any deliveries made or attempted to this apartment in the last twenty-four hours?'

'Not on my shift, and there aren't any notes in the log on that.'

'But other deliveries, to other units?'

'Certainly, several. Each would be cleared individually. No one's sent into the residences without clearance. If a resident isn't at home for a delivery, we hold the package at the desk. Visitors are also cleared. No one can access the elevators or stairs without their key card or clearance.'

'A lot of visitors in a building this size.'

'Yes. But the safety, security, privacy, and comfort of our residents are our priorities.'

'Once they're cleared, anything to stop them from accessing another floor?'

'They'd need a key card. If I clear someone for level twenty, they're restricted to that level.'

'But the residents aren't restricted.'

'No.'

'In the event of fire or another emergency?'

'All elevators and exits are automatically opened. That didn't happen. It would have been logged. So would any anomaly lasting five seconds. If the feed had a glitch, the glitch – type, time, duration – would be recorded. We're a Five Lock building, Lieutenant, the highest security rating given.'

She linked her hands together as she looked around the bedroom. 'I'm at a loss.'

'No building's a hundred percent secure,' Eve commented. 'Somebody gets their pocket picked, somebody makes a copy of their key card for their newest lover, whatever. Do you know every person who lives here, by sight and name?'

'Yes. Yes, I do.'

Eve stopped, turned, interested. 'Seriously?'

'It's my job. We're currently at ninety-three percent occupancy with six hundred and thirty-four units occupied, eighteen hundred and sixteen residents – including live-in staff. We employ more than three hundred full- and part-time staff to serve and service the building. Not including outside marketing and seasonal workers and subcontractors on our call list.'

'Huh. Who lives in the unit across the hall from this one?'

'Ms Yuri and Mr Simston, and Ms Yuri's mother, Mrs Yuri – a widow – and Georgie, their Yorkie. They're currently in Aruba, but are expected back by late afternoon tomorrow.'

'Unit 3100.'

The first glimmer of a smile dawned in Rhoda's eyes. 'Ms Karlin, Mr Howard. Newlyweds. They were married last fall. Ms Karlin divorced Mr Olsen shortly after I began work here four years ago. He was granted custody of their Persian cat, Yasmine. Unit 3100 hosted a dinner party last night. Catered.'

'How many guests?'

Rhoda closed her eyes a moment, nodded to herself. 'Dinner for twenty. Cocktails at seven-thirty. Catered by Jacko's, arrival at six. Florist delivery, that's Urban Gardens . . . four-thirty. That's approximate.'

'Roarke knows how to pick them.'

'I do,' he said from the doorway.

'Sir.' Rhoda turned to him. 'I'm so sorry.'

'There's nothing to apologize for. I'd like you to review the overnight feed, mark anyone you don't know. The lieutenant will need a list of residents, staff, logged guests, delivery companies, and so on. You know what to do.'

'Yes, sir. I'll have a copy of the feed ready for you and the police.'

'I have it. Do you need more from Rhoda at the moment?' he asked Eve.

'Just one more thing. Other than the newlyweds, any other parties here last night?'

'Six catered, and three others. And a number of drop-bys. I can have all of that for you.'

'Okay. I'll let you get to it.'

'Sir. We could lose a lock on our rating.'

'One thing at a time,' Roarke told Rhoda, giving her shoulder a pat to move her along.

When she left, Roarke watched Eve continue to search.

'I think he had almost as many clothes as you do,' she commented. 'Just the one safe, in here, I came across on my sweep. It's open. I can't tell if they had the code or broke in.'

Roarke slipped inside, crouched down to examine the safe. He took out one of his toys, ran some sort of scan.

'Scan,' he told her. 'Eight-digit code, and it was opened with a reader. It's a simple lock. I expect someone like Banks would have had the code tucked somewhere so he wouldn't have to remember it, but this was scanned. The bulletins haven't disclosed cause of death.'

'Broken neck – manually. Dumped in the water. Made to look like a mugging – took his coat, shoes, valuables. No 'link on the body.'

'They didn't bother to make this look like a burglary,' Roarke said. 'He has jewelry in here, his passport, which is always worth a bit of something on the black market. And there's art and other easily liquidated things throughout the place. Likely he had some cash in here, and that's gone. But cash can't be traced, so why not?'

'You're pissed. Me, too. But it's not that challenging to get into an apartment, even in a secure building, when you know the occupant's dead or going to be. Can you take that toy, see if the locks were compromised, or if that's a straight entry, too?'

'I can.'

He left her. By the time he came back, she'd moved on to the sports closet.

'Jammed and scanned – bedroom level.'

She stopped, eyes narrowed. 'So they didn't wait to do it the easy way, with his key card and codes off the body. Broke in before they killed him. Why is that? Because it's easier to cross a lobby to an elevator before, say midnight, than it is at after three in the morning. A lot of people still coming and going at, like, ten, eleven at night. Parties, heading out for a drink, coming in from dinner and all that. Several parties happening in the building, and that's going to be fairly routine. Caterers, deliveries, guests.'

'Dallas – Hey, Roarke.' Peabody stepped in. 'Nothing in the guest room or home office. Not even a used memo cube.'

'Fast, sloppy, and so far thorough. Take the master bath.'

She dug into a ski jacket. 'He left the building about nine, had them order a cab. From the contents of his stomach, he went to a high-end cocktail-type party. Had sex with a redhead.'

'That's specific.'

'Stray pubic hair. We have him picked up by another cab – we've got the address and time – and dropped off near the JKO. TOD just after three, so he met his killer or, more likely, killers there. One of them has the skill to snap his neck, they team up, haul him over the fence into the reservoir, where he's spotted about two hours later by a couple of underage drinking buddies who jump in to pull him out.'

She moved on to a wet suit.

'Meanwhile, they stripped anything valuable from the

body, including his pocket e's, so we have no way to trace who he talked with or when. They're not stupid.'

'Got something!' Peabody walked back in with a memo book in a waterproof bag. 'Inside the toilet tank – classic.'

'And for a reason,' Roarke agreed when Eve took it, opened the bag.

'Passcoded.'

Roarke held out a hand.

'Seal up first.'

He sighed, but obeyed. Then fiddled with the book for about twenty seconds. 'Rudimentary block. Open now, and ... ah. What you have here is an on-the-go sort of bookkeeping. The books for the laundering service is how it looks.'

'Any names?' Eve demanded.

'It doesn't look like it. Numbers. What went in, and when, what came out and when. His fee, profit. It's more a little pocket guide than actual accounting.'

'If he kept those books here, they're gone now,' Eve con-cluded. 'Maybe the art gallery has records. And names.' She took the device back, resealed it, dropped it in an evidence bag, sealed and labeled.

'If they missed this, maybe they missed something else. Peabody, while we finish here, have Baxter and Trueheart hit the art gallery. Get the warrant, have them transfer the electronics to Central, and take a good look around the gallery. Interview any staff, and get the names and contact info for other employees.'

'I'll be down with Rhoda and our security,' Roarke told her.

On their arrival, Eve sent the sweepers to the second level while she and Peabody went through the main.

She yanked out her comm when it signaled. 'Dallas.'

'Baxter. Here at the Banks Gallery now. Banks had a run of bad luck, Loo. He got himself dead, had his apartment broken into. And it turns out, his art gallery, too.'

'Ah, fuck!'

'Yeah, I hear you. Cleared the d and c unit out of the office here, and all the other electronics. The hot artist chick in charge today says they don't open until one on Tuesday, but when she heard about Banks being dead, she thought she should come in, check on things, maybe notify the other artists and all that. She'd just called in the break-in when we got here.'

'And the art?'

'She doesn't think anything's missing, but she's doing an inventory. They've got stuff in what she calls a holding room. She says she has to go by memory mostly, as the records were on the comp that's gone. And that's a little problem, as Banks had a habit of rotating.'

'The art?'

'He'd see something he liked, take it for his place, keep it awhile, rotate it back. He'd get bored, is what she told us. Have a couple of the artists hang stuff in his place, bring stuff he had in here, hang it, like that. He never bought any-thing – she tells us – for his personal collection. He called

206

it marketing. How he'd hang it in his home for friends to admire. Still, she says, not everything came back, and as she's done some of the hanging over there, not everything stayed in his place, either.

'She tried to keep her own list on her PPC, but she says it was hard to keep up.'

'Okay, get what you can, have the sweepers send in a team. Get contacts for the artists and anybody else who worked there. I want EDD checking the security.'

'Feed's gone.'

'I figured. Have them nail down what time the security was compromised. And . . . when you're done, bring her over here, to his apartment. I want her to look at the art, see if she can pin down anything that she thinks should be here and isn't.'

When she clicked off, she circled the living area, studied the walls. The empty walls.

'Peabody!'

With rapid clumps, Peabody hurried in.

'What did they do in the turnover here that they didn't do on the bedroom level?'

'Ah . . .'

'They didn't pull the art off the walls upstairs like they did down here. You look down here, you might think they were looking for a safe or hidey-hole behind a painting. But if they did the same upstairs, they didn't take the paintings down. Why is that?'

She wandered. 'Why is that?' she repeated. 'No holes or hooks in the walls, but lots of paintings.'

'You hang them from that fancy trim. It's called a picture rail so you can hang art – either with invisible wire or decorative chains. Change it out when you want, shift it around without damaging the walls.'

'Right. So there's no way for us to tell where this stuff was hung, if it's all still here.'

'His insurance would have records.'

'Not the way he worked it. He'd take stuff from the gallery, use it until he got tired of looking at it, switch it out. And sold some of it under the table. Straight profit in his pocket.'

She crouched down for a better look at the figure studies dumped on the floor. 'Did they take a painting or two? Why? He's got expensive wrist units and cuff links in the safe they opened, but they left them. Did they take any paintings? Did they take one because they thought: Hey, that would look frosty over my mantel? Maybe. It's worth finding out.'

Eve took one last look around. 'Greed,' she said. 'It's all about greed. Let's go see what Roarke and Ms Memory Bank have for us.'

She found Roarke and Rhoda in the security hub. It was – no surprise – not just state of the art, but likely the state the art aspired to. A little mouse-faced man worked with them. Though he was dressed all in gray, she recognized the jiggle-bop of an e-geek.

'Rhoda has your copy,' Roarke said. 'We're going through the feed of your time frame, with Rhoda noting down residents, guests, staff, and so on for you.'

'That's helpful.'

'Our man Bingley here is combing through for abnormalities in the system that might have gone undetected.'

'Elevators and stairwells are priority.'

'I got that. I got that. Got that.' Bingley murmured it like a chant as he jiggled in his chair.

Eve judged he topped out at about five-five, maybe a buck and a quarter. His straggly hair and wispy beard were as gray as his clothes. His knobby-knuckled fingers worked keyboard and swipe screens with an agility that would have made Feeney beam.

She shifted her attention to the monitors, noted the time stamp. Twenty-two-forty. Scanned the people coming, going. Spotted some of Jacko's crew leaving. She'd met the caterer and his team on another investigation. Those she could eliminate. Also low on the list, the couple coming in – both wrapped in furs with twin looks in their eyes that said: Next stop, sex.

Then the teenager, boots, trendy flak jacket, earflap hat, with a mop-haired dog on a leash.

She studied the solo male – late thirties, grim-faced, flapping top coat, rolling overnighter. Maybe.

'Who—'

'Look here, look here, pally!'

Roarke leaned over Bingley's sloped shoulder at the man's exclamation. And said: 'Ah.'

'Ah what?' Eve demanded.

'Blip, blip, lights out, smooth ride.'

'What does that mean?'

'Reset,' Roarke ordered. 'Roll. Pause. And yes, very bloody clever.'

'Got juice,' Bingley said. 'No dope.'

'Yes, indeed. It wouldn't register as a glitch or disruption.'

Eve resisted, barely, tearing at her hair or punching something. Maybe someone. 'What wouldn't, for fuck's sake?'

'The blip. Just under three seconds.'

'Two-point-six,' Bingley said.

'Exactly. A shutdown of the elevator cam – elevator four. Then he shut the lights off in the car, unjammed the cam. Under three seconds isn't long enough to register. The light? What have we there, Bingley?'

'Goes dark for nine-point-eight seconds.'

Roarke turned, worked another comp. 'Short, singular event, logged twenty-two-nineteen. The system flagged it, but as it was of short duration, cited as on watch.'

'What floor? What floor did he get on?'

'Fifty, rode two floors up to Banks's bedroom level. He had to turn the cams back, you see, or the system would alert. But the lights? That's building maintenance, and as they resolved so quickly, it's simply on watch.'

'What about getting back down? What time, what floor? He could have exited from the main level. Watch for both levels.'

'No blip. See, pally?' Bingley said to Roarke. 'No blip, lights on.'

'I see, yes. We don't have the same routine for an exit. In

210

fact, what I'm seeing is no one accessed an elevator on that floor until eight sharp this morning.'

'Who? Where's the feed?'

'She's got the cranks,' Bingley commented to Roarke. 'Often.'

'Your deal, pally.' He cackled softly, brought up the feed. 'Rhoda?'

She swiveled over. 'That's Mr Clarke, 5203 – two-level unit – and his two children, their nanny. He'd be leaving for work, the nanny would be walking the children to school.'

At Eve's insistence, they checked the feed, both levels, elevators and stairways, until noon, with Rhoda providing names and apartment numbers.

'Everyone,' Rhoda concluded. 'Everyone who exited belonged on their level. There's no one out of place. I'm sorry.'

'We'll run them all,' Eve said. But it didn't fit, just didn't fit. 'Because how the hell did he get out and down?'

'Coulda flown,' Bingley said with a grin. 'Flap, flap. Hey, pally?'

Rather than respond, Eve just narrowed her eyes. Then she turned on her heel. 'Peabody!'

As she strode out, Bingley's grin widened. 'Plenty cranks, pally.'

'Not this time.'

Roarke caught up with her at the elevator. 'Obviously he didn't flap his way out, but.'

'But. We're going to check the terraces, both levels. He

could've been an ice-for-veins son of a bitch and rappelled down, at least a few floors.'

They got on the elevator. 'What's with the "pally"?'

'Bingley considers me bright enough, but young and with much left to learn. He's a bit odd, but knows what he's about.'

She thought it through on the ride up. 'He doesn't have to live on fifty or fifty-two, or live here period – though that would be handy. He could have blended in with guests or caterers, even faked a delivery. Get to the unit, resident says this isn't my package. Sorry, will check with my dispatch, and you're in. Slide out anywhere. We'll go over the feed, and we'll find him, but it won't be quick.'

They got off, walked back to Banks's apartment, straight out to the main floor terrace.

'This level makes more sense. Why add another floor?'

Though it made her stomach pitch to look down, she gritted through it, examined every inch of the terrace wall before calling out a sweeper.

'I'm looking for any sign some asshole rappelled down from here.'

She went to the second level, repeated the process.

In the end, with negative results on both, she circled the bedroom. 'If he didn't go over, he went through, and if he went through, he'd show on the elevator or stairwell feed. He doesn't. Maybe . . . Could he get down to another level through the guts of the building?'

'If anyone other than maintenance attempted to access

the guts, as you say, it would generate an alarm. If anyone attempted to circumvent the alarm, it would have to be done from another area, and would require more skill than I suspect these people have, and a great deal of time and very good tools.'

'Well, he fucking didn't go flap, flap.'

'A parachute?' Peabody suggested. 'It's crazy, but maybe he jumped, floated down.'

'It's New York, but even so if some dude drops down out of the sky with a chute, somebody's going to report it. He had to ... Wait. Wait. The apartment directly across. The people there aren't back until tomorrow. Check the locks,' she told Roarke. 'Check to see if the locks have been compromised or opened in the last eighteen hours.'

Roarke checked the bedroom level, went down, checked the main. Looked back at Eve.

'You may often have the cranks, but you are my clever girl. Jammed and scanned and opened.'

'Which constitutes a crime. Gives me probable cause to enter. Open it up, pally.'

On a half laugh, he bypassed the alarm, the locks, nudged the door open for her.

The wall of glass stood unframed, letting in the gloomy March light.

'That's an odd place for an empty frame.' Eve gestured to the frame – like the others in Banks's main level – lying on a multicolored rug. 'Terrace doors are open just a crack.'

She stepped to them, eased them open, stepped out into the incessant drip of rain.

'He has to know the apartment's empty. He knows the building. Lives or works here, or he knows Banks well enough to have spent time in his place, spent time here. He does what he needs to do across the hall, brings the painting over here, takes it out of the frame, rolls it up. Easier to carry that way.'

She crouched down by the wall. She didn't need the sweepers, not when she could clearly see the digs and scrapes on the decorative stone.

'Got balls,' she stated. 'Fifty-one floors up, but over he goes.' Gearing herself up for it, she stood, leaned out and over.

'He goes off near the end of the wall. Maybe straight down, or if he's done climbing, has good equipment – and I'm betting – he can swing over. To his apartment, an accomplice's, another empty one.'

'He retracted the hook, so yes, good equipment,' Roarke put in. 'You'd go down between terraces, you see. Wouldn't do to have someone spot you, would it? With the right equipment, you could retract, move horizontally or down as your needs demanded. You might slip into another unit, one unoccupied, and walk straight out that way.'

Eve glanced back. 'Sounds like the voice of experience.'

He only smiled. 'Does it?'

'I need to get back to Central, check in with my team, brief Baxter and Trueheart. I need everything Rhoda can give me.'

'You'll have that.'

'Appreciate the assist. Peabody, get the sweepers out here while I get what we need. I'm going to take it all home as soon as I clear the decks at the cop shop. You're going to start running guests, visitors, outside vendors from last night. I'll take the residents.'

Eve blew out a breath. 'Let's get to work.'

12

Baxter gave Eve a list of artwork the hot artist chick knew Banks had taken from the gallery. Though incomplete, it gave Eve a start.

She updated her board and book, wrote her report, and sent copies to Whitney and Mira. And glanced over when she heard the dancing clicks coming toward her office.

Mavis Freestone swirled in. A long, shiny coat of popping pink covered with electric-blue lightning bolts lay open to a crotch-skimming skirt that fluttered more pink over striped tights and thigh-high shiny blue boots. Her hair twirled up, gold streaked with both colors, then poufed back into a pink ponytail.

She bounced right over to Eve and wrapped her in a fierce hug that smelled of cherry lollipops.

'Hi,' Eve managed.

'Hi to you. And that's for the top secret Peabody and McNab project. You're the ultra maggiest of mags, Dallas.'

'It's not that big a deal.'

Mavis drew back, eyes – purple as plums today – shining.

'It's the mega deal of deals. Wait till you see the gown Leonardo's altering and customizing for her. He's doing it himself because that's my moonpie. Got minutes?'

'Sure, a few.'

'Bella's out entertaining your troops, but she's got something for you.'

'Okay.'

'Maybe you could ...' Mavis gestured toward the murder board.

'Oh, right.' She covered it.

'Ice. Second.'

Mavis dashed out, and as she dashed back, Eve heard Bella's cheerful jabbering.

The kid wore what Eve decided was a Mavis and Leonardo-style slicker. More pink, lots of shiny, and decorated with rainbows. She, too, wore boots, with multi-colored bows in lieu of laces, along with a frilly skirt and a dazzling smile.

She wiggled out of Mavis's arms, chanting: 'Das, Das, Das!'

Then launched herself at Eve with a height and velocity that made Eve think the kid might develop one hell of a standing jump shot.

She hauled Bella up because what choice did she have? Said, 'Hey.'

'Das!' Bella threw back her head, laughed like a lunatic so her blond curls shook against the pink unicorn clips tucking it back from her ridiculously pretty face.

Bella caught Eve's face in her hands, shook her head, then linked arms tight around Eve's neck. Sighed. 'Das, Das, Das.'

'We haven't said anything – unless in sort of code – about top secret because somebody could blab,' Mavis explained. 'But I'm pretty sure she knows something happy's coming, and you're the reason.'

'I'm not. I just—'

Bella leaned back, kissed Eve's cheek. Earnestly she babbled, patting her hands on Eve's face, then brushing them into Eve's hair. She pulled one of the unicorns out of her curly mop, and with a kind of ferocious concentration, shoved it into Eve's choppy hair.

'Oh hey, I don't—'

'Pretty!' Bella beamed sunshine smiles. 'Das pretty.' And kissed Eve again.

'My Bellamina, that's so sweet, and generous. She's learning to share. It's important to share.' Mavis spoke directly and very deliberately to Eve – with the pretty scary addition of a steely mom stare.

'Right.' And now, Eve thought, she had a freaking pink unicorn in her hair.

'And that's not even the present. I guess that's an extra. Bellissima? Do you want to give Dallas her present?'

'Das!' She wiggled down. ''Res'nt, Das. Bella do. Pretty!'

Mavis took a roll of thick paper tied with a ribbon out of her enormous bag, handed it to Bella.

Smiling, lashes fluttering, Bella held it up to Eve. 'Bella do. Das.'

Eve sat, untied the ribbon, unrolled the paper.

Blobs of color, splotches of more, covered it along with finger swirls and prints, dots, and shaky lines.

She said, 'Wow.'

'Bella loves to paint. Finger painting's her specialty. When I told her we were coming to see you today, she wanted to make you a painting.'

'It's great.' And rivaled, she thought, one of Jenkinson's most eye-burning ties for impact.

Bella crawled up into Eve's lap, wiggled her butt down. She took Eve's hand so they pointed together.

'Das,' she said. 'Ork. Somshit. Gah-ad.' She tapped, then moved up. 'Das Ork how.'

'Sss,' Mavis prompted.

'How-sss. Like cas . . .' She looked at Mavis.

'Sil.'

'Cas-sil.'

'It kinda is,' Eve agreed, a little surprised she could interpret the words, even if she still saw only blobs and splotches. 'It's really great, kid.'

More babbling, along with hopeful blue eyes. This time Eve had to look to Mavis.

'She's hoping you'll put it up.'

'Oh. Ah, yeah, sure. I . . . I'm going to take it home. I have to show it to Roarke, and we'll put it up.' Somewhere.

'And Somshit?'

'Yeah. Him, too.'

'Gah-ad?'

'The whole deal. It's great,' she said again because, strangely, it sort of was. 'Thanks.'

On a happy sigh, Bella laid her head against Eve's shoulder.

'We have to go, my Belle, and Dallas has to work.'

'Want Das.'

'We'll see Dallas soon, but we have to go home, finish packing for our trip.'

'Go whoosh!' Bella scrambled around to face Eve, jabbering and howling with laughter.

'She loves to fly and go on trips.'

'Where are you going?'

Mavis hauled Bella up. 'To New LA. The Oscars, remember?'

Stupid, stupid Oscars. 'I didn't know you were going.'

'Not just going. I'm performing.' In a rare show of nerves, Mavis pressed a hand to her belly. '"Hold on Tight" is up for Best Song, and they asked me to perform. It's not going to take it – I think "Take Your Rest" has it locked – but . . . Jeez, Dallas, I'm performing at the freaking Oscars. I'm a little terrified.'

'You'll kick ass.'

'Ass,' Bella echoed.

'Sorry.'

Mavis shook her head. 'I can use the kick ass. And I'm going to try to do that.' She tipped her head to Bella's. 'Who'd've thought? Who'd've thought I'd ever have the chance to kick it at the Oscars? And I wouldn't if it wasn't for you.'

'Oh, bull ... ony.'

'Primo save. It's true. You and Roarke opened the door, and here I am. I'm never going to forget it. So, you better watch.'

'Wouldn't miss.'

'You watch,' Mavis repeated. 'Because I'm going to kick it. For my Bellamina, for my honey bear. But this time? This time most of all for you and Roarke. Gotta jump, we're leaving tonight. Tell Dallas bye, baby.'

'Bye, Das!'

'Flip side,' Mavis said. 'Cha.'

Bella blew kisses over Mavis's shoulder as they clipped out.

Eve looked down at the finger painting. A castle-house, Roarke, a fat cat, and, okay, Somshit.

You just never knew where life would take you.

Or death, either, she thought.

She gathered her things, headed out. Despite the tie – yellow flowers over a sea of green that made her eyes want to bleed – she walked to Jenkinson's desk.

'Anything hits I need to know, tag me. Otherwise, handle it. I'm working from home.'

'Sure thing, boss.' His gaze drifted up; his lips twisted into a smug smirk.

'What?'

'Just thinking how you rag on my ties, but you got a pink unicorn in your hair.'

'I – crap!' She reached up, dragged it out. 'Not on purpose. Yours is deliberate.'

Because she couldn't just ditch it, she stuffed the clip in her pocket and tried to stride out with dignity.

By the time she got home, Eve had a reasonable plan of attack for the work. She walked in just as Summerset walked down the stairs.

His eyebrows arched up. 'Has there been an alien invasion? Perhaps a zombie apocalypse?'

'We've got the zombie right here.' She stripped off her coat, tossed it over the newel post as he continued down. Then she dug into her file bag. 'I'm supposed to show this to you.'

She unrolled the painting, held it up. 'Mavis brought the kid by. It's her work – the kid's, not Mavis's.'

He smiled – and that was creepy. 'Yes, I see. Very colorful.'

'It's the house, and ... the rest of us.' Eve tapped a blob. 'She says this is you.' And waited a beat. 'Somshit.'

He laughed – and that was way creepy. 'I'm flattered.'

'Well, anyway.' Eve rolled it up again. 'She wants me to put it up somewhere.' This time she waited longer than a beat.

'Naturally. It's a long tradition in many families to display a child's artwork on the friggie.'

'Why?'

'The kitchen's often considered the hub or heart of the house. Though that might not be the case for you, I would think your office kitchen would serve.'

'Right.' She started up the stairs, stopped when he spoke again.

'The unrestricted love of a child is a precious gift.'

'I get that.'

'I thought you would tell him, was sure of it. I was wrong.'

She didn't have to ask what he meant. 'I didn't have proof,' she began, and he said nothing. 'And what good would it have done, for him, if I'd told Roarke I suspected the man he thinks of as his father killed Patrick Roarke?'

'I thought you would tell him,' Summerset said again, simply. 'Due to – beyond our personal ... friction – your duty to the law, and your loyalty to Roarke.'

'Those are exactly the reasons I didn't tell him.'

'I don't understand you.'

'Guess not.' She started to continue up, stopped. 'Okay, here it is, then it's done. I believe absolutely in the law, the need for it, the rules of it, the need and rules of it that lead to justice. I'd be nothing without believing that. But that was a different time and place, and circumstances. You had no one in authority you could trust to serve and protect, to stand for you when a fucking monster threatened to rape, torture, and kill two children. He'd have followed through on that threat because there was no one to stop him. You did. Roarke's here because you stopped Patrick Roarke, because you protected the child he was at that time, in that place, in those circumstances. That's enough for me.'

'There were no cops such as you in that time and place.'

'Times change.' She continued up. 'Put it away.'

'Perhaps I can,' Summerset agreed.

She stopped one more time. 'You don't get points for teaching him to be a better thief.'

That creepy smile snuck back. 'His talent there was innate.'

She shrugged. 'Hard to argue.' And walked up to her office.

When Roarke came in two hours later, she'd gone through a pot of coffee and set up a trio of auxiliary boards. She sat at her desk, boots up, eyes closed.

'I'm not asleep.'

'All right then. You've been busy.'

She opened her eyes, studied the new boards as he did. 'One for residents – including day staff – one for hotel employees – including subcontractors. One for visitors and outside vendors, delivery people who came in during the relevant time frame.'

'That would be near to three thousand people, I expect. You're handling all this?'

'Peabody's got the hotel staff, and since Baxter and Trueheart are finished with the art gallery, they're taking the vendors and deliveries, the visitors. I want the visual, and I'll eliminate as they do.

'Screwed up your schedule today,' she said.

'A breach in my security screwed up my schedule, and now that it's nearly on track again, I want a glass of wine and some food.'

'Gotta feed the cat,' Eve said absently. 'He came in a little bit after I did, settled down for one of his marathon naps, so Summerset wouldn't have dealt with it.'

She rose, wandered to the boards. 'I've eliminated a good chunk of residents. Kids, elderly, women. Both wits were absolute on the male. And there are more than a few whose out-of-town status checks out. I've crossed off a couple more with solid alibis. Still working on that.'

'Here. Diffuse the coffee you've been pounding.' He handed her the glass, kissed the top of her head. 'I'll take half after we've had some dinner.'

'It wasn't really a breach in your security.'

'Close enough.'

She followed him into the kitchen, and the cat – sensing the dinner bell – came with her. 'You can't have alarms going off every time a light flickers,' she pointed out.

'True enough.' He stopped to study the finger painting she'd stuck on the friggie. 'This is . . . interesting.'

'Mavis brought Bella by my office and the kid gave me this, wanted me to put it up. Summerset said this is how it's done.'

'Ah. A bold use of color and texture. Perhaps she's a budding student of the Pollock school.'

'It's the house.' Eve stepped up, tapped the painting. 'And this is me, you, the cat, Summerset.'

Roarke looked closer, then stepped back, trying distance. 'You see that?'

'You don't?' Then with a laugh, she got the kibble. 'The kid explained. Did you know Mavis is performing at the Oscar deal?'

Roarke angled his head, still studying the finger painting. 'I did, yes.'

225

'I should've known. It's a big deal for her, so I should've known.'

'You don't pay attention to such things, and Mavis wouldn't expect you to. You pay attention enough to hang this artwork, and that's considerably more important, I'd think.'

'It's not exactly the heart of the house though, is it?'

He turned to her, slid a finger down the dent in her chin. 'This house has many hearts.'

Her face cleared. 'It does, doesn't it?'

While the cat attacked the kibble – with a chaser of salmon – they had stew, a comfort at the end of a dreary day.

'How would you have gotten in there?' she asked him. 'Into Banks's place, if you didn't live in the building?'

'Likely I'd have had time to plan – so there are a number of ways. But in this case, we're talking of the moment.' He considered as he ate a good, chunky chicken stew generous with dumplings.

'I wouldn't have complicated it with elevator security and jammers. How long, after all, did it take you to track his coming and going?'

'I still don't know who he is.'

'But you already know his methods, his skills, and you know he entered the building by normal means.' He gestured to her board. 'He's on one of them.'

'Okay, so what's the alternate method?'

'Up the outside.'

'Get out! It's over fifty floors,' she pointed out, and got a shrug.

226

'The height's hardly a deterrent with the proper tools. With electronic gloves, booties, it's simply a matter of choosing your time, then moving steadily up. Again, between the glass to avoid being spotted. I'd have done it after midnight, and when I'd reached the terrace, dealing with those locks is, well, cake as we say. Nothing nearly as complex as the main doors.

'Go in,' he added, topping off the wine, 'do my search. Not sloppily. Why alert the cops the moment they step in the door? Be subtle about it – after all, no one's going to disturb me, and I'm not meeting the man I intend to kill for some time yet. Take what I need, as well as any cash I find, as it's not traceable. I don't bother with a painting. Then I take my leave the same way.'

He toasted her with his wine. 'However, if I'd targeted such a place, it would be for the valuables, so I'd take what I came for. The method would be the same.'

'You've actually done that? Climbed up a building?'

'It's exhilarating. The dark, the air, the life going on below, and on the other side of the wall. All unaware of you. And unlike you, I enjoy heights.'

She thought about it as she ate. 'They're not professional thieves. Already knew that, but what you're saying caps it. They worked out what to do on the fly. It worked, but you're right. They're on the board. Along with a couple thousand others, but they're on the board.'

'Before they went into that apartment to remove whatever Banks might have that connects them to him, your suspect range was a great deal wider.'

'That's a point.' She polished off her stew. 'Now I'm going to narrow it.'

With focused work she eliminated more than two hundred on her board. Deleted names from the other boards through reports from the rest of the team.

She started a priority list on anyone who'd had military or paramilitary training or had relatives who did.

Roarke worked along with her, then broke to take a scheduled tag from Hawaii. When he came back, she had her head on the desk.

Out, he thought, and ordered her machine to continue her work on auto.

She stirred and mumbled when he lifted her out of her chair. 'I'm good.'

'Good and tired.'

'I've got eighteen on the priority list. There are going to be more.'

'You'll get back to that after some sleep.' He carried her to the elevator, ordered their bedroom.

'I'm closer than I was.'

'My book says you'll be closer yet tomorrow.'

He sat her on the side of the bed – the cat was already sprawled dead center. Pulled off her boots, ordered the fire on.

'What if a big gust of wind blew you off the side of the building?'

Back to that, are we? he thought. 'I'd have been very annoyed.'

'I mean . . .' She pulled herself up to strip off her weapon harness. 'Did you wear a chute?'

'That would depend on the job.'

Groggy, she undressed, pulled on a sleep shirt. 'Who's the one who . . .' She made a whoosh sound, flipped out her fingers, mimed climbing a wall.

He thought it a wonder he followed her. 'Spider-Man.'

'Yeah, yeah. He's a good one. Smart-ass kid. At least you didn't go swinging around buildings on web ropes.'

Something in his smile had her eyeing him as she crawled into bed. 'You didn't do that. There aren't really web ropes.'

'There are cables, pulley systems – and those are stories for another time.'

He slipped in with her, wrapped an arm around her to tuck her close. 'Go to sleep.'

'You never did that in New York. I'd've heard about it.'

'Not if I did it right.' He kissed the back of her neck as she dropped off. 'And I did.'

When she woke in the morning, he sat drinking coffee, watching the financials with the cat stretched out beside him.

She sat up. 'It wasn't a Spider-Man suit.'

He glanced over. 'Wasn't it?'

'It was black – but he has a black one, too, I guess. It's confusing. But it had an *R* – for Roarke – instead of the spider deal. And you're swinging over the damn city and climbing up buildings, and there *was* a big gust of wind. It scared the shit out of me. Don't do that again.'

'I'll resist. Though you do have the most fascinating dreams.'

She grabbed coffee, gulping it as she headed for the shower.

When she came back, he had breakfast waiting, more coffee, and had banished the cat to the spot in front of the fire.

The oatmeal didn't surprise her – winter couldn't end soon enough – but at least it was just a cup of it and it came with bacon and eggs.

'We're in for a bright, if blustery, day,' he told her.

She thought of the financials on the screen. 'Anything up there these guys would be interested in?'

'There's always something, but there's nothing major coming to boil at the moment.'

'You're always buying stuff – companies.'

'And you're worried they might try for one of mine. We've taken precautions – and all my people are accounted for.'

'You've got a lot of people.'

'And still, they're accounted for. Add to it, I don't have anything brewing in New York right now. A thing or two pending overseas or off-planet, but nothing here.'

'And you're not going anywhere, like to oversee one of those pendings?'

'No travel plans for several days.'

'If that changes—'

'I'll let you know.' He took her hand, kissed it. 'Don't worry. I won't be tempting any wind gusts.'

'Okay.' Satisfied, she finished breakfast, got up to dress.

Since he didn't comment on her choice – brown trousers and jacket, navy sweater – she figured she'd at least scaled the high bar of his fashion sense.

'I'll be at Central through most of the morning. I've got off-case work I let go yesterday, and I want to finish as much of the eliminations and priorities as possible before I start interviews.'

'I'll be at my own HQ. And if you start looking seriously at any of my people, I'd like to know it.'

'It's not going to be one of your people.' She scooped up her pocket debris. 'I have to eliminate, but it won't be. A subcontractor, possibly, but not one of your hotel staff. Your screening's tougher than the NSA's.'

'And still.' He rose, gripped her hips, kissed her. 'Take care of my cop.'

She framed his face, kissed him back. 'Don't climb any buildings.'

'Only by the stairs.'

'Good enough.' She started out, glanced back over her shoulder. 'You looked good in the suit.'

She took the flash of his grin with her out into the bright, blustery day.

Thinking of him as she started the drive to Central, she considered exactly what he'd said.

If he'd targeted a place like Banks's, he'd . . . take what he needed, wouldn't have bothered with a painting.

Yeah, the painting bugged her. Why take it – then try to hide that fact by waiting until you were in the escape location before taking it out of its frame? He/they didn't, as Roarke would have, go the subtle route in the search of the apartment, but took the framed painting across the hall before removing it from the frame, discarding the frame.

Why?

Because it mattered, she decided. *I'd take what I came for*, Roarke had said. The painting was something they'd come for. It mattered.

She tagged Baxter from her wrist unit.

He said, 'Yo.'

'Pick up the iced artist.'

His smile spread. 'I like a sexy start to the day.'

'Keep it in your pants, horndog. I need her to go over her own lists again, incomplete or not. Link it up with the record of the artwork – in the main level of the crime scene. One's missing. What is it? Who painted it? Not painted,' she corrected. 'Drew. Drew what? When and where did Banks acquire it?'

'I've got a list of what he took from the gallery – officially. She added to that, ones she knows he slipped out of there, but she knows she didn't catch them all.'

'I want her to look again anyway. Focus in on the figure-study types. For right now, we don't care about paintings – landscapes, portraits, whatever. It's the black and whites, the nakeds or mostly nakeds.'

'It bugged her,' Baxter commented. 'She figured if she'd had the gallery comps, she'd have been able to pin it down, or get closer to pinning it.'

232

'That's the point of taking them out. We're going to have to rely on her notes, her memory. You and Trueheart work with her to match up what's on the lists, and what's not. Whatever they took mattered.'

'I'll tag the boy, swing by and get him. We'll scoop up the icy one, take a trip back uptown.'

'I need to know as soon as you get anything, even a maybe.'

She ended the transmission and spent the rest of the drive calculating what a drawing of a naked person had to do with murder and money.

13

She went straight to her office, made herself ignore her board. With coffee, she spent the thirty minutes she'd given herself before shift to catch up on her department's caseload – open and closed. She read reports, signed off on requisitions, and dealt with the top skim of the most urgent administrative duties.

The rest could wait.

When Eve walked into the bullpen, Peabody stood at her desk unwinding one of her boa constrictor scarves. A single glance – and the fact that her eyes didn't start to melt – showed her Jenkinson and his tie, Reineke and his socks weren't at their desks.

'They just caught one,' Peabody told her. 'Construction crew on Tenth found a DB in their dumpster. You clocked in early.'

'Paperwork.' She tossed a disc onto Peabody's desk. 'That's your half of currently viable suspects. Start a second run, see if you can eliminate any, or bump any up the list. Baxter and Trueheart are picking up the art gallery woman.'

'Suspect?'

'Not at this time. I want her to look at the artwork again, her records. Why did they take a figure-study deal? Which one did they take? Who drew it?'

'I figured souvenir. Potentially valuable.'

'Then why not take it out of the frame on-site? Why take it across the hall to remove it?'

'Maybe ... once he got it over there, he realized it would be easier and safer to take the rolled canvas than the whole deal.'

'Possible,' Eve conceded. 'It's possible he was that stupid and impulsive.'

'But you think he was buying time.'

'Why not drop your ass down from Banks's apartment? Why break into another and go down from there — after removing the artwork from the frame, ditching it in the other apartment?'

'The empty apartment,' Peabody agreed. 'One where the residents aren't coming back until later today, so it would be a day, potentially, before we realized the artwork was taken.'

'It's what plays. I think he took what he'd come for. The electronics, anything that linked him and his partner to Banks. And the artwork.'

Taking her seat, Peabody spitballed back. 'Banks owned a gallery, worked with artists. Maybe one of the killers is an artist, or connected to one. He could be the artist, and wanted his own work back.'

'Keep that in mind when you work on the list. Detective Carmichael, Santiago, I've got Baxter and Trueheart in the field. Next DB's yours.'

Eve went back into her office, locked the door. The trouble with working in a small space, she thought as she glanced around, was the limited hidey-holes. But for this project, she'd use that to her advantage.

She got out the candy bar she'd brought from home, stood on her desk to attach it to the inside of a ceiling tile. An easy find, oh yeah, but . . .

She fastened a button alarm, carefully, so carefully, to the joint of the tile. Lift that sucker a fraction, and the shrieking whistle should scare the unholy crap out of the thief even as its blue dye exploded all over the fucker's face.

Satisfied, looking forward to retribution, she jumped down, unlocked her door.

Armed with more coffee, she settled down to work on her half of the list.

She got a solid ninety minutes in, shifting several names to what she considered a secondary list: *low probability*. And a third list she termed *possible*.

That left her with more than sixty as *most likely*.

Still too many, but they'd set up interviews and get some face-to-face.

She reread the tox report on Banks, who'd been flying high on wine, Erotica, and Zoner when he'd wandered like an idiot into Central Park at three in the morning.

She'd eliminated the delivery girl who'd brought Paul

Rogan muffins, his driver (though no car service had been utilized on the day of the bombing) as connected.

That left her more than sixty to interview, and a sexy artist chick who might, potentially, identify a missing piece of art.

She grabbed her 'link when it signaled, saw Harvo on the readout.

'Give me a name.'

'Hi back.' Harvo's hair, currently short, spiked into lethal points, and blazing orange, threatened to melt the screen.

'Hi. Give me a name.'

'Delores Larga Markin. Want the rest?'

'Whatever you've got.'

'Being me, I got it all.' A heart-shaped blue stone winked on the left side of Harvo's nose as she turned to read from her own screen. 'Female – and a natural redhead – age twenty-eight. Sending you her address and contact info now. She's the younger of two daughters. Mom's Carlotta Larga, empress of footwear.'

'Footwear has an empress?'

'You've probably worn her, seeing as you married the sexy rich guy. I've got a pair of the knockoffs myself. Anyhoo, the empress has been married to Phillipe Larga for a zillion years. One marriage, only marriage for both. The daughter – our redhead – is also a designer for Larga's secondary line, Alores, named for both daughters, Alora and Delores. They're all stupid rich. The redhead's been married to Hugo Markin, a scion – frosty word, *scion* – of Roger Markin, the casino king, for a couple years.'

'Gambling,' Eve mused aloud.

'Roll those dice,' Harvo said cheerfully. 'Spin that wheel. Obviously if redheaded Delores lost her hair of intimacy in your dead guy's hair of intimacy, they were having intimacy.'

'Obviously. Thanks for the quick work.'

'Hey, this was breezy. Next time give me a challenge.'

'I'll work on it.'

She clicked off, started a run on the redhead and the scion. Then picked up another tag, this one from Trueheart.

'Sir. Baxter's still with Ms Kelsi. She can't be absolutely sure, but she thinks the missing artwork might be from one of three artists.'

'Three?'

'She thinks – again, not a hundred percent – Banks took those three off the books. We took her back to Banks's apartment for another on-site look. None of them are here at the crime scene. She needs to get back to the gallery, check there, but she's pretty sure it's one of these three. Angelo Richie, Selma Witt, Simon Fent. All the art in that area of the crime scene are what she calls, ah, figure studies.'

'Naked people.'

'Yes, sir. And black-and-white studies, like charcoal or pencil drawings and that sort of thing. She knows these three artists used that, ah, form and medium for some of their work.'

'Take her back to the gallery, see if she can pinpoint. And get me more data on whoever she pinpoints. All three, if that's the closest she gets. I want locations and contact info on the artists asap.'

'Yes, sir.'

Something there, she thought when she clicked off. Something. And she'd pull that line as soon as she finished pulling the one on the Markins.

After finishing a run on both, she got up, grabbed her coat. 'Peabody,' she said as she swung through the bullpen. 'With me.'

Coat in hand, scarf already winding, Peabody hustled to catch up. 'I've got ten dropped down to the bottom of the list. I get why you had them on there, but—'

'That's on hold. Harvo ID'd the redhead.'

'The ... oh, *that* redhead.'

'Delores Larga Markin.'

'Wait, Larga? Shoe Larga's daughter? Oh, Largas are like art for the feet, like a song, like a poem.'

'I bet they're like shoes.'

'Seriously the ult in footwear.' Peabody jumped into the elevator, struggled into her pink coat. 'If I ever have five or six figures to spare, I'd buy a pair. But even the second line's out of my reach, even on sale. But maybe ...'

'Maybe we could also put your shoe fantasies on hold. Second-gen Larga's married to a Hugo Markin. Daddy owns casinos. A lot of them. They tend to gamble in casinos. Check one. It turns out Markin also has several relatives in or retired from the military. Check two. Since his wife likely lost her pubic hair to Banks at the party before he died, it's probable Markin knew Banks. Check three.'

For once, the elevator didn't fill to capacity, so they rode it straight down to the garage. 'The Markins live in the same building as the party hosts. We'll kill two birds with one arrow and talk to the party people.'

'And that's sort of check four.' Peabody climbed into the car. 'It's stone. You kill the two birds with one stone.'

'Have you ever tossed a rock at a bird?'

'No!' Appalled in her Free-Ager's heart, Peabody strapped in. 'That's just mean.'

'And ineffective, I bet, since birds can fly. An arrow's got to be quicker than heaving a rock that's big enough to take out a couple of birds at a time.'

'But still,' Peabody murmured.

Eve whipped out of the garage. 'Baxter and Trueheart are taking the gallery woman back to the gallery. She's got three possibilities for the painting.'

'It's not a literal rock or actual birds.'

'What?'

'Nothing,' Peabody decided. 'Do you want me to run the artists?'

'Trueheart's doing that, and we'll save time if she pins it down to one.' As she drove, ignoring the blasts of ad blimps and the farts of maxibuses, Eve decided it was as good a time as any.

'Nadine's taking the rocker to this Hollywood thing.'

'I know.' Peabody gave a grin and the eye-roll

equivalent of *hubba-hubba*. 'He is frosty extreme, and seriously into her.'

'I don't want to hear about their sex life.'

'Not that kind of into. Although ... Anyway, going as a couple's a major BFD for Nadine, I think.'

'Whatever. She's taking him, but she has room on her transport and in the hotel.'

'You're going! You're going after all?' Peabody bounced in her seat, actually clapping her hands together. 'You're going to walk the red carpet of all red carpets! This is—'

'Oh, hell no. Giant hell no. She's got room for you and McNab. Feeney cleared it, so you can take off on Friday afternoon, report back Tuesday morning.'

Peabody said nothing, absolutely nothing. And stared straight ahead.

'What's the problem?'

'I ... I think I stopped breathing for a minute. You're giving me time off to go to the Oscars? Nadine's going to take us, and let us stay with her? Her and Jake the rock god?'

'She's got room.'

Peabody kept staring ahead. 'We're in an active investigation.'

'I've got Baxter and Trueheart. And, strangely enough, I managed to close cases before I took you on. You're not on the roll this weekend anyway,' Eve continued, 'so I cut that OT out of my budget.'

'This is ... I can't think of a big enough word. I can't

think straight enough to make one up for it. As long as I can remember I've watched the Oscars and all the beautiful clothes, the people.'

'Free-Agers watch Hollywood?'

'We're not like monks, and I bet monks watch the Oscars, too. My granny? Man, she never misses. She has a big Oscar party every year. I still sort of watch it with her and the rest. I set up my home screen, have the family on my tablet so we all watch. Granny's brutal when somebody wears something she thinks is stupid. It's the best. And now I'm going to – Oh my God, what will I wear? I don't have anything that's Oscar worthy.'

'Roarke talked to Leonardo, so Leonardo's covering that, for both of you.'

'I . . . ' Now she turned her head, stared at Eve. 'I'm wearing Leonardo to the Oscars?'

'Why do people say that? You're not draping a big Leonardo all over you. Christ. Jesus Christ, if you cry the deal's off.'

The tears came anyway. 'I have to. Just for a minute. I know it'd be like torture for you. But for me? It's like this amazing dream. I'm not even going to say I wish you were coming because, torture. That's how much this means to me.'

'If it means so damn much, why didn't you say so before?'

'You gave us Mexico. You gave McNab time to recharge when he needed it. I'm not going to ask my partner, my LT, my friend, to do me another solid right on top of that.'

She let out a breath, scrubbed the tears dry. 'Add to it, I never thought about going, not seriously. It's so ... beyond. It never really landed that we could.'

'Well, now you are.'

The building had its own parking. Eve had the gate scan her badge, followed the instructions for the visitors' section. Pulled into a slot.

'Now get your head in the game.'

'I will.' But Peabody put a hand on Eve's arm. 'I wanted to be a cop. I studied you, and I wanted to be a New York cop. A Dallas-worthy cop.'

'For Christ's sake.'

'Just one minute, okay? When you pulled me into Homicide as your aide, that was the biggest moment of my life. I've had other big ones. McNab, making detective, helping take Oberman down. All the bad guys but her especially, because she's the opposite of what we are. This doesn't come up to those because they're life-changing. But outside of life-changing, it's the biggest. Thanks.'

'Nadine's the one hauling you.'

'She'll get a whole bunch of thanks, too. And Leonardo, and Roarke. You first.'

'Okay, good. Now done.'

They got out, started the walk toward the elevator. 'I've got to do this one thing.'

'If you try to kiss me,' Eve warned coldly, 'I will mess you up.'

'I'm not even going to threaten to kiss you, or kiss

you in my head — that's how much this means to me. But I have to—'

In the garage, Peabody threw her arms in the air, tossed back her head, and screamed. The sound echoed, ping-ponged, and made Eve's ears vibrate.

'Okay. Whew.' Peabody huffed out another breath. 'Now, head in the game.'

'Every dog in this building is barking. Glass has shattered. Small children are hiding under their beds.'

'Maybe.' Peabody pressed the call button. 'But it had to come out so I could get my head in the game.'

'It better stay there,' Eve warned and, using her badge to bypass the lobby, called for the Markins' floor.

The elevator opened in the center of an area with wide hallways leading to each of four corner units. And each, she assumed, had private, fully secured elevators of their own. She crossed to the southwest facing unit, rang the bell.

Please state your name and business.

Clipped and brisk, Eve noted, and answered in kind.

'Lieutenant Dallas and Detective Peabody, NYPSD.' She held up her badge. 'We need to speak with Mr and/or Mrs Markin.'

Your identification is being scanned … Your identification has been verified. Please state your business.

'We'll state our business with Mr and/or Mrs Markin. Open the door or we'll arrange to have one or both of them transported to Cop Central for interview.'

One moment.

'Why are comps always so damn nosy?' Eve wondered.

It took more than a moment, but the double doors opened. Since the woman inside hit about forty, wore what Eve thought of as domestic black, she deduced housekeeper.

'Lieutenant, Detective, if you'll wait in the anteroom, I've notified Mrs Markin's admin. She'll be with you very shortly.'

The housekeeper walked away, leaving them outside another set of open doors. What Eve had assumed was the private elevator stood to the right with fancy, decorative ironwork over a door of dull gold. On the opposite wall wide, sliding doors reflected the same tone. For coats and wraps, Eve imagined.

Through the open doors, the living area spread big as a ballroom with floor-to-ceiling glass offering the stupendously rich person's view of the city, the great park, and, on this clear day, the Hudson. Staircases swept in fluid curves on either side of the glass.

An enormous mirror ornately framed in that dull gold ranged over a flickering fireplace with a surround of polished stone the color of tropical seas.

Sofas, chairs, benches reflected the fluid curves of the staircases, the colors of the surround and the mirror frame. A piano, blizzard white, stood under the curve of the right staircase. It held a large, clear glass ball filled with blue stones and flowers from the palest blue to a purple so deep it read black.

From the high ceiling hung a many-tiered chandelier formed with hundreds of dripping glass teardrops. Eve decided if it ever fell, it could easily kill a good fifty people standing under its spread.

A woman came down the right sweep. Dark skin, a curling mass of bronze-tipped dark hair, a voluptuous figure in a suit of poppy red. Early thirties, Eve judged. Not beautiful, but arresting.

She crossed the wide space on towering heels of blue and green swirls over the poppy red.

'Lieutenant, Detective, I'm Amelia Leroix.' Her voice carried a faint accent. European, Eve thought as she shook the extended hand. Probably French.

'Mrs Markin is in a meeting. She's working from home today, and is still in a meeting. I hope I can help you.'

'We'll wait until she's out of the meeting.'

'I see. Then allow me to take your coats.'

'We're good.'

'Perhaps I can arrange for coffee? Tea?'

'You could arrange for us to speak to Mr and/or Mrs Markin.'

'I'll let Mrs Markin know you're waiting. I'm afraid I don't have Mr Markin's schedule. I believe he's also working from home today, but I'll have to check.'

'We'd appreciate it.'

'Please, come in, sit down. I'll need a moment.'

Eve didn't miss the flicker of resignation on Amelia's face as she turned toward the left sweep of stairs.

Different wings, Eve thought. For business meetings, or altogether?

Peabody wandered over to the glass wall. 'That's one serious view. And the terrace has to add another two hundred square feet of living space in good weather.'

'Making ankle-breakers pays.'

'Did you *see* the assistant's shoes? I bet those were from the hand-painted collection.'

While Peabody enjoyed the view, Eve studied the room. Some framed photos – but none of the married couple together. The art struck her as safe and tasteful, and she didn't see anything wrong with that. Despite the size of the room, it felt comfortable, at least marginally welcoming.

She turned as the man she recognized as Hugo Markin came down the stairs. He wore a silver-blue sweater to match his eyes and casual, well-tailored black trousers. He wore skids – pricey ones the same color as the sweater. His hair, waves of streaky blond, flowed back from a vid-handsome face.

His smile held buckets of charm. A blue stone ring shot fire from his extended hand.

'Lieutenant Dallas, what a pleasure. I'm an enormous fan. In fact, I'll be in the Highland Center on Sunday, cheering for your Oscar win.'

'It's not my Oscar, win or lose.'

'So modest. Ah, Detective Peabody, another pleasure. Let's sit, have some coffee, and you can tell me what brings you to see me today.'

'We can start with Jordan Banks.'

'Such a shock!' He gestured them to seats by the fire. 'Do you know I spoke with him the very night he died? At a party in this building. But then, I'm sure you do know. What can I tell you to help?'

'How well did you know him?'

'Not terribly well, really. We did play golf a few times – in a foursome. And would see each other at parties. Mutual friends and acquaintances. I might see him, now and again, if we were both at one of our casinos – my family's casinos – at the same time.'

'Did he often frequent your casinos?'

'I couldn't say, frankly.' In a picture of ease, Markin draped an arm over the low back of the sofa. 'I recall seeing him a time or two. I think he enjoyed roulette, but that's my best recollection only.'

'What time did you leave the party?'

'It must have been around one.'

'Was Banks still there?'

Markin shifted as if thinking, but the gleam in his eye told Eve he was amused by the questioning. 'I'm not sure. It's a large apartment. Not as large as this, you understand, but large enough. And it was a very . . . festive gathering. People spread all over. They have two levels rather than our three, but considerable opportunities to spread out, or enjoy a more intimate tête-à-tête. I believe Jordan indulged in an intimate tête-à-tête with my wife the night he died.

'Ah, here's our coffee.'

A man in domestic black wheeled in the tray.

'Black for the lieutenant, cream with two sugars for the detective.' Markin smiled again. 'I told you I was a fan.'

As the man poured, Delores Larga Markin came down the stairs. Her luxurious red hair spilled over the shoulders of a gray suit, high-necked, military in cut, with a double row of silver buttons down the jacket.

She wore silver booties with needle-thin heels and a line of red braiding up the sides. Square-cut diamond studs flashed at her ears, her only jewelry.

'Ah, here's my beautiful wife. Come meet Lieutenant Dallas and her stalwart sidekick, Detective Peabody. Renaldo, another cup.'

'No, thank you, Renaldo. I have another meeting shortly. I'm sorry I'm so pressed for time today,' she said to Eve.

'Oh, you can always squeeze out a bit more for interesting company. That will be all, Renaldo. Sit, sit, Dello.' He patted the cushion beside him. 'I was just telling our guests about you and Jordan. You know, it occurs to me you must be the last woman to give him a ride before he died.'

Delores simply stared at him. Then she sat, keeping at least a foot of space between them. 'Would you give me the room, Hugo? I'm sure you can make yourself available to Lieutenant Dallas if she needs to speak to you again. You have so much free time.'

'Why not?'

'Another couple questions before you leave, Mr Markin.

Your whereabouts this weekend. From Friday night through Monday morning.'

'That's quite a length of time. Wasn't Jordan killed Monday night, or rather early Tuesday?'

'Can you give us your whereabouts over this past weekend?'

'If I must. Spot-checking our casinos in the south. Mississippi, Georgia, Florida. I barely made it back in time for Thad and Delvinia's party.'

'You have several relatives in the military, active and retired.'

'Do I?' He sipped his coffee. 'I suppose you're right. After all, we still call my grandfather "The General."'

'You're not interested in the military yourself?'

'Not in the least. I'm a lover, not a fighter. Isn't that right, Dello?'

She didn't spare him a glance. 'You're a man of tactics, Hugo, without a clear strategy to guide them.'

'Still, I have you, don't I? I'll just be upstairs if I'm needed. Absolutely thrilling to meet you both.'

As he walked upstairs, Delores crossed her legs, let out a breath.

'You're here about Jordan.'

'We'll start there.'

'I'm sorry he's dead. It would be foolish to deny, since Hugo was so helpful. I had sex with Jordan on Monday night, at the party. Thad Trulane's and Delvinia Otter's party.'

'Your husband didn't seem surprised or overly concerned about your relationship with Jordan Banks.'

'I wouldn't call a brief sexual encounter a "relationship," but no, Hugo's neither surprised nor concerned. Hugo and I haven't been intimate in over a year. Our marriage is nothing more than a legal contract at this point.'

She sat, her back ruler straight, her face calmly composed. Unless, Eve thought, you looked carefully. Then you saw misery beneath the polish.

'We each go our own way,' she continued. 'If you suspect him of killing Jordan out of a jealous fury, that wouldn't be the case. Frankly, fury's just too much effort for a man like Hugo. I didn't particularly like Jordan.'

'But you had sex with him.'

'Yes. I went to the party because I like Delvinia, I wanted to blow off a little steam, and because I didn't know Hugo would be there. I hadn't seen him for several days.'

'Is that usual?'

'Yes. We go our own way, as I said, and generally stay out of each other's way. When I saw him there, it annoyed me. And I had impulsive, if briefly satisfying, sex with Jordan. Then I left, came home.'

'And your husband?'

'I don't know. I don't know how long he stayed, when he came back, if he came back alone or with someone. That's how it works for us.'

'Why?' Peabody shifted. 'You don't like your husband. Why are you living with him?'

'My parents are adamantly opposed to divorce. They'd be very disappointed to know I've had sexual relations outside of marriage, but divorce would be even more disappointing. Hugo was a mistake, but he's my mistake. Right now, I'm living with the mistake. He's well aware why I do.'

She looked away then, toward the expansive, exclusive view of New York. 'I think it amuses him.'

'How well did he know Jordan?'

'Well enough. My impression is Jordan set out to seduce me because I was the wife of a friend – however casual a friend. They share some qualities, some interests. Sports, travel, gambling, women.'

'The stock market?'

Puzzlement drew her eyebrows together. 'The stock market. I couldn't tell you about Jordan, but Hugo doesn't trouble himself with that sort of thing, to my knowledge. He has people who trouble themselves on his behalf.'

'Art?'

'Jordan, of course. Hugo? Not particularly. Oh, Hugo's educated and can talk art. But he doesn't have any real interest in it. In anything really but what gives him pleasure. He's lazy – a cardinal sin in my family, but he hides it well. I can't give him an alibi for Jordan, but I can say, killing someone? Far too much effort, and he certainly wouldn't exert that effort on my behalf.'

'Where were you all weekend?'

'Amelia can tell you the details and timing precisely, but on Friday, my mother, sister, and I – and our support staff – traveled to Paris to meet with some accounts. We came back Monday morning.

'I hope you find who killed Jordan, but I didn't know him well enough to help you. I'm sorry, but I do have another meeting.'

When she rose, Eve and Peabody followed suit.

'Do you know your husband's family?'

'Many of them. Hugo's not like most of them, actually. His grandfather, "The General," said to me on our wedding day that I'd be the making of Hugo.'

Her mouth twisted into a tight, bitter smile. 'He was wrong.'

'Is he close to any of them?'

'It's hard to say. If someone can be useful, Hugo is clever at exploiting a relationship. Until they're no longer useful.'

'Okay, thanks for your time. Do you know if the party hosts are in residence today?'

'No, they're not. It was a bon voyage party. Delvinia and Thad left the next day for Turks and Caicos. They'll be yachting through the spring.'

14

'"Yachting through the spring."' Eve just shook her head as they rode the elevator down to the garage.

'Does Roarke have a yacht?' Peabody wondered. 'Not that either of you would yacht through the spring or whatever.'

'No to both. He's not big on boats.'

'A yacht's kind of a super boat. Anyway, Hugo's kind of a shit.'

'He's a complete shit. And he still checks off a lot of boxes. He doesn't give a rat's ass about anybody but Hugo, enjoyed putting his wife in an awkward position with the cops during a murder investigation. Let's check out his travel over the weekend. Convenient he got back in time for the party, one Jordan went to. I never like convenient. It brushes close to coincidence.'

'I think she was being straight when she said he's too lazy to kill somebody.'

'As she sees it,' Eve said. 'Which doesn't mean he wouldn't be an accessory. He didn't snap anybody's neck, but I bet he wouldn't mind watching it done. I bet he wouldn't mind setting some family up, using somebody to blow up a bunch of people, if he got some juice out of it. Pleasure and greed – I think he lives by both.'

'And he's a shit,' Peabody said as they crossed to the car.

'Exactly. We're going to track down the couple yachting till spring. Maybe both killers partied first. I don't think so, but maybe.'

She drove out. Then, as it was on the way, stopped at Banks's art gallery.

'Let's see if we have anything here.'

She double-parked, ignored the outrage of horns and shouted expletives as she flipped up the On Duty sign.

'Shouldn't be long.'

The Banks Gallery was a glossy little place tucked amid glossy little boutiques and glossy little cafés.

A sign on the door read *Ferme*, but the lights shined. Eve gave the glass door a few good raps.

Trueheart strode into view, spotted them, came straight to the door. He unlocked it, pulled it open.

'Lieutenant. We weren't expecting you.'

'In the neighborhood. What have you got?'

'Maisie's – ah, Ms Kelsi's still stuck on three possibles. In fact, she's leaning toward a fourth now that she's looking at her notes and checking artists' web pages.'

'Let me talk to her.'

He guided them through – a lot of movable walls covered with art. Some of it incomprehensible to her, some she thought nice enough. Banks had definitely favored naked people, but he'd displayed landscapes, cityscapes, seascapes, still lifes.

She didn't get the still-life tag. Weren't all paintings still?

Trueheart led the way into an office. It hit glossy, too. Obviously Banks had liked his fancy comforts. The big sofa, the big chair, the big desk. Lots of naked people on the walls here, and a full-size AutoChef.

Baxter sat on a rolling chair hip to hip with the iced artist chick.

From the length of bare leg showing under the desk, Eve judged her as tall, and clearly thin as a whip. Her hair had that just-out-of-bed tousle in cool, cool blond, and her eyes held an emerald pop of green.

She spoke in a breathy, I'm-so-aroused voice Eve imagined had Baxter's blood simmering.

'I really think … maybe.'

She looked up, blinked those emerald eyes. 'Oh, I'm so sorry. We're closed.'

'Maisie, this is Lieutenant Dallas. And Detective Peabody.'

'I see.' She rose – and yes, a lot of long leg in a short, tight black skirt. 'I'm really sorry I can't be sure about the artwork. Jordan …'

'It's not speaking ill of the dead, Maisie,' Baxter said gently. 'It's helping find out who made him dead.'

'You're right. He just took artwork when he felt like it. He usually brought them back every few weeks. A rotation. He should have recorded it all – he excused it by calling it marketing. Having guests over, potential clients, showing

256

off the work in his home. But that wasn't the reason, and he didn't care about excusing it.'

Maybe she spoke in a breathy baby-doll voice, Eve thought, but she wasn't anyone's idiot.

'Your work?'

'Mine, too. I could've objected, but I needed the job here, and wanted the exposure. Most of the artists displayed here feel – felt – the same. He took a steeper commission than the standard, but he also took a lot of new artists who couldn't get into other galleries. It was a trade-off.'

'He piss anyone off?'

'Routinely.' She smiled a little. 'Not enough to kill him. With him gone, the gallery's going to close. That doesn't do any of us any good.'

'Okay. Can you show me the art you think might be the one?'

'What I did was dig up some old files – mine,' she added. 'I minored in office management, which is how I got the job here as gallery manager. Anyway, sorry. I tried keeping my own files, and I've been trying to coordinate them with what I can pull from the web pages of artists we've featured.'

'That's good,' Eve told her.

'It's been nagging at me. I just couldn't let it go, so I remembered the files I'd stored at home. I was just about to tag David when he tagged me because I thought, maybe . . . '

She lifted her hands. 'I can't get it below these three – and now there's another I think . . . maybe. Not all artists are good at the business and marketing sides, so their web pages aren't well organized and updated, so there's that issue. The other problem is, I haven't been in Jordan's place for months, and I know he switched things out since. A few times since. But these . . . '

She brought one up on the wall screen from her tablet. 'This is Selma's. Selma Witt. It's her *Woman at Rest*. Selma's very good. She works primarily in acrylics, but does some excellent charcoals and pastels. I know Jordan took this one out, but that was last fall – maybe even the end of last summer. There's no record of him bringing it back, or of it being sold. It's not in the gallery. The thing is, he didn't usually keep anything as long as that.'

Eve studied the work – the drawing of a woman in bed, reclining against a mound of pillows and on tangled sheets.

Eve closed her eyes, put herself back in Banks's apartment, tried to bring back the black-and-white art on his walls.

Should've paid more attention, she thought. They all looked so much the same.

'Give me another.'

'This is Simon Fent's work. He's . . . Well, he's not as good as Selma, but he does show promise. There's still a student's hesitancy in his work, a failure to commit to the vision, but Jordan liked it. It's the only one of Simon's we took on.'

'Keep going.'

She brought up another, and Eve lifted a hand. 'This one. Wait.'

She turned away for a minute, tried to bring those damn

walls back, the black frames, the black-and-white figures in them.

Turned back.

'This one. Third from the entrance door.'

'This is Angelo Richie, one of his early sketches. He actually gave this one to Jordan – or Jordan said he did. As a thank-you for giving him his first gallery sale. Even this earlier work? You can see the talent. His people move, they breathe. These are lovers, and you see the joy. *Reunited*, it's called. They've come together again after being separated, and—'

'Fine. I want his contact info. This artist.'

'He and Jordan had a falling-out, a couple of years ago. Angelo pulled all his work from the gallery. I heard he went to Italy to paint. I don't have his contact, but he's back in New York. He's right on the edge of breaking out as a major artist. Actually just over the edge, and getting a lot of attention. He's having an opening at the Salon – and that's big in our world – tonight.'

'You sure about the piece, LT?'

'As sure as I can be,' she told Baxter.

'Angelo Richie. SoHo address,' Peabody announced. 'The Salon's in Greenwich.'

'They'd be loading in,' Maisie told her. 'The art, for tonight. I didn't know Angelo all that well, but I know he'd be at the gallery during load in.'

'Thanks, you've been a big help. Wrap it up, Baxter.'

'I liked the painting. Well, it's really a sketch,' Peabody

said as they went back to the car. 'It's romantic and a little heartbreaking.'

'I doubt the killers took it because it appealed to the romantic inside them. Let's see if the artist has any idea why.'

She flicked on her in-dash when it signaled. 'Dallas.'

'Hey, Lieutenant,' Santiago said. 'I know the next DB's ours, but we really think, considering, these are yours.'

'These.'

'Five. Including the guy in the suicide vest.'

'Where?'

'It's a high-class kind of art place called—'

'The Salon.'

His eyes narrowed. 'You going sensitive on us?'

'Secure the scene. We're on our way.' She hit the sirens, shoved into traffic. 'Have you ID'd the DB in the vest?'

'Wayne Denby. One of the three owners, and the gallery director.'

As Peabody tightened her seat belt, Eve two-wheeled it at the corner, snaking her way west. 'Get uniforms over to his residence. Now. Probability is high there are hostages in distress inside. Tell them to break down the door, my authority. Relay the home address to Baxter. I want him and Trueheart there. Now, Santiago.'

She punched vertical over an all-terrain whose driver considered lights and sirens someone else's problem, screamed around the next turn to barrel south.

'Fuck, fuck, fuck,' Eve cursed while Peabody used a run on Denby to keep her mind off the potential of a bloody, bone-breaking crash inside a vehicle doing ninety through arrogant traffic.

'Wayne Denby, age thirty-eight, owns the Salon with two partners. Married to Zelda Este Denby, thirty-four. Eight years in. One son, Evan, age five.'

'Same pattern.' Eve threaded between a couple of Rapid Cabs, caught a glimpse of the passengers in the back. One grinned wildly while he took a vid of her car screaming by.

'Solid married guy,' Eve continued, adding a horn blast to the sirens as a couple of I'm-in-a-fucking-hurry pedestrians tried to dash across the intersection as she sped toward them.

Both scrambled back – and one shot up both middle fingers.

'He'll have been a devoted husband and father,' she said, blood hot, mind cold as she crossed into the Village. 'Family centered. Single-family home, good security.'

She slammed the brakes, fishtailed to a stop an inch from the barricade and the line of people ranged behind it.

'I'll get the field kits,' Peabody said as they jumped out either side of the car.

Eve elbowed her way through the lookie-loos, around the barrier, badged past the beat droids on crowd control.

The Salon, housed in a classy corner brownstone, displayed a painting of a woman, dark hair flowing, sheer, ankle-length red dress swirling as the artist caught her in a spin, her arms lifted.

A jagged crack shot across the sun-filtering glass. The

painting had fallen off its easel hard enough to snap the corner of the frame. Eve read the artist's signature in the opposite corner.

Angelo Richie

A uniform opened the door. 'Lieutenant. They're back through that archway to the left.'

She could smell the smoke, the blood, the acrid stink of burning – plaster, wood, flesh.

The archway had been white. Gray smeared it now, under blood splattered like red rain. She stepped up, studied the carnage. What was left of five people scattered over the floor. What had been flesh, blood, bone, muscle lay in pieces, charred and black. Paintings, some nearly obliterated, others in scorched tatters, scattered with them.

Fire damage crisped sections of the walls, the floors, the ceiling. Fire-suppressant foam still dripped. Ash had filtered into piles, some soggy with foam.

A piece of what she identified as a metal ladder impaled one of the victims.

Sealed up, faces cop-blank, her detectives recorded the scene, marked body parts.

Careful of her steps, Detective Carmichael crossed to Eve. 'Has to be your guys.'

'Yeah.' She took her field kit as Peabody stepped up beside her, began to seal up. 'Tell me what you've got.'

'Art opening tonight for Angelo Richie. They were

loading in this area. The other owners were here – one, Joe Kotler, was in the back office working, the other was in the front area with one of the assistants. We have them all in the back, but according to the two out front, Denby came in. He told them to stay where they were. His partner – that's Ilene Aceti – says she was so stunned by his tone, how he looked, she just stood there for a minute. Then she told the assistant – Cista Daub – to hold on, started to go see what the hell. And boom. Just like that. She was close enough it lifted her off her feet, tossed her in the air. She's got a broken arm – already treated by the MTs. The assistant fell – just bumps and bruises there.'

She paused to take a water bottle out of her pocket, drink. 'Aceti, broken arm and all, got up, rushed toward this area. Active fire at that point. She yelled for the assistant to get out, tag nine-one-one, and ran toward the back as Kotler came rushing out. The sprinkler didn't engage, or the alarm. He grabbed a tank of suppressant, managed to put out the fire before it spread beyond this area.'

'No sprinkler, no alarm?'

'Nope.' Santiago walked over. 'We haven't checked that yet. We'd just finished another call, about six blocks from here. Unattended death, looks like natural causes,' he added. 'So we responded to this one. Smoke hadn't cleared when we got here. Pretty good bet this was yours.'

'We contacted Salazar – since she had the other, too. She and a team are on the way.'

'Good.'

'Since the fire was out, we asked the smoke eaters to hold off until we finished. You know what they can do to a scene.'

'Yeah. Do we have the names of the other DBs?'

'The artist, Angelo Richie, two assistants, Trenton Bean and Loden Modele, and an intern, the nephew of Kotler, Dustin Greggor. Kid was nineteen, and Kotler's pretty messed up over it.'

'Five people,' Eve stated. 'And two injuries.'

'I'd say lucky if I believed in luck,' Carmichael commented. 'Aceti's assistant said they expected a couple hundred at the opening tonight. If these fuckers wanted to screw with the gallery for whatever motive, that would have screwed a lot harder.'

Eve scanned what remained of the paintings. 'I think they got what they aimed for. Peabody, contact EDD. I need some geek to – Never mind,' she said as Roarke came in. 'We've got an on-site geek.'

She walked to him, might have objected when he gripped her hands but for the fierce look in his eyes.

'What? And what are you doing here?'

'I had business downtown, was heading this way when the alert sounded. It wasn't hard to deduce, and you add the missing painting. I saw your car out front just minutes after the alert.'

He let out a quiet breath. 'I didn't know if you'd been here when the bomb went off.'

He released her hands to skim one of his over her hair,

then flicked a finger down the dent in her chin. 'You might have been here,' he murmured.

'I wasn't.' Understanding, she gave his hands a firm squeeze. 'Five people were – including the guy in the vest. Family man, one of the owners.'

'And his family?'

'I've got uniforms, Baxter and Trueheart, on that.'

He looked through the archway, said nothing for several seconds. 'There's no water damage. The sprinkler didn't engage?'

'It didn't. Neither did the fire alarm.'

'As I'm here, would you like me to check on that for you?'

'That'd be handy. They had an art opening scheduled for tonight – a pretty big one. Artist – the same one who did the missing figure study – was Angelo Richie.'

'Richie? That's a pity. He had talent.' Roarke brushed a hand down her arm as if just needing the contact. 'We have one of his paintings – *Woman in Moonlight* – in a guest room.'

'We do?'

'We do, yes. I spotted it on a trip to Italy a year or so ago.'

'He and what was probably a bunch of his paintings, or what's left of him and them, were in there.'

'I see.'

'I bet you do. What's the point of blowing up an artist and a bunch of his paintings? An artist I'm told was about to hit it big?'

Roarke shifted his gaze back, met her eyes. 'You're a quick study, Lieutenant. What would you name as motive?'

'Leverage.'

'Exactly. A young, very promising artist dies violently and tragically before his first major American opening. And much of his work dies with him.'

'His surviving work shoots up in value,' she finished.

'It certainly will. Anyone who bought – or stole – any of his previous work would see a substantial return on the investment.'

'The one they stole? That's a bonus point. This was planned well before they killed Banks.'

'No doubt of that.' He took her hand again. 'I'll check on that system for you.'

He started to step away, but her comm signaled. 'Dallas. When?' She listened, eyes narrowing. 'How bad is the wife? Yeah, got it. Have EDD check every damn thing. Have Child Services hang with the kid until. Stick with them, Baxter.'

She shoved the comm back in her pocket. 'Kid was sedated, lightly.' She turned to include the detectives in the update. 'Unharmed, a little dehydrated, scared shitless. Wife took a beating – face mostly. They broke two of her fingers. She's about twelve and a half weeks pregnant.'

'Ah, fuck that,' Santiago said and kicked the bottom of the arch.

'MTs say she's stable, but they're taking her in for tests, more fluids, whatever they do. Kid was restrained to the bed in his room. The wife in a utility area. Home invasion happened early Tuesday morning. The wife thinks about four, four-thirty.'

'That's fast work,' Roarke added.

'Yeah, terrorize Rogan into blowing up the Quantum meeting Monday morning, collect the winnings, most likely. Then move on Banks, who's stupid enough to put a target on his back. Steal the painting and electronics and/or records that connect you, head over to the next mark, and get to work.'

She circled the room. 'Banks wasn't planned, but they fit him in. They had to deal with him before they moved to the next mark. Cut off that loose end first – and get the bonus point.'

The smell of death was everywhere, lives snuffed out in an instant.

'Eighteen people now, but it's not about racking up the body count. If that interested them, they'd have waited and had Denby strapped up tonight when the place was full of art lovers.'

She looked at the charred remains. 'It's not about people at all. It's about profit. Nothing else. Peabody, let's talk to the witnesses. Carmichael, Santiago, stick for Salazar.'

They spoke to the assistant first, who shook and wept and added little. Peabody arranged for her to tag her roommate and to be transported home.

Eve stepped into the back office for the next round. 'If I could speak to you next, Ms Aceti.'

'I'm not leaving Joe.' She sat beside him, the hand of her uninjured arm clutching his. Her broken arm was splinted with a temporary cast and resting in a sling. 'I won't.'

'All right. We'll talk right here, all of us.' She sat across from them. The woman had some facial nicks, a few tears and scorch marks on her shirt and trousers. She'd tied her hair – long enough to hit her waist with copper streaks through inky black – back from a face ivory pale with shock. Her deep-set brown eyes blazed against it.

Her partner sat, slumped, dazed, eyes swollen from weeping. His skin, nearly the color of the woman's streaks, made Eve think of Leonardo. He wore his hair in dozens of intricate braids.

His black turtleneck and silver-studded black jeans smelled of smoke.

'I know this is a difficult time, and again, I'm sorry for your loss.' Eve glanced over briefly as Peabody came in, sat. 'We have to ask questions.'

'I have questions,' Aceti said with an edge of fury. 'I have questions, too. And I'm telling you right now, Wayne would never, never do this unless . . . We've all known each other since college. We loved each other, do you understand?'

'I do. We—'

'It's like what happened at Quantum. It's all over the screen about somebody hurting that man's family, threatening them until he – did what he did. It's the same! I need to know about Zelda and Evan. I won't tell you a goddamn thing until you tell us about Zelda and Evan. She's pregnant.'

Aceti's lips trembled. 'She's pregnant.'

'And she's stable. The MTs treated her, and she's been taken to the hospital.'

'The baby?'

'As far as I know she and the baby are stable.'

'Evan. He's only five.'

'He wasn't hurt. Scared, but not hurt. You need to talk to me, both of you.'

'They were supposed to leave yesterday morning. They were supposed to be away until later today. We had everything under control here for tonight. And they were taking Evan to Disney for an overnight treat, and to tell him he was going to have a baby brother or sister. They didn't know which yet. They hadn't told anyone else but me and Joe, and their parents. They wanted to tell Evan first. We thought they were away, having fun, and all the time, they must have . . .'

She leaned toward Eve, aggressive, fierce. 'It's not Wayne's fault.'

'No, it's not. You may be able to help us find the people who are at fault.'

'Wayne's dead.' The aggression died as she sat back. 'We were the Best People at his wedding, Joe and I. We started this place together. We made it into something.'

'Tell me what happened.'

'I didn't expect him for a couple more hours. We had everything in place. Just a matter of loading in. We'd already diagrammed where we were placing the paintings, the sketches. I was in the front with Cista, and we were going over where we'd set up the bar, the refreshments. Angelo, the artist, was in the gallery loft – with Trent and Loden and

Dustin. They'd removed the art we'd had displayed there, had begun placing Angelo's work. Joe was in the office.'

'Were you open to the public?'

'The Salon's closed on Wednesdays. We try to schedule openings for Wednesday nights so we can do the loading in. The show would run for four weeks, but the opening's when you draw the biggest crowd, and the media, the art critics. We're – we're known for our Wednesday night openings. Wayne came in.'

Her voice began to shake. 'He came in, and he looked pale, sick. I started to say something, and he snapped at me. He never snapped, but he did. "Stay out here. You and Cista stay out here."'

She blew out a breath. 'I just stood there, so stunned because he had snapped and looked sick. Angry, too. Then I got a little angry myself. What the hell was this? And I started across the room. The explosion – it was terrible. It was like being picked up and thrown by some huge, hot wave. I just flew, then I felt this awful pain. My arm. And Cista was on the floor, too. I could see fire, smell it. I was so scared. I yelled at her to get out, to call for help, and I started to run back for Joe.

'He came running out. The sprinklers didn't come on. Joe said, "We have to put the fire out," and he ran back. We have an emergency fire suppression tank in the back. He put out the fire. He walked right through the arch and put out the fire. But . . . '

'It was too late,' Kotler whispered. 'Too late. I didn't

know Wayne was … I didn't know until Ilene told me. Dustin. I knew Dustin was … My nephew. He's only nineteen. Gap year. He just wanted to work here before he started college. My nephew Dustin.'

He began to weep, harsh, gulping sobs. Aceti put her good arm around him, drew him against her. Then she, too, began to weep.

Eve gestured to Peabody, moved with her to the door.

'See if you can get any more out of them. About the artist. If they sold any of his earlier work, who bought it. You know what to ask.'

She stepped out, took a breath of air that wasn't thick with grief. Roarke tucked away his PPC, moved to her.

'Remotely compromised, the fire suppression system and its alarm. Nothing else. They never tried for the locks, or the cameras. The suppression system's been off since early this morning. About five A.M.'

He glanced toward the door, and the sound of weeping. 'Nothing shatters lives like violent death.'

'No. I need to talk to Salazar.'

She walked to the archway, and with a word to one of her people, Salazar came out. 'The morgue's picking up their pieces. We're picking up ours. And I can tell you, just by the eyeball, it's going to be the same bomb maker. Military grade. We've got his signature now.'

'Can you trace the components?'

'We can try. The fricking black market on this is a maze. And if he's got any brains, he's not getting everything from one source. I think he's got brains. I'll push on my end the same as you'll push on yours. You know the thing about making bombs, Dallas?'

'They go boom.'

'Yeah, and the juice of making the go-boom, the intricacy, even the risk it goes boom on you? It's addicting. He's got two under his belt – at least. He's going to build more.'

'I know it. He's having a hell of a good time, and making a steady profit.' She took a last hard look as the morgue team bagged parts of human beings. 'He's going to have a fucking downturn. I swear to God.'

15

Eve went by the Denby residence, the expected single-family home in the West Village. All three floors already swarmed with sweepers.

No basement, she noted, but a large utility area. And there they'd bound the battered, terrified pregnant woman, tied her to the exposed pipes under a work sink.

Eve crouched down, examined the blood smears on the pipes. And the scratches – fresh – along the thick joint. She found a screwdriver, also blood-smeared, on the floor.

'Got her hands on this somehow.' Curious, Eve opened a drawer on an old cabinet beside the sink. 'Out of here. A few household tools in here. She must've gotten it out, tried to use it to hack through the pipe.'

'If her hands were bound to that pipe, she must've used her foot. Her feet.'

Eve nodded as she straightened. 'Yeah, managed to get the screwdriver out of the drawer, nudge it over, over until she could reach it with her hands. Had to take time and a lot of sweaty, uncomfortable effort.'

She stepped out, into the kitchen, and found Feeney walking in.

'They said you were down here.'

'And they said EDD was here. They didn't say the captain.'

His droopy eyes hardened. 'I wanted to handle this one myself. It's pissing me off.'

'Get in line.'

'Remoted it,' he told her. 'In layers, just like before. System wasn't as high-end as the last one, but it's damn good. Good toys is what they've got, Dallas. They paid for good toys and somebody who knows how to modify and enhance them. Or they've got the skills to build the toys.'

'Maybe, maybe they've got the skills, but they're not B and E pros. Not thieves, professionally.' She moved with him and Peabody through the house. 'Easy valuables, including jewelry. Upstairs you've got suitcases already packed, and some things left out probably going in last minute. Safe upstairs in the master? Better jewelry and cash inside.'

'Was it open?' he asked her.

'No. I'm getting pretty good at opening safes, so I did. It's just a glorified lockbox. They spent more on art, from the looks of it, than shiny bits, but there were some in there. And the cash. Not thieves,' she repeated.

'They like scaring and hurting people,' Peabody put in. 'Thieves just want to get in, score, get out. They like terrifying a family, and making the father the sacrifice.'

Frowning, Eve turned to her. '"Sacrifice"?'

'He is, isn't he? He's their human bomb.'

'Yeah. Yeah.' She paced the living area. Photographs, a few toys, a lot of art. 'Flip that. He's the hero. Saves his family. He's the hero who sacrifices himself. Maybe it's a Mira thing, but . . . Maybe one or both of them had a father or authority figure who sacrificed himself.'

'Or didn't,' Feeney added.

'Or didn't. Let's look at Markin's military relatives' records. Could be. We're going back to the lists. If not Markin, they're on the board. At least one of them's on the board. Let's hunt these fuckers down before they do this to another family.'

'You really think they'd do it again?'

'They like it, remember?' Feeney answered Peabody.

'Add to it, they must have had at least one contingency. If they couldn't torture Rogan and Denby into it, they'd have another ready to go.'

'We'll take their e's in,' Feeney said. 'We'll see if we can get a cross-match on anyone who's on the first target. Anything that crosses, we'll find it.'

'They knew enough about both of them to play the game. Paths crossed somewhere.'

Stock market, business mergers, art, military, explosives, Eve thought as she drove to Angelo Richie's loft. Where was the line that ran through them all, connecting them?

'Just to get on and off it,' Peabody said, 'with this second hit, I understand I can't take off for the awards. McNab, either. We need to stick on this.'

'We're not going there yet.'

275

'I just want to say the job comes first. So . . . I'm going to check in with Baxter, get the status on the wife and kid.'

'Do that.' She wasn't going to think about it, Eve determined. Personal issues had to wait. Because, yes, the job came first.

'Banks was a link,' she said, more to herself than to Peabody. 'His relationship with Karson on the first, his connection to Richie's work on the second. That makes him the linchpin on both. What else does he connect to?'

'The wife's stable,' Peabody announced. 'So's the fetus. They're keeping her on hospital bed rest for the next twenty-four. The kid's fine,' she continued. 'The wife's parents have him. Baxter and Trueheart were able to get statements, and they're on their way to Central to report.'

'Give them Richie's address, have them head there instead. Gambling. Another link – Banks to Markin. It's all gambling – stock market, art world. Maybe the next is more direct.'

'Blow up a casino?'

'I don't know what that gets you.' Eve, hunting for a parking space, felt both shock and glee at spotting one nearly in front of Richie's building.

Maybe it was a loading zone, but she snagged it.

'A competitor's?' she continued. 'Still, that's not quick profit in your pocket. And first, we need a back check on people who bought Richie's work, so we need the galleries or art brokers, whatever else he used to market them.'

She stepped onto the sidewalk, studied the squat, square block of the building.

It sat back from the sidewalk with a scrubby patch of winter yellow grass fronting it. The building itself – four stories – appeared to be built of cinder blocks painted a quiet green. Some old factory, she assumed, repurposed to lofts and sturdy enough to have survived the Urbans.

As they started over a concrete walkway, Peabody considered, 'If he went to Italy to live and work for a stretch . . .'

'Yeah.' Eve could feel the headache coming on as they walked to the steel entrance doors. 'It means dealing internationally, and that's going to slow it all down. Roarke has one of the paintings. Richie's.'

'He does?'

'He said it's in one of the guest rooms.' She scanned the call buttons – fifteen – then the security. Low-end, bordering on pitiful. 'Something . . . *Moonlight*.' Pulling out her master, she breezed through the locks, into a kind of vestibule with a muscular freight elevator. '*Woman in Moonlight*.'

'Oh! I know that one! I didn't know who painted it, but it's in where we usually stay when we hang overnight. It's really beautiful, all blues and silvers and mystical.'

When, after eyeing the freight elevator, Eve aimed for the stairs, Peabody just thought: Loose pants. And started the trudge up four levels.

'Whatever. He's got one, maybe he can help pin down other sales. Especially since these bastards will have multiples.'

Rather than the graffiti, the stray used condom, the smell of beer vomit she expected in a low-end downtown building, murals roamed along the walls. Scenes of green parks or fanciful castles with fountains, fire-breathing dragons, winged nudes.

'I bet Richie wasn't the only artist living here. It's probably something like a commune.'

'Only two units on this level,' Eve noted when they reached the fourth. Music thumped against the door of the unit on the right. She turned to Richie's, mastered through.

She wasn't surprised, and as her hand was already on her weapon, drew it. Inside the large space with its wide front-facing window, canvases hung in tatters. Others lay scattered on the floor, destroyed by sharps or a stomped foot.

'Clear it.'

A quick job, as other than the main space, the loft had a single bedroom and bath, a small kitchen.

'Eliminate as much of his work as you can.' Disgusted, Eve shoved her weapon in its holster. 'The value of what you've got goes up.'

'It's a crime. I don't mean to throttle back on the human lives taken, Dallas, but to destroy art like this? No way they're art lovers. No way they could do this if they were. The art's just—'

'An investment, and they maximized their profit. Let's nail down the timing. When they got in, when they got out. Because if they took the trouble to steal one of Richie's pieces from Banks, I'm betting they took some from here, then wiped out the rest. When did Richie leave here for the Salon, when did they cut Denby loose to go to the Salon?

We've got Denby's arrival time, the bombing, so when did they fit this in?

'Field kits, Peabody.'

She moved across the hall, jammed a finger on the buzzer.

With music still thumping, the door swung open. 'Look, Lollie, I told you – Sorry. I thought you were someone else.'

The woman hit about five-three with well-muscled arms and a mermaid tat along her left biceps exposed by a black tank. She had her dark blond hair bundled up under a flowered kerchief and wore baggy gray pants tucked into steel-toed boots. Goggles hung by a strap around her neck.

She held a wicked-looking chisel.

'Lieutenant Dallas, NYPSD.'

'Okay.' She stuck the chisel in the short leather tool belt at her waist. 'Why?'

'Do you know Angelo Richie?'

'Sure. He lives across the hall. Again, why?'

'He's dead.'

The woman laughed. 'What are you talking about? He's over at the Salon loading in for his opening. He has a major show opening tonight.'

'Not anymore.'

The first sign of anxiety clouded soft, hazel eyes. Her voice sharpened with it. 'What the hell are you talking about?'

'How well did you know him?'

'You tell me what you're talking about first.'

'There was an explosion this afternoon at the Salon. Angelo Richie and four others were killed.'

'Explosion. Like – like a gas explosion? I don't . . . Wait, just wait.' She turned, dragging off the kerchief. A lot of tangled, tousled hair fell.

Eve stepped in, noted the space nearly mirrored Richie's. This one appeared to be divided into stations, one with stones – raw stones – and one on a workbench with mallets, more chisels. A half-formed face emerged from the pillar of stone.

Another area held welding tools, another had a worktable, stacks of metal.

'Could I have your name?'

The woman turned back, face pale, breathing ragged. 'What?'

'Your name, please.'

'I'm Astrid. Astrid Baretta, but I only use Astrid. Angelo's really dead?'

'Were you friends?'

'I guess we were. I—' She broke off, covered her face with her hands. 'I admired his talent. He has real talent. He's arrogant and full of himself, but why wouldn't he be? We both shared a pretty serious work ethic. I sculpt. And I . . . I guess I should tell you I slept with him now and then. Nothing serious, but, well, it was handy for both of us.'

'When did you see him last?'

'I slept with him last night. A kind of good-luck fuck. Oh God, that sounds terrible.' Tears swirled now. 'I didn't mean it that way. I was happy for him, you know? I took over a bottle of champagne, and we drank it, and had sex, and I came home. I've been working all day, so I didn't see him before he left to load in.'

'Is that one of his paintings?'

Astrid nodded when Eve gestured to a study of a woman with gold and green hills behind her back as she stood in a garden with a basket on her hip and her face lifted to the sun.

'Yes. He painted it when he lived in Italy. That's Tuscany, one of my favorite places. I bought it shortly after he moved in here.' She let out a sigh. 'I could afford it, and this space. Family money. It's why I only use my first name. I really want to make my own name. Got a ways to go yet.

'But Angelo? He was going to bust out. He was already getting serious attention. And he had years and years ahead of him. And now, he's gone? Right at the start of his rise? A fucking gas leak?'

'It wasn't a gas leak.'

'I don't understand. You said explosion.'

'Would you come across the hall?'

Eve led the way to where Peabody conducted a search.

Astrid didn't gasp. She moaned, a deep, guttural moan. 'No, no, no. Who would do this? Who could do this? His work. Monsters. Fucking monsters.'

Tears didn't just swirl now, but streamed.

'Who would do this?' Eve echoed.

'I don't know. I don't know anyone who'd do this.' Weeping, she knelt down, touched a ripped canvas. 'I hope they burn in hell for it. Maybe, maybe some can be restored. They'd never be the same, but there are some good restoration artists. He didn't deserve this. He didn't—'

She broke off, and those tears shut off like a tap turned. 'Not a gas leak. What kind of cop are you?'

'We're Homicide.'

'Murder.' With the hands balled and shaking at her sides, Astrid got slowly to her feet. 'You're saying someone murdered Angelo.'

'And four others.'

'An explosion? Somebody set off a bomb. At the Salon. His work there. His work here.'

Her face went as hard as the stone on her workbench. 'Oh, I see. I see. Three reasons, there are only three reasons I see.'

'What are they?'

'Somebody's just crazy – straight crazy. Somebody crazy jealous because he was about to bust out. Or somebody who figures a dead artist's work – especially if a lot of it is gone – is worth a hell of a lot more than a live one's.'

'Do you know anyone who fits any of those reasons?'

'I don't. I'd tell you if I did. I'd help you hunt them down myself.'

'Who had access to this unit?'

'Just Angelo. Like I said, we slept together sometimes – and we both slept with other people sometimes. I had to knock or buzz. As far as I know, so did everybody. He didn't have any close friends, not really. But he didn't have anybody who hated him, either.'

'Did he ever mention Jordan Banks?'

'Not to me.'

'Hugo Markin?'

'No, sorry.'

'Wayne Denby.'

'Sure. He's one of the owners of the Salon. I actually met him a couple times. He came over to talk to Angelo about which paintings to include in the show, and the fact is, he had a better sense of the flow than Angelo – and Angelo knew it. He's all right, isn't he?'

'No.'

Her lips parted, trembled. 'He had a kid. He talked about his little boy. He was leaving here, he said the first time I met him, to meet his wife and his little boy, taking him to a – a puppet show.'

'Did you see anyone in or around the building today who shouldn't have been? Did you hear anything?'

Astrid shook her head as tears swirled again. 'I've been working all day, I like the music loud. But – Lollie. Maybe Lollie. She watches the street a lot, for inspiration.'

'Which apartment?'

'I'll take you down. Please, I have to do something.' She stared at the torn and sliced canvases. 'I have to do something. I'll take you down.'

'Peabody, keep the scene secured.'

'Affirmative. I let Baxter know the situation. They should be here any minute.'

'Let's go, Astrid.'

'It's just one flight down. I thought you were Lollie when you buzzed. She's been poking at me all day to come down to help her pick out an outfit for tonight. We were going together. She's just had yet another dramafest breakup with her latest guy, so she's— I'm babbling. I'm just pushing out words so I don't think too hard.'

'It's okay.'

The third floor held six units. Astrid walked to one Eve judged to be directly below Richie's main studio space.

The woman who answered wore a paint-splattered white smock over black skin pants. The smock didn't disguise the curvy body beneath.

Her hair streamed in multicolored braids around a stunning face dominated by enormous eyes of tawny gold.

'Finally! Come see which— Oh, sorry. Hi!'

She beamed a smile at Eve.

'Lollie, this is Lieutenant – sorry, I forgot.'

'Dallas.'

'Lieutenant Dallas. She—'

'Oh sure, like the one in the vid. Hi!'

'Not like a vid,' Astrid began.

'Sure it is. I watched it last night and ate a *pint* of ice cream because I felt sad and pissy about Franco. They had an *And the Winner Is* marathon going. I watched a lot of it. Are you going to model for Astrid? That's just entirely frosty. You've got a terrific face.'

'She's not here about that. Sorry,' Astrid said to Eve, and took Lollie by the shoulders. 'Shh. This is bad, Lollie.'

'What's bad?'

'Angelo. He was killed.'

'Don't say that, Astrid. Don't say that. He's getting ready for his opening.'

'It happened at the Salon.' She walked Lollie backward into a room less than half the size of the studios above. An easel with a canvas stood by the big window, a drop cloth beneath. Eve saw the half-finished cityscape as Astrid steered Lollie to a chair.

'Somebody's playing a nasty joke,' Lollie insisted.

'No, it's not a joke. And, Lollie, you're not going to get hysterical or dramatic. This is important, so you're going to wait for that.'

'But . . . Angelo.'

'You talk to Lieutenant Dallas for Angelo. I'm going to get us both a drink. I guess you can't have any wine.'

'No,' Eve confirmed. 'Go ahead.'

She pulled up a stool, faced Lollie. 'When did you last see or speak with Angelo?'

'Just this afternoon. I think it was afternoon or nearly. I hadn't been up too long. I watched that marathon and ate too much ice cream, and I don't have clocks. I don't like to worry about time, but I think about noon. Because of the light.'

'Where did you see him?'

'I was having my energizer, and I saw him leaving, from the window. I opened the window – the small one on the side – and called out. I said: "Good luck, Angelo," and he blew me a kiss. He blew me a kiss, and walked away. I have to cry, Astrid.'

'That's okay, but no hysterics.' She handed Lollie a glass of straw-colored wine, knocked back half a glass herself.

'Did you see anyone in or around the building who shouldn't have been?'

'No. I painted right there. I can see out the window.'

'You're right below his studio. Did you hear anything up there?'

'No. Well, the men who came for the other paintings. I heard the elevator go up.'

'What men?'

'From the Salon, I guess.'

'What did they look like?'

'I don't know, really. I was painting. I just saw the car stop – and I didn't want it in the painting.'

'What kind of car?'

'I guess it was a van, really. A black one. I blocked it and them out because they'd throw off the balance of my painting.'

Eve took a stab. 'Were they old men?'

'I don't . . . They didn't move like old men. I guess I didn't see their faces. They had sunshades on – it's a bright day. And hats. And I was blocking them out. Then I heard the elevator go by and up. It makes a lot of noise.'

'How long after Angelo left?'

'Oh, awhile. Closer to now than then. I don't have clocks,' she said, eyes shining with tears. 'I'm sorry.'

'That's okay.'

'I sort of heard them up there. You don't really hear a lot, but a couple of times I thought they dropped something or stomped around. And then I heard the elevator coming down. Then I saw them carrying out some of Angelo's paintings. It made me think about the opening. I tagged you right after, Astrid, about what to wear.'

'What time?' Eve snapped at Astrid.

'Was that the first time you tagged me, Lollie?'

'How many times did I?'

'Four.'

'The first time was when I saw Angelo leave. I guess maybe it was the third time. Sorry.'

'It's okay.' Astrid rubbed Lollie's shoulder. 'I think that was about two-thirty or three. That's my best guess. The first time was about eleven-thirty, so that would be when Angelo left. And the second was a little after one – because I had to take a break. And the third would have been after two-thirty, but I think before three. Because the fourth was just a few minutes before you came to the door, and I actually looked at the time. It was nearly five.'

'That's helpful. Lollie, what else can you tell me, about the men or the van?'

'I wish I knew more. I don't think they were old because they walked fast. I wanted them to – I just thought: Get out of my painting. The van was new, I think, or really clean. Shiny, and I didn't want shiny.'

'Did it have windows on the sides?'

'No. Just that solid black, and it spoiled—'

'Anything written on the side?'

'Oh, like a company? No. Just black. I know that for sure.'

'How about the hats? What kind of hats?'

'Ooooh.' She gulped wine, closed her eyes. 'I think ear-flaps? I think. I paint landscapes and cityscapes. If I paint people they're just part of the scape – and not detailed. I look closer at things than people because I don't paint people. But they weren't old, and they had on black like the van. Sunshades, for certain. And I think earflap hats. Maybe gloves? I think maybe. I just didn't look at them. They were in the way. And they were only in the painting for a few seconds each time.'

'I'm going to show you a picture. Tell me if you think this might be one of the men.' Eve brought up Markin's ID shot, laid her thumb over the data.

Biting her lip, Lollie studied it. 'I want to say yes because I want to help, but I just don't know. I want to help. I modeled for Angelo. He paid me fair, and it helped me buy paints. I want to help. I'm so sorry.'

'You have helped, both of you.'

'We helped, Astrid.' Lollie turned her face into Astrid's shoulder.

Eve left them, went back upstairs where Baxter and Trueheart worked with Peabody.

'The sweepers are heading in,' Peabody told her.

'We've got an estimated time frame. Richie left about eleven-thirty. The nine-one-one on the bombing came in at fourteen-forty-six. Best estimate for the killers walking out of here with some of Richie's paintings is between fourteen-thirty and fifteen hundred.'

Baxter shook his head. 'No way they tore up all these paintings, loaded up whatever they took in that amount of time – post bomb time. Fifteen minutes? They had to get in, get up, do all this, pack up paintings, get out.'

'That's right. They had Denby wired, so they could watch him. Cut him loose, followed him or dumped him near the Salon, continued here. It's just a few blocks. They were probably in here, packing up what they wanted when the bomb went off. Then they tore up the rest. No need to tear up the rest if Denby didn't follow through. They'd still have a few more paintings, so that's a win either way.'

'Security's crap here,' Baxter considered. 'Wouldn't take much to get through it. Hop the elevator. Already packing material here, just use it, bust things up, cart things out. Transport?'

'Black panel van. Shiny. That's all the wit's got. Two men – in black – sunshades, earflap hats. It's a bright, breezy day, so that's not going to stand out. She didn't get a good look, didn't pay attention, but we've got a black van, the timing, and that's more than nothing.'

'I'll get uniforms to canvass,' Baxter said.

'Do that. Trueheart, start checking rentals of late-model black panel vans.'

'Yes, sir.'

'Baxter, give me what you got from the wife and kid.'

'Same description as the first round. Black clothes, hoods, white masks, black gloves. The wife woke up to a punch in the face in the early hours of Tuesday morning. The husband's unconscious, and one of them punches her again while the other drags her husband to the foot of the bed, binds him to it – he's gagged already.

'She tells them to take whatever they want while they're restraining her to the bed. She saw them snap something under the husband's nose to revive him. He's struggling, one punches her again, tells the husband to sit still, be quiet, or he'll hit her again. Then the other brings in the kid – screaming, crying for his mother. It's like a replay, Dallas. They lock the kid up and away – don't gag him so his parents can hear him crying. The only variation? When they threaten rape, she tells them she's pregnant, begs them not to hurt her little boy or the baby.'

'They hadn't told many people,' Eve concluded. 'The killers' research missed that.'

'They didn't hit her much after that, backed off the rape threats. But . . . ' Baxter hissed. 'Fuckers. The last thing they said to the husband before they dragged her out, locked her downstairs? One pulls out a knife, tells the husband if he doesn't do what they need him to do, he'll slit the little boy's throat. It'll be fast, won't hurt much. But then he's going to cut the baby out of the wife. She'll die slow, and the baby? They'll just have to see.'

Eve walked to the window, stared out. 'Any connection to Rogan, his wife, kid? To Karson?'

'None we've found so far. She didn't know any of them. The kid did say that the one who watched him most read him a couple stories.'

'Not the one who talked about carving a fetus out of the woman.'

'No, the other one.'

'Softer touch. The other one likes the violence, the power of it. Still, they let them live. That's not going to hold if they start on another family. That's going to break, and soon. Trueheart?'

'I've got a couple, Lieutenant. I want to check the suburbs and into New Jersey.'

'Good thinking. Line them up, go run them down. Peabody, let's go harass a few people on our list. Baxter, hold the scene for the sweepers, then start running down the rental vans.'

She started down the steps. 'Do a geographic on the list. We'll take the first couple between here and Central, or close to that. Then you head home, and so will I. We'll try cutting down the list before we start interviewing tomorrow.'

Unless something broke, Eve thought, they were in for a long night, and a longer day after.

16

After interviews, briefings, paperwork, and reports, Eve dragged into the house. And Summerset loomed.

'You're quite late tonight. Nothing lasts forever, I suppose.'

She raked him with tired eyes. 'You've lasted. Gotta be two or three hundred years by now.' She stripped off her coat, tossed it over the newel post, trudged her way upstairs.

When she walked into her office, Roarke and the cat walked out of his. 'There she is.'

'What's left of me.' As the cat rubbed against her legs, she shrugged out of her jacket. Even excellent material and a perfect fit could morph into the misery of a straitjacket after fifteen hours.

Roarke took the jacket before she tossed it at the handiest chair. 'First things,' he said. He took a little case out of his pocket, flipped it open.

Eve scowled down at the tiny blue pain blockers. 'Do you have stock in those things?'

'I ought to by this point. Let's deal with the headache I can all but hear banging, and take five minutes.'

'I could use five minutes.' Though the headache wasn't banging – it was more a muted thumping – she took the blocker, let him nudge her to the sofa. 'You've been working, too.'

'I have, yes, after Summerset and I had a meal together, and he told me a bit more about his holiday.' As he spoke, Roarke shifted Eve, began to knead her shoulders. 'He and Ivanna enjoyed the time together.'

'How am I supposed to ditch the headache if I'm thinking about Summerset sex?'

'I didn't mention sex.'

'It's implied.'

'And if you push that line, we'll both have headaches. To add to these rocks in your shoulders.'

'Crap day. Pretty much crap day.' And wasn't it just fine to lean back into those talented hands? 'I ate. I pulled a Roarke and ordered in pizza for the team.'

'So you said when you texted you'd be late. Points for you.' He leaned forward, laid a kiss on the back of her neck. 'Why don't I get you a glass of wine, and you can fill me in.'

'I'd rather have a beer. I'd rather have coffee,' she added, 'but you'd make those noises about needing a break from coffee. At least beer's a cop drink.'

'I'm no cop, but I'll have one with you. We've still some of Will Banner's brew. That's definitely cop beer. How would that do you?'

'Down to the ground, thanks.'

Already the headache had receded to an annoyed

murmur. The rocks in her neck and shoulders had broken down into irritating pebbles.

The man had a way.

So when he walked back with the beer, sat, she curled into him, wrapped around him.

'Here now,' he soothed.

'It's nothing wrong. It's just ... good to be home, and here. I can take the long, crap days, the multiple DBs in the long, crap days. I can even take feeling like I'm getting basically nowhere after the long, crap days because it's good to be home, and here.'

She tipped her head back, kissed him, then shifted back to sit hip to hip. Took a swig from the pilsner he'd poured. 'Beer's good, too.'

'It is. And I'll wager you've gotten beyond nowhere.'

'It doesn't feel like it. And less like it after each notification. Four today seeing as Baxter notified Denby's wife.'

'How is she?'

'Holding steady. They didn't fuck her up as much as they did the first one. Broken nose, couple broken fingers. They mostly kept the pounding to her face, especially after she told them she was pregnant. They didn't spend as much time on the Denbys. It may be Denby broke sooner than Rogan, or it may be they wanted to hit the loading in instead of the actual opening.'

'You lean toward the first,' Roarke commented.

'Yeah, not only because I think Denby broke sooner, but because they found out they had a pregnant woman on

294

their hands. I think they moved up the timetable. They still accomplished what they wanted, but it meant adjustments, and a daylight B and E.'

She drank again. 'I'm skipping around.'

She walked it back to the home invasion, moved through the destruction of Richie's paintings in his studio.

'We're still checking on rentals of black panel vans, but so far they're all legit. Maybe they own one, or have access to one, or just boosted one for a couple hours and nobody noticed.'

'Will you have your witness at the loft work with Yancy or another police artist?'

'Maybe, but I don't think we'll get anything there. She couldn't even give us skin color, height, nothing. She's three floors up, not paying any attention. We're lucky we got anything. Sweepers' report lists twenty-two canvases destroyed from the loft – fifteen completed, the other seven partials. And nobody but dead Angelo knows how many more were completed, how many they took with them.'

'If that was always the plan, they may not have had a stash of his paintings ahead of the game.'

'Yeah, that's another bitch. Still, you know people in the art-collecting world, and people who know people.'

'I'll poke around there. I can tell you that there will be an immediate boost on the value. As soon as the details and circumstances of his death, and the loss of much of his work, gets out? Well, there are certain collectors who'll pay considerably more due to those circumstances. Particularly.'

'Maybe you know some of those sick bastards?'

'I may know a few, and of more. If this is the plan – and it follows, doesn't it? – they'd have to know at least one.'

'Yeah. They have a connection. Business world/stock market, art collecting. Gambling. I can't figure what's next. They had to have at least one contingency plan, one alternate mark if neither of these worked out. And since they both worked, why not go ahead with the contingency?'

'Some quit while ahead,' he reminded her, but she shook her head.

'Not these two. And it'll be quick, that's pattern, too. Bang, bang, bang. How much did you pay for the painting you've got?'

'Happily, I looked that up, as I thought you might ask. Fifty thousand euros. It's insured now for a hundred twenty-five USD. He was moving up.'

'How much do you figure it's worth now to one of those sick bastard types?'

Roarke took a considering sip of beer as he calculated. 'I expect I could sell it through standard means tomorrow – after the media play – for a quarter million. Through less standard means, if I waited a few days more? As it's learned just how many of his originals exist? Half a million.'

'A hell of a return quick and fast, right? And if you have multiples, some or likely most of which you stole – so no outlay – potentially millions.'

'Smart money would wait a few years, let the legend

ripen – and as he had exceptional talent, died young and tragically, it will. Then you'd turn a painting like ours for several million.'

'They won't wait. Maybe – maybe – they'll hold on to one or two because they like to gamble. But it's quick profit first. The quick score. They've had feelers out, or they're putting them out now.'

'Sell the stocks, sell the paintings,' she mused, 'take the cash. Pure profit. That's where we have to focus. It's the greed that'll get them. That's the focus until I can figure out their next target.'

'The problem with tracking the stocks is the use of side sales, day-trading, numbered accounts, working it offshore and off-planet. And selling off in smallish, strategic bits rather than large lumps. The large lumps are fairly easy to track back to their sources – even considering all the above. And I've found those.'

'Why haven't I heard that before this?' Eve demanded.

'Because they're going to lead you nowhere. Like your rental vans, they've proven legitimate, and nothing that crosses your investigation. Still, I have them for you. You've been a bit busy today.'

'Yeah. Yeah. Sorry. Thanks. I mean it.'

'And what is it besides fatigue and frustration weighing down on you?'

'Eighteen dead's a lot of weight.'

'What else?'

She drew a breath. 'I told Peabody Nadine could

take her to the Oscar thing. And McNab. How you and Leonardo are handling the wardrobe part of it. So she – Jesus.'

After staring into her glass, she put the half glass of beer aside, pushed up. 'She didn't say anything at first, then she does the stand-up thing. Can't leave in the middle of an investigation, so I knocked that back. Then she started blubbering. Just blubbering, and telling me how this is some lifelong fantasy dream deal for her. She's out of orbit about it, so out of orbit she even shuts up about it so she doesn't piss me off.'

She hissed, dragged her hands through her hair. 'Then, boom.'

'And that changes things.'

'Christ, yes. She already brought it up – job comes first. No whining about it.'

'That's our Peabody,' he replied.

'I said I wasn't going to think about it yet – we just keep going. But the job comes first. If we can't wrap this up, or if they hit again? I can't cut her loose. I'm not just her friend, she's not just my partner. I'm the boss. I have to do what I have to do.'

'You do, yes.' He rose. 'The job, the dead, the victims all come first. She'd never question that. She's a good cop, so they all come first for her as well. But—'

'There can't be any buts on this,' Eve began.

'But,' he repeated, moving to her, laying his hands on her shoulders. 'I'll be your Peabody.'

'It's not—'

'I'm not a cop,' he interrupted. 'But I have certain skills, and in this particular case, certain connections and insights that should be useful. They're yours while you need them.'

'You've got your own work to deal with.'

'There's nothing that can't wait. Your job may not come first for me, but you do. And Peabody, Nadine, Mavis? They matter a great deal. Beyond that, the victims matter to me as well. You'd do what needs doing, and you'd carry the weight. You'd carry it longer than Peabody, who'd never blame you or the job. So I'll be your Peabody.'

Her chest burned. 'You'd look stupid in that damn magic pink coat of hers.'

'Well now, I've my own, don't I? So you'll work with an expert consultant, civilian, for a few days if needs must, and the woman who matters to both of us can fulfill that lifelong fantasy without guilt.'

He took her hands. 'And I'll enjoy hunting down a pair of murderous, greedy bastards with my clever cop. There's a win for me.'

'What about all the planets and their satellites you're scheduled to buy?'

'Word is they'll still be there next week. If not? Well, look at the money you'll have saved me.'

Eve squeezed his hands, hard. 'She'll blubber again.'

'I won't. And there's a win for you.'

'Okay.' She moved into him. 'But I'm going to work the hell out of the ass she's obsessed with before she leaves.'

Turning, she looked back at her board. 'And if we pin *their* asses, so much the better.'

'Tell her that,' he suggested. 'Send her a memo, take the weight off altogether. You'll both work clearer.'

'I guess we would. I'll do that, then I've got to write a couple reports, update my board.'

'I believe I'll renew acquaintance with a few sick bastards I know in the art world. And since you've no intention of finishing your cop beer, as you'll go for coffee, I'll take it with me.'

She got the coffee, composed the memo.

From: Dallas, Lieutenant Eve
To: Peabody, Detective, Delia
Re: Official Leave
This confirms the leave previously discussed and approved. You are granted official leave of seventy-two hours, commencing Friday at sixteen hundred hours. I will work with my expert consultant, civilian, during that period on current investigations, and any other official business that may ensue during said period.

That's it.

Between this time and the commencement of official leave, be prepared to work your ass off. If I hear any shit about my decision and directive, I will kick whatever is left of your ass.

And done, Eve thought, and began outlining reports. It took twenty minutes for Peabody's response, during which time, Eve concluded, her partner had struggled with righteous objections, resolved herself, and blubbered.

> From: Peabody, Detective Delia
>   To: Dallas, Lieutenant Eve
>   Re: Official Leave
>   Sir. I'm grateful to you for granting this leave, and
> to the expert consultant, civilian, for making said leave
> possible during the course of a challenging investigation. If
> circumstances require this leave to be rescinded, I am prepared
> to return to duty at any time during the seventy-two hours.
>   I am fully prepared to work my ass off until it's as skinny
> as yours. (I wish.)
>   Thank you.

She had to smile, then rose to update her board.

She stood back, studying the new faces as Roarke came in.

'I had one faint glimmer,' he began.

'I'll take a faint glimmer.'

'A contact with – we'll stick with "sick bastard" for now – indicates he received a query several weeks ago. On the dark web, which the sick bastard frequents.'

'About Richie's paintings?'

'About a hypothetical. If the artist of a certain painting, worth an estimated amount, were to die a sudden and tragic death with much of his work destroyed in this tragedy, would the sick bastard be interested in bidding on the painting.'

'That's pretty damn vague. Yet specific.'

'My contact claims he asked for more specifics – after all, if he didn't know the artist in question or the painting, he couldn't speculate. However, several others expressed some interest.'

'It's a sick bastard world.'

'And yet, without sick bastards where would we be? The upshot, for the moment, is the hypothetical refused specifics, instead boasting he'd provide them in the spring. Advising the sick bastards to prepare for bidding.'

'Weeks ago. So they knew about Richie, knew about the plans for the opening, likely had Denby selected as the trigger.' She circled. 'That, the showing and all of the hype around it, would have been set. A date, specific.'

'For marketing, and the hyping, to give Richie time to finish work, to select it. Yes. And no, the meeting for the merger wouldn't have been set weeks ago. It would have been in the works, certainly. But the very definite date and time wouldn't have been set until closer to that date and time.'

'They ended up having to go back-to-back. Probably wasn't their first choice, but to cash in on both, they had to go with the one-two. Still stupid.'

When Roarke took the coffee from her hand to drink it himself, she only scowled a little. She figured she owed him.

'You know the smarter, easier, more direct way to blow up the artist and most of his work? You send Denby to his studio, not to the Salon.'

'Hmm. You know, you're right about that,' Roarke agreed. 'Except, of course, they wouldn't have been able to steal several canvases.'

'That tells me they don't, or didn't, have enough scratch to buy up paintings. They had it for the stocks, but not for the paintings. And they could – what you called it – do the margin thing on the stocks. They didn't have a big hunk of money for stocks and paintings, so they had to do it the stupid way.'

'Stupid, but effective,' he pointed out.

'It still tells me they don't just want money. They need it. Not saying it's not down to basic greed, but to gamble on these deals, they had a relatively small stake. They had to steal the paintings. And they knew they were going to weeks before the opening. Weeks before the meeting at Quantum was set in stone.'

She frowned back at the board. 'It's not a lot, but it's more.'

'And you have more here. Your interviews?'

'Low probability on the left. The three higher on the right. I'm not sold on the three. Except this one.' She tapped a face. 'He has a brother-in-law who's retired army, and a sister – not the one married to army – who's an art broker, based in Florence. And when we interviewed him, he came off nervy and evasive. Something shady there.'

'William O'Donnell.' Roarke studied the ID shot, sipped more coffee. Said, 'Hmm.'

'What?' Instantly, she swung around, eyes narrowed

and focused. 'What kind of *hmm* was that? That was a, you know, some kind of *hmm*.'

'Obviously, I'll need to guard my *hmm*s in the future.'

Eve drilled a finger into Roarke's chest. 'You know this guy?'

'I don't know William O'Donnell, but I knew a Liam Donnelly. Back in Dublin in the bad old days, and here and there a few times since.'

'He's got fake ID? Son of a bitch.'

Even as she swung again toward her command center, Roarke took her arm. 'Hold on a minute.'

'He may be a friend of yours, but—'

'Not a friend so much as a former colleague, we'll say. He was a decent B and E man. Had some years on me when we both ran in Dublin. We had a few . . . enterprises in common over the years. Where did you find him?'

'As William O'Donnell he's a mechanical engineer at Econo.'

'Is he now? He always did have a hand for mechanics, as I recall. I'd heard he'd retired from those other enterprises. Or for the most part.'

'Decent enough at B and E to get through security at Rogan's, at Denby's? A one-eyed moron could get through the security at Richie's building.'

'He'd have improved considerably to have gotten through my system at the Rogan's house, but it's not impossible he did. What is? He'd never be a part of murder. In tormenting women and children. It's not Liam, not at all.'

'People change.'

'So they do, as you and I illustrate very well. But the core rarely does. It's not Liam, Eve. He had a mother and three sisters he adored. I'd wager he still does. The only time I ever saw him use violence was when a . . . compatriot slapped a bar girl. Liam stood, lifted his chair, and slammed it into the idiot's face. Broke several teeth, as I recall. Then he hauled the man up, ordered him to apologize. No one strikes a woman when Liam Donnelly's about, he said. He never carried a weapon other than a pocket knife.'

'I need him in the box.'

Roarke sighed. 'Give me his contact information to speed it up, and let me speak with him.'

'So he can rabbit before—'

'Bloody hell.'

She saw the flash of hot temper before he turned, paced away. And her own rose to meet it.

'Eighteen dead. Your old pal's a suspect. I'll have him in the box.'

'You know, sometimes the fucking cop is a keen pain in the arse.'

'I'm always the fucking cop.'

The flash of heat had cooled, she noted, and gone brutally cold when he turned back to her.

'And that I know very bloody well. Do you think a man I haven't seen in a fecking decade matters more to me than the eighteen blown to bits? Is that what you think? How do you live with a man such as me?'

'I think old ties can squeeze tight.'

'So tight I'd betray you?'

'Don't put that on me.' The insult boiled under her skin. 'I didn't say anything about betraying.'

'But that's what it would be. If you don't trust me to stand with you for those eighteen, then what the bloody hell are we doing?'

'Back on me,' she said, bitterly.

'And if you put him in the box, a man with a past and false papers, what will happen to him? If he's innocent of the rest, as I know he is, what will happen? Deportation at best, prison at worst, because you won't trust me to hold up my end.'

'If he rabbits?'

'He may have already, but it won't be because he had any part in this. I'll talk to him, and while I do, you run Liam Donnelly. See if you find anything more than I've told you. See if you find a man who'd beat women, frighten children, or drive a father to kill and die.'

'If you're wrong?'

'I'll use every resource I have, and I've more than he, believe me, to hunt him down and put him in your bleeding box with my own hands.'

'Make it fast,' she snapped and, still fuming, went to her command center to do the run.

She had to use Feeney's baby, the IRCCA, as she needed the international run. She found Donnelly easily enough, and his spotty juvenile record. Petty theft, some car boosts.

306

Then it appeared he'd gotten better at his work. Only suspicions of burglary or theft, and always in empty houses or businesses. No muggings, no person-to-person crimes. One arrest tossed for lack of evidence. And one conviction in his late twenties.

He did three years for that one, and then poofed.

But she found not a single citing of violence, of weapon possession.

She pushed on his family, saw his mother lived in Queens near the sister and the retired army. Another sister lived in New Jersey – also married with family – and the third currently lived and worked in Italy.

Nothing criminal on any of them. She couldn't decide if that equaled relief or annoyance.

Then Roarke came back, and she found the annoyance easily.

'He was nervy,' Roarke said as he moved to the cabinet for wine, 'and evasive, as he knew your reputation. He was frightened. He knew about the bombing, of course. He works at Econo, as you know.'

Roarke poured wine while she sat and said nothing.

'He never thought the cops would give him more than a cursory glance, as he had no connection to the meeting or anyone in it. When you interviewed him this evening, he was shaken. He has a wife and three children, as you also know. He met his wife as William O'Donnell, twelve years ago. After he'd come to New York – before he was . . . retired. He retired after their first child was born – that's nearly eleven years now. And before they married, he told his wife about Liam and the time he'd spent in prison and the rest. She married him anyway. But they haven't told the children, you see.'

He looked at her now as he sipped the wine. 'And he was afraid you'd push deep enough to see through the identification he's used all these years, the life he's built. He was afraid he'd have to leave his family, or decide to uproot them all and run.

'You can contact his sister in Italy. He says if Richie was becoming important, his Colleen would know, and would help you in any way she could. He hopes you wouldn't need to speak with his brother-in-law, who knows nothing of his life before, as it could cause friction in the family, but he won't run. He trusts me enough not to, as I told him I trusted you weren't interested in uprooting three children or punishing him for false papers.

'He's terrified,' Roarke finished. 'But he's putting the life he's built in your hands because I asked him to.'

He crossed to her. 'So where does that leave us, Lieutenant?'

'You say you understand the job comes first, then you slap at me when it does.'

'And you ask me to work with you when it suits, but yank back when my way of doing the job veers from yours. Even,' he said before she could speak, 'if both ways put those who've died first and foremost. Pushing at Liam would have eaten up your time and energies – as it already has more than it needed to.'

'Chasing him down if he was part of this would've eaten more.'

'True enough, but he's not. And you're too good a cop to have looked into his past and thought otherwise. We both know there are ways of doing the job other than pulling a man out of his house and grilling him in the box. And both of us, Eve, skirt our particular lines when we have to, or when the other needs it.'

'It's easier for you.'

He angled his head. 'Do you think so?'

She let out a breath. 'I like to think so. I don't like thinking how many times you've compromised or moved your line. It makes the scales too uneven.'

'They're level enough from where I stand. What I can't tolerate is thinking your trust in me has limits.'

'It doesn't. Fuck.' She had to put her head – throbbing again – in her hands. 'It wasn't not trusting you. It was not trusting some guy you acknowledged was a thief – a guy who checked off several boxes – just because you have some fond memories.'

He drank more wine. 'If I jiggle my line a bit, we can call that fair enough. But I'd never jeopardize your investigation over fond memories.'

'He was the best shot I had so far. Markin's another, but I haven't been able to pin it down. Now this guy is off the list. I'm still checking out his alibi.'

'I'd expect no less. Nor would he. I'll go make another couple of contacts. And you should drink some water.

It'll help revive the blocker a bit to push back the fresh headache.'

'It's annoying when you look in my head.'

'I just have to look in your eyes. I know how they look when they're fighting pain. Drink some water,' he said, and left her.

17

When he judged he'd done all he could for the night, Roarke found Eve asleep at her command center.

Second night running, he thought. She would push herself to exhaustion, carrying the weight of eighteen dead. And no point, he decided, in beating against that wall. That was the woman he loved, no matter how much she could – and did – infuriate him.

He glanced at the work on her screen, noted she'd juggled, yet again, names on her list. From most to least probable.

She'd do better, he knew, when she conducted her face-to-face interviews. She had a master's skill in reading people, the nuances of tone, gestures, a look in the eyes, a turn of phrase.

Oh, she had her blind spots, he thought, but then he did as well. Still, he didn't care for it, not one bit, when one of those blind spots centered on him.

However irritated he remained, he gathered her up.

She jerked, might have struck out. Fortunately for both of them her reflexes remained keen.

'I was just—'

'Past the point where coffee can keep you going,' he said as he carried her to the elevator.

'I drank the water.'

'Good.'

He carried her into the bedroom, where Galahad was already sprawled on the bed, belly-up like roadkill. After sitting her on the side of the bed, Roarke sat himself to take his boots off.

His boots, she thought, not hers. Maybe a small, stupid thing, she considered, but she knew a flick in the eye when it stung her.

She was, as he'd thought himself only minutes before, very good at reading nuances.

'If you want to stay pissed off—'

'It isn't a matter of want.'

'Fine. If you're *going* to stay pissed off, I can stay right there with you.' She yanked off her own boots, tossed them aside before she shoved up to strip off her weapon harness.

'I took him off the list, didn't I? I'm not going to report him over the fraudulent ID. But you should tell him he's on my scope now.' In angry clicks and bangs, the contents of her pockets hit the dresser. 'So if he's not retired, or he gets a yen to come out of retirement, I'll bust him. And that'll be on him.'

Roarke rose to take off the sweater he'd changed into after his workday. 'I did.'

'Fine. Good.' She dragged off her belt with a snap like a

whip. 'And goddamn it, if I didn't trust you, you wouldn't get within fifty klicks of an investigation.'

'Unless it suited you.'

Hot, molten, *flaming* fury erupted against his cold and bitter ice. 'Bullshit.' She stalked over to him. 'Bullshit, bullshit.' Shoved him. 'Bollocks.'

'Careful.' His voice, dangerously quiet, only pumped up the heat for her.

'Oh, bite me.' Shoved him again. 'I opened the door, and I can close it because I'm the one with the badge. I'm in fucking charge. I opened it, and I leave it the hell open *because* I trust you. So knock it off.'

Viciously pleased to see flashes of heat melting the arctic ice in his eyes – damned if she'd be the only one on boil – she pushed again. Then added an insulting gesture he'd once pulled on her. She flicked his shoulder.

'There, I knocked it off for you.' And there it was, the hot blue center of the flame. She started to flick his other shoulder. He grabbed her hand; she lifted her chin.

And they lunged at each other.

They landed on the bed in a grappling heap. The cat didn't just leap up, he hissed, nearly spat before he stalked away. Ignoring him, they rolled over the bed, fighting for dominance.

Until she grabbed Roarke's hair by the fistfuls and dragged his mouth down to hers.

A brutal meeting of lips, teeth, tongues became a greedy ravishing. Temper-fueled lust scorched through blood, burning away any thought of care, of caution, as he tore her sweater away, yanked down her tank.

And when that greedy mouth fixed on her breast, the shock of sensation held her on the tenuous edge between pleasure and pain. She clung there, breath tattered, a red haze of need clouding her mind, and her body alive, wildly alive.

Her fingers dug into his back, his hips, nails biting. She wanted flesh – the feel, the taste of flesh – wanted him – hard, hard, hard – inside her. She scissored her legs, shifted the balance to roll again, fought to strip him, strip herself, to take what she wanted.

Take him. Be taken. And now.

He reared up, and now his hand took her hair, yanking her head back to expose her throat. Fed there while his hands moved roughly down her body, that long warrior's body he craved like his next breath.

When his fingers speared into her, she came on a cry that held triumph and shock. And wanting both, more of both, he drove her up again.

In that instant, that glorious instant when she went limp, before she could gather and rise again, he shoved her onto her back. Plunged into her.

One instant, one more instant while they both gripped that toothy edge, while they hung together in air too thick to draw in, where their eyes met – flaming blue, molten brown.

They took each other, driving, driven in a fever of need, a mad thirst for more, still more. Lost in the storm, he muttered in Irish, words both incoherent and savage.

When pleasure, building, building, impossibly building, peaked, it slashed like a blade.

She lay under him, weak, dizzy, empty of anger. And somehow tendrils of sorrow trailed in to fill the void.

'It's not you I don't trust. It's never you.'

'It's never me you want to distrust,' he countered. 'But there are still times, just now and then, when those cop's eyes are on me and say different.'

He rolled off her. 'The heart and the brain don't always mesh, do they? I know your heart, darling Eve, but your brain still has some mysterious corners.'

They'd scattered clothes over the bed. He considered just kicking them to the floor, but as he needed a minute to settle himself, he rose to dump them in a handy chair.

When he turned back to the bed, she'd rolled onto her stomach, and slept.

Heart, brain, body, he thought, all meshing in this case with pure exhaustion.

He drew the covers over her, slipped in beside her. And waited for sleep to come.

The air smelled of smoke, blood, burnt flesh. She saw the charred remains, the blackened severed limbs where skin had bubbled off the bone. The blood – black as tar – splashed over the walls like a vicious painting.

One wall, blinding white, held all the names of the dead beneath the spatter.

Eighteen, and room for more.

Two men stood in the room, men dressed in black with white masks. They spoke in whispers, words she couldn't quite hear. She reached for her weapon, but it wasn't there. Not her sidearm, not her clutch piece. Prepared to take them on unarmed, she charged.

But what she'd seen as shadows stood as a wall. Impenetrable.

Desperate, she searched for a door, an opening, found none. She moved back through the dead to give herself room, ran full out, throwing her body up at the last minute to strike the wall with a violent kick.

It repelled her like a hand swatting at a fly. She tried again, again, slamming the wall with kicks and punches until her fists left smears of blood.

The men simply watched her from behind their masks.

One laughed, then slapped the second on the shoulder in a gesture of shared humor.

'Well now, how long you figure she'll keep up with all that?'

She heard Ireland – thicker, deeper than Roarke's. It made her stomach flutter in a kind of sick dread.

'That one? Always was a stubborn little bitch.'

Now her stomach twisted as dread dropped to fear and resignation. The men pulled off the masks – no need for them, after all.

She stood facing Richard Troy and Patrick Roarke with a shadowy wall between.

'The boy always was a fuckup,' Patrick Roarke claimed.

'But still he's got my looks, so you'd think he could do better than that one. And a cop for all of that as well.'

'She's a killer.' Troy smiled wide and bright. 'I'm dead proof of it.'

'That right. You're dead,' Eve said. 'Both of you. A long time dead.'

'But there are so many more like us,' Troy reminded her. 'We just keep coming, little girl. Beat yourself against the wall of that, and we still keep coming.'

'There are always more like me.'

'Look around you. Can't keep the dead from piling up, can you now?' Patrick Roarke laughed, then as the shadows shifted, poured whiskey from a bottle into two glasses.

As they clinked glasses, drank, she saw they stood in a room with a bed, and on the bed a figure struggled. She couldn't see through the shadows, but saw the movements, heard the screams muffled by a gag.

'And more to come.' Troy lifted his glass in toast to another wall.

It cleared to show the people behind it. And her heart began to pound in her chest.

Peabody, Mavis, oh God, the baby, Feeney.

She rushed, beat against the wall.

Nadine, Baxter, Leonardo, McNab. More. Everyone, everyone who mattered. Summerset, Whitney, Trueheart, Charles, Louise, Crack. Her whole squad, Reo, everyone milling around the room as if at some goddamn party.

Mira, Dennis Mira, Morris.

317

Every time she blinked, more appeared in the room.

Though she beat on that wall, shouted, no one heard, no one saw.

Everyone, everyone who mattered to her. But the one who mattered most.

'Where's Roarke? Goddamn you, where's Roarke?'

She rushed back – the figure on the bed. God, oh God.

The two men sat at a table, counting money with a mountain of it at their backs.

'You can never have too much of it, can you, Paddy?'

'No indeed, Richie, no indeed. And the getting more's the fun of it.'

Shifting shadows. She started to call to Roarke, to swear to him she'd find a way to get to him. But when the shadows cleared, she didn't see him. She saw herself, bound to the bed, struggling, terrified.

The red light blinked on and off, on and off as it had a lifetime before in a horrible room in Dallas.

'More fun this way.' Troy wagged a thumb to the next wall. 'Look who's joining the party.'

The moan rolled out of her soul. Roarke stepped in – everyone, everyone, everyone who mattered – with the suicide vest locked around him.

On a scream, she launched herself against the wall. She felt her arm break – the snap of a twig – and threw herself against the wall again.

'Roarke! Don't, don't, don't. It's a lie. Look at me. Roarke!'

Spiderweb cracks sizzled over the wall. As he reached

for the button, she screamed again, reared back to charge through the cracks.

'Stop it now. You stop it. You need to wake up. Christ Jesus, Eve, you bloody well will wake up!'

She snapped back, saw his eyes. Just his eyes. On a choked sob she grabbed at him, pressed to him. 'You can't. You won't. Swear you won't. You have to swear to me.'

'Stop now, stop. It's a dream, just a dream.'

'You can't – You're wet. Is that blood?' She shoved back, ran her hands over him.

'Of course it's not blood. It's only water. I was having a shower,' he said, calm and gentle as he stroked her back. 'I heard you screaming. And now I'm dripping all over you. Let me get that throw over you.'

'Just hold on.' Shaking, she wrapped her arms around him again. 'Just hold on.' The cat bumped his head against her so she reached down to try to soothe. But her hand shook violently.

'You need to slow down your breathing. Slow breaths, baby. A bad dream, nothing more. I'm right here. I'm just getting the throw. You're freezing.'

'No, no. Don't let go.'

'Look here, look at me now.' He tipped her head up. 'A dream, all right? You understand me?'

'It felt real. I could feel . . .'

His heart squeezed when she gripped a hand on her own arm.

'Were you back in Dallas?'

'No. Yes. Not exactly.'

'You need to get warm, then you'll tell me. Here now.' He pulled the throw over, wrapped it around her.

'You're cold, too. And wet. I'm sorry.' She gathered the cat up, stroked him. 'I'm sorry.'

'You hold on to him – you could both use it. I'll get you a soother.'

'I don't want a soother.'

'We'll split one.'

She pressed her face to Galahad's fur. 'You need to get warm.'

'I'll just get a towel, then we'll split that soother and you'll tell me.'

With her face still buried, she nodded.

He ordered the fire on as he walked to the bathroom, ordered the jets he'd left running to shut down. Then he dropped his forehead to the glass tiles and took his first true breath since he'd heard her scream.

Screaming, he thought, as if someone hacked at her with an axe. And so deep in that nightmare she'd been mired, he hadn't been able to pull her out at first. She'd just screamed. Even when her eyes had flashed open, wide and blank, she'd screamed.

He dragged a hand through his dripping hair, grabbed a towel to drape over his hips, and went back to her.

She hadn't moved an inch.

He programmed the soother to split, brought the glasses over to sit on the bed with her again.

'Drink some, and tell me.'

She didn't argue.

'I think I knew it was a dream at first. At first. It was a crime scene. The bodies – after the explosion – but all of them. Just all those pieces of people, and the whiteboard with their names. All their names. I know their names.'

He took her hand, kissed it. 'Yes.'

'Then I saw the two of them – black clothes, white masks – talking – whispering. But I didn't have my weapons. I didn't have them, so I went at them to fight, to take them down, but . . . You couldn't see the wall. I could see through it, and they were on the other side. I couldn't get through the wall. They saw me, and I could hear them, and I knew . . .

'They took off the masks, but I already knew. Richard Troy and Patrick Roarke.'

Sorrow clouded his eyes as he stroked a hand on her cheek. 'We'll never altogether be done with them, will we?'

She shook her head, told him the rest.

'The room, the other room, so many people. Every time I looked, more people. But not you. I thought you were in the room with the two of them. A prisoner. And I would've gotten you out. I would've found a way.'

'Of course you would.' He kissed away the tears on her face. It broke his heart when she wept.

'But it wasn't you.' She had to fight to breathe again, to hold back the horror. 'When I could see through the shadows, it wasn't you. It was me. And then I knew. I knew what they'd done. Then I saw you, in the room with everyone, everyone who matters. I saw you, and the vest.'

Because it threatened to swamp her again, she drank the last of the soother. 'I screamed for you – you couldn't hear me. I beat on the wall, and tried to break through. It started to crack, but you were reaching for the button. I had to get in, had to get in. If I couldn't stop you . . . I couldn't stand being without you. I can take anything, but I couldn't take that. You have to swear to me.'

'*A ghrá*, it didn't happen. And it won't. Didn't we already say we'd find another way?'

She gripped his hand until her knuckles went white. 'You have to swear to me. You have to believe I'd find a way to get out, and swear to me you'd never push the button. Swear it.'

'And if it had been me, a prisoner?'

'You'd find a way.'

He leaned over, touched his lips to hers. 'And there you have it, so I'll say again what we said before. We'd find a way. I'll swear to you, and you'll swear to me. There's trust between us, isn't there? We'd find a way.'

'Yes.' She let out a breath. 'Yes. I swear it.'

'And so do I. Those fucking bastards, and any like them? They won't win. We won't let them.'

She rested her head against his shoulder, and let it go.

'You were already up.'

'A holo conference. I'll reschedule, and we'll get a bit more sleep.'

Meaning, she knew, he'd put his work aside, stay with her in hopes she'd get more sleep.

'No, I'm getting up. I'll feel better if I get going, get something done. You need to put on one of your emperor suits.' She ran a hand down his bare chest, felt his heartbeat. 'I'm going to get a workout in, sweat the rest out of me.'

'All right then. I'll be an hour or so,' he added as he moved to his closet.

She sat as she was, wrapped in the throw, holding the cat while he selected a suit. 'You're still a little pissed off, but now you're worried on top of it. It's hard to be both.'

Oh aye, his cop knew her nuances, he mused as he chose a shirt, gray as storm clouds. 'I'll manage.'

'Because you're good at multitasking.'

'There is that,' he agreed, reaching for the tie he wanted that slashed bold blue over storm-cloud gray. He wandered closer to the bed as his clever fingers fashioned the tie into a perfect Trinity knot. 'It's also that over and under and through being a little bit pissed off and worried with it, I love you with all I am, and ever hope to be.'

Her eyes stung again, but she kept them trained on him. 'There is that.'

He smiled, leaned down to brush his lips to hers. When her arms wrapped around him, he sat, drew her in. 'Rescheduling's not a problem.'

She shook her head, but burrowed for one more minute. 'No, I'm good. Besides, you went from naked to god of all he surveys in about six and a half minutes.' Easing back, she tapped the complicated knot of the tie. 'How'd you do that without even looking?'

'Talent.'

'Well, go do your business-god thing with your classy tie. I'll see you in an hour or so.'

'Or so.' He pressed his lips to her brow, left her.

She sat another moment, stroking the cat into thunderous purrs. She'd told him she wanted a workout mostly to stop him from worrying. Still, maybe a good sweat would drown the dregs of the dream.

Rising, she knocked back a quick shot of coffee, pulled on a tank, baggy shorts, and running shoes while Galahad watched her.

'I'm fine,' she told him. 'Or I will be. You could use a workout yourself, pudge boy.'

He blinked his bicolored eyes, rolled over to stretch out on his back. Cat of leisure.

She took the elevator down. In the gym she programmed the beach, took a minute to just bask in the sights, sounds, and feel of blue ocean, white sand. And with the surf rolling, she ran three miles full out. Somewhere in mile two, she stopped thinking.

With her skin cased in a good, healthy sweat, she guzzled water, then turned to weights, lifted until her muscles trembled.

As she stretched, she eyed the sparring droid. She wouldn't have minded a good, vicious bout, but she'd nearly hit the hour.

'Next time.' She pointed a finger at the droid. 'I'm kicking your ass.'

Upstairs she found Galahad had deserted his post. Probably down with Summerset for breakfast, she decided, and hit the shower – and there she washed away the last of the dream in blissfully hot water, steam, pulsing jets.

By the time Roarke came back, she'd pulled on black trousers, a crisp white shirt, and her weapon harness. Breakfast sat under warming domes.

'Were you a benevolent god or a wrathful one?'

'A bit of both. Keeps them guessing.' She looked herself, he thought, strong and ready. Most of the worry he carried drained.

He poured himself coffee, topped off hers. It didn't surprise him to find waffles under the domes.

He sat with her. 'And what's first on your agenda today?'

'Briefing. I'm going in early to set that up, and to work out the interview assignments.' She drowned her waffles in butter and syrup. 'With two teams, we should be able to knock a good chunk off that list. Or pin somebody to the freaking wall.'

'I'll hope for the latter. What would you like me to do for you today?'

'Just focus on world domination.'

'I always do, as I find it entertaining and profitable. But multitasking, I'd enjoy an assignment.'

'Follow the money. Yeah, yeah, you always do that, too.' She ate waffles. 'Every day would dawn brighter with waffles.'

'We haven't quite hit dawn yet.'

'When we do, it'll be brighter. Anything you can scrape up on the stocks, the art. If we don't make real progress today ...' She stabbed another bite of waffle. 'Eighteen dead. When I weigh that against the line crossed by using the unregistered, the dead win.'

'It's likely I'd find more without being hampered by CompuGuard.'

'Yeah, and it wouldn't be the first time. I need to push the interviews first. If I thought they were done, if I didn't feel dead certain they've got another scheme in the works—'

'You could push through it your way. And you'd find them, I've no doubt of it, sooner or later.'

'It's the later that's burning my gut. Contingencies. They had to have them, at least one contingency. One more they could work either to replace one that went south, or for the triple play.'

'You think they'd always planned for three, even four,' Roarke concluded.

'They had to rush the timing of the first two when the merger meeting scheduled on top of the art opening. They probably planned to hit both, but with a little more time between. And then a third. They're gamblers. Three's a lucky number, right?'

'All numbers are lucky when you hit them. But,' he added, 'the gamblers I've known – the professional, the passionate, the addicted – they're a superstitious lot. Added to it, they'd believe in the streak.'

'These two are on one. Another stock or art deal? Those are most logical. But I can't find anything that fits, not in New York. How many major mergers, how many artists on the brink? Not that many right in New York City, not on top of each other.'

'You'd have to consider international,' he pointed out. 'Even off-planet. The world's full of mergers and emerging artists.'

'Yeah, and I can't eliminate that altogether. But they have to stalk the target, his family. They have to watch and research. They have to be as certain as possible he'll push that button. Now, maybe one of them goes off to wherever to do the legwork, then the other comes in to double-team the family. But that splits them up, and I think they're too dependent on each other.'

She polished off the waffles, opted for another hit of coffee.

'One of them's softer. He doesn't wrap the first kid up tight before they leave, and he reads stories to the second kid. How does the dominant one trust the softer one not to fold unless he's there, propping him up, keeping the buzz going?'

'And how,' Roarke considered, 'does the softer one make sure the more violent doesn't cross the line if he's not there to keep him steady?'

'Exactly.' Shaking her head, she rose. 'So no, bad risk to separate. And why extend the target area, adding expense with travel, rooms? If they have jobs, how do you get that kind of time off? And this is New York. Anything you need to find, you can find it here.'

She picked up the jacket – black, leather flaps on the pockets, thin leather cuffs on the sleeves – pulled it on over the weapon harness. 'The work's figuring out what or who needs to be destroyed so they can make a profit, and how to connect a devoted family man to that what or who. Eliminate the stock market, the art world, and calculate where they'd try next.'

She studied him as she filled her pockets. 'You're not their kind of gambler,' she considered. 'When you gamble in business, you know the odds, the ups, downs, ins and outs. You know the players and the house. You usually are the house. When you gamble for play, it's just that. Play. But still, you gamble. That place you bought in Nebraska, for instance, because we sort of made a bet.'

'No "sort of" about it, and it's coming along quite nicely.'

Her eyes narrowed. 'Real estate's a gamble.'

'Ah.' He sat back, intrigued. 'Interesting. And yes, it certainly is.'

The idea had a little buzz going in the back of her brain. 'Blowing up that wrecked farm out in Nowhereville – what would that get you?'

'If I'd insured it well, there'd be that, but you'd only go there if, for a variety of reasons, getting rid of it gets you out of debt or a deal.'

'Okay, shift to a building here in New York.'

'Do I own it?'

'You? Probably. Them, less certain. What would they gain by blowing up a building – or a person or persons involved in that building?'

'Well now, it's a puzzle you've given me without many of the pieces.'

'Quick profit. Nothing long-term.'

'Insurance again, but it takes more than a man in a suicide vest to destroy a building. Damage it, yes. Enough its value goes down. You could pick it up cheaply, but that's a long-term investment, and that piece doesn't fit. Kill the people who own the building? What does that get you? An interesting puzzle.'

'You own a lot of buildings, and you have a lot of people working for you.'

Now he rose, walked to her, ran his hands down her arms. 'And I have security, the sort they'd never get through.'

'You don't have security on every place you go – a lunch meeting at a restaurant, a meeting at another building.'

'Few have access to my schedule on any given day,' he reminded her. 'Summerset, Caro.'

'The people on the other end of the meeting,' she countered. 'I don't see the finished puzzle, either, but say, maybe, we have a few of the pieces here, you could do me a big favor.'

'What would it be?'

'Mix things up today. Change the schedule around. And check on your people, especially any who have access to your HQ, your office. And since you're you, you can run a check on people on the other side of the meetings you've got on your plate. Anybody who hasn't come into work today, or for a couple days.'

'I can do that, especially if it stops you from worrying. And I'll play with this puzzle. Real estate's a world I know.'

'Good. I'm going to head in, get a jump start.' She leaned in to kiss him. 'Take care of my business god. Please.'

'Done. Take care of my cop.'

When she left, he checked the time. Far too early to disturb Caro and begin the shuffling of the day's schedule. In any case, he had another meeting. As he headed to his office, he decided after that and before the post-dawn day began, he'd work a bit on the puzzle.

18

For the second time since the investigation started, Eve drove to Central before sunrise. She wondered if she could train her body and brain to subsist on four or five hours of sleep most nights, like Roarke. Then she could make the commute before the streets clogged with traffic, the skies filled with noisy ad blimps.

Still, she'd rather not finish off the four or five hours with a nightmare.

He'd be careful, she assured herself. It wasn't as if her dreams were prophetic. Her subconscious ruled there, and sometimes it pushed the worst of her thoughts and fears to the surface.

Love pushed the button, she thought. In her dream, in reality. Who else who loved so deeply had these murderers-by-proxy targeted?

Most likely a male, a father of at least one young child. No, she considered, almost certainly only one young child. More than one complicated it, made it more difficult to restrain and control.

They'd stick with an only child unless they didn't have a choice.

Most likely male, married, a father – one kid . . . twelve or under, she thought. Older, again, more difficult to control, not as helpless. And most likely a father between the ages of thirty-five and forty-five. It could tip slightly over either end, but that was the sweet spot in her mind.

Single-family home. Multifamily brought in complications again. Proximity to neighbors, more chances of being seen or heard.

Successful man with at least some power and status in his business or employment. Someone who wouldn't be questioned when walking into the key area.

And she'd bet, just bet, one or both of the killers had crossed paths with both targets. Not friends, she thought as she swung into the garage at Central. Not directly connected. But they'd crossed paths. Golf, tennis, the gym, a favorite restaurant, the theater, the vids, buying a damn tie or a pair of shoes.

Easy to cross paths with Denby, she thought as she walked to the elevator. You just had to stroll into the Salon. An art lover, or just a browser. A salesman, another artist.

Chewing on it, she got in the elevator, headed up.

She ignored the cops nearing the end of their shift who trudged on, and the LC with the black eye and split lip who stood stoically on legs scraped raw at the knees.

Because the LC smelled of stale sex and resignation, Eve got off and took the glides the rest of the way to Homicide.

In her office, she updated her board and book to reflect the night's work. She reupped her hold on the conference room, sent memos to her team to report there.

She shot off a text to Feeney asking him to attend the briefing if it worked with his schedule.

After running a probability – ninety-six-point-eight – she sent an inquiry to Mira asking for confirmation or rebuttal on her belief that both killers would remain in New York, in close proximity, and keep their targets in the city.

Couldn't be a hundred percent, she mused, but if Mira agreed, it added weight.

As the sun came up, filtered light through her skinny window, she reviewed her squad's caseload – what remained open, what had been closed. What looked to be going cold or heating up.

Made notes.

Finally she gathered what she needed – including a pot of real coffee – and walked to the conference room.

In the quiet she set up the board, lining up the data on interviewees by priority. She earmarked Hugo Markin for a second pass. Not just because he was a prize dick, she told herself. But because there was something there. She felt it in her gut.

Though she'd have preferred to toss the job to Peabody, she struggled her way through programming the data she wanted to put on-screen.

Just as she finished, Feeney walked in.

'You couldn't have gotten here fifteen minutes ago?'

'Why?'

'Nothing.' On a huff of breath, she shoved her hands through her hair, relieved to have the programming off her task list. 'You're here early.'

'A second ago I was fifteen late. Is that real coffee?'

'Yeah.'

He helped himself. 'I got a shit-ton of paperwork piling up. Figured I'd come in early and deal with it. Now I've got an excuse not to, and real coffee. It's a good day.'

He drank half the mug. 'Before they get their lovebird asses in here, are you still cutting Peabody loose tomorrow?'

'Yeah. I was going to cancel it – had to – but Roarke stepped in. He'll cover for her. How did I get to the point I'm letting a civilian cover for my partner?'

'It's the right civilian.'

'Yeah, but still … Shit. Do you have to pull McNab back in?'

'Nah. I've got enough boys to work his stuff. You can have Callendar if you need her, since she's got a good rhythm with you and the rest. The wife says I gotta watch this year, and won't take no.' He grimaced into his coffee. 'I gotta watch a bunch of Hollywood types in fancy getups making speeches and shit. I blame you.'

'Me?' Shock, insult vibrated. 'Blame Nadine.'

'I blame her, too.' He looked at the board, scanned the names, the faces. 'How sure are you they're on there?'

'At least one of them's there. At least one. You don't break into one of Roarke's places – and this one was high-end – unless you live there or have legit access. I think he or they live there. Know the building, knew Banks. That's what plays, and since it plays, these are the ones who best fit the profile.'

She got more coffee as he studied the board. 'I have to watch, too.'

'Your own fault.'

'It's Nadine's fault,' Eve insisted, with considerable frustration. 'I was doing the job. She wrote the damn book, then the script thing. And if she wins this thing? Every time I think it's going to ease off – there are people saying: Oh, I read the book, saw the vid. Big fan! Like I give a cold *crap* about any of that. If she wins this damn thing, it's going to be an even bigger pain in my ass.'

She cut herself off mid rant when Whitney stepped in.

'Sir.'

'Lieutenant, Captain. I noted you'd reserved the conference room. I'm only here for a short time this morning, as Anna and I are attending Derrick Pearson's memorial.' He walked to the board as he spoke. 'He's one of eighteen now.'

'It's a tough one, Commander,' Feeney said.

'Yes.'

They went back, Eve knew. Way back. But it wouldn't be Jack and Ryan under these circumstances.

'Are these your primary suspects?'

'At this time, yes, sir.'

'From your last report, you've found no direct link to either Paul Rogan or Wayne Denby.'

'Not to them or to any of the victims as yet.'

'Not to Derrick,' Whitney murmured. 'So if I happen to see one of these faces at the memorial . . .'

'I'd very much appreciate it, should that transpire, if you would bring said individual into Central.'

Whitney smiled, grimly. 'You can count on it. I'll stay for the briefing, or as much as I can. Is that real coffee?'

'Yes, sir.'

She moved to pour him some herself, heard Peabody's clump, McNab's prance. 'Peabody—' Eve's brows drew together at Peabody's overbright eyes and wildly patterned scarf. 'Before you settle in, go program another pot of coffee from my office.'

'You got it! Good morning, Commander! Hey, Feeney! Be right back!' Exclamation points struck every couple of words before she all but bounced away.

McNab lifted his skinny shoulders in a gesture as sheepish as his smile. 'She's a little buzzed,' he explained to Eve.

'She's what?'

'Departmentally approved booster,' he said quickly. 'She put in a long night because, grateful – me, too – about the Oscar thing. Beyond mega thanks on that, Dallas.'

'Don't mention it. I'm fucking serious.'

'Okay, but see, she gets a little hyped on the boost, but more, before I caught her, she'd dipped into our emergency stash of espresso. It's like gold, you know – we bought it for each other at Christmas. Anyway, she took a shot of that, so she's pretty buzzed out.'

'Keep her under control,' Eve warned.

'Trying.'

Eve pressed her fingers to her eyes. When Baxter and Trueheart walked in, she hoped they'd balance things out.

Then Peabody came in. She'd ditched the scarf and the pink coat. Eve almost preferred them to the screaming red sweater with fussy pink flounces at the cuffs, the shiny, electric-blue jacket, and, *Jesus,* neon green pants with frigging pink flowers down the sides.

'Peabody.' Baxter let out a half laugh. 'You look like a garden.'

'It's almost spring! Coffee!'

'None for you,' Eve snapped.

'Aw!'

'Water,' she ordered McNab. 'Only water.'

'On it.'

'Sit.' She pulled the pot from Peabody, who, she noted with resignation, also smelled like a garden. 'I'm going to summarize where we are, then we'll move on to where we're going. Before I do: Feeney, anything?'

'Entry to the Rogan and Denby houses by the same methods. We've found nothing on either man's communications or data systems, their house systems, office systems, the devices of family members, that connect them to the bombings. EDD concurs with Homicide that these individuals were coerced and not complicit.

'Banks,' he continued. 'The more we look, the shadier he comes off. We got nothing linking him directly with the bombings at this point. If he wasn't dead, he'd do a nice long stretch for fraud, embezzlement, money laundering, and more petty shit, but he's dead. He had some gambling debts – nothing big enough for spine-crackers – but there might be a connection there. You got that in the last report.'

'We'll follow it up,' Eve confirmed.

'McNab's got some he dug out last night.'

'We've got a tag coming in on Banks's house 'link,' McNab began. 'He had one in the pantry deal in the kitchen they missed when they turned the place.'

'A house 'link in the pantry?'

'Yeah,' he told Eve. 'A mini I guess he had in there for the droids to use. On the night of his murder, just before midnight he got a tag on it. No message when the 'link went to the answering system. Another tag to Denby's house 'link two hours earlier. A hang-up when answered from the residence. Another to the Richie apartment minutes before the bombing at the Salon, and one more to Rogan's house 'link on the night of the home invasion at twenty-two-ten. A hang-up when answered.'

Subtly, he pressed a hand to Peabody's bouncing knee, kept talking. 'All of these tags were made from a cloner. We can't trace the device, but we've been working on tracing the locations of the transmissions. We nailed Richie's first – he only had the one house 'link, and apparently didn't really use it. The transmission came from right outside the building.'

'Making sure nobody was in the unit,' Eve concluded.

'Maybe Richie had a friend over, a woman in there, what-ever. Just making sure the space was clear.'

'We figure, yeah, as we've nailed down Banks. Lived alone, too, rarely used the house system. Transmission in this case? From inside the building.'

'Inside.'

'Yes, sir.'

Eve looked back at the board. 'One of them lives there, was on a guest list or vendor employ. But lives there works best. Banks contacted them that day. It's a big stretch to believe his killers just happened to be going to a party in his building, or to a job there. Security's tight there, as good as it gets. We bump down the guests and the vendors. We're going to interview the ones that fit profile, but they're not priority. How about the others?'

'I nailed down Rogan's early this morning. Transmission from a block south of the residence. Denby's I worked some on the subway. I'm close. Give me another twenty, and I'll have it.'

'Take the twenty, confirm, but it'll fit pattern. The important one at this time? The one made from inside the building.

'Okay, let me wrap up where we are,' Eve began, pausing as Whitney rose.

'That's all the time I have this morning. Detective McNab, good work.'

'Thank you, sir.'

'Lieutenant, hunt them down.'

'Yes, sir.'

He stopped by Peabody's chair, glanced at McNab as Peabody beamed, drumming her hands on the seat of her chair in a quick rhythm. 'Departmentally authorized?'

'Yes, sir,' McNab said. 'Absolutely, sir. We put in a long night.'

'Make sure she takes a half dose next time.'

'It was the espresso chaser, Commander.'

Whitney shook his head. 'That would do it,' he said and strode out.

Peabody let out a giggle, slapped her hand over her mouth. 'Sorry,' she mumbled behind her fingers. 'Not funny.'

Eve said nothing, decided to handle the screen herself. She ran through each crime scene, the evidence, conclusions, progress.

'We've found no evidence linking any of the eighteen victims to any of the crimes under investigation. Our links remain Karson to Banks, Banks to the suspects. Banks to Richie. Richie to Denby. Our focus now will be the names on this board who live in Banks's building.

'You have the profiles, and I've assigned interviewees to each team. We have to consider they're not done. They have another target, one they've already researched and may move on at any time. Look for connections to real estate deals.'

'"Real estate"?' Baxter repeated.

'It's an angle. Or we might look for anything connected to some innovation about to launch. New tech, for instance.

Something or someone who, if taken out, means profit for the suspects. A deal brewing. Something coming out or up soon. They're on a hot streak. It's possible – I think low probability, but possible – this moves out of New York. Don't discount it. Focus on what's going on here, but don't discount that.'

She flicked images on the screen. 'Karson leaked to Banks, so look at familial, romantic, spousal connections. Information that could be passed, however casually, to someone with a connection to the suspects. Somebody cheating on a spouse or lover can be pressured into giving out information. Look for that.'

She turned off the screen. 'Let's get to it. McNab, you nail that location, I want it.'

'Kiss bye!' Peabody puckered up. McNab gave her a sappy smile – before remembering himself and sending a pleading look toward Eve.

'Detective Peabody! I will personally dump you in the tank and sweat that booster out of you if you don't maintain.'

The pucker dropped to a pout.

'With me. Now. No "kiss bye," goddamn it.'

Peabody trotted behind Eve. 'I just feel so good! I can't stop! My brain's all full of colors!'

'Your body's covered in them. It makes my eyes throb. Get your coat and cover up the worst of it, then sit down and be quiet. I need to talk to the rest of the squad because people just keep killing people.'

'That makes me sad.'

'Go be sad and quiet at your desk.'

Since her eyes already throbbed, Eve ran through the current caseload with Jenkinson and his psychotic rainbow tie, Reineke and his kittens on Zeus socks.

She shifted to Carmichael and Santiago, caught them up on the Denby arm of the investigation, segued to their current hot – the bludgeoning of a funky-junkie in Battery Park.

By the time she wrapped it up, she assumed Peabody had lost her sad, as her partner chair-danced to some internal beat. Sometime in the last fifteen minutes, she had applied a shiny coat of bright pink lip dye.

'Stop jerking off and get your ass up.'

'You bet!'

Eve strode to the door, through it. Then, teeth gritted, went back to see Peabody standing at her desk, all smiles. 'Jesus Christ, Peabody. With me.'

'Okeydoke!' She trotted along. 'Say, Dallas, have you ever noticed—'

'No. Don't talk.'

She hummed instead. Eve opted to stick with the miserably crowded elevator all the way down, as the noise level drowned out the chemically induced joy.

In the car Eve drew a deep breath. Tried one more. 'If you don't pull it together, I'm going to leave you locked in the car while I conduct interviews.'

'Uh-uh, partners. Ass to work off. I can't stop!' she added with just a little hint of panic as Eve pulled out. 'Part of my brain's going, Oops, crap, why! But the rest of it's all happy and everything's so bright! See, look! That woman's walking a puppy. She has red boots! I like red boots. Aw, I wish we could get a puppy! I'd name her Cuddles, and— Ow!'

Shoulders hunched, Peabody rubbed the arm Eve punched. 'I can't help it.'

'Try harder.'

'See, what happened is we worked really, really late because, murders and going to the Oscars. Oh, I want Nadine to win so bad! I can't wait to see— Ouch!'

'Keep it up and you'll need body paint to cover the bruises.'

'I'm just saying it's like we only got two hours down, and then I couldn't turn my brain off because, murders and the Academy freaking Awards! Okay, ouch. But I'm saying everything was just fuzzy this morning, and I needed to give you one hundred percent. A hundred absolute percent. So, booster. But then it didn't feel like it worked. All fuzzy. So I thought about the espresso, and maybe it did work some because it's crazy stupid to chase the boost with espresso. It's the real. McNab and I splurged. I *love* McNab! Ian McNab is my BFF – boyfriend forever! And we— Ow, ow, ow.'

'Stop talking. Stop. I get what happened. I get why it happened, which is why I'm not searching for a blunt instrument to beat you bloody with before I dump your broken body out on the street to be run over by a maxibus.'

'Maybe I should take some Sober-Up. It's not like being drunk, but maybe—'

'No. Nothing else goes in. Except water.' Eve programmed just that from the in-dash. 'Drink.'

'I already sort of have to pee.'

'Good, the sooner you flush it out, the better.'

'Where are we going? Can I pee where we're going?'

'Yes. Drink. Mikhail Kinski, resident of Banks's building. Age forty-six, former army, rank captain. Divorced. One hit on domestic violence. Works security for Dobb–Pinkerton Financial.'

Peabody nodded, tapped her temple. 'Got it.'

'Good, because we're there.'

'Really good! Because now I sort of more than sort of have to pee.'

Eve found a second-level street slot. 'You put on your cop face, and you zip it. You observe on this one, and that's it. Unless somebody jabs a spike up your ass, I don't want to hear anything coming out of your mouth with an exclamation point at the end.'

'That would really hurt.'

'And I can find a spike. Believe it.'

She hoped the short walk, the fresh air, and the flushing would bring her partner back.

The lobby looked rich, with its towering green marble columns and acres of gold leaf. While Peabody goggled like a damn tourist, Eve ignored the ornate decor, the scores of people – most in black – clipping and striding to and from elevators with their ear-links and micro PPCs.

'There.' Eve pointed toward a sign for restrooms. 'Make it fast.'

'Yay.'

As Peabody bounded off to pee, Eve headed straight to the security podium. Held up her badge.

'Where would I find Mikhail Kinski?'

The woman, black-clad, muscular, aimed a suspicious eye at the badge before pulling out a scanner. She seemed a little disappointed when it read green.

'Mr Kinski is in Security Hub A. You'll need to be escorted to that level.'

'All right.' Eve stepped back, keeping one eye on the restroom and hoping she didn't have to go in there and yank Peabody away from primping in the mirror while she sang a happy tune.

Fortunately for her partner's life expectancy, Peabody came trotting out. She had a big grin plastered on her face, but maybe, just maybe, her eyes were a little less manic.

'The bathroom is *swank*.'

'Great. Lose the smile.'

Peabody shifted to an exaggerated glower. It might've been effective, Eve thought, without the pink lip dye. Still, better than the smile.

Eve watched the man stride off a single, secured elevator. She recognized Kinski from his ID shot. A well-built man with close-cropped silver-blond hair, icy blue eyes, and the edgy cheekbones of a Nordic god, he walked with that purposeful stride straight to Eve.

'Badges, please.'

Eve offered hers, elbowed Peabody until she remembered hers. He drew out a mini scanner, verified.

'What can I do for you, Lieutenant, Detective?'

'We can talk about that here in the lobby of your work-place, or we can go somewhere more private.'

'Give me a broad stroke.'

'The murder of Jordan Banks.'

He nodded, one decisive movement, then turned to lead them to the secured elevator.

'We can speak in my office. This will have to be brief. We have a full system test in twenty minutes.'

He used a card swipe and a thumbprint to engage the elevator. The ride down was short and smooth.

They emerged into a short hallway with double doors, fully secured and monitored by cams, at the end. Kinski turned to the left, used the swipe and his print again to open a door into a small, spartan office dominated by double wall screens.

He walked to sit behind a simple desk, gestured at the two metal chairs. 'Have a seat. This should be brief, as I didn't know Jordan Banks.'

'You live in the same building, two floors down.'

'So I learned when I read of his murder. There are over eighteen hundred people living in that building, Lieutenant. Do you assume I know all of them?'

'I'm only concerned about Banks.'

'I didn't know him. I never met him. I may or may not have seen him at some point over the twenty-eight months I've lived at that address.'

'That would be shortly after your divorce.'

Kinski's eyes went to blue stone. 'Yes.'

'Can you verify your whereabouts from twenty-one hundred Monday night through oh-four hundred Tuesday morning?'

'I was at home from approximately twenty-one hundred Monday night until oh-six-thirty Tuesday morning.'

'Alone?'

'Yes.'

'Can anyone confirm that?'

'I left this building at nineteen hundred hours, walked to Hannigan's Irish Pub on Forty-first to have dinner with a friend. I left about twenty-thirty and walked home to arrive at approximately twenty-one hundred.'

'Long walk.'

'I like to walk,' he said evenly. 'After I arrived home, I remained home until the following morning. My apartment security will verify the time I arrived, and the time I left.'

'You work in security, Mr Kinski. I imagine you have access to a lot of interesting toys, and you have the knowledge and skill needed to use them.'

'My job makes me a suspect in the murder of a man I didn't know?'

'This is an inquiry. I haven't read you your rights. Being security – you are head of Level A?'

'I am.'

'Being that level of security in a building that houses financial institutions would likely give you a working knowledge of finance. The market. Maybe some inside information.'

His gaze remained level, stony. His voice matched it. 'Now you're accusing me of, what, insider trading? I've had enough of this fishing expedition. A man's murdered in Central Park, his valuables taken before he's dumped in the reservoir. The media terms it a mugging. At least I see you're not stupid enough to dismiss it as such.'

'Why would that be stupid?'

'His neck was broken — manually, according to the reports. I doubt your average mugger's had the kind of combat training that particular skill requires.'

'But you have.'

Still hard, his gaze never strayed from hers. 'I have. I live in the same building, I work in security with a background in military service. I've been in combat. I was home, alone, on the night in question.'

'You also have a charge of criminal violence on your record.'

As the angry flush rose up to his hairline, the first hint of frustration eked through. 'I did not strike my ex-wife. I have never put a violent hand on any woman outside of training or combat when they were soldiers. If you looked deeper, you'd find my ex-wife is currently in court-appointed re-habilitation for drug and alcohol abuse, and I won't discuss that any further.'

He rose. 'I have work. I'll escort you out.'

Eve rose, gestured for Peabody to do the same. She waited until they were back in the elevator to look up at Kinski's rigid face. 'Ever been to the Salon?'

She saw the flicker in his eyes before they narrowed. 'The art gallery, the one bombed yesterday? By one of the owners. What is this?'

'You didn't answer the question.'

'No.'

'You had some training in explosives during your time in the army.'

He started to speak, then pressed his lips together. When the door opened to the lobby, he stood, straight as the soldier he'd been. 'If you need to speak with me again, I'll engage a lawyer.'

'That's your right,' Eve said easily, and felt his eyes boring into her back as she walked across the lobby.

'That shook him up,' she commented. 'He checks some boxes, no question. No real buzz, but boxes checked. Need to verify the wife's rehab.'

'I'll do it.' Peabody's voice held quiet – no exclamation point. 'I'm so, so sorry. It's mostly worn off. I mean, I feel pretty energetic, but the whoopee's about gone. I'm so sorry, Dallas.'

'Forget it.'

'No, seriously. The last thing you needed was me flying around on a mental trapeze. I'm embarrassed, but even more just sorry.'

'Fine. If you're so sorry, get rid of that stupid lip dye.'

'What lip dye?' Peabody asked as they walked up to the car.

'The one on your lips.'

Obviously baffled, Peabody flipped down the vanity mirror when she dropped into the passenger seat. Her gasp sucked up most of the oxygen in the car.

'Oh my God! When did I do that? I don't remember doing that. This is all wrong.' She started digging in her bag. 'I bought this on impulse, but it's not my color. It looks terrible on me. I tossed it in my desk drawer weeks ago.'

'So your main concern is it's not your freaking color?'

'It's not!' Peabody pulled a tiny, wet tissue out of a pack, rubbed it vigorously over her lips. Balled it up when it turned pink, pulled out a second. 'And, come on, I'd never wear something called Sexcapade Pink on duty. I'm a cop!'

In this case, Eve accepted the exclamation point. 'Good to have you back.'

19

They interviewed three more at places of employment. Two of the three had ready alibis – to be verified for both the weekend of the home invasion and the night of Banks's murder. The third claimed to have been at home with a cold from Saturday through Monday, and provided the name of the herbalist he'd used for remedies and relief.

'You can fake a cold and a trip to an herbalist,' Peabody commented.

'Yeah, you can. And it's a squishy alibi to have handy if you're hiding something. We'll keep him on the high side of the list. We'll verify the alibis, check off the herbalist. We're going to head to the apartment building, knock on some doors of the work-at-homes or not-workings.'

'Can I have coffee now? I drank a gallon of water,' Peabody claimed when Eve gave her a silent stare. 'I peed out a gallon when you count I've peed at every stop we've made. The boost is gone, I swear.'

'If you start talking about puppies, I'll punch you again.'

'Deal.'

Peabody programmed coffee for both of them, drank hers while working her PPC. 'We've got two still up on the list out of five – once I verify the alibis. I think they're going to hold. I've got Baxter and Trueheart's update on here. One out of four – and the one's bumped down a couple notches.'

'Confirming Kinski's ex is an addict in rehab doesn't take him off the hook,' Eve considered. 'But it does lead me to speculate that rather than spousal abuse he may have been defending himself against a juiced-up attack or trying to keep her from using. He still checks the boxes.'

'We talk to some of his friends, coworkers, his army CO.'

Eve nodded. 'Next step on him. Then there's Markin, because something's there. The wife says he's too lazy. Maybe he's lazy, but it doesn't mean he wouldn't go into something like this for the fun of it.'

'Bored rich with a mean streak.'

'Exactly.'

She pulled up in front of the apartment building. The doorman, all courtesy, hustled over to open the car door. 'Good morning, Lieutenant. What can we do for you?'

'I've got some people to talk to.'

'No problem. Rhoda will get that going for you.'

The efficient Rhoda ran down Eve's list of names. 'Mr Skinner's out – dentist appointment. I can let you know if he comes back while you're here. Mr Lorimer left just after eight for some outside meetings. He didn't indicate when to expect him back, but again, I'll let you know. Both Mr Abbott and Mr Prinz left for the gym – they go to the same one and are friendly – they're usually back by two. Everyone else should be in residence.'

'Good. I have two detectives who'll be here sometime this afternoon with another list of names.'

'I'll be happy to clear them.'

'Appreciate it.'

In the elevator, Peabody said, 'This is a nice place. Classy.' She lifted her shoulders. 'Roarke.'

'Yeah. We'll start at the top, work down.'

At their first stop, Clinton Wirely welcomed them with considerable enthusiasm. Fit and fifty-ish, with gold-and-silver-tipped brown hair, avid green eyes, he sparkled with delight.

'This must be about The Unfortunate Mr Banks – it sounds just like a title of a story. Please, sit, sit, sit.'

'You knew Jordan Banks.'

'Not a bit, but I know both of you. I'll be positively glued to the screen Sunday night. I adore the Oscars, and throw a little gala of my own for friends on the night. I'm just devastated I can't offer you coffee. I'm a tea drinker. I have fresh, organic papaya juice that's amazing when mixed with some sparkling ginger.'

Before Eve could refuse, Peabody piped up, 'I'd love some juice, thanks.'

'Wonderful. You just make yourselves at home. I'll be back in a snap.'

He sort of whirled out in his knee-length striped sweater and black skin pants.

'Sorry, I could really use the juice.'

Eve took the time to study the living space. Not as grand as Banks's, but with that same view out the glass wall. Lots of art, she noted, lots of color. Pillows shaped like birds, curved sofas, fancy dust catchers arranged just so, fresh flowers.

Wirely came back with a pitcher of – as advertised – sparkling juice over ice, a trio of glasses, and a plate of thin, frosted cookies, fancy napkins.

'In case you change your mind,' he said to Eve. 'I wondered if the police would talk to residents. I'm so excited you are – I know that's just terrible of me. The poor man's dead, after all. Not to speak ill of the dead, but he was a bit of a scoundrel, wasn't he?'

'You said you didn't know him.'

'I didn't, but I know *of* him. I'm an unapologetic gossip,' he added as he poured the juice. 'I'm friendly with a number of people in the building. After all, we're neighbors. And we do love to dish. I can't say he came up very often while he was still among the living, but since?' He cast his gaze up to the ceiling. 'My, my, and my.'

'Such as?' Eve prodded.

'Well.' Eyebrows wiggling, he offered the plate of cookies. 'I'm sure you know, but in case. A womanizer. He had the most delightful lady friend – I did meet her once in the elevator. That poor woman who was hurt in that hideous explosion this week. Willimina Karson. She's the head of Econo. I read she's going to fully recover.'

He patted a hand on his chest. 'So relieved. As I said,

delightful. And just lovely. And I'm told while he had this delightful woman, he pursued others. Including our own Ankah – that's Ankah Si? Gorgeous creature who happens to live just across the hall. He tried his charm on Ankah, sent her flowers, asked her to dinner – all while involved with the lovely Willimina. Our Ankah flicked him off.'

Smiling, he flicked his fingers with their short, neat, buffed nails to demonstrate. 'She has good taste in men. Now this I did know while he was among the living, as Ankah was quite insulted, and told the story at one of my little parties. Then after The Unfortunate Mr Banks's demise, I heard Ankah was far from the only one.'

Eve let him ramble some about what he'd heard: the women, the drug use – terrible for the body and soul! – the gambling.

'You seem to know quite a bit about a man you never met.'

'Oh, my lovely, I keep my ears open. I may not know everything about everyone in the building, but I'll wager I know at least a little about most. It's all grist for the mill. I write short stories. It's my passion.'

'I thought you were a lawyer. A legal and financial consultant – estate-law specialist.'

'That's duty, not passion. I'm the oldest son of two great legal minds, and I did what was expected of me. Quite well, too, if I say so myself. I do continue to serve clients, but I've cut back considerably, and take time to write.'

'Your brother's in the military.'

'Goodness, you know quite a lot, too. Yes, second son,

semper fi. A marine like our grandfather, our uncle – also second sons. Lawyers and soldiers populate my family. We're not allowed to be lazy and suck, you could say, on the family money teat. We earn our way, unlike Mr Banks, from what I hear.'

Rather than answer, Eve glanced around. 'You have a lot of art.'

'Another passion. What's life without art, after all? Dull and gray and flat. You must agree,' he said to the currently colorful Peabody.

'I do, completely. I guess you know Banks owned the Banks Gallery – an art gallery.'

'Yes, but owning and working are different things, wouldn't you say?' He added a sly smile. 'I'm told he didn't put much effort into the working end of the matter. I must stroll in there one day just to see what I see. I imagine he has a nice collection himself. Is it true someone broke into his apartment? That's the rumor, but no one can confirm. Apparently the place is all sealed up. Like a crime scene.'

'We need to keep people out of a victim's residence,' Peabody evaded. 'Until we're sure we've gathered any possible evidence.'

'Of course. That's very sensible.'

Peabody studied the art. 'Do you have any Angelo Richies?'

'Oh.' Wirely slapped a hand on his chest. 'That is a tragedy. A true tragedy. When I heard about the bombing at the Salon, I nearly collapsed. I've bought several paintings there. I deal through the lovely Ilene, as we struck an immediate

356

simpatico – though I knew Wayne. I'm sick, just sick to think he's gone. And Angelo Richie, such a talent. Do you know I planned to attend his opening last night? My current beau is out of town, but I planned to attend with several friends.

'I don't understand a world where people would torment a good man like Wayne, a loving husband and father. In all truth, hold a weapon to a little boy's head so the father sacrifices himself. Kills others. A blazing talent in its youth like Richie, the others. The art.'

He dug out a silk handkerchief, dabbed damp eyes. 'The second time in a week, they say on the reports. Another father, more death. It's not a world I understand when there's such beauty and joy to be taken and shared.'

'Yeah. Since you shared an interest in art, I'm surprised you never met Banks. Same building, same interest.'

'And now I never will.'

'Why don't you tell us where you were on the night of the murder. From eight Monday night until four Tuesday morning.'

Those avid green eyes widened, and once again Wirely slapped a hand to his chest. 'I'm a suspect? Why, this is marvelous! I know, I know, it shouldn't be, but it simply is. An old queen like me, a murder suspect. Should you read me my rights?'

'Do you want me to?'

'It would be exciting, but it's not at all necessary. I was at home – though I did pop down to see Milicent and Gary. They're in 4904. Lovely people. We had a drink and a visit.

I think it was about eight when I went down. I'm sure I was back here by nine-thirty, as I wanted to make myself a snack and watch *Valley of Tears*. I'm just addicted to that show, and its first run of the new episode came on at ten.'

Pausing, he tapped a finger to his chin. 'Let me see now, after that – elevenish, I wrote for an hour, as I expected a call from my beau at midnight, or shortly after. He's on tour – with Ankah. I met him through Ankah, they're musicians. My beau is a cellist. He's adorable. We talked for nearly two hours, then I snuggled right in and went to sleep. I stayed in until, oh, about noon the next day. I had lunch with friends at Bistro on Madison.'

'That's a long conversation, two hours.'

'Well, it wasn't all talk.' He gave Eve a smile as silky as his handkerchief. 'We – how to explain delicately – pleasured each other remotely. It's a five-week tour, after all.'

'I need your friend's name.'

'Nigel Tudor. He's adorable, as I said, and would certainly confirm. But I did record our … conversation. Audio and video. For the lonely nights? It's time stamped. I can make a copy if that helps.'

'We'll just talk to Nigel, thanks. His contact?'

Wirely rattled it off. 'Do give him my love.'

'Okay. How about the weekend prior?'

'Well, Nigel left for tour on Saturday, so we had a gathering Friday night for him and Ankah. I suppose we said goodbye to our last guest about one in the morning. Then Nigel and I … '

'Snuggled in,' Peabody suggested, and had him beaming at her.

'Yes, we did. My adorable beau and Ankah left at ten sharp on Saturday, and I confess I brooded for the next hour or so – before Pitty and Charo dropped by and dragged me off for a spa day to cheer me up. They're delightful creatures, and we had a lovely day. We had cocktails afterward, and met some other friends for an early dinner before going to see the most dreadful play.'

He let out a sigh, shook his head. 'Don't go to see *Goodbye, Jessica, Goodbye*. Trust me. We went down to the Blue Note afterward for drinks and music to cleanse the palate. I don't think I got home until after three. I did drag myself out to Hildago's brunch on Sunday, about elevenish? Then I came home and stayed home. Got some writing done, took a nap, that sort of thing.'

'Okay. Thanks for your cooperation.'

'Absolutely my enormous pleasure. I can't wait to see what you're both wearing on the red carpet Sunday.'

'Her, not me.'

'Ah, well. I'll look for you, Detective Peabody. I hope you'll both come back. Remember, if there's something I don't know about someone in the building, I can probably find out.'

'We'll keep that in mind.'

Eve stepped out, walked toward the elevator.

'You don't want to check with Milicent and Gary and all the rest?' Peabody asked.

'He's covered. He's too smart to lie about something that easy to verify or tear down. And he's no killer.'

'I liked him.'

'He's sly, gossipy, and a self-proclaimed "old queen." I kind of liked him, too.'

They wrapped up three more, none of whom were as interesting or chatty as Wirely. As they headed for the next, Peabody pulled an energy bar out of her bag.

'I need a little . . . lift. Don't want to say *boost*. Want?'

'What is it?'

'Ah, Fruity Nut Carbo Burst – with chia seeds and flax.'

'I thought they made sheets and underwear and stuff out of flax.'

'It's a food and fiber plant.'

'You're telling me you're eating something that's used to make underwear? Why not just gnaw on your own underwear?'

Peabody took a determined bite of the bar. 'On days – which is most – we don't stop for so much as a limp soy fry, it's tempting.'

Eve stepped off the elevator, said, 'Loose pants.'

'That's an upside. It's really chewy,' Peabody managed around the next bite of bar. 'About three out of ten on the taste scale, but really chewy.'

'Swallow your underwear,' Eve ordered, and pressed the buzzer on the next apartment.

'Trying,' Peabody muttered as Eve studied the apartment security.

Not top grade, she noted, but close. And the comp response came smooth and female.

Good afternoon. Please state your name and the purpose of your visit.

'Lieutenant Dallas, Detective Peabody, NYPSD.' Eve held her badge up for the scan. 'Police inquiry.'

Thank you. Your identification has been verified. Mr Iler will be with you in a moment. Please wait.

Lucius Iler, Eve thought. Age forty-four, third-generation money — antique trade. No marriage, no offspring. Registered day trader. Brother (deceased), uncle, grandmother, two cousins, and a stepsister in the military.

A lot of boxes checked, she mused as she heard the locks disengage.

Vid-star polished, she thought when Iler opened the door. Chestnut waves spilling artfully around an angular face sporting the perfect (and deliberate) amount of scruff. Turquoise eyes, heavily lashed, transmitted interest and curiosity as a little dimple winked on the right side of his mouth with his polite smile.

'How can I help you, officers?'

'We'd like to come in and speak with you, Mr Iler.'

'What about?'

'Jordan Banks.'

'Who? Oh, oh, of course. I don't know how I can help with that.'

'Can we come in?'

'Sorry, sure.' He backed up. 'I'm a little distracted. I wasn't expecting cops at the door. I guess no one does.'

'Criminals sometimes do,' Peabody said, earning the little dimple.

'I hadn't thought of that. So … I guess we should sit down.'

Eve supposed it was only natural for someone with a family antique business to fill his home with them. The generous space offered plenty of room for large tables, free-standing cabinets, fussy chairs, and sofas. A lot of gleaming wood and rich fabrics with an enormous, softly faded rug centering the space.

Like Banks's, this unit boasted a fireplace. Silver candle-stands and a tall painted vase graced the mantel over it.

Behind them a long, oval mirror, framed in more gleaming wood, reflected the room.

Most of the art showed landscapes that struck Eve as European. Sunbaked houses jogged up and down hillsides, charming cottages sprang out of woods and gardens.

He didn't offer refreshments, but after gesturing to chairs, sat – a slender man in a white cashmere sweater and tailored black pants.

He tapped his fingers together. 'What can I tell you?'

'Did you know Jordan Banks?'

'I did – slightly. We met some time ago. I'm not sure when, exactly. Maybe a year or so? At a party. We had mutual friends, it turned out. Thad and Delvinia. And somehow or other it came out we lived in the same building. New York's really a small world. We chatted awhile. He owned an art gallery, and my business is arts and antiques, so—'

'I thought you were a day trader.'

'Oh.' His fingers tapped together again. 'That's more a hobby I enjoy. My family business is arts and antiques, so as Jordan and I had that mutual interest, we talked shop for a while, exchanged business cards.'

'Did you follow up on that?'

'"Follow up"?'

'Connect again?'

'I did visit the Banks Gallery – his art shop – and we had a drink. His gallery focuses on current art and artists, and my interests are in older works. But we had a drink once or twice, or I might see him at a party and chat.'

'Ever been to his apartment here?'

'Yes, actually, to see his art collection, and naturally, I reciprocated. We might have been art lovers, but our tastes didn't strike the same chord.'

'Were you at the party on Monday night hosted by your mutual friends, Thad and Delvinia?'

'No. I was sorry to miss that. I was on a road trip – only returned that evening, and much too tired to pull it together and head out to a party.'

'A road trip?'

'North. Through New York State, into New England. Antiquing – really I suppose more of a busman's holiday.'

'How long were you gone?'

'I took a long weekend. Frankly, I wanted a little break,

so I drove north.' He spread his hands, tapped his fingers back together. 'No real plan other than to stop here and there, look at antique and collectible shops. I don't, in general, do any of our buying, but I do scout now and then. Primarily our antiques come from Europe, but we do buy and sell Americana as well. You never know what treasure you might stumble on in some little shop.'

'And did you?'

'Did I what?'

'Stumble on any treasures.'

'Not this time. But, as I said, it was really a busman's holiday. An excuse to get out of the city.'

'And you got back Monday evening.'

'That's right. I'm not sure what time. I unpacked, had a drink to unwind.'

'And then?'

He shifted, looked mildly annoyed. 'I can't tell you exactly. Took a shower, puttered about, read a little, as I recall. I went to bed early. It's lovely to get away, but there's nothing quite like your own bed.'

'Did you speak to anyone, let them know you were back? Answer messages that might have come in while you were away?'

'No. As I said before, I was tired. I really don't understand why you need to know all of this.'

'Jordan Banks was murdered in the early hours of Tuesday morning.'

'Yes, so I heard. What does it have to do with me?'

'You knew him. He was murdered after leaving a party of your mutual friends. These are routine questions in a murder investigation.'

'I wouldn't know, as I've never been questioned by the police.' His tone cooled, considerably. 'Frankly, it feels intrusive.'

'I'm sure it does. Do you know Hugo Markin?'

'Hugo? Yes, I know him and Delores – his wife.'

'Willimina Karson?'

'I met her when she was involved with Jordan. I wouldn't say I know her, but I've met her.'

'Paul Rogan.'

He stared into Eve's eyes, tapped his fingertips. 'No, that's not a familiar name.'

'Wayne Denby.'

'I don't think so. I meet a lot of people.'

'Angelo Richie.'

'No, I don't think . . . wait. The artist. I know of him and his work. He was just killed, wasn't he? It's tragic.'

'For him,' Eve agreed. 'For an art collector who bought his work before he started to rise – that would mean increased value. Wouldn't it? Speaking as someone in the arts and antiques, business.'

He shifted again. 'That's a cold and calculating perspective.'

'But accurate?'

'Yes, very likely.' His fingers tapped, his gaze strayed, fixed over her shoulder. 'I don't see what that has to do with Jordan's murder.'

'Banks had a Richie figure study in his apartment.'

'Did he? I doubt I'd have recognized the work. But surely you're not suggesting Jordan was killed over a charcoal figure study by an emerging artist.'

Eve smiled. 'People kill for all kinds of reasons. Do you gamble, Mr Iler?'

'Gamble? Occasionally. Who doesn't?'

'Did you ever gamble with Banks?'

'Not that I recall. Lieutenant, I met the man a handful of times over the last year or two. We weren't close friends. If that's all, I—'

'Just a couple more. You have a number of family members in the military.'

His lips quivered a little so the dimple flickered like a twisted nerve. 'You looked into my family?'

'Standard procedure, Mr Iler. I want to say I'm grateful for their service, and very sorry for the loss of your brother.'

Even as his shoulders relaxed, Eve saw genuine emotion come into his eyes. 'Thank you. We've very proud of our long family history of serving. My brother, Terry ... Captain Terrance James Iler gave his life serving.'

'A terrorist attack on his base while he was stationed in Seoul. Four years ago, wasn't it?'

'Yes, and still as fresh as yesterday.' Iler looked away. 'He was due to come home the following week. He told me – I spoke with him only hours before he was killed – he planned to ask Felicia to marry him. He never got the chance.'

'Felicia?'

'Felicia Mortimer. They'd been involved for quite awhile, and Terry told me he planned to buy a ring, ask her to marry him when he came home. He never came home.'

His throat worked as he looked away again. 'He saved lives that day. He gave his life to save others. He was a hero.'

He held up a hand. 'I'm sorry, it's still raw. I suppose it always will be. I hope you'll excuse me now.'

When he rose, Eve got to her feet. 'Again, we're sorry for your loss. Thank you for your time.' She turned for the door, stopped. 'I nearly forgot. If you could give us the names of the places you stayed over your long weekend, it would tie that off.'

'What possible difference does it make?'

'For our report.' She studied him, smiled blandly. 'Checks all the boxes.'

'I have no idea. I told you before, I didn't have a set plan. I just stopped when the mood struck. New England's ripe with odd little B and Bs. I can't remember the names.'

'That's okay. You'll have the paper trail – credit card data.'

His jaw tightened like a drum. 'I didn't use credit or debit. I used cash.'

'Really? No record for expenses, taxes?'

'I explained – clearly, I think – it was really a holiday for me.'

'At a charging station for your car, a meal on the road?'

'Cash. You said Jordan was killed Tuesday morning. What does where I stayed or ate over the weekend, or any of it, relate to that?'

'Loose ends nag at me. If you happen to remember one of your stops, just let me know. I'll tie off that loose end. Thank you again.'

With Peabody, Eve strode to the elevator. 'He's not the smart one.'

'No. No, he is not,' Peabody agreed. 'A lot of that was rehearsed, probably in the mirror.'

'Over-rehearsed, at that. And he's not real good with the — what is it? — ad lib. Too much information gushed out to demonstrate cooperation at the beginning. He never once expressed any regret his fellow art lover got himself murdered. Never asked any questions pertaining to. Comes from being a sociopath — just can't relate.'

'Gushing's right. Just how did he know the Richie in Banks's apartment was a charcoal?'

Eve smiled, shot a finger at Peabody. 'Bang. Doesn't say, Oh yeah, I saw a Richie up in Jordan's apartment. Doesn't say, Yeah, yeah, Jordan mentioned he had a charcoal by Angelo Richie. Instead he pretends it takes him a minute to place Richie at all, then doesn't connect him to Banks — smarter if he had. But he knows what he took out of the apartment Monday night, so it's on his mind, and he just rolls it out.'

'I thought you might haul him in after that.'

'I could sweat him. We could break him. And we'd nail him on eighteen murders, forced imprisonment, and so on. But I don't know, yet, if he'd flip on his partner, and we want them both.'

'We could flip him.'

Eve shook her head. 'Depends on the partner. What we're going to do is break from the interviews while we contact Captain Terrance Iler's CO at the time of the terrorist incident. Let's make sure Terry's dead.'

'Jesus, you think his dead brother's not dead and his partner?'

'Let's confirm. And we need to contact this Felicity Mortimer. Maybe have a chat there. That's why we need to break off the interviews until we do.'

She stepped off the elevator, walked to the desk. 'Rhoda, is there an office we could use?'

'Of course – just one minute.' She tapped her earpiece. 'Adam, cover the desk for five, please. Thanks. Come with me,' she told Eve. 'You can use my office.'

She led the way back, paused outside a nice little break room. 'Would you like anything?'

Since she wanted to keep her thoughts cool, Eve opted for cold. 'I could use a tube of Pepsi.'

'Detective?'

'Same for me, but diet.'

'The chicken noodle soup's very good. You've been here over three hours,' Rhoda pointed out. 'Without a lunch break.'

'Roarke approved,' Eve commented, and made Rhoda smile.

'My office is the second on the left. I'll just bring in the soup and drinks.'

20

She had to admit Rhoda was right about the soup.

While she ate, Eve tracked down Colonel Xavier Unger, had a long chat while Peabody did the same with Felicia Mortimer.

When Eve finished, she sat back, stared up at the ceiling and thought it all through. She sat up again when she heard Peabody end her conversation.

'Report.'

'Felicia met Terry when he was stationed in Germany, and she was doing some postgrad work. She's a linguist – a UN interpreter now. They hit it off right away, both native New Yorkers, both living in Germany. Started dating. Got serious enough she put off coming home until he had leave. Meet-the-family time on both ends. Long-distance relationship, but it held. He got assigned to South Korea. They met twice while he took R & R in Tokyo, had more time when he came home on leave. She'd have said yes.'

'Impressions.'

'She loved him, would have made herself into a military

spouse, and she felt they'd build a solid foundation away from his family. She liked them – apparently his mother particularly. She found his father too controlling, emotionally distant, and – from what Terry told her – he was always expected to serve.'

'Another second-son thing?'

'Maybe. Sort of. She said his older brother – that's our guy – wasn't athletic or tough as a kid, and Terry was. Older bro, a little frail, but very protective of little bro. Used to read him stories.'

'Is that so?'

'Yeah. Terry Iler was almost ten years younger than his older brother. The parents traveled a lot, so it was nannies, staff, and big brother. It sounds like Iler took the big brother job seriously. So Terry went into the service because it was expected, but according to Felicia, he thrived there. He found his place there. The old band of brothers thing – sisters, too. He loved the army, made captain inside four years. When he was killed, she says her whole world fell apart. She spent more time with his family after that. She and Iler leaned on each other. She went to grief therapy, gradually pulled out of it.

'Nearly three years after he died, she met someone. They got married last summer.'

'There's a trigger. The bitch isn't honoring hero baby brother's memory. Decides to have a life.'

'Is he a memory?' Peabody asked.

'Yeah. His CO not only has confirmation – DNA – but

saw Captain Iler pulling wounded to safety before Iler rushed back for more. The second explosion took him out. CO's a solid eyewit on it.'

'So the hero dead brother isn't the partner.'

'No, but the partner's military. That's the connection, the bond between them. Iler's weak, and not as smart or clever as he thinks. He has money, he knows art, he knows the market enough to play in it, but he's never been in combat, never trained, never laid out or been in an op. The partner's that end of it. The partner knows explosives. The brother died in an explosion, and the target of the attack on the base was ordinance as well as personnel. A lot of the men and women who died or were wounded in the attack were trained in demolition and explosives.'

'Band of brothers.'

'You're the sharp Peabody today. The brother of my brother's my brother. What brings these two together – greed, profit, gambling. But now we've got more. The grieving brother with the often-absent, controlling father.'

'If the father hadn't controlled and expected, maybe the brother doesn't join the army and end up dead.'

'Keep ringing that bell. The father's to blame for the loss of the child. The mother doesn't stand between to protect. Will the father give his life for the child? Let's find out. And, hey, might as well make some money on it.'

She checked the time. 'I want to run this through with Mira. Set me up on that, then let's get these interviews done.'

'We've got Iler.'

'Now you lost valuable points. The partner may be here, on the list, in the building.'

Peabody scowled. 'I didn't think of that.'

'It's fifty-fifty. We've got to run it all the way.'

'You made Iler nervous, Dallas, pushing on the weekend.'

'I wanted to make him nervous. If he's nervous enough, maybe they don't try for number three. I'm putting eyes on the building – outside. We've got Rhoda and her team inside. Set me up with Mira while I talk to Rhoda and get the cop's eyes going.'

She strode out, gestured Rhoda over. 'I'm putting a surveillance team outside.'

No hitch in Rhoda's stride, she merely nodded. 'I'll let the doormen and security know.'

'Who takes over for you when you go off shift?'

'Aaron Vogal's our night manager.'

'Is he as good as you?'

Rhoda smiled. 'I trained him myself. He's excellent.'

'I need steady, and discreet.'

'You'll have both.'

'If Lucius Iler leaves the building or has a visitor, I need to know. Immediately.'

'Mr Iler,' Rhoda murmured. 'I see.'

'I hope you do. You're not to confront or alter your behavior in any way. I need to know who comes to see him.'

'Mr Iler has a number of friends, and business associates. He works most often out of his apartment, so he has a number of visitors.'

'Male. Can't give you an age range at this time. He might give you the impression of a soldier, military training.'

'That narrows it somewhat, but Mr Iler has a number of clients, friends, connections who are or were in the military.'

'Okay.' She'd go through the visitors' logs again, Eve decided. 'If anyone meeting that description visits him tonight, have security notify the surveillance team, and tag me immediately. I – Hold on,' she said when her 'link signaled.

The readout had her cursing under her breath. 'Not now, Nadine.'

'Don't hate me.'

'Don't make me hate you.'

'I pulled a prime spot on *Knight at Night*.'

'Congratulations. Go away.'

'Don't cut me off! I *am* going away, that's the point. I can't wiggle out of this, even if I wanted to. I have a boss just like everybody, and she wants me out there.'

A very bad feeling began to creep in. 'Out where? *Knight*'s out of New York. I know this.'

'Usually, yes. But she's out of Hollywood all this week because, Oscars, Dallas. And I have to get out there. I had to bump up the shuttle, add a night to the hotel.'

'You're fucking kidding me.'

'I'm not, and I'm sorry. Sincerely because you're doing a solid friend thing here, and now it's more.'

'When?'

Nadine, face a little frantic, held her breath a moment. 'We have to take off in two and a half hours. I'm sorry!'

Eve closed her eyes and, while Rhoda looked on, lowered her head to pound it lightly on the counter.

'Dallas! Dallas!'

'Shut up a minute.' Eve gave herself a couple more pounds, sucked in a breath. 'Fuck.'

'I know, I know. Leonardo's going to do their fittings and adjustments out there anyway. They just need to pack and be at the shuttle in ... an hour forty-five. I'm sorry, really. I don't want to let her down, and it's on me if you can't cut her loose, but—'

'They'll be there.'

'Oh, thank God. We owe you. We all owe you.'

'You're damn fucking skippy you do,' Eve snapped and clicked off. 'Sorry,' she said to Rhoda.

'Think nothing of it. Could I get you a blocker?'

'There isn't one big enough.' Eve strode back toward Rhoda's office as Peabody started out.

'It took some doing with her admin, but Mira's clear in thirty, in person or via 'link.'

'Good. You have to go.'

'Talk to Mira?'

'No. Nadine has to leave in two and a half hours. You have to get to the shuttle in an hour forty-five.'

'But it's tomorrow.'

'Now it's today. Tag McNab on the way. Go.'

'But, but, Iler. I can't just—'

375

'Look at my face.' Eve jabbed spread fingers at her own eyes. 'You're now on leave. Get the hell out so I can work. One more word, just one, and I haul you out bodily.'

Peabody pressed her lips together, then thumped a fist to her heart.

'Yeah, yeah, get out. I'm busy.'

Peabody rushed to the door and, figuring she could probably outrun Eve with the distance and the adrenaline, called out, 'Thanks, boss!' Kept going.

'You're fucking welcome,' she muttered, kicking Rhoda's desk before she could stop herself.

She tagged Baxter first.

'Just finishing up interview three on-site.'

'When you wrap it come down to the manager's office. Rhoda will show you.'

'Ten tops,' he said, clicked off.

She blew out a breath, tagged Roarke, got Caro.

'Hello, Lieutenant.'

'Caro, I'm sorry.'

The stylish, ever-efficient Caro only smiled. 'It's no problem at all. He's in a meeting. He should be out in a few minutes, but he said to put you through at any time if you needed to speak with him immediately.'

'Not immediately. If you could tell him, when he's free, Peabody's schedule moved up. She had to leave. I'm at the apartment building. Banks. Things are moving. He can reach me when he has a chance.'

'I'll take care of it. We're all pulling for Nadine.'

'She's lucky they're not pulling her out of the East River. Thanks.'

Taking a breath, rubbing her temples, she started outlining a takedown plan, grabbed her 'link again when it signaled incoming.

The colonel had come through with her requested list of military personnel on base at the time of the attack.

A lot of military personnel, she thought. But she could eliminate females, the dead, anyone on active duty. He'd be retired, she thought. Or discharged – honorably or not.

Could be older than Iler, she considered, as the dominant partner. Or ... Baby brother. The dominant still, she thought, but also a kind of surrogate.

She looked at the little screen on her 'link, then with envy at the generously sized wall screen. And went out, once again, to Rhoda.

By the time Baxter and Trueheart joined her, she had a pot of coffee, and a good chunk of her elimination done and displayed on the wall screen.

'That's real coffee,' Baxter said. 'I can smell the real.'

'Rhoda had a stash.'

'You should marry her,' he told Trueheart as he poured out mugs.

'I have a girl.'

'Keep the girl, marry Rhoda. She has amazing powers.'

'If we have that settled.' Eve kept working as she spoke. 'We have the art and finance half of our suspects nailed down in Lucius Iler, apartment 5005.'

'You got him. Hot damn!' Baxter lifted his mug in salute. 'Is Peabody hauling him in?'

'No, he's in 5005. I've got uniforms in soft clothes watching the building, and Rhoda – of the amazing powers – in the lobby, should he decide to leave. Peabody's on her fricking way to fricking Hollywood.'

'She is?' Trueheart's earnest face broke into smiles. 'I thought it was tomorrow.'

'It was. Now it's not. Sit. Listen.'

She caught them up quickly.

'He'll have contacted his partner,' Eve concluded. 'No way to prevent that. The partner may rabbit, but I don't think so. He's a soldier.'

'Leave no man behind.' Baxter nodded.

'They're brothers – as least in Iler's mind. They go, they go together. The probability's high the partner's on the list on-screen – all of them were on base at the time of the terrorist attack. I've eliminated females, deceased, active duty. They've been at this for months, so it's extremely unlikely the partner's active duty. Trueheart, pick this up. Cross-check these names with the list of residents. If they both live here—'

'We can wrap this up,' Baxter finished, 'and go out for burgers and brew.'

'If we have that kind of luck, I'll buy both. I've got a consult with Mira in a few. Rhoda – and I concede her amazing powers – has it set up so we can do it on-screen here. That way I don't have to relay to you afterward.'

'Maybe I'll marry her,' Baxter considered.

'She's too smart for that.'

'I overcome female brains with my smooth charm and sexual prowess.'

'He really does,' Trueheart agreed as he worked.

'It's a skill.'

'Save it until we bust these bastards. Roarke's on his way in.'

'Peabody's stand-in.'

'While Trueheart's doing the cross-check, give me what you got.'

Baxter huffed out a breath. 'Goose egg. Nobody we interviewed fits, nobody pops.'

'If I'm not on the hook for burgers and brew, we're back at that. But we focus on military history. The partner could have changed his name.'

'If he lives here, or comes to see Iler frequently? Rhoda.'

'And/or the night manager, the doormen. So you're going to generate ID shots of the list currently on-screen.'

She checked the time. 'After the consult.'

With Mira on-screen Eve ran through the data, impressions, conclusions, while Mira sat at her desk at Central sipping tea.

'The less physically adept older brother, proud and protective of his younger sibling,' Mira began. 'Both of them often left in the care of staff while their parents traveled – with the father a dominant figure, one who controlled and demanded. The father did not, certainly in Iler's mind, offer unrestricted, selfless love – and may, in fact, have been critical of, demeaning to, the more frail, unathletic older son. While the mother, in his view, cared less about tending and protecting her children than pleasing her husband, and perhaps herself.'

'It's envy? Targeting the family-focused parents?'

'It's certainly a motivator. The younger brother grows up, becomes the soldier, as expected. He forms new ties – new brothers, in a sense. He falls in love, another replacement. Iler, rather than building his own relationships, keeps his brother as the center. On a very real level, he sees himself not just as his brother's keeper, but as his father figure. But he can no longer protect his brother, who dies a hero.'

'As a soldier,' Eve put in. 'Because the father demanded it.'

'Yes. Iler can't blame himself. He has no capacity for self-blame. The father should have protected the child, but caused his death instead, and lives on. The woman his brother loved, a link to his brother, moved on, chose another. Women are weak, calculating, without loyalty. He feels, as much as he's capable of feeling, only for the child. His loyalty has transferred to his partner, his brother substitute.'

'The partner, the dominant, feeds all of this.'

'Unquestionably. Let the father prove he'd protect the child. The gamble for profit? It's the risk that feeds both of them. Iler, physically frail as a child. I believe he would have worked hard to build himself up. He'd be a risk taker – physically – a gambler physically and financially. An addict to risk and reward.

'The partner, a soldier,' Mira continued. 'Trained to accept risk and violence, to lay down his life if needed. He survived the attack, but a man he admired – or at least respected – didn't. You're right, he could be younger. Still the dominant either way. But he would have been Terrance Iler's subordinate. Not just Captain Iler, but *his* captain.'

'Responsible for the lives of his men. Like a father's responsible for the child.'

'Yes. He likes violence, enjoys it. Another addiction.'

As she wrapped it up, Roarke stepped in.

'Thanks for the time.'

'Keep me updated,' Mira told her. 'When you have one or both of them in Interview, I'll observe.'

'I will.' She ended the consult. 'Trueheart.'

'No matches, Lieutenant.'

'There goes the brew and burgers,' Baxter lamented.

'Generate the ID shots. Let's take a walk,' she said to Roarke.

She wanted some air, needed to move – and didn't mind a bit if Iler happened to look out and see her on the street.

'You're banking rent from a sociopathic killer.'

'Ah well,' Roarke responded. 'It happens.'

'Lucius Iler.'

'Iler Antiquities?'

'That's the one. You know him?'

'I don't, no, but I've purchased a thing or two from the company over the years.'

'Oldest son,' she began, and told him.

She broke off long enough to contact Officer Carmichael, currently stationed in a fancy tea shop across the street.

'He's up there, sir. He came out a couple times on the terrace. Looked upset. He's doing some day drinking. Last time he came out he had his 'link, talked a lot. Seemed to calm down some.'

'Keep on it.'

Roarke strolled back toward the building with her. 'So, basically, Iler's killed eighteen people, terrorized two families because his own parents didn't give him enough hugs, his brother died saving others, the woman his brother hoped to marry didn't grieve for the rest of her life.'

'Add in an addiction to risk and gambling, greed, and a partner who strokes his twisted resentments, yeah. That's about it.'

The hem of Roarke's coat snapped in the March wind; his hair streamed in it. 'It'll be a pleasure to watch you take them both down, and to play a part in it. Why is Peabody on her way to California today?'

'Nadine. She got a spot on Annie Knight's freaking Oscar week show out there, and had to bump everything up.'

'Was this before or after you found Iler?'

'After. I don't want to talk about it,' Eve stated. 'And don't even think about kissing me when I've got two pairs of cops' eyes on this building.'

'I doubt they can read my thoughts at this distance.'

'Cops' eyes,' she repeated, and stood for a moment longer in the noise and the wind.

'What would you like me to do, as your Peabody?'

'The first thing I'm going to say is I don't know what you pay Rhoda, but she should get a big, fat bonus.'

'Consider it done.'

'Depending on how things go, I need Baxter and Trueheart to get back to the interviews – focusing on military backgrounds, but not exclusively. He could be using fake ID and data. I'll need to take some interviews to get it done. While I am, I need you to start full-spread runs on the names I've culled out from the terrorist attack.'

'I can do that.'

'He may or may not go by the same name now, but you should look for the shaky. Maybe a questionable psych eval, particularly after the attack. Medical discharges, dishonorables.'

'Training in explosives?'

'Possible. Just as possible he developed those skills and interest after the attack. If he was married – doubtful, but a maybe – he's divorced. If he's employed, it's in security, or that's my most probable. He could be a cop, goddamn it, but if he went there, he's former because this takes too much time – plus, the second hit came too hard up on the first. Too much leave time for a cop unless he's pulled a sick-out or hardship leave. Don't discount the cop angle just because it pisses me off.'

'I won't. You've dismissed the tactic of taking Iler in, sweating it out of him?'

'I still may. Let's see what we get from the ID shots and the runs first.'

She went back and found a silver-haired man on the desk.

'Lieutenant, sir, Rhoda's back in her office with your detectives. No one has come in to visit Mr Iler.'

'Good.'

In the office Rhoda sat studying the screen while Baxter handled the programming, one ID shot at a time. She started to rise when Eve and Roarke came in, but Roarke gestured her down.

'Take your time,' Baxter told her. 'You see a lot of faces on any given day. Remember, if anyone seems a little familiar, we'll earmark it, come back to it.'

'Not that one,' she said. Baxter moved to the next.

'Visitors' log?' Roarke asked.

'I'm cross-checking on the portable.' Trueheart sat behind the desk. 'Not just exact names, but any that use the same initials, same first or last.'

'Keep at it,' Eve ordered, then turned to Rhoda. 'He may have changed hairstyle, color. Grown a beard, shaved one off.'

At the end of the first long round, Rhoda picked out five possibles.

'I'm worried I've pulled those out because they remind me of someone else.'

'Take a break,' Eve told her.

'Oh, but I—'

'You'll come back to it fresher if you take a couple minutes. Baxter, dispense some of the smooth charm and coffee for Rhoda. Hold the sexual prowess.'

'Sometimes it just ekes out. How do you take your coffee, Remarkable Rhoda?'

'Black, thanks. When you have real, why add to it?'

'My kind of woman. You aren't married, are you?'

'Not at the moment. You're all trying to settle me down, and I appreciate it. Knowing I've had almost daily contact with one of the men who's done all of this?' She accepted the coffee, drank. 'It's unnerving.'

'Your nerves look steady to me.' Eve glanced at Roarke. He sat, working on his PPC. Already running the five possibles, she thought.

He made an excellent Peabody.

'Let me see them again. Not him,' Rhoda said as the first displayed. 'I realize now he looks a little like – and this is embarrassing – Scott Trevor from *Galaxy Force.*'

'You watch *Galaxy Force*?' Baxter shot a finger at Rhoda. 'Addicted.'

'We need to have drinks and talk. And you're right. He could be Scott Trevor's older cousin. How about this one?'

She studied, closed her eyes, refocused. 'Could we hold that one, come back to it? I'm just not sure.'

'No problem.' Baxter switched to the next.

'There's just something . . .' She closed her eyes again, sat quietly, then opened. 'Oh. Oh, I see. He's shaved his hair. He's shaved his head, and there's something, else, something, I'm not – his nose. His nose is thinner now. Thin and straight – it looks as if it's been broken and set poorly in this picture. He usually wears sunshades, even when he comes in after dark, almost always wears them. That's Mr Nordon. Oliver Nordon. He visits Mr Iler, most often in the evening so I wouldn't see him then, but I've seen his name on the log. And I've cleared him myself when he comes during the day. Mr Nordon.'

'Got it,' Trueheart said. 'Got him. Sergeant Oliver Silverman, under Captain Iler in Seoul.'

'Sergeant Oliver Silverman,' Roarke continued, 'age thirty-two at the time of the attack. Wounded therein — broken leg, severe burns on torso, arms. Ah, shrapnel damaged his genitals, resulting in partial amputation and the fitting of a prosthesis.'

'Youch,' Baxter mumbled.

'Both medical and psychiatric evaluations determined Silverman should be honorably discharged.'

'Something else there. If he'd wanted to stay in, they'd have found a place for him unless they deemed him unfit. Wounded warrior.'

Roarke nodded at Eve. 'I can look deeper.'

'Later. Do you have a current ID shot of Silverman?'

'Went off the grid after discharge.'

'A lot do, Lieutenant,' Trueheart said. 'Plenty of sidewalk sleepers are vets.'

'Yeah. But that's no sidewalk sleeper. Run Nordon,' she told Roarke.

'I am. Oliver Nordon, age thirty-six, freelance security consultant, residential and commercial.' He glanced at Eve. 'Good call, Lieutenant.'

'Give me an address.'

'It's 563 West Sixty-third.'

'Baxter, warrants for Iler and Silverman/Nordon. Search and seizures on both locations. Use Reo, she's fast. Trueheart, I want cops – team of four – sitting on Silverman's address five minutes ago. In body armor.'

'Yes, sir.'

'Two more uniforms to this location,' she added. She snapped into the communicator already in her hand. 'Feeney, eyes and ears, 563 West Sixty-third. Apartment number?' she asked Roarke.

He didn't look up from his PPC. 'No. Townhome, three stories.'

'You catch that?'

'I ain't deaf,' Feeney said.

'Suspect data coming to you . . .'

'Now,' Roarke finished.

'He'll be armed, Feeney, and he's fucking dangerous. Full body armor for your team. I'm tagging Salazar. He'll have explosives.'

'I'll tap her.'

'Warrants are in the works, uniforms en route to cover. Bomb sniffers, Feeney. Nobody takes the door until the sniffers clear it. And I want residences and businesses on both sides of the target location evacuated. Baxter, status!'

'Reo's pushing it.'

She snatched the 'link from his hand. 'Push faster, harder.' Tossed it back to him. 'We'll do the takedown here, then be at your location.'

She clicked off, narrowed her eyes at the image on-screen.

'Here's how it's going to go,' she said, then outlined the two-pronged op.

'She's marvelous,' Rhoda murmured.

Roarke merely smiled. 'Isn't she?'

'Warrants coming through. Baxter, Trueheart, take your positions. Carmichael, Shelby, you copy?'

'Roger that.'

'Roarke, with me. You can take the block off the fiftieth floor, Rhoda,' Eve told her when they reached the elevators. 'Just this car for now.'

'Good luck,' Rhoda called out as the doors shut.

'This one shouldn't give us too much trouble. But you never know.'

'It's Silverman you're worried about, and I agree. By the way, you weren't wrong about Markin.'

'Markin? He's in this?'

'Not this, no. It's embezzlement he's in – from his wife's personal account, and her business. I poked around a bit, since we started our day so early.'

'Huh.'

'She hasn't noticed yet, but she will. Or her accountants will. I wonder if her parents might be a bit more understanding about her divorcing him under the circumstances.'

'It might be kind of fun to take him down myself instead of passing it along. Like a – that thing – palate cleanser.'

They walked down to Iler's apartment. Eve buzzed.

No comp inquiry this time, she noted. He'd shut it down.

'Check it, open it,' Eve said.

Roarke took out a device, ran it over the door, the locks. 'It's clean. No explosives.'

In less time than it took to talk about it, he melted through the locks. They stepped in as Iler swung a leg over the terrace wall.

As Eve charged forward he grinned, then began a rapid descent on his climbing cable. He kept that grin aimed up at her, riding down with a large backpack, a second hefty bag strapped cross-body.

Dropped down to the sidewalk. Surrounded by cops.

'Another good call, Lieutenant.'

'He had to be ready to go. Once he told his partner how I pushed about the weekend, even a pair of morons could figure out we'd linked Banks's murder to the two explosions. And Iler had the crappiest of crap alibis for the time in question.'

She rolled her shoulders. 'One down, one to go.'

21

Roarke drove so she could keep current with the team.

'Getting you eyes and ears now. Place looks locked down tight – privacy screens engaged,' Feeney told her. 'And, lookee here, he thinks he's going to block us out with some filters. Give him hell, Callendar.'

'Giving him all kinds, Cap. Burning through.'

'Sniffers?' Eve demanded.

'Starting to sniff now. Okay, through the filters, going eyes first. Got a basement level, starting there and working up. Callendar, make me proud. I'm going to talk to the sniffers.'

'Basement's clear, Dallas. Going up. Hey, did you know McNab can do cartwheels?'

'What?'

'He did a triple heading out the door – first level, nobody there – for Hollywood. I scored it an eight-point-five out of ten because, a little wobbly on the third. Second floor, clear. Bunch of us are having a viewing party at the Blue Line on Sunday so – Target is clear. No heat source. No humans. No bad guys. Sorry.'

'Not only that,' Feeney said as he climbed back in the EDD van, 'he's got the place wired.'

'Are you clear?' Eve demanded.

'Yeah, yeah, we're clear. Salazar and her team are working on it. What's your ETA?'

'That would be now,' she said, jumping out of the car as Roarke pulled behind the van.

The explosion had her cursing, surging forward toward Salazar's barricade. Roarke yanked her back before she could plow through.

'What are you going to do?' He kept his hand clamped around her arm.

She yanked out her comm. 'Salazar! What's your status?'

'Five-by-five. Stay out,' she added. 'We've shut down the booms on the doors, the windows. Checking for trip wires, flash bombs.'

'I'm coming in.'

'That's a negative. This is my purview, Dallas. Don't get in my way, don't distract my team. We need to clear this location.'

'You're right.' She walked back to the van. 'What can you tell me?'

'Big boom, third floor. Nobody was up there,' Callendar added. 'The team had entered, cleared first level and were up to two.'

So Eve waited, knowing Salazar's kind of work couldn't be rushed. She paced, ignoring the gawkers who never tired of gawking, the media hounds who'd scented a story.

'Baxter, go handle the media. Brush them back, but not too hard. We might need them if Silverman's in the wind.'

Now she did push through as Salazar stepped out, giving the all clear.

'Fucker had the place wired, top to bottom, inside out, and sideways. We got them all. The one that detonated was on a timer. Looks like he piled every electronic device in the place onto the third floor, set his charges. That's where he had his workshop, so a lot of that's gone. He built the vests up there.'

Despite the wind, Salazar, baking in her protective suit, swiped at sweat. 'Looks to me like he cleared out all the way – empty safe, not a stray sock left in the bedroom closet. I'm going to say he took some toys with him. We'll go through what's left.'

'Thanks. Feeney, take a look at what he blew up, see if you can salvage anything.'

'That'll be a trick,' Salazar commented. 'The wreckage is on the second floor now, seeing as the boom blew a hole in the floor of the third.'

Eve stepped into a white-walled, narrow foyer. 'Find out who owns the property,' she told Roarke.

'Iler bought it about a year ago. I already checked,' he said when she gave him a glance. 'He's claimed a loss on his taxes for maintenance and repair, with a rental income of two hundred a month. That's so far below market for this sort of property in this neighborhood to be laughable.'

She moved into the living area. 'So he bought the place

so Silverman would have a place to stay, charged a minimal rent so the tax guys wouldn't poke in too deep.'

'Precisely.'

She studied the space – the same white walls, unadorned. Floors that could have used some work, riot bars on the windows.

'He didn't spend much time down here,' she noted. 'Two ratty chairs, an old table, no screen, no stuff, but a lot of dust.'

She continued through – empty dining area, empty sitting area, a kitchen and powder room that showed no signs of regular use.

Still, she'd send the sweepers through every inch.

They climbed the stairs to the second floor. The ceiling of a bedroom gaped open, a hole with about a six-foot diameter. Fire suppressant dripped from the edges. The charred rubble, stinking of smoke and fried wiring, lay in piles on the floor.

Feeney in his shit-brown coat, Callendar in her boldly striped one stood in identical poses – hands on hips – and frowned.

'Got our work cut out for us, Cap.'

'We get anything out of this shit pile, we'll be miracle workers.'

As Eve watched, they looked over at each other, grinned.

'Does that mean you're going to work miracles?' Eve asked.

'It ain't going to be easy, and it ain't going to be quick.

But you never know till you know. You feeling lucky, Callendar?'

'I'm an e-dick, Captain. I wake up feeling lucky every freaking morning.'

'Use your lucky feet to walk down to the van, get our toys and tools. We'll scan this shit pile in place before we call in some boys to haul it to the lab.'

He looked back at Eve when Callendar bounced out. 'Not quick,' he repeated. 'Not easy. It's fried, blown to hell, and got suppressant clogging over that. Could use you,' he said to Roarke.

'Right now he's Peabody.' Eve looked down at the shit pile, shook her head. 'Do what you can.'

Of the remaining two bedrooms, only the master had furnishings.

'The sergeant kept things squared away in his personal space,' she noted as she walked through with Roarke. 'Bed's made — military precision there.' She drew out the drawer of the single nightstand. 'If he kept anything in here, he took it.'

She opened the footlocker he'd used in lieu of a dresser. 'Same here.'

'Bathroom's scrubbed to a gleam,' Roarke told her. 'Some cleaning supplies in the vanity, a couple of towels, bar soap in the shower, and nothing else.'

'I'd say he kept a kit for toiletries, shaving, that kind of thing. Salazar's not wrong about the closet,' she said as Roarke joined her. 'Bet your fine ass he had a go bag, so he grabbed it, whatever else he wanted, cleared out the safe. Smart, smart not to leave so much as a stray sock behind. But we'll find prints, hair. He didn't have time to wipe the place down.'

'Going by the furnishings, or lack thereof, he likely had few possessions.'

'Sleep, shower, dress.' Eve circled the room. 'Plot, plan, be ready to bug out. What kind of towels?'

Roarke smiled at her. 'Organic cotton.'

'Bed linens, too. So he learned to appreciate the finer things.'

She walked out, and up.

Smoke and fire suppressant still stung the air on the third level. She could look through the hole in the floor to where Feeney circled the pile of rubble as he waited for Callendar. Black streaked the white walls, and flying shrapnel had punched some holes in them.

'This is his lair, this is where he lived.' She stepped up to the remnants of a workbench, crouched. 'A solid one, a damn good one. Like organic cotton. Couldn't take this – or those vises that blew off and into walls. Got most of the tools and supplies, though. Some still here – that's for Salazar.'

'He built his bombs here,' Roarke agreed. 'And lived with them. The big wall screen, the good leather sofa and chair – or what's left of them now. That was once a high-end AC and friggie.'

He picked up a bottle – cracked, but not shattered. 'Twenty-year scotch. Unblended. That's a finer thing.'

'I leave Iler shaking – on purpose. He contacts Silverman, panicked. Silverman calms him down. Here's what we do. Has Iler give him enough time to pack up, to set explosives and clear out. Iler packs up, too. Neither one of them's smart enough to understand I'd have Iler under surveillance, but smart enough they don't want anybody to know he's running. They need some time, so he's going to be real clever and belay his way down to the street.'

'Which is a git move on the face of it in any case.'

'Oh yeah, but he is a git, and Silverman's not much smarter. Smart would've been for Iler to wait a few more hours. Wait until, say, two in the morning, then drop his ass down to the street, where Silverman's waiting for him in the black panel van.'

'You've booked a private shuttle,' Roarke continued. 'You get out, get gone, taking your profits to somewhere without extradition – which you should have arranged at the very start of the whole business.'

'Not smart, but there are eighteen dead, and I've still only got one of them.' She stepped back up to the hole in the floor. 'Feeney!'

'Yo!'

'I'm heading back to Iler's. He didn't blow up his equipment, and he's no pro. He might have left a trail.'

'We're going to scan this shit pile. I've got boys coming in for it. We'll be right behind you when we're done with this.'

'Good enough.' Eve straightened, looking around once more. 'We need that trail,' she said to Roarke. 'Because what I don't see in here, or anywhere where Silverman worked and lived, is any remnants of a suicide vest. He'd have had another one in the works, or ready to go. He took it with him.'

'He's lost his partner,' Roarke pointed out.

'It won't stop him. And without Iler, there's nothing to stop him from killing the wife and kid of the next target.' She dragged her hands through her hair.

'He wired the place, hoped to blow some of us up. Failed. Blew up his data, but we may get something out of it. Eventually. He must've had a meet spot with Iler. A time and place, but Iler didn't show. He has to know we have Iler.'

'More inclined to run then.'

'No, no, no. More inclined to finish. He's volatile. Why the fucking hell take time to blow up the whole damn house? He didn't use ninety percent of it, but Salazar said it was wired top to bottom. He only needed to blow his data, his records.'

'Well, he's a madman.'

'He's a madman, and the brother of his brother's in a cage. That may mean the access to at least some of the money's compromised. The money, that's Iler's area. Iler had the painting on him when we took him, half a million in cash, and the codes and IDs for three accounts.

'He's got to finish it, do the next, at least the next. Cash in, cash out. Look, we've got to split this after all. I need you to go to Iler's, see what you can do to find that trail. I wanted to let him sweat a few more hours, but I have to start working him. I need to get him in the box.'

'All right. I'll grab a ride with Feeney.'

'Thanks. I'll keep in touch.'

As she jogged downstairs, her 'link signaled a text.

Peabody, she noted, and scanned it on the move.

We're here, and it's already mag to the ex. But we want to know, just have to know – Did you get them?

Eve answered fast and brief. **Iler's in a cage, about to go in the box. ID'd the partner, working on bagging him. Too busy for details.**

Peabody's response came in seconds. **You'll break Iler like a twig. Let me know when number two's in the bag.**

Eve shoved her 'link in her pocket, and prepared to break Iler like a twig.

He'd lawyered up, but she'd expected it. She knew Richard Singa, the high-dollar criminal attorney, and had faced off with him before.

Iler sat silent and smug – from the smirk – when she came into Interview with Baxter.

'Record on. Dallas, Lieutenant Eve, and Baxter, Detective David, entering interview with Iler, Lucius, and his legal counsel on the matter of case files H–32019, H–32024, H–32029, and related matters.'

She sat, folded her hands on those case files. 'Mr Iler, have you been read your rights?'

Singa lifted a finger. 'We acknowledge my client was properly Mirandized.'

'Mr Iler, you've been charged with conspiracy to murder,

first-degree, eighteen counts, possession of and intent to use explosive devices to cause physical harm, enforced imprisonment, six counts, accessory to assault, four counts, endangering a minor, two counts, and various charges of fraud, tax evasion, breaking and entering—'

'Lieutenant.' Now Singa lifted both hands, peered at her with dark eyes over a broad nose. 'Obviously my client not only disputes all charges, but was, as we all know, nowhere near the scene of the tragedies at Quantum headquarters or the Salon gallery. And as the security in your own husband's apartment building must clearly show, he did not leave his own residence on the night of Jordan Banks's murder. Therefore, I must insist we dispense with this absurdity.'

'Has your client informed you by which method he attempted to elude arrest?'

Singa's gaze remained direct and dispassionate. 'While my client's practice of climbing and belaying was unwise in that particular location, you have no evidence this was an attempt to elude. Mr Iler had no reason to expect arrest, as he's committed no crime.'

'He had the artwork he stole from Banks's apartment in his possession.'

'My client maintains he purchased the artwork from Mr Banks.'

'So he'll provide a receipt for the purchase?'

'A cash deal,' Singa said smoothly, 'between friends.'

'And when was this cash deal between friends made?'

'Several weeks ago.'

'That's bullshit. I personally saw said artwork on Banks's wall on the evening before his murder.'

Singa hesitated — the faintest flicker across his eyes. 'Are you an expert in figure studies, Lieutenant? In Angelo Richie's work? Otherwise, it's easy to mistake one for another.'

'I have a witness who is an expert on both. So there's that. Your client also had a half million in cash, his passport, codes for numbered accounts, clothing, and other personal effects on him at the time of his arrest.'

'It's hardly against the law to carry cash, a passport. As to the codes and accounts, we will submit that, perhaps, my client attempted to game the system — as many do. Such matters hover in a gray area, and we will cooperate fully with any levy of taxes and/or fines, should they be warranted.'

At that, Baxter grinned, looking directly at Iler. 'Is your suit here telling you that you're going to lose up to seventy percent of what you squirreled away — and likely do a little time in a white-collar cage?'

The smug look dropped away as Iler swung toward Singa.

'We'll discuss that later,' Singa told Iler. 'For now, we again insist these false and damaging charges be dropped.'

'I'm not going to—'

'Later,' Singa snapped at Iler, and Eve chose her moment to drop her own bomb.

'Sergeant Oliver Silverman.' She waited a beat as color drained out of Iler's face. 'Aka Oliver Nordon. We've already paid a visit to the place you bought him. You've got to be good pals for you to let him have it for a couple hundred a month in rent.'

'How did you – I don't—'

'Quiet.' Now Singa clamped a hand on Iler's arm.

'Eighteen people, Iler. Eighteen. Because the only person you had the capacity to pretend to care about gave his life to save others. Because you chose to use his memory to make a profit, to have some fun, to get some sort of twisted payback. Whose idea was it to use loving fathers to get that payback, make that profit? Yours or Silverman's? It could matter. Your lawyer will tell you it could matter to how hard this goes on you.'

'My client has invoked his right to remain silent, and his right to legal counsel.'

'Yeah. Who's next, Iler? What family did you and Silverman plan to destroy next?'

'I don't have to talk to you. I want this to stop,' he told Singa.

'Give me the name.' Eve pushed forward. 'Right now we've got people combing through Silverman's place, combing through yours. Believe me, we'll find it. We'll wrap you up and toss you into a concrete cage off-planet.'

Every ounce of color bled from his face, and his eyes went wide and glassy. 'No, you won't. You will not. You can't prove any of this. We weren't there.'

'Stop talking, Lucius. I need to consult with my client.'

'Consult all you want, it won't change a damn thing. Off-planet, the rest of your life.'

'Look at him.' Baxter laughed as he and Eve rose. 'He's starting to think he can make a deal. Eighteen people dead, and he thinks he can deal it down because he's got money.'

'Not as much as he thinks, seeing as the IRS is going to take most. He's damn near tapped out anyway. Did you know that, Singa? Better get your retainer up front.'

'And your client?' Baxter added. 'He'd better pack some insulated johnnies. Those off-planet cages are cold, baby. They're cold.'

'Interview paused. Record off.'

As they stepped out, Mira came out of Observation.

'Did you see his face when you said "off-planet," LT?'

'Yeah.'

'We can use that. We can hammer that.'

'I agree,' Mira said as she joined them. 'He doesn't believe he'll be punished. He's convinced nothing will happen, but even the thought of, the remote possibility of being locked up off-planet frightens him. It's a lever.'

'Yeah, and we'll use it. Singa's going to keep him clamped down, clammed up. He didn't know about Silverman, but he's getting that out of Iler now.'

She paced away, paced back. 'And you know what he'll do? He'll start rolling the line that Silverman coerced his client, lied to him, forced him, threatened him.'

'Fuck that.'

She nodded at Baxter as she paced. 'Yeah, fuck that, but it's what he'll do. He'll string it out, jockeying for a deal, and he'll start with immunity – Yeah, fuck that sideways,' she said before Baxter could. 'I've got another way, maybe. I've got another lever.

'Baxter, do you know anybody in the IRS with some punch who's not an asshole?'

'I might know somebody.'

'Tag him.'

'Her.'

'Of course her. I want a jump on the slaps for those dark accounts. And given that he's currently charged with conspiracy to murder, etc., etc., they might freeze everything. No access to funds until the IRS completes their investigation, blah, blah.'

'Could work.'

'I've got another button to push.'

While she pushed another button, Roarke worked with Feeney and Callendar.

'Fucker's got enough electronics to open his own shop,' Feeney complained.

'That could make me like him, if he wasn't a fucker.' Callendar jiggled while she worked.

'A fucker he is,' Roarke agreed, 'but a smart enough one, or paranoid enough, to have filters and fail-safes on every bleeding thing. We'd do better with this in the lab, as even when we get through on something, the scanning and decoding from here will take hours – and that's piece by piece.'

Feeney chugged out a breath. 'You're right on that. We'll haul it down to Central.'

'My lab's closer,' Roarke pointed out, which had Feeney rubbing his chin.

'You're right on that, too. Still, we've got the portables he had with him to get through, and that shit pile from Silverman's.'

'Split it up, Cap?'

Feeney grunted at Callendar. 'Yeah, shit. I hate missing out on any of it, but that's the way to do it. I'm going to have some boys head up, tag, and log all this and haul it to your lab. You take that, and my boy and I here will head to Central with the rest.'

'Girl, Feeney. I keep telling you, I'm a freaking girl.'

'Boy, girl, what's the diff?

'Boy, penis. Girl, vagina.'

The tips of Feeney's ears pinked. 'Don't start that. An e-man's an e-man, whatever their works.'

Feeney pulled out his comm, walking away with his pink-tipped ears to start it rolling.

'I don't mind being one of his boys,' Callendar told Roarke. 'I just like to rag him, watch him get all hunchy.' She looked around the living area where they'd pulled out and set up all the electronics. 'It's a lot.'

'Less fun if it's easy.'

'Straight up.' She offered her fist to bump. 'Wonder if Dallas is having fun yet.'

*

404

Eve gulped coffee as she waited for the results from her button pushing. Losing time, she thought as she stared out her window, watched evening rolling toward night. All because some pricey lawyer with a sociopath for a client would play every trick in the hat, use every evasion on the field to get some sort of win.

Baxter came in, pointed at her AC, got her nod. 'Good news first. My friend at the IRS is very, very interested in Iler, and is pushing the paperwork through the system, the legal areas to do just what you want. Freeze it all.'

'What's the bad?'

'Singa just pulled the plug for the night. His client's exhausted, requires his full eight hours of rest before resuming interview.'

'Goddamn it. I knew that was coming, but goddamn it.'

'The maybe good news in the bad? Singa didn't look happy. In fact, he looked pretty seriously pissed off.'

'Not good enough.' Frustrated, she gave her desk a quick kick. 'Right now, he's pulling in his own investigators, and they'll be all over trying to get data on Silverman. He'll use, or try to use, everything he gets to deal down Iler. Silverman could be on his way to Argen-fucking-tina.'

'But you don't think so.'

'No, I don't think so. I think it's a hell of a lot worse.'

She stared at her desk 'link, willing it to signal.

'Maybe, maybe I can break through. But if he's got Iler locked for the night, I can't break until morning. Eight hours. Fine. Not a second more. Go get Trueheart, go get something to eat or whatever. Go home. Keep in touch with the IRS skirt, let me know if that moves any. Be back here at four hundred. We'll put him back in the box at oh-four-thirty.'

Baxter grinned. 'That's just nasty. I like it. Are you heading out, too?'

'Waiting for a tag back. If this works, we'll break Iler by five hundred.' She looked back out at the dark. 'I hope to Christ it's soon enough.'

At least she didn't have to deal with Summerset by the time she finally made it home. As Roarke had texted he'd tackle Iler's electronics in his lab, she tossed her coat over the newel post, headed straight up.

There he was, in full work mode. He'd changed into a black sweater, had the sleeves shoved up above his elbows. A strip of thin leather secured his hair back in a short tail.

She assumed there was logic and order in the lineup of Iler's many e-toys, just as she assumed the same about the codes, images, symbols rolling over Roarke's multiple wall screens.

The cat found it all fascinating, or so it seemed, as he squatted on a stool and watched. He gave Eve a glance with his bicolored eyes when she walked in, then went back to his evening's entertainment.

'Anything?' she asked.

'A considerable lot, actually.' Roarke continued to work, swiping screens, tapping keys and controls. 'You'll have him on tax evasion. I pushed through some files, got enough to see that, then moved on, as it's not your priority right now.'

'It's not, but still.'

'Insider trading as well – and you might find it interesting he paired up with Hugo Markin there.'

'I do, but.'

'Not priority, understood. Which is why those files are earmarked for another time.' He paused the work, rolled his shoulders. 'If he'd applied himself, he might have had a very successful career in cyber security. He's buried data deep, encoded it well. It's a job of work getting down to it.'

'You're better than he is.'

'I am.' Now he put his hands on her shoulders. 'We are. I can see by the look in your eyes you didn't get what you need from Iler. You will.'

'I will. I'm working an angle.' She picked up the water on his workstation, drank deep. 'He's lawyered up, which is no surprise. Sharp, high-priced lawyer, also no surprise. He's not talking. I could get a few rises out of him, but the lawyer shut him down. He's scared of being locked away off-planet, though. Got annoyed at the idea of a white-collar cage, but scared, shaky at the threat of off-planet. Off-planet's the key,' she said as she wandered the room.

She drank again. 'He hadn't told the lawyer about Silverman, I got that, too. So the lawyer shuts it all down – consult with client, client needs his eight hours down. Fuck, fuck, fuck.'

'The rules are often infuriating.'

'Maybe, maybe if I can keep shoving the off-planet up his ass, dangling Silverman, maybe he starts to crack even with the lawyer running interference. But now we wait – until we toss him back in at oh-four-thirty.'

With a laugh, Roarke ordered up another water. 'That won't sit well with Iler or his lawyer.'

'One thing, it gives me time to work an angle. The father. I get the father to understand his son's going down, one way or the other – and Silverman's going to benefit from Iler's loyalty. And funds. I'm working on blocking those funds, but the father has plenty I can't block.'

'So you convince the father to block that stream.'

'Yeah, no money for you if you continue to protect Silverman, if you don't reveal the name of other targets. If he flips, talks, I deal. On-planet incarceration.'

'A cage is still a cage,' Roarke said, but Eve shook her head.

'You didn't see his face. Mira agrees, says he might be spacephobic. Have you found anything about him going off-planet – business or pleasure?'

'I haven't, now that you mention it, not as yet.'

'I think I can use that fear, and the father. One son smearing the honor of the dead son. This goes to court, all that publicity, all that humiliation for the family. But the father's in freaking France. I got the father's lawyer, got him to contact Reginald Iler, get it going. I've been haggling with the lawyer off and on, maybe making progress. But the senior Iler's going to freaking sleep on it, and because of the damn rotation of the stupid Earth he's like hours ahead. Behind.'

She closed her eyes. 'No, ahead, so I can't lock it up until right before I get Iler junior back in the box.'

She two-pointed the empty tube of water into the recycler. 'Screw science.'

'You need pizza.'

The thought nearly perked her up. 'Maybe, but I have to tie up some contingencies with Reo.'

'You can eat pizza while you tie. I'll eat while I work on this.'

'Pizza?'

He pulled her in for a kiss. 'In solidarity.'

22

She ate pizza while she worked out tactics with Reo. Apparently it looked good, as the assistant prosecutor ordered up some of her own.

Despite the gray sweatshirt, the tousled fluff of blond hair, and the lack of makeup, Reo had the appearance of a delicate Southern belle.

Eve had reason to know that appearance masked – often strategically – a sharp mind and steely will. In court, Cher Reo could and did eviscerate a witness on cross without breaking a sweat.

At the moment, she bit neatly into her second veggie slice. 'I'll be there at four – God help me – A.M. Singa's going to be pissed, but he boxed himself in on it. He should've stalled you a couple of hours, then pulled out for the eight straight.'

'Silverman threw him off his game. He needs to research the asshole, get his investigators on it. If he wants to use Silverman as a cover for his worthless client, he has to lay out a plan first.'

'Maybe he's working late and eating pizza,' Reo

speculated. 'Anyway, if Daddy Iler contacts you before his nine o'clock time, let me know. Either way he leans, I can work it.'

'I will.'

'See you in the morning then. We'll nail his ass, Dallas.'

'Fucking A.'

She rubbed her eyes, started to program more coffee, when Roarke stepped in.

'I have something for you. Iler purchased a new model black panel van – loaded. An Essex Sprinter, license Echo-Zulo-Baker-five-seven-eight.'

When she reached for her comm, Roarke held up a hand. 'Hold on, save yourself time and order up a search along with your APB. He's also paying rent on a private garage.' As he gave her the address, he walked over to pour wine. 'As I haven't found, as yet, another storage facility, and you haven't found, as yet, the Richie artwork they stole – or what Iler purchased – and I found two he bought legitimately in Italy four years ago – they might have used the garage for both purposes.'

She wanted to do the search personally, bit back the impulse by reminding herself of priorities. 'I'll get a team to the garage now, get out the APB on the vehicle. This is good.'

He waited until she had before nudging the wine on her. 'We'll take five, you and I – and while we do,' he continued before she could object, 'I'll tell you I've been in touch with Feeney.'

'What's he got?'

'I'd imagine a raging headache by this time. He, Callendar, and two others have been working on cleaning, scanning, piecing together. It's slow, tedious work. The odds are long they'll get much of anything, you should know that. If anything can be recovered, they will. He and Callendar are going to take four hours in the crib, then get back to it.'

'Okay.'

'They've dug into the portables Iler had – and there you've got the financial information, his own portfolio, that sort of thing. Nothing on his contact lists, as yet, no link to Silverman. However, they dug up the 'link conversation with Banks.'

'You should've led with that.' She popped up, paced to the board. 'That's big.'

'He deleted it, but nothing's ever gone. Deleted, added some filters, and so on. It took some doing, but you have the conversation.'

'I need to hear it.'

'It's on your unit now.' Roarke leaned over, cued it up.

She heard Iler's voice answer cheerfully. *Well, hello, Jordan.*

Hi there. We need to chat.

About what?

About Quantum and Econo, about stocks and explosions.

After a tangible hesitation, Lucius answered, *A terrible thing, isn't it? Another disgruntled employee. Your ex was injured, wasn't she?*

Cut the bullshit, Lucius. I've had the cops at my door, and they

412

wondered — pointedly — if I'd shared any of the information Willi passed on to me with anyone.

Listen, Jordan—

No, you listen. I told the cops I hadn't, played it cool. But that can change. I did you a favor, Lucius.

I paid for the favor.

Not enough. If you want me to hold the line I've taken with the cops, I want a cut of what I imagine is a substantial profit. Let's say two hundred fifty thousand. Consider it insurance.

This is ridiculous. You can't prove you told me anything, and you certainly can't prove I had anything to do with what happened at Quantum.

Do you want the cops poking around, Lucius? I covered for you, and I'll go on covering for you. For a cut.

I had nothing to do with—

Don't care. Pay the insurance, Lucius, in cash, and your worries are over.

We need to discuss this. Not over the 'link.

Happy to. I'm at Thad and Delvinia's bon voyage right now. You can meet me here.

Not in public, for God's sake, not at a party. Let me think. I'll get back to you.

'Follow-up conversation coming next,' Roarke told her.

You took your time, Banks answered.

I needed time to think. And I needed time to put some cash together. I can give you a hundred — and that's simply to avoid the bother of police prying into my business. I don't appreciate this, Jordan.

413

We'll consider that a down payment. You've got a week to come up with the rest. Bring it to the party.

I certainly will not. I still have to get it, and I won't be seen with you. Our friendship's over, Jordan. I'll meet you at three A.M., Central Park. By the JKO.

Dramatic! I love it. See you then – have the money. Oh, and, Lucius? We were never friends.

'Idiots,' Eve said and shook her head. 'Both of them. Banks threatens Iler with exposure, then meets him, middle of the night, middle of the damn park. And Iler doesn't throw his 'link in the damn river after beating it with a hammer.'

'Custom 'link, platinum casing. Cost him about ten thousand.'

'Which makes him an idiot on that, too. This is going to wrap him, at least on Banks.' As she spoke, she copied the transmission, sent it to Reo.

'You're not overly worried about wrapping Iler. You know you'll break him. And you know you'll get him to flip on Silverman eventually. It's the eventually that worries you. It's the thought you might have to put others on your board before the eventually that worries you.'

'I'm hamstrung until the damn Earth rotates. But we've got the vehicle ID'd, we've got a location on the garage, and we might find something there that points to the other targets. Maybe there aren't other targets.'

'You're saying that to not add pressure on me.' He bent over, kissed the top of her head. 'I'll get back to it.'

'Listen, I suck at the e-stuff, but I can follow directions.

I've run out of what I can do here.' Frustration rippled as she looked around her command center. 'If they find anything at the garage, I'll hear about it. If they find the vehicle, I'll hear about it. I'll work with you until I do. I can do drone work.'

'I'd say you'd be better off trying for at least a couple hours' sleep, but you won't. All right then, if I can be your Peabody, you can be my drone.'

It didn't take long for her to figure out he tossed her busywork. Still, he kept her busy, and maybe it saved him some time and trouble.

She knew when he had the bit between his teeth because he muttered, swore, and his Irish thickened.

For herself she settled into the mind-numbing job of scanning codes, looking for – or waiting while the computer looked for – matches or patterns.

If one popped, she toggled it to Roarke so he could do whatever came next. She had no idea what the whatever might be, but a few times when she toggled something over, Roarke made the kind of noises she interpreted as progress.

She wondered if brains actually could spill out of the ears, and she sent Roarke another section.

'Ah, well now, that could be useful,' he mumbled. 'Pry this bleeding bitch open just a bit more. Aye, that's clever, but not fecking clever enough, is it then?'

She rose, turned to the friggie because she realized she'd finally hit a point she'd never believed possible to hit. She couldn't handle more coffee.

She got water for both of them.

'And there, you shagging, cross-eyed whoremonger, I've got it.'

Half-asleep, too used to his mutters to think anything of them — though *whoremonger* was new — she held out the water.

He flicked her away. 'Not now. There it is. Hiding out, tucked away in a bunch of bollocks. Not clients, no, they're fucking not clients.'

She heard it now — not frustration or inching progress, but pleasure edging toward triumph. 'Who?'

'Not done. Quiet. It wants to go sick if I get too close, and we won't have that. Standard virus is all it is. Just kill it, and then . . . There you are.'

'Who?' she demanded again. He shot whatever he'd found to a wall screen.

'Paul Rogan,' he read. 'Along with his wife, his daughter — and considerable salient information. Then the same for Wayne Denby.'

'Target list, two more. Jesus Christ. Tyber Chenowitz — wife, six-year-old son. That address—'

'Is all but around the corner.'

'Send the second — Miller Filbert, Lower East — to Baxter. Now, now, now. How fast can you get me eyes and ears on Chenowitz?'

'I've what you need in the lab here.'

'Get it, then let's move.'

As Roarke shot the data to Baxter, Eve dragged out her comm. 'Alert Lieutenant Salazar,' she demanded on the move. 'Two locations require E and B units.' She snapped information to Dispatch as she bolted down the steps, then contacted Baxter herself while she dragged on her coat.

He didn't bother to block video, so she got a good shot of his bare ass – not bad – as he scrambled out of bed.

'Got the address. On my way in five.'

'Get Trueheart, get there. Tag Feeney for eyes and ears. I've got another one I'm handling. Salazar's alerted. Wear vests and helmets. I'm sending uniforms, both locations. The van's a black Essex Sprinter, new model. Echo-Zulu-Baker-five-seven-eight. Watch for it. Do not enter until Salazar's team clears. That's an order. Move.'

She turned when Roarke jogged down to her with a field bag.

'I can get your eyes and ears, and I can scan for explosives.'

'Even better.' She ran outside, jumped in the car. 'Here's what we do. Go fast, but quiet. If he's there, if he has them, sirens might make him cut his losses. If he's crazy enough to hit another without Iler, knowing how close we are, he's crazy enough to kill the family. He'll sure as hell try to use them as shields.'

Roarke punched into vertical rather than waiting for the gates to open fully.

'I think I know the house. It's back off the street and gated, like ours. I'll need to bypass the security as, again, if he's there, he may have reset it as a precaution.'

It took under two minutes to get there. Roarke pulled up out of the range of the gate cameras.

'I'm going to jam them long enough for me to bypass. We'll go over the gate, then I'll reset.'

When he got out, she contacted Dispatch, ordering backup to wait outside the gate until she cleared them through.

'Done.' Roarke slid behind the wheel again, took vertical over the iron gates. Reengaged the gate system.

He stopped in the shadows.

The house, about twenty feet back from the gates, stood three stories, with pillars framing a wide front porch. A large section of the roof jutted out, flattened. She could see in the security lights the rise of dwarf trees.

She'd seen that roof garden, she realized, from the roof dome of their own house. A spilling water feature down the west wall, a kind of fancy shed she imagined held tools for the raised wooden beds full of growing things and color in the spring and summer. Chairs and umbrella tables in season, too, so as to enjoy the views in the garden and beyond. Big colorful pots to hold the trees and viny things winding up decorative supports.

No lights on the roof now, or on the main floor. But she noted them filtering through some of the windows on the second floor.

'There's a vehicle around the side – I can see the lights bouncing off the chrome bumper, but I can't get a good look. Work on the alarms, the eyes and ears. I'm going to move closer, check it out.'

She got out of the car, eased the door shut. Keeping low, weapon drawn, she jogged toward the house.

The black panel van sat close to the side of the house, out of sight from the street. She shined her penlight over the tags for confirmation.

She jogged back to Roarke.

'He's in there. Get those eyes in, tell me where.' Once again, she pulled out her comm.

'Salazar.'

'My location. His van's outside this location. Lights second-floor windows. I've got an e-man getting me eyes.'

'I'm heading to you. Don't enter until we clear.'

'We can scan for boomers. He's got three people inside. What's your ETA?'

'Ten minutes.'

'Don't take the gate until we give the green. Contact Baxter, tell him it's going down here.'

'Ten minutes, Dallas.'

She clicked off. 'Roarke.'

'Four in the room directly above, with the lights on. One has to be the child from the size of the heat read. One is sitting, one is lying down. One's standing – moving, back and forth.'

'Get us in there, quiet.'

'Scanning first. Because if it's wired, it won't be quiet at all. The door's clean. Another moment or two on the rest.'

'Be ready. We get upstairs – quiet. If I can take him out without endangering the civilians, I will. I need you to hang back in case I can't. Let him think I'm alone. If and when I lower my weapons, it's a signal you've got a shot. Take it.'

'All right, we're clear. I'll be scanning as we go. He may have set booby traps.'

She went in low, Roarke high. The moment they crossed the threshold, a light in the wide foyer flashed on.

She swung around, back-to-back with Roarke, weapon sweeping.

'Motion lighting,' he whispered. 'Fuck me. It's not to do with the alarm. It's set up so if someone comes in late, or goes down in the night, the light comes on for them.'

'If he sees it—'

A scream, agonized, ripped out. As Eve bolted toward the stairs, a woman's terrified voice shrieked, 'No! No! Please, don't hurt my baby!

A man's voice joined it, and a child's desperate calls for his mother.

She caught the sound of running footsteps, and the child's sobs overhead, swung first to the right and the master.

The woman struggled desperately against the binds that tied her to the bed. Blood seeped from her nose; her right eye was blackened, swollen closed. The man, equally bloodied, twisted against the ropes as he tried to worm his way across the floor to his wife.

He wore a suicide vest.

'Help us!' The woman wept as she scraped her wrists and ankles raw. 'He has my baby. He took our son. Help us.'

'Get her out.' On the floor, the man stared up at Eve with pleading eyes. 'Get my wife out, save our boy. He's got the detonator. There's no time.'

'Get her out,' Eve ordered Roarke, punching her comm to give Salazar and the backup the green. 'If you can do anything about the vest, do it. Otherwise, just get her out, wait for Salazar.'

She rushed the steps, weapon sweeping – heard a door slam. On the third floor, she paused, checking right, left. Family area, she noted, but two doors to the left, one to the right, all closed.

She drew a breath, held it. Listened while trying to tune out the weeping, begging rising up from the second floor.

She heard it, muffled, distant, but she heard the boy call out, again, for his mother.

Up, she realized. Roof garden.

She sidestepped left, angled to the first door, went in low. Bathroom, clear. Moved to the next.

Another set of stairs, straight up with a door at the top. She eased her way up, thinking of the man with the detonator. Nothing to lose now, no way out now. He'd press the button if she played this wrong.

She hit the door, swept, and caught sight of him through the denuded branches of ornamental trees, the kid flailing against him. He swung around, laid a combat knife against the boy's throat.

'I'll slice him. You hit me with a stream, I'll still slice him.'

All in black, but he hadn't bothered with the mask this time. Why bother? she thought. He'd intended to kill them all anyway.

'There's no way out, Sergeant.'

'I'm taking the fire stairs down.'

'Not with the kid, not with the detonator.'

The boy stopped fighting, stopped crying. His eyes went wide and blank as a thin dribble of blood slid down his neck.

'I'll slice the kid, blow up the other two. Or I take him down with me. He lives, they live. I go.'

Riot gear, neck to boots. Even with a full stream, she wouldn't take him down with one, maybe not two. And if she tried, the kid was done. She could see that in Silverman's eyes.

'Is this what Captain Iler stood for?'

'He's dead, isn't he?'

She eased closer, eyes locked. 'Is this what he died for?'

'He died for nothing! I served, I damn near died, and what did I get for it? Thanks for your service, you're finished. Do you *want* to see him bleed out?' he demanded as she took another step.

Once, she'd been too late to save a child from the knife. Not this time. Goddamn it, not this time.

She heard the sirens – backup coming in hot – and so did he. When his grip shifted on the knife, she aimed there.

The stream caught the kid – just the outer edge of it. His body jerked. As Silverman fought to control it and his shaking knife hand, Eve charged.

He dropped the boy, turned into the attack, tossing the knife to his left hand, slashing. When the knife skidded off the coat, she tried for a head shot, took a hard left jab in the face. He followed through, knife and fist, taking them both down in a bone-rattling heap.

She lost her grip on her weapon, rolled to clamp both hands around the wrist of his knife hand before he stabbed the toothed blade into her face. Breath whistling, she got a knee into his gut, used momentum to roll him off. As he sliced down again, she got a kick into his shoulder, sprang up, leaped over his sweeping leg as he did the same.

The boy lay in a trembling heap as they circled each other. She judged her weapon somewhere to the left, and her clutch piece useless. If she tried for it, he'd be all over her.

She danced back as he crouched, passing the knife from hand to hand. Danced back, away from the kid, with Silverman's eyes gleeful on hers.

'You should've let me go. Now I'm going to stick this knife in your guts, rip it through, and spill them out.'

She swung into a back kick, vaulted over a raised bed that smelled of earth and green. As she landed, she grabbed a pot with something spearing up hopefully through the dirt, flung it at him. Though he danced aside, it caught his cheek on the fly, left a raw scrape before it hit the painted concrete and shattered to shards.

The sirens screamed closer. Did he hear them? she wondered. She didn't think so. He was in the zone now. The killing zone.

She leaped onto another bed, pushed off, leading with her feet. Both landed, a human battering ram, center mass. The force sent him staggering back, and the knife clattered away across the concrete, balancing the odds. Still, he shook off the blow, came at her.

He had her by maybe seventy pounds, a combat-trained vet. He aimed a fist at her throat; she dodged, took it on the shoulder. Pain rang down her arm in clamoring bells.

She stopped feeling the blows – the ones delivered, the ones suffered. As she blocked, punched, she tasted her own blood, smelled his. Then he threw her back, slammed her into the trunk of one of the trees. Her vision grayed for just an instant, and she saw him yank the detonator out of his pocket.

He grinned as she leaped up, as she gathered to charge. And he pressed the button.

Eve, already in motion, saw the shock on his face as nothing happened. She rammed him like a bull, grappled with him, then flipped herself back.

Now, she thought, blood in her throat. Fucking now.

She balanced on one leg, shot up with the lifted one to slam two rapid kicks into his jaw. As he stumbled back, she leaped up with the other, plowed it into his midsection.

Mouth bloody, he came at her and, with her muscles relaxed, she whipped kicks at his shins, knees. She heard feet pounding up the stairs, ignored them as she used stiffened fingers, clenched fists to punish soft tissue – ears, eyes, throat.

It rushed through her, the power, the pain, the punishment.

'Get the kid,' she called out to whoever rushed up behind her. 'I've got this.'

As she coiled to finish it, Silverman made a desperate leap for the wall of the rooftop. Eve lunged forward, grabbed his wrist, slippery with sweat and blood, with both hands.

He dangled there while her muscles screamed in protest. Four stories up. It might not kill him, but she wasn't going to risk it.

'You don't get off this easy.'

'I'll take you with me.' Throwing up a hand, he grabbed her arm, dragged.

She dug in as the toes of her boots slammed the wall. She wouldn't go over, she would *not*, but she wouldn't be able to hold him much longer.

Roarke reached down beside her, adding his weight, his muscle. When Silverman continued to pull, to fight, Roarke ended it with a vicious, short-armed punch.

As he went limp, they hauled Silverman back over the wall.

Adrenaline gone, pain blooming everywhere, she slid to sit, back to the wall. Her breath whistled harsh out of aching lungs.

Roarke knelt beside her.

'Ten minutes,' he said. 'It couldn't have been ten minutes before I got up here, and look at you.'

'Yeah, well.' She swiped at the blood dripping out of her nose. 'Look at him.'

She did. He lay dazed, surrounded by a half dozen cops all with weapons drawn.

'The kid,' she said when Baxter crouched in front of her.

'Trueheart's got him, taking him down to Mom and Dad. He's fine. Got a scratch. Just a scratch, some bruises.'

'He caught the edge of my stream.'

'He's fine, LT. Lucid, a little shocky, scared. But he's fine. Now, you? Ouch. Do you want to wrap him up?'

She shook her head, winced when it spun a little. 'You take him. He's going to need medical, then he's in a cage until I'm ready for him. My weapon—'

Baxter handed it to her. 'We'll bag his knife. You cut any?'

'No. I don't think. Wrap him up, Baxter.'

'You got it, boss.'

'Magic coat,' she murmured to Roarke as Baxter moved away. 'I don't think he even noticed the blade wasn't getting through.'

He dropped his brow to hers a moment. She let him have the moment, took it for herself. But pushed back when he started to lift her.

'You're not carrying me out of a scene loaded with cops.'

'Then you're not arguing about a trip to the nearest health center.'

'Let's just start with the on-scene medical. Okay?'

'We'll start there.'

23

She suffered the exam, the treatment, the blockers, ice patches, healing wands. But drew the line at the pressure syringe and tranqs.

'I've got to finish this,' she argued. 'I can't finish it if I'm dopey.'

'You could do with the tranqs and sleep,' Roarke argued back. 'You've got your men in cages. A few hours won't change that.'

'I need to finish it while they're on the ropes. If the father comes through — and he's due to make contact within the hour — I need to push it, end it, close it. I don't want them figuring out how to slither out of any of it.

'After,' she promised. 'I won't need a tranq to sleep. You drive, okay? You can fill me in on the way to Central. I've got cops taking statements from Chenowitz and his family. I can follow up there later.'

He studied her face, the mouth still raw and puffy, the eyes — both — with purpling bruises to match the marks on her jaw.

'I shouldn't let you win this one.'

'I took everything but the tranq. That oughta count.'

'I suppose it does.' He slid an arm around her, took some of her weight as they walked to the car.

'When he pulled out the detonator, my heart stopped.' She eased carefully into the car. 'My life stopped. I knew you'd have gone back for Chenowitz. No way you'd have left him in that vest.'

'She wouldn't leave him,' Roarke replied. 'Jolie, his wife. She'd have run out the moment I cut her loose – to get to her son. I convinced her she'd put the boy in more danger, that you'd protect him.'

'You had that right,' Eve agreed.

'But then she wouldn't leave her husband. He begged her to, but she wouldn't, so I had a choice. Knock her unconscious, carry her out, or deal with the explosives then and there. A bit tricky, but not as complicated as I'd feared,' Roarke explained.

'He never anticipated anyone attempting to defuse. Especially this one. He was going to kill them all,' Eve stated as a fact.

'Now they're safe. Salazar rushed in moments after I defused, locked it in a bomb box, and that's that,' Roarke concluded.

'Tuned them both up this time. Iler wasn't there to cool him off. And he'd have sent Chenowitz out at dawn, down to the building Iler bought – in the Nordon name – where a crew of about six, maybe eight would be setting up for rehab. Five more charges set in there, Salazar said, for a chain reaction.'

'Buy a property, over insure it, destroy it, collect. Classic,' Roarke said. 'Chenowitz – the successful builder, devoted family man – blows up his own crew.'

'It didn't matter that he'd never be able to collect on this one. He'd have won, completed the mission, and that's what counted. In his mind, the military let him down, betrayed him. His brothers, his family, all Blue Falcons.'

'"Blue Falcons"?'

'Military term,' she told him, closing her aching eyes for a moment. 'Stands for *buddy fuckers*.'

'Ah. And in his mind, Silverman was the buddy who'd been fucked.'

'He and Iler fed off each other. Iler's got the funds, the financial know-how, Silverman's got the tactics, the explosives training. And they both used what they had to twist the memory of a hero, for fun and profit.'

She took a long breath. 'I need to round up Reo, Mira, send an update to Whitney.'

'You should text Peabody, let her know you've got them both. It's still shy of midnight on the coast.'

'I don't want to hear about time zones.'

She made the tags, sent the update, wrote the text, then eased out of the car – as carefully as she'd eased in – when they reached Central.

'It's going to take me awhile,' she began. 'I know you'll

want to observe when I have them in the box, but you should find a place to chill until then.'

'I'll wander up to EDD.' He took her weight again as they crossed to the elevator and in. 'I can let Feeney and Callendar know in more detail what I've pulled out of Iler's e's. I'd wager they're back at it.'

'Good thinking.' She leaned against him. 'You make a hell of a Peabody.'

'The highest of compliments.' He tipped her face up, kissed her bruises. 'I should have punched him harder.'

'Just hard enough.' She stepped to the doors when they opened on her level. 'Tell Feeney I still want whatever he can dig out.'

'Understood.'

She glanced in both directions, saw the all clear as the doors started to close. 'I love you.'

He stopped the doors with a hand. 'Come in here and say that.'

'Later.'

Since there was no one to see, she limped toward Homicide, and into her office. She got coffee, sat at her desk. Then laid her head on it, said, 'Son of a bitch!'

She let herself have a couple of good moans, maybe a quiet whimper, then pushed herself up to drink the coffee, write up the report.

When her desk 'link signaled, she smiled at the readout. Reginald Iler. And here we go, she thought.

'Lieutenant Dallas. Thank you for contacting me, sir.'

He had a hard, handsome face, shrewd, dark eyes. 'You look as if you've been in a brawl.'

'I have been. With Sergeant Oliver Silverman. He's now being treated in our secure infirmary and booked as your son's coconspirator on eighteen counts of murder, and related charges.'

'I've never heard of this man. This is—'

'Your surviving son has heard of him, and, in fact, knows him very well. As I explained through your attorney, Sergeant Silverman served under your younger son, Captain Terrance Iler. Mr Iler, your son and Silverman will do eighteen life sentences, consecutive. I'm going to make absolutely sure of it. I no longer need your cooperation in this matter.'

'Now just a damn minute.'

Gave you too many minutes already, she thought.

'I don't need it because I have the evidence, and very shortly I'll have full confessions. However, if your cooperation, as I outlined through your attorney, saves the families of the victims more grief, saves the State of New York time and trouble, I'll take your cooperation into consideration as regards where your son serves those eighteen consecutive life sentences. Your choice, sir. You'll have to make it here and now, as I'm about to bring your son back into Interview.'

Later, she sat in the conference room working out strategy with Baxter, Trueheart, Mira, Reo. She came a little painfully to attention when Whitney walked in. And – ah, Jesus – Anna Whitney beside him.

'We won't get in your way,' Whitney said. 'How much longer do you need?'

'We've just finished, Commander. I'm having both suspects brought up into separate Interview rooms. Baxter and I will work Iler, as we teamed on him earlier. Trueheart and I will work Silverman.'

'You can wait in the lounge, Anna. I'll have someone come for you. My wife,' he explained, 'would appreciate observing the start of each interview, if you have no objections, Lieutenant.'

'No, sir.'

'You're wondering,' Anna said to Eve, 'how I'll handle the sort of language, the descriptions of violence that go into an interview. I'm a cop's wife,' she said simply. 'Seeing them in the box will give me some peace. Being able to tell Rozilyn I saw them will, eventually, give her and her family some peace.'

She touched a hand to her husband's arm. 'I'll be in the lounge.'

Eve remained standing when Anna walked out.

'Everybody clear?' she asked. 'Any more questions? No? Then let's get this party started.'

She and Baxter started with Iler, and his attorney led off with a bite.

'I will file a formal complaint against both of you,' Singa began. 'Demanding my client submit to Interview before five in the morning is absurd.'

'He had his eight, Singa.'

'Clearly, this timing violates the spirit of that law.'

'Clearly, you should have thought about the timing before you demanded the eight at twenty hundred hours. File all the complaints you want. We have business to get to. Mr Iler—'

'You will address me,' Singa reminded her. 'My client has invoked his rights.'

'Oh yeah, slipped my mind. I also meant to mention that fee of yours again. You got that up front, right? A good chunk? How much do you charge an hour?'

'That's none of your concern.'

'You're right. It's yours. You might be somewhat concerned to learn your client's broke. No money, no access to same. All accounts have been frozen – by the IRS, pending further investigation.'

'They're pretty excited,' Baxter added. 'Even more since we broke through your filters and coding. You've been a very bad boy, Lucius. There are IRS agents having wet dreams right now, and you're the star.'

'That freeze also pertains to any funds Mr Iler may have advanced you, Singa, on his behalf, as all his moneys, properties, possessions are now in that freeze. The IRS will be in touch with you.'

'And you know, once they "get in touch," they just love to poke around.'

'Yeah, they do,' Eve added with a broad, toothy smile. 'And in case either of you are thinking of a rich daddy? You can forget it. Reginald Iler and I had a long conversation.'

'You had no right.' Iler tried to push to his feet, rattling his restraints. 'No right to involve my father.'

'You had no right to murder eighteen people, to destroy eighteen families. Which one of us do you think is going to pay?'

'You're cut off, sonny boy,' Baxter added. 'Daddy's closed the family bank – and that includes any interests you may hold in various arms of the family business. You got zilch.'

'I want to talk to my father. Now.'

'Sorry, you don't get it. You're under arrest. Your wants aren't of concern. Your attorney is, of course, free to contact the senior Mr Iler. Though I believe Senior Mr Iler will be disinclined, at this time, to communicate. At all. At least until I speak with him again.'

As she spoke to Singa, she hardened her look, her tone. 'When I do, if I tell him your client has given a clear and full confession on all charges, given us clear information on all details of his crimes, and the crimes of Sergeant Oliver Silverman, Mr Iler may be inclined to pay the legal fees and expenses incurred by his son to date. Though it sounded to me as if he'd negotiate same, and hard.'

She shifted to Iler. 'You think Singa's going to work pro bono on a case he has to know by now is locked? Eighteen consecutive sentences, off-planet.'

'I'm not going off-planet. I can't go off-planet. I have a condition. Richard, you said—'

'Did he tell you he could work it? Have that part off the table? Not happening, you fuck. The PA's holding firm

434

there. If the psych exam finds you have a "condition," you'll be properly sedated for the trip to Omega. You've got one shot, and one shot only. Full confession, every detail, and you serve your time on-planet. Hedge, bullshit, lie, evade, we're done.'

She leaned closer. 'You make me sick – and your lawyer just adds to it. But he's doing his job, so I can swallow that down. You did what you did to make money, to gamble, to pay back your own father because your fucking inner child's so needy. So lie to me, you piece of shit, and I'll personally watch them strap your unconscious ass in the shuttle to Omega.'

'This isn't right.' Iler's eyes went damp as he turned to Singa. 'You said you'd fix this. You said—'

'Quiet, Lucius. Lieutenant, I need to consult with my client.'

'I bet you do.' Eve rose, gestured to Baxter. 'Oh, just one more thing, as it may play into your consult. We've got Silverman. We took him down after he broke into the home of the next target on your list. Like Baxter said, we cut through your filters. The Chenowitz family is fine. Silverman?'

She ran a hand over her own bruised face. 'We had a little altercation. He looks a lot worse than I do. You take your time. I need to chat with him anyway.

'Lieutenant Dallas, Detective Baxter exiting Interview. Record paused.'

When the door closed, Baxter gave Eve a light punch on the arm. She hissed in a breath.

'Shit, sorry. It's just — that was righteous. I think I liked the look on Singa's face even more than Iler's. You could just see him watching all those juicy billable hours drain away.'

'Iler will fold. Singa will advise him to because, billable hours and the fact we've got Silverman. He'll use the on-planet deal as leverage. He'll do part of our job for us on this.'

'Take a break,' she told him as Trueheart came out of Observation. 'Grab some coffee, stay close. Okay, Trueheart, let's go kick some ass.'

'I checked on the kid, well, the whole family, but I wanted to make sure August was doing okay. He got on the 'link to thank me for taking him to his mom. And he said — I thought you'd like to know — a ninja woman saved him.'

'"Ninja woman."' Eve let out a snorting laugh. It hurt her bruised chest a little, but it was worth it.

She opened the door to Interview B. 'Record on,' she said and recited the salient information into the record.

Silverman sat, arms crossed, face a mass of bruises.

'I've got nothing to say. I'm waiting for my attorney, so you can kiss my ass.'

'Your court-appointed?' Eve responded, then smiled. 'Oh, I bet you mean that high-priced criminal attorney you contacted after booking, the one shuttling in about now from Philadelphia. Too bad we're going to have to inform him you have no available funds.'

'I've got funds. I've got resources. Fuck you.'

'You've got nothing. Accounts frozen. Iler's got nothing.

And his daddy won't pay. Not one thin dime. If you're thinking of trying to find a way to turn those Richie paintings into quick cash, you can forget that. They've been confiscated from the garage Iler rented.'

She dropped into a chair. 'EDD's putting your comps and devices back together in the lab. Of course, it's more out of a sense of pride at this point, as we have all we need. For you? Well's dry. You have a right to an attorney, and since you can't afford one, one will be appointed for you. You can wait in your cage while we get that going.'

His eyes, surrounded by bruises, stayed dark and sharp on hers. 'Fuck the lawyers, fuck the courts, fuck you.'

'I think he's a little upset he got taken down by a woman, Lieutenant.'

She shot Trueheart an easy smile. 'You think? He got most of his dick and one of his balls blown off. He can pump the chemical testosterone and steroids all he wants. They don't make him a man.'

'You shut your dick trap.'

She pushed her face into his. 'Make me.'

'Now, Lieutenant, come on. Ease back.' Trueheart patted her arm. 'He was wounded serving his country.'

She shrugged, sat back. 'Do you want the lawyer, Silverman?'

'Didn't I say "fuck the lawyers"? Did I bust your eardrums when I punched that bitch face?'

'I can hear you fine. You're waiving your right to an attorney? You need to say it for the record.'

'I don't need or want a goddamn shit-ass lawyer. I'm a soldier. I can take care of myself.'

'You *were* a soldier,' Eve corrected. 'Now you're a murderer. Is that why you went to Iler? I bet his brother talked about him – the big bro who read him stories, looked after him when they were kids. Did you figure you'd find a brother in Iler?'

'Captain Terrance Iler was the best man I know. And those sons of bitches killed him. He dragged me out. I told him to leave me, but he dragged me out, and he went back in, and they killed him.'

'Is this how you honor his sacrifice?' Trueheart asked, his voice church quiet.

'Fuck sacrifice. Fuck the army. Those sons of bitches blew themselves up to kill us, but there's always more. I was ready to go back, take some bastards *out*. They say I'm not fit to serve? They say the bombing scrambled up my brains? I ended up on the street thanks to them.'

'You used your compensation, your pension, to buy drugs, and what you had left, you gambled away,' Eve reminded him. 'You refused to continue treatment at any VA facility, or utilize the assistance offered to veterans.'

'Fuck all of that.' His mouth twisted so violently into a snarl, the healing bottom lip split open again. 'Do you think I'd take their pity?'

'It's gratitude for service,' Eve corrected. 'But rather than take it, you targeted innocent people, and took lives.'

'Innocent is bullshit. Nobody's innocent.'

'What made Paul Rogan guilty?'

'Which one is that?'

Eve's gut clenched at the careless question. All the dead were the same to him. 'The first. The man whose wife and daughter you tormented until he blew himself up, as well as others at Quantum HQ.'

'Fucking pussy is what he was. Cried. Begged, pleaded. It's called tactics, moron. It's called putting the pieces in play.'

'So Rogan and Denby were pieces to be put in play?'

'Worked, didn't it?' He lifted his hands, spread them, made a *boom* sound. 'The rest, collateral damage. You think I give a shit about any of those rich bastards in their big houses? They're no better than me.'

A vein beat at his temple – snaking, pulsing toward his shaved skull.

'I put my life on the line for them, and it got me squat. So I took what I was owed.'

'You built the bombs, the vests that you forced Rogan and Denby to wear.'

'Nobody held a bang stick to their heads.'

'You just beat their wives, threatened to kill their children. You built the bombs, the vests,' Eve repeated.

'I got the training. Didn't make the cut, and that was a pisser. I knew what I was doing. I trained myself more after they booted me back to the world. I could've taken out more than I did, but Lucius wanted to keep the casualties down. He's got soft spots.'

'How'd you pick the targets?'

'What do you care?' He smirked. 'Got blowed up, didn't they?'

'It took some doing, some work, some smarts. Why don't you tell us how smart you are, Sergeant?'

'Shit. Rogan was easy. That asswipe Banks fed Lucius some intel on the merger – rich bastards getting richer. We're just sitting around one night, me and Lucius, drinking and bullshitting, and he says how we could make a windfall buying up some of the stocks. We started playing with it, then we could see how it could work.'

'And how was that? Why Paul Rogan?'

'Lucius wanted to pick a father. He's got a hard-on for his own, right? He wanted to see, like an experiment, if a father would give his life for his kid. His brother gave his life for his men. It's like the same, so we started working on it. Rogan fit the bill.'

'I'm going to say Lucius worked up the jammers, the way through security.'

Silverman jerked a shoulder. 'He's got a knack. Took him weeks, but he figured it out.'

'You handled the parents, he handled the kids.'

'No hurting the kids, that was his line.'

'But the women were fair game.'

'You gotta incentivize people. They don't believe you'll follow through, they don't follow through.'

'Lucius set up the fake accounts, buried them, bought up stocks,' Eve prodded.

'He's got good brains for that shit. He's an asshole on tactics, but he knows his money shit.'

'How much did you make?'

'One-point-three.' When he grinned, a little blood dribbled down his chin. He swiped it away. 'More money than I've seen in my life, all at once.'

'And still not enough. Did you always plan to steal the Richie from Banks?'

'That jerk-off? Lucius said we'd consider that the jerk-off's fee. We had some already, and we'd have more after we got the art guy to blow up the artist and a bunch of his faggy art shit.'

'But Banks pushed his way into it. You had to kill him.'

Silverman eased toward Eve. 'If I could've gotten my hands on you just right?' He bared his teeth as he twisted his hands, made a crunching sound. 'Stupid fuck walked right into it. Lucius was a little shaky after I did it, but he held up.'

'The two of you dumped Banks's body in the reservoir.'

'It's called teamwork.'

'Lucius had already broken into Banks's apartment for the Richie artwork.'

'That was slick.' Admiration gleamed in those dark eyes. 'Damn slick. He's got skills, and we both figured we might as well have it.'

'It's a tight timeline, Rogan to Banks to Denby.'

'Tighter than we figured, but we worked it. Gotta think on your feet in the field.'

You're not thinking so much now, Eve decided. Now

you're bragging. 'Where was Lucius supposed to meet you, after I paid him a visit, got him all worked up?'

'He's not used to dealing with cops. We were supposed to meet at the garage. I figured it went south when he didn't show.'

'Did he know you planned to move on Chenowitz?'

Silverman responded with another smirk. 'He'd have known when we got there.'

'Did he know you planned to kill the wife and kid this time?'

'Look, I let him have his way before on that, and that's why it went FUBAR. We left them alive. Dead don't talk.'

'You'd be surprised.'

'Where were you going to go?' Trueheart wondered. 'You knew your partner was compromised, you knew, had to know, we were coming for you.'

'Private shuttle, dickwad. We got the scratch for it, and enough to buy some pilot's silence. We get to Port-Salut – no extradition, tropical, beaches? All the money we need. We get there, we're home free. Fat fucking City.'

'There won't be any beaches for you, Silverman,' Eve said.

He shot up his middle finger. 'Do you think I care about doing time? I'm a goddamn soldier. Nothing you can throw at me I can't handle. You won't break me.'

Eve stood. 'I just did. Detective, have the prisoner taken back to his cell. You're a disgrace to everything Captain Iler stood for, fought for, died for.'

'You don't know dick about squat.'

'I know you. I've seen you before. I'll see you again. You're nothing special. Dallas, exiting Interview.'

She stopped outside the door, scrubbed her hands over her face. Coffee, she thought. One more hit, then she'd go back on Iler.

Mira stepped out of Observation, laid a hand on Eve's shoulder, rubbed gently. Eve sent a leery glance at the medical bag in her other hand.

'You need another round with the healing wand and ice patches.'

'I need coffee.'

'You can drink it while we have that round. Save time,' Mira added. 'Don't argue with a doctor. You played him perfectly.' She steered Eve toward Eve's office. 'Tapped into his anger, resentment, manhood, ego. He may have emotional issues resulting from the attack, his injuries, and the loss of fellow soldiers.'

'Screw that. He—'

'Wait.' She nudged Eve onto her desk chair, opened her doctor's bag. 'His emotional issues don't negate his actions. He showed no remorse. Look up. In fact,' she continued as she ran the healing wand over Eve's bruises, 'he showed pride. He was, knowing he had no escape route, pleased to share details. To brag. In a very real way, he considers himself now a prisoner of war. He needs to be on suicide watch. He will try to self-terminate, whatever he claimed about not breaking.'

'Yeah, I already planned for that. I need that coffee.'

443

'One second.' Mira applied the ice patches, walked to the AutoChef. She handed Eve coffee. 'I'm going to close the door and do the rest of you.'

'It's not that bad.'

Mira simply walked to the door, locked it. 'Strip off the jacket, weapon, shirt. I don't want to recommend to your commander that you should be taken to a health center.'

'Goddamn it.' Outgunned, she pushed up, started to jerk off her jacket. Everything twinged and pinged at once.

'Here.' Mira slid the jacket off. 'We'll get this done, no fuss, then you'll finish your job.' She helped Eve out of her harness, her shirt. Then sighed.

'Not that bad? Really, Eve, damn it! Did the MTs say ribs are broken?'

'Bruised. Just bruised.' She clamped her teeth down as the healing wand could sting on deeper injuries. 'Maybe a hairline fracture. Maybe.'

'Internal injuries?'

'No. I swear. Roarke wouldn't have let me skate out of there and straight here. I've got strains and sprains in places I didn't know could get strains and sprains. The son of a bitch can fight.'

'Obviously so can you.'

She closed her eyes, ordered her body to relax, to accept the treatment. 'Roarke's Christmas present – dojo, training – holo and in the flesh with the master. I let it come. I was a goddamn crane, and a snake, a freaking dragon. Had the tiger coming, but he tried to take a header off the wall.'

'I have to admit, I'd like to have seen that. You're going to need another treatment in three hours.'

'Okay.'

Mira kissed Eve's cheek. 'I mean it.'

'I know it. Or you'll rat me out to Whitney.'

'And Roarke.'

'Figured.'

She had to admit she felt better after Mira got done with her. With Baxter she walked back into Interview A with Iler. Singa remained counsel of record.

'Record on, resuming interview. So here we are again. I have to tell you – full disclosure, because why the hell not – Silverman rolled on you like a pig rolls in shit.'

'He wouldn't do that.'

'You think he gave a rat's ass about you?' Baxter demanded with a laugh. 'You were a vehicle, a piece on the board.'

'I think he liked Lucius here okay,' Eve added. 'And he admired certain skills. Like building jammers, figuring out how to get through security systems. While he built the bombs. He knows he's done.'

She looked at Singa. 'Just like your lawyer knows I'm not bullshitting. He gave us everything, like how this all started after Banks fed you some inside scoop on the merger. You and Silverman sitting around, drinking and shooting the shit, and you.' She pointed at Iler. 'You come up with the idea.'

'No, I—'

'Lie, it's done. Maybe you were just bullshitting, playing

what-if, but it started rolling from there. I don't need any-thing from you.'

'We have a deal on the table,' Singa said.

'Yeah, I talked to APA Reo, and we agreed to go ahead with the deal. Save time and grief, just like I said before. One lie, deal's void. Was that also made clear?'

'It was,' Singa agreed. 'Lucius, you need to cooperate.'

'I said I would.'

But he sat, silently.

'Did you know he dragged the Chenowitz kid – August, six years old – up to the roof of the house, held a knife to his throat? Drew blood? He'd planned on killing the kid anyway, so no harm using him as a shield.'

'He wouldn't do that. Ollie wouldn't do that.'

Eve slapped both hands on the table. 'You *know* he would. You know it. You could pretend otherwise as long as it all worked for you and you banked that profit. But you fucking knew what he was inside.'

'I would never harm a child.'

'Just terrify them.'

'I did what I could to keep them calm,' Iler countered. 'I'd never have allowed Ollie to physically hurt one of the children.'

'How did you plan to stop him?'

'He'd listen to me. We're a team. The point is, and it's important: I never killed anyone.'

'Eighteen.'

'No, you see, those men, those two men made a

choice. They had a choice. They could have gone to the police instead.'

'And had their families killed.'

'No, no, no, that was a bluff. Just a bluff.'

'"A bluff."' Eve opened the file, tossed out photos of both crime scenes. The charred bodies, the pieces of the dead. 'A bluff.'

'They had a choice,' Iler insisted. 'They could have called the bluff. I admit we bear some responsibility, but—'

'"Some responsibility."' She lunged up, lunged across the table. 'You had him wired, had him wear a recorder so you could see – and so he could hear his wife and child screaming. You beat the women, threatened rape.'

'I never touched them. I swear it. I swear it. I agree Ollie could go too far, but I held him back.'

'Did you hold him back when he snapped Banks's neck? Lie to me, you fuck. Please lie.'

'I – he – Jordan was blackmailing me.'

'You killed him for it.'

'Ollie did. I could never—'

'Did you help dump his body in the water? Lie to me,' she urged.

'I didn't know what else to do.' Tears started seeping down his face. 'I didn't know.'

'Did you and Oliver Silverman break and enter into the residence of Paul Rogan, Cecily Greenspan, Melody Greenspan Rogan with the intent and purpose of imprisoning said family?'

'I . . . yes.'

'Did you or your partner physically assault both adults?'

'Yes.'

'Did you or your partner batter Cecily Greenspan and threaten to sexually assault her?'

His shoulders shook with sobs. 'Yes, but—'

'Did you, over the course of time from the early hours Saturday through Monday morning, threaten, assault, and coerce Mr Rogan, keeping his child separated, causing her to cry out for him, with the purpose of making him choose to carry an explosive device into the Quantum Air headquarters, to wear said device into a scheduled meeting, to detonate said device, killing himself and others in order to save his family?'

'We were bluffing.'

'Did you threaten, repeatedly, to kill Rogan's wife and child if he did not carry out the bombing?'

'Yes, yes, yes, but—'

'I'm going to start considering your stupid *buts* an evasion and negate this deal. I would love to think about you living the rest of your worthless life off-planet. Deep space, no air unless they pump it in.'

'Please.'

'Did you and Silverman arrange to meet Jordan Banks at approximately three A.M. in Central Park, and did you stand as an accessory to his murder by Silverman?'

Iler buried his face in his hands. 'Yes. Please stop.'

'When we're done.'

And when they were done, she called on Mira to give Iler a sedative.

'I want to high-five,' Baxter told Eve, 'but I can't work up to it. He was pathetic. Just goddamn pathetic.'

'Go home, get some sleep instead. Good work.'

'Yeah. Hey, Trueheart,' he called as his partner came out of Observation. 'Let's you and me hit that diner you like, have ourselves a big, greasy breakfast. Get the taste of this out of our mouths.'

'Works for me. Do you want to come, Lieutenant?'

'No, thanks. Good work, Trueheart.'

She started to turn toward Homicide when Anna Whitney came out, flanked by Roarke and the commander.

'Jack's annoyed with me,' she said briskly. 'I'd agreed to stay only for the first few minutes of each interview. But I wouldn't leave. I couldn't. I'm going to see Rozilyn now. Thank you for finding justice for a good man.'

'Yes, ma'am.'

'Jack.'

'All right, all right. Go home, Lieutenant.'

'Yes, sir. I'm just going to write this up, connect with Reo, then—'

'No. I'll write it up.'

'You? But—'

His eyebrows lowered. 'Do you doubt I can handle that duty, Lieutenant?'

'No, sir.'

'You're dismissed. You're on medical leave until the

start of your shift on Monday morning. You're off the roll. Understood?'

'Yes, sir.'

'Good work, Dallas. Fine work. If I see you here five minutes from now, I'll kick your ass.'

He took his wife's hand, walked away.

'I'd say that was clear enough.' Roarke took Eve's.

'He probably hasn't done this kind of paperwork in ten years. Twenty.'

'Let's get your coat.'

'I should be able to tie up my own ends.'

He kissed her hand before she could snatch it away. 'Lieutenant, do you want your ass – which is surely already carrying bruises – kicked by your commander?'

'No.' She let Roarke help her into her coat. 'No,' she said again.

'Let's go get some sleep. Unless you'd like a big, greasy breakfast first.'

'Sleep. Good work, Peabody.'

'Thanks.'

He got her down to the garage, into the car. Before he'd pulled out, she was getting a head start on that sleep.

Epilogue

She slept for twelve hours, woke starving, and ate like a horse. Because it ached enough – and Roarke wouldn't take no – she agreed to a soaking treatment, more wanding, the ice patches.

She snuck into her home office long enough to read Whitney's work. Had to admit he did the job well. Maybe she wanted to fiddle, just a little, but she had a feeling the commander would notice.

And maybe kick her ass.

Sprawled on the sofa with Roarke, she dropped off again while watching a vid, slept straight through – dreamless – until nearly noon.

She swam, dozed, snuck in a quick check with Reo. Both prisoners would get their psych evals, their sentencing hearings – and the PA's office expressed full confidence Iler would be remanded to an on-planet maximum security prison, while Silverman would make Omega his new home.

Eighteen consecutive life sentences.

Satisfied with that, Eve took a walk around the grounds

with Roarke. Then ate a huge bowl of spaghetti and meatballs.

Submitted to more ice patches.

Breathed a sigh of relief on Sunday when Roarke finally pronounced, 'You'll do.'

She did well enough to indulge in a fairly energetic bout of sex.

And felt in tune enough to bitch when he settled her down in front of the screen.

'Why do we have to watch all this pregame stuff?'

'Because I'm not going to miss watching our great good friends on the red carpet of the Oscars. You've got enough popcorn to give you solace.'

Maybe.

She didn't see the point in strutting around in fancy duds, striking poses on some swatch of red while entertainment reporters in more fancy duds cooed and giggled and asked lame questions.

'There's our Peabody.'

'What?' She looked up, focused on the screen.

Peabody — Jesus — in some frothy pink (naturally) number that bared good, strong shoulders and sparkled in the sunlight.

'How come it's daytime? It's nighttime.'

'Rotation of the planet, darling Eve. It's still about rotation.'

'Right. She looks good.'

Her hair all fluffy and curly.

'Where the hell did she get those rocks she's wearing?'

'On loan – from you. McNab looks good as well.'

Duded up, she noted, in a dark blue tux – made McNab-ish with a plaid vest, a screaming red bow tie.

She spotted Mavis – how could you miss her? – in a sweeping blaze of red and white. As she twirled for the cameras, the sweeps separated like blades of a fan. The heels of her red shoes towered with sparkling laces crisscrossing to the knee. Beside her, Leonardo wore one of those long tux jackets that skimmed to his knees in some sort of metallic fabric that shifted from emerald to sapphire.

He held Mavis's hand as she bubbled for the reporter. 'I can't wait. It's total dream come abso-true time. I'm nervous, but I'd be in the basket without my honey here, and our pals. Here's Nadine. She's wearing my honey, too. Nadine!' Mavis gestured. 'You want to talk to Nadine, right? Nadine and Jake. He's mega frost, isn't he?'

'Elegant,' Roarke decreed as Nadine stepped up. 'Just exactly right.'

Eve guessed so. She'd gone sleek and classic and deep gold. Not sparkling but gleaming and slithering down to a kind of liquid trail behind her. Diamonds dripped from her ears and formed two wide cuffs on her wrists. Beside her, Jake went for the rocker-style formal. Leather tux jacket and boots, plain white shirt, long tie worn loose at the neck.

'She's nervous,' Eve noticed.

'She is, yes, but it wouldn't show unless you know her. Handles herself very well, don't you think?'

'Mavis is keeping it bouncing. It helps.'

'You completely have to buzz with Peabody and McNab. Hey, Peabody! Come on up!' Mavis urged.

The camera panned for a split second to Peabody's stunned, somewhat terrified face before Mavis bounced right down. She grabbed one of Peabody's hands, one of McNab's, bounced right back.

'Detectives Peabody and McNab, NYPSD. Best fricking PSD in the universe of PSDs. We're having the most magalicious time together. Come on, we gotta do a shout-out. Hey, Dallas! Hey, Roarke! You better be watching.'

She laughed, circled her arms around Nadine and Peabody. 'Shout-out. Come on!'

Nadine laughed, losing that edge of nerves in her eyes.

They shouted out.

'There you are. Now you can say, with perfect truth, you watched and you heard.'

'Yeah.' Eve munched popcorn. 'And I'm not there answering stupid questions and wearing one of those outfits. It works.'

Plus, she figured she could catch some more z's while people droned on. And on.

The cat curled up at the small of her back. She had a bowl of butter-and-salt-drenched corn, and she could snuggle into Roarke, just close her eyes.

She woke, mumbling, when Roarke elbowed her.

'Mavis is about to perform.'

Eve blinked at the screen. 'Everybody's inside.'

'And have been for about a half hour. Nothing went on of interest to you. Shift over, will you, pour us some more wine.'

Eve shifted, poured, yawned, sipped wine.

The stage went dark. A drum began to beat. A spotlight flashed on a single figure.

Mavis didn't wear the gown now, but a skin suit of silver lights on black, silver knee-high boots.

She hit the first note, a howl rising from guttural low to wailing high.

Then she rocked it, dancing over the stage in that single light, belting out the song. She pointed, another light, another figure, and another, another.

'Jesus,' Eve murmured as her oldest friend fronted a dozen dancers on the stage in perfect and complex choreography. Singing in a voice straight from the gut.

'She's good, really good. When did she get so good?'

'She doesn't have to shock for attention. She already has it. She's quite marvelous really, and always was in her way.'

Eve watched, transfixed. The other lights winked off, one by one until Mavis stood alone again. Another howl, and the stage went black.

'Listen to them. They're cheering for her, all for her. You always knew,' Eve told him.

'I knew she could perform,' Roarke said. 'And I knew we'd do well enough when I signed her. But I'll admit she exceeded expectations.' He turned, brushed his lips to hers. 'Need another nap?'

455

'I guess that woke me up. Shit. Here's to Mavis freaking Freestone.'

Roarke clinked glasses. 'I believe we should switch to champagne.'

'Why the hell not?'

He got up for a bottle, for flutes. Popped it. He poured, then settled back in again. 'I'm going to think more seriously about putting in that home theater.'

'This is nice.'

'It's very nice, but so would that be. Dear Christ.' He sat up, gulped champagne after absently eating some of the popcorn. 'Why the bloody hell do I do that? Every bleeding time.'

'I don't know what your problem is. It's delicious. But more for me.' She ate a handful.

'You'd eat cardboard if it was covered in butter and salt.'

'Corn's better.'

'That corn? Marginally. Ah, Nadine's category's in the next segment.'

'It is?'

'Best adapted screenplay.'

'Right. I wish it was over with. What are her odds?'

'According to the buzz, it's mixed. Stiff competition in both writing categories.'

'Both?'

'Original, and adaptation,' Roarke explained, and caught himself before he reached for more popcorn. 'She's adaptation – screenplay based on her book.'

'Got it. Still wish it was over. Getting this far's a big, right?'

'A very big. Here come the presenters. There are six in her category nominated.'

'How do they ... Shit, they said her name. There she is. Mavis is back, that's good. And she's got everybody else right there, so ... '

She narrowed her eyes, studying Nadine as the other nominees came on in adjoining squares. Looks calm, Eve thought, but she's not.

Get it over with. Why don't they stop talking and get it—

'And the Oscar goes to, Nadine Furst, *The Icove Agenda*.'

'Holy shit. Jesus, she won? She won?'

'This is a moment.'

Eve watched, dumbstruck, as Jake planted a big one on Nadine, as Mavis bounced and squealed, as Peabody actually jumped up to dance.

And Nadine, elegant and sleek – hands shaking some – walked to the stage, climbed the stairs. Hugged two people she probably didn't know. Clutched the gold statue.

'Oh,' she managed. 'God. I'm just ... I wrote something in case – and I left it in my purse. So here goes.'

'She's crying a little,' Eve noted. Nadine was thanking the Academy, the cast, the crew, the director, her friends. 'And talking really fast.'

'She only has so much time.'

'Now ... We gave you a shout-out, Dallas and Roarke, on the red carpet. Here's another. You're the reason, both of you. But, Dallas, as much as you're going to hate this – being Dallas – this is as much yours as mine. I'm putting it in my place, but it's yours, too. I'm sharing this amazing award with the smartest, bravest, most dedicated cop and frustrating person I know. Thanks. Holy crap! Thanks!'

'And that,' Roarke said, 'is my very favorite acceptance speech in the history of them.'

'Jesus.' Eve scrubbed at her face. 'Between her and Mavis, they've got me dripping. I'm glad for her, I really am. I have to be. But, Christ on a tricycle, Roarke, this is going to be a pain in my ass. As if it wasn't enough of one before.'

He laughed, hugged her in. 'Just think what a pain in your ass it'll be if it wins best picture.'

'Don't say that. Don't think that. Don't put that out there.'

'To Nadine,' he said. She huffed, but clinked.

'Okay, but that's it. One's enough. No more.'

'Well, we'll wait and see, won't we?'

The Icove Agenda took five Oscars, including best adapted screenplay, best director, best cinematography, best actress, and the big guns. Best picture.

A little shell-shocked, Eve dragged herself into bed.

'It'll never end now. Never end.'

On a laugh, Roarke snuggled her in, kissed the back of her neck. 'There, there.'

'Bite me,' she muttered.

She closed her eyes and, consoling herself that the job would keep her too busy to worry about it, willed herself to sleep.

EXCLUSIVE EXTRACT

Read an extract from

Connections in Death

The new J.D. Robb thriller

1

The legalized torture of socializing lined right up with premeditated murder when you added the requirement of fancy shoes.

That was Lieutenant Eve Dallas's stand on it, and she should know. She was a murder cop in fancy shoes about to socialize.

Moreover . . . Whoever decreed that fancy shoes for females required sky-high skinny-ass heels rendering said shoes useless for any practical purpose – including walking – should be immediately subjected to every known manner of torture, legal or otherwise.

Surely by the almost-spring of 2061, in the freaking United States of America, useless skinny-heeled shoes should be banned. Beaten with hammers, set on fire, then banned.

She walked in those damn shoes toward a swank penthouse, a tall, lanky woman in a slinky jade dress that shimmered with her movements while a fat teardrop diamond shot fire from the chain around her neck.

The short, choppy brown cap of her hair set off the diamonds winking none too quietly at her ears. Her long brown eyes narrowed with dark thoughts.

Just who came up with the concept of the cocktail party?

Eve wondered. Whoever did, by her decree, should join the originator of fancy shoes in the torture chamber. Who the hell decided it would be a freaking fantastic idea to create a custom where people stood around, usually at the end of a workday, making small talk while balancing a drink in one hand and a plate of tiny, often unidentifiable food in the other?

And, oh yeah, whoever came up with small talk as a social imperative? Straight into the torture chamber.

And while we're at it, throw the sick bastard who added the requirement of a gift every freaking time you turned around right in there with the others. Because a sane person didn't want to have to think about what the hell to buy somebody who invited them to a damn party. A sane person didn't want to *go* to a party at the end of a workday and stand around in shoes with stupid skinny heels and balance weird food while making idiotic small talk.

A sane person wanted to be home, wearing comfortable clothes and eating pizza.

'Finished yet?'

Eve glanced toward the ridiculously handsome face of her husband – the guy responsible for the slinky of a dress, the damn shoes, and all the diamonds. She noted the amusement in those killer blue eyes, in the easy smile on that perfectly sculpted mouth.

It occurred to her that not only would Roarke enjoy the upcoming torture, but he could have deemed and decreed all the rules of it himself. He was lucky she didn't pop him one.

'Need a few more minutes for the internal monologue?' he asked, the Irish in his voice just adding more charm.

'It's probably the most sensible conversation I'll have all night.'

'Well now, what a thing to say. Nadine's first party in her new home will be full of your friends. They, and she, are smart, interesting people.'

'Smart people are home drinking a brew and watching the Knicks kick some Kings ass on-screen.'

'There'll be plenty of games yet to come.' He gave her butt an affectionate pat as they approached the outer doors of Nadine Furst's penthouse.

'And,' he added, 'Nadine deserves a party.'

Maybe, maybe she could concede that one. The ace on-screen reporter, bestselling author, and now freaking Oscar winner had earned a party. But she herself, murder cop, lieu-tenant murder cop, deserved maybe wishing a hot case had fallen in her lap at the last minute.

As Nadine earned her cred on the crime beat, she ought to understand.

Eve turned to face him again – that carved-by-romantic-angels face framed with black silk. In her fancy shoes they stood pretty much eye-to-eye.

'Why can't a party be brew and pizza and the round ball game on-screen?'

'It can.' He leaned over to brush his lips on hers. 'Just not this one.'

When the doors opened, the quiet, classy corridor filled with voices, music. Quilla, Nadine's teenage intern, stood in a black dress with a silver buckle at the belted waist, short-heeled red booties. The purple streaks in her hair glittered.

'Hey. I'm supposed to say good evening and welcome. And can I – *may* I' – she self-corrected with a roll of her eyes – 'take your coats?'

'How do you know we're not crashing?'

'Besides how I know you?'

Eve nodded. 'Besides.'

'Because lobby security has the guest list and all, and you had to clear through it to get up here. And if you're some doof who slipped by or lives here or whatever, Nadine would have you booted. The place is full of cops.'

'Good enough,' Eve decided as Roarke handed over their coats.

'You look lovely tonight, Quilla.'

She flushed a little. 'Thanks. Um, now I'm supposed to tell you to go right in, have a wonderful evening. There's a bar and buffet in the dining area as well as waitstaff passing food and beverage.'

Roarke smiled at her. 'You did that very well.'

'I've done it about a million times already. Nadine knows a shitload— I mean, a lot of people.'

'"Shitload" covers it,' Eve said. And as they moved through the foyer, through the open doors, was just a little horrified to see she knew most of them herself. How did that happen?

'Dig the dress, Dallas. The color's, like, bang.'

'It's green.'

'Jade,' Quilla qualified.

'Exactly.' Roarke sent Quilla a wink.

'So anyway, I can take the gift, too, unless you want to

give it to her, like, personally. We've got a gift table in the morning room.'

'"Morning room"?'

'I don't know why it's called that,' Quilla said to Eve. 'But we're putting the hostess gifts in there.'

'Great.' She shoved the fancy bag at Quilla.

'Chill. Okay, hope you have a kick.'

'A kick at what?' Eve wondered as Quilla headed off.

'I think it means have a good time. Which should speak to you,' Roarke added, 'as you enjoy kicking things.' He trailed his fingers down her back. 'Let's get you a drink.'

'Let's get me several.'

The passage to the bar, however, proved fraught with obstacles: people she knew. And those people had something to say, which cornered her into saying something back.

She was spared cold-sober small talk by passing waitstaff and Roarke's quick hands. His quick thinking and smooth moves also saved her from the chatty chat of one of Nadine's researchers.

'Darling, there's Nadine. We need to say hello. Excuse us.' With a hand on the small of Eve's back, he steered her away.

Nadine stepped in from the terrace. Eve deduced the party do – lots of tumbling curls – as Trina's handiwork. Though far from Nadine's usual polished, professional style, Eve supposed the streaky blond curls suited the dress. Strapless, short, snug, in hot-tamale red. Those cat-green eyes scanned, landed on Eve and Roarke. She met them halfway, rose to the toes of her skyscraper red heels, and kissed Roarke enthusiastically.

'I'd say this proves our place is perfect for entertaining.'

'"Our place"?'

Nadine smiled at Eve. 'Well, it is Roarke's building. A lot of your crew's out on the terrace. It's heated, and there's a small bar setup, another buffet.'

Despite the fact that friendship often baffled her, Eve knew her job. 'So where is it?'

Nadine fluffed her hair, batted her eyelashes. 'Where's what?'

'Well, if you don't want to show it off—'

'I do. Yes, I do.' Laughing, Nadine grabbed Eve's hand. With the skill of a running back, she snaked through people, wove around furniture, bolted up the curve of stairs and into her pretty damn swank home office. It held a couple of sofas in classy blue, chairs that picked up the classy blue in a swirly pattern on white, tables in slate gray that matched the T-shaped workstation in front of a killer view of New York City.

A square recessed fireplace flickered in the left wall. The gold statue stood on the mantel above it. Eve moved closer, studied it. Weird-looking dickless gold dude, she thought, but the nameplate read NADINE FURST, and that's what counted.

But if they weren't going to give him a dick, why didn't they give him pants?

'Nice.' Curious, she lifted, it, glanced over her shoulder. 'It's got weight. Blunt-force trauma waiting to happen.'

'Only you.' Nadine slid an arm around Eve's waist. 'I meant what I said in my acceptance speech.'

'Oh, did you say something?'

Nadine added a solid hip bump, and with a laugh, Eve set the award down again.

'It's all yours, pal.'

'Not nearly, but – I get to look at it every freaking day. So.' Turning, she reached out a hand for Roarke's. 'Let's go down and drink lots of champagne.'

Jake Kincade stepped into the doorway. The rock star, and Nadine's heartthrob, said, 'Hey.'

His dark hair spilled and swept around a strong face currently sporting a three-day scruff. He wore black – not a suit, but black jeans with a studded belt, black shirt, and black boots Eve admired because they looked sturdy and comfortable.

How come, she wondered, *he* got to dress like a real person?

'How's it going?' he said to Roarke as they shook hands. 'Looking prime, Dallas. Got to gander the gold guy? He's shiny, but you gotta wonder. If they weren't going to suit him up, why not give him his works? One or the other.'

'Good God,' Roarke murmured.

Jake flicked him a glance. 'Sorry.'

'No, not at all. It's only, I know my wife and have no doubt she thought exactly the same.'

'Maybe. More or less. It's a reasonable question.'

'At least Jake didn't look at it and see a murder weapon.'

The creases in his cheeks deepening, Jake grinned down at Nadine. 'Maybe. More or less. Anyway, you got another wave coming in, Lois. How does anybody know so many people?'

Now Roarke laughed, took Eve's hand. 'I'm beginning to think it's a good thing I saw her first.'

'Lots of cops,' Jake said as they started out. 'Other than that trip to Central, I haven't seen so many cops since ...' He looked at Eve. 'I probably shouldn't mention the time I was sixteen and used fake ID to get a gig in this club that got raided.'

'Did you kill anybody?'

'Nope.'

'We'll let it pass.'

'Speaking of cops, did you know Santiago can rock a keyboard?'

'Ah . . . he plays piano?'

'Wicked,' Jake confirmed. 'Renn brought his keys – the whole band's here – and the chick cop pushed Santiago into getting down. Chick cop's got pipes.'

'She can sing,' Nadine interpreted for Eve. 'And that's Detective Carmichael, Jake. I asked Morris to bring his sax,' Nadine added.

'Let me tell you, the dead-doc can smoke that sax. Hey, there's one of my breed.'

Looking down as Jake did, Eve saw Mavis, a fountain of pale, pale blue hair, a frothy pink dress with a short, flippy skirt, blue shoes with towering heels fashioned out of a trio of shining silver balls. Beside her, Leonardo resembled some sort of ancient pagan priest in a flowing vest shades deeper than his copper skin. His hair showered down to his shoulders in what looked like hundreds of thin braids. At the moment, Mavis talked to – bubbled over more like – a tight little group.

Feeney – the captain of the Electronic Detectives Division – wore the same rumpled, shit-brown suit he'd worn to work. Beside him stood Bebe Hewitt, Nadine's big boss, in shimmery silver pants and a long red jacket, looking fascinated. Then big-eyed teenage Quilla, towered over by Crack. The sex club owner also wore a vest. His stopped at his waist with lethal-looking studs on the shoulders, leaving his chest and torso bare except for muscles and tattoos. Beside him, a woman – unknown – smiled easily. She wore classic New York black and had a face made exotic by knife-edged cheekbones and heavy-lidded eyes.

'The kid's a little young for a cocktail party,' Eve commented.

'You're never too young to learn how to host an event, or how to behave at one,' Nadine countered. She glided down the rest of the steps and over to greet Mavis.

'The kid's all right,' Jake said to Eve. 'Giving Nadine a run.'

'Is she?'

He grinned with it. 'Big-time. Campaigned to come tonight, and tossed out how she could do a three-minute vid report on the party – soft-news clip. The Quill's got it going.' He tapped his temple.

'I got a couple earsful of your An Didean project, Roarke. She's keeping her own ear to the ground there. I'd like to talk to you about that sometime.'

'Anytime at all.'

'Hey, Dallas.' Mavis did a little dance on her silver balls, grabbed Eve in a hug. 'This party is whipping it.' She added a squeeze for Roarke, for Jake. 'All my fave people, add food and adult beverage, and it's going on. I heard there's jamming on the terrace. Am I going to get in on that?'

'Counting on it,' Jake told her. 'How about we check out the venue?'

'I'm in.'

'I'll get the drinks,' Leonardo said.

After Leonardo kissed the top of her fountain of hair, Mavis beamed up at him. 'Thanks, Honey Bear. Check you all later. I'm heading to the music.'

Feeney shot a finger at Eve. 'Did you know Santiago can burn up the keys?'

'I heard that.'

'Light under a bushel.' With a shake of his head, Feeney took his rumpled suit out to the terrace.

'Bushel of what?' Eve wondered.

'I'll explain later. It's lovely to see you, Bebe.'

'And both of you. I'm grateful, Lieutenant, for the work you and your detectives did in the Larinda Mars investigation.'

'That's the job.'

Bebe nodded, looked down into her drink. 'We all have one. Excuse me.'

'She's taking on too much of the blame.' Nadine looked after her as Bebe slipped away.

'It wasn't on her.'

'No.' Nadine nodded at Eve. 'But she's the boss. I'm just going to smooth that out. And send somebody with another round of drinks.'

Crack shot his eyebrows up. 'Cops do bring a party down.'

The woman beside him gave him a sharp elbow. 'Wilson!'

He only laughed. 'You looking fine for a skinny white girl cop.'

'You don't look half-bad for a big black man dive owner.'

'Down and Dirty ain't no dive. It's a joint. Yo, Roarke. I want you to meet my beautiful lady. This is Rochelle Pickering.'

Rochelle extended a hand to Eve, then to Roarke. 'I'm so happy to meet both of you. I've followed your work, Lieutenant, and yours, Roarke. Especially in regard to Dochas and An Didean.'

'She's a shrink,' Quilla announced, and Crack grinned at her.

'Kid shrink. Watch those steps, shortie, or she could come for you.'

'As if,' Quilla muttered, but melted away into the crowd.

'Wilson.' Rochelle rolled her eyes. 'I'm a psychologist, specializing in children. I've actually consulted at Dochas.'

'I'm aware,' Roarke told her, which had her blinking at him.

'That's . . . unexpected.'

'Our head counselor speaks highly of you.'

'She's a marvel.'

As promised, another tray of drinks arrived.

'I just have to take a moment,' Rochelle continued. 'It hardly seems real I'm standing in this amazing space. That I'm meeting both of you. I met Nadine Furst and Jake Kincade, God, Mavis Freestone – who's exactly, just exactly, as delightful as I'd hoped she would be. And Leonardo, someone whose work I drool over. And I'm drinking champagne.'

'Stick with me,' Crack told her. 'The sky's got no limits.'

Eve had questions, a lot of questions. Such as, she'd never known anyone to call Crack by his given name. What made this woman different? And how did a kid shrink hook up with the streetwise owner of the D&D? And when did Crack go all – what was the word? Smitten, she decided, the word was *smitten*. When did he go all smitten?

The Eve Dallas series

Eve and Roarke are back in Connections in Death – out February 2019